Praise for
LIFTED FROM THE WATERS
by Culpepper Webb

"In Mississippi, we know about inspiration: everywhere we look is the next evocative setting; everyone we meet is the next engaging character. But where does the writer's voice come from? We have an embarrassment of literary success to lead us and guide us, but where do we look to find the way to tell our story? Culpepper Webb's storytelling is a clear new voice in our literary landscape. It is a knowing and touching voice, rich with cadences comforting and familiar, effortlessly flowing from the times and terrain marking the journey. *Lifted from the Waters* is a marvelous book."

—Ward Emling
Director, Mississippi Film Office

●　　●　　●

"*Lifted from the Waters* is a Southern epic, one of those rare literary-but-entertaining novels that holds your interest even as it touches your heart. Its lead character, Gunter Wall, is one you'll not soon forget. I thoroughly enjoyed this book."

—John M. Floyd
Award-winning Author of *Rainbow's End*
and *Midnight*

●　　●　　●

"This fictional autobiographical memoir brings an awesome authenticity to the times, places and happenings that shape this story.

The protagonist has woven a personal and sentimental account of his life against a backdrop of some of the monumental events of the period—the devastating Mississippi River flood of 1927, the Great Depression of the thirties and, most dramatically of all, the battles of World War II and its aftermath.

It is a remarkable account of one man's heartbreaking tragedy, extraordinary courage and exemplary resilience, but in the end it is an inspiring testimonial to his personal faith."

—William Winter
Former Governor of Mississippi

●　　●　　●

"I enjoyed reading *Lifted from the Waters* so much that I read it in one weekend. I found the characters of the book easy to relate to, and the author's storytelling made me feel like I was right there with them. I could almost smell that home cured ham with biscuits! I definitely recommend it as a great read."

—Phil S. Walker
Senior Pastor of Ridgecrest Baptist Church
Madison, Mississippi

LIFTED
FROM THE
WATERS

A NOVEL

BY

CULPEPPER WEBB

Pecan Row Press

Jackson, Mississippi

ISBN: 978-0-9795187-2-0
LCCN: 2010921586

Library of Congress Cataloging-in-Publication data
  Webb, Culpepper
  Lifted from the Waters / written by Culpepper Webb
  1. Men authors — Fiction. 2. Book Clubs
  (Discussion Groups) — Fiction.
  I. Webb, Culpepper. II.Title

Cover photograph by Michael E.Whitten Jr.
Author photograph by Harold Head

Pecan Row Press
www.pecanrowpress.com
Info@pecanrowpress.com

Printed in the United States of America

IN HONOR AND MEMORY OF

Jimmy Blanks
Billy Byrd
Milton McMullen
James Webb
John Webb

ACKNOWLEDGEMENTS

Just as Gunter Wall of *Lifted from the Waters* did not overcome his life challenges without the help of others, the book you are holding did not reach your hands without the care and attention of many. Ronda, my wife, has for the past decade allowed me the moments of solitude to pursue my passion of writing. Some men spend extended periods of time playing golf, hunting or fishing. I write, and Ronda has granted me that privilege. Her encouragement from the halfway point to the finish line of this book was immeasurable. She heartened me in times of self doubt.

Lifted from the Waters was originally written in pencil on legal pads. Fran Gatewood, my typist translated (I carefully chose this word to describe my handwriting) longhand into printed form, which was then test read by several. I thank each of you who read the manuscript then candidly shared your opinions. Your collective insight helped me to make needed changes.

The refined manuscript was read by Alice Nicholas. Her enthusiasm and vision for the book convinced me her company, Pecan Row Press, was the best route for the book's future. Her commitment to this project has been immense, her dedication to all aspects of the project extensive.

Susanne Lakin, my content editor, carefully guided me on theme and concepts, word by word challenging me to do my God-given best in telling the story of Gunter Wall. She did so without trying to change the nature or character of Gunter. In fact, I am convinced that through her guidance his nature is conveyed far more convincingly. Susanne, thank you.

Indelibility of both content and quality was a great concern of mine. Ann McNair, the senior editor, quelled my concerns by meticulously putting the finishing touch on these one hundred thousand words. I am at peace.

In my mind's eye I desired to paint the picture of a man who endured the Great Depression and whose life was spared in battle in World War II, later to be "lifted" from near despair to serve. *Lifted from the Waters* granted me that opportunity to convey my respect and appreciation for those such as Gunter Wall, many of whom are deceased. Memories of men I have known inspired me to write. Finally, at times people use the phrase "thank God" in a trite or casual fashion. I prayed fervently during the writing of this book and my thanks to God is neither trite nor casual.

Enjoy the read. It is my hope that you will find value in doing so.

Sincerely,
Culpepper Webb

PROLOGUE

Around here, there is only one river: the Mississippi.

Last time it covered all the land was 1927, when the levee broke not far from where we were living and less than thirty miles from where I stand today. The flood is an event in my life I've tried countless times to forget, but can't—even though it happened over seventy-nine years ago, when Dad lifted me from its waters with his massive hands. Some events in life are too profound to forget, regardless of the passage of time.

Yet, I no longer wish to forget. In fact, today I want to remember it in minute detail, to taste the muddy water in my mouth and lungs, then cough it out, the grit remaining. The flood is the deep-seated point of my early recollections of Mama and Dad and my older brother Everett—the Walls. People I loved and to this day love in my memories. I long to see them again. I truly do.

Growing up, there was nothing but cotton in the fields. Spent my first four years right in the middle of a cotton patch in a shack we didn't own, on land that wasn't ours. I could see forever across the flattest land God ever created, silt piled upon silt by the annual flooding of the river.

I lean against the Explorer and gaze across open land at the half-exposed November sun, this month the sun against sky more vivid than any other, a respite from the haze of summer and the dreary clouds of winter and early spring. A whippoorwill just within the woods sings his summons, calling me to enter. The near-vacant field is scattered with the scraggy cornstalks that survived the plowing under. They are this morning little more than silhouettes against the rising sun.

Cornstalks. Never thought I'd live to see corn as our main crop.

Never thought I'd live to see a lot of things, and at times never thought I'd live *period*—my brushes with death numerous when I was young.

Look, the sun is now a complete ball, no longer touching the horizon. It rose so quickly. I have no time to tarry; Robert Rugetti's grandson, Eddie, will be here sometime this morning to hunt rabbits with his young beagle, and my solitude will be broken. Got to get to the woods—and here I am standing with my mind drifting, same as it has for the past two weeks. Here I go, handle to the bag containing my canvas chair in one hand as I close the back door with my other. No need to lock, just get to the woods, the gravel under my soles now turning to johnsongrass.

This has to be the place that Dad, Everett, and I—and later young Tom—usually entered the woods. It's been so many years, so difficult to remember. Even the road I came in on this morning was dirt in those days, not gravel. The walk's not bad so far, no briars yet. Don't have to go but a few feet anyway. For some reason, if only out of habit, Dad—and later, I—would always come back and find a log to sit on near where we entered the woods. We would sit on it and eat cured ham and biscuits. I get hungry just thinking of the taste of salted ham.

Today I was scared I wouldn't find a downed log, so I brought a chair. Might not be quite the same, but at my age I'd probably fall off a log anyway. The spot must have been right along here. Why, that looks like a tree downed by nature years ago no more than twenty feet away, but it's so covered with briars I can hardly tell. Yes, it's a log all right, just enough opening in that briar to see bark. Guess I'll set my chair up facing it. Would you look at that sweet gum tree afire with yellow and red leaves! I've got a full view of it, too.

I adjust myself on the chair, plant my hands in the pockets of my jacket that's layered atop my sweater, and try to get my feet right. I put on two pairs of socks this morning. My feet are always getting cold. It's been like that all the way back to age four. Wonder if it's psychological. They are even a bit chilly now.

So here I am. Been planning this all week. Got the idea for coming out here the day of the funeral two weeks ago. My mind has raced since that day, one minute thoughts of the past, next the future, then back to the present, all within a moment of time. At first I simply wanted to come here to stir up memories, but as the days passed, coming here has taken on a new dimension.

I'm not depressed, nor without hope, but I am lonely—the loneliest I've been in my entire life. Spent fifty-five years with her and now . . . and now I'm tearing up again just thinking of her. How many times have I done that?

At first I merely wanted to revive my memories, relive my life. But the past few days I've wanted more. I've craved an affirmation of my life, in some strange way comparing myself with Dad, Everett, James Street, Missouri, and other men. I know that it's not right. I am Gunter Wall, not them. But each of them affected my life so profoundly. Dad rescued me physically with his hands and emotionally with his heart. He just went about his life living the phrase James Street taught me: "Always do the right thing." James Street followed his motto with humility, not going about tooting his own horn. Oftentimes that was simple, clear cut, do it or don't do it, knowing when I deliberately failed or just came short, or when I succeeded with distinction; and other times my life's entanglements were complex, my walking the tightrope between two choices, having to decide which side to walk toward—not falling in the process. Along the way I was lifted by others or by God, elevated to continue the path of my life's journey. There are few who have treaded this earth who have been lifted more than I.

How ingrained within me is that phrase, *always do the right thing?* This morning in the dark, no moving vehicles for miles around, I turned on my left blinker before leaving an asphalt road with half the asphalt missing to go onto a single-lane gravel road. Did it simply because I was supposed to.

Why, years ago, right after the war when I was still in Japan, Missouri drove over five hundred miles one way to comfort my folks, let them know I was going to be all right. He couldn't have been more than twenty-three at the time—quite a caring man. Yes, Everett, my brother, he saved my life. And young Tom—so young. At times I still have a pain to the lowest depth of my chest when I think of him. The touch of each of these men goes beyond my surface to my soul.

And there was Mom and . . . can't even say her name without opening the floodgates and I don't need that right now. Need to squash my thoughts of her for the moment.

I do so wish to see my life, the important parts, the events and people that shaped and molded me, see them all with a fuller vision.

God, help me to clearly see my life, the significant events—remove the clutter in my mind, like the tearing away of those tangled briars before me so I can see the log one end to the other. You know better than I what was important. By seeing, I think I will better understand my life. I was rescued from near death three times before I finished high school and was brought back to the journey of my life's path as a young man by my father, by a mentor, by my wife—and by you. I've been lifted when I needed lifting, but did I lift, did I lead, did I do what was right for others? I was granted so much.

I close my eyes, no sounds around save a bird chirp here and there. I'll wait, listen.

What is that noise I hear building within my mind? Sounds like roaring water. And a dog's bark—then abruptly none. The roar is turning to a rumble, almost deafening. A door now before me is shaking, the hinges coming loose—the Mississippi is coming straight at me! My chest is swelling to near explosion with anticipation, nervousness, alarm—but not dread.

I've lived this before.

ONE

Mama and Dad tower above me, Everett not so much so. Breakfast is usually biscuits and sausage or cured ham, and today it's cured ham that I am tearing out of the biscuit with my front teeth, tasting all ham and no biscuit, just the way I like it.

"Gunter Wall, watch your manners," Mama says. "You're not a horse or a cow."

I nod and keep chewing on the ham, only slower. My, that salt-covered ham is good. I'm hungry.

Don't know why, but I'm looking around the room at white-painted boards running ceiling to floor, the floor just boards without paint, same as those on the outside of the house. There's a black woodstove to the side of the wall with the coffee pot on top, next to the basin on the counter with a pump to its side. On the floor to the front of the basin is my stool. I love to pump water. Hanging from the ceiling is a kerosene lantern burning bright. There are no cobwebs in the corners. Mama goes after cobwebs with the broom like she does everything, crumbs of biscuits on the floor included.

Across the table Dad is chewing a biscuit, his face long, no smile, same as yesterday and the day before. That's not like him, but it's been raining over a month and he can't go to the fields to plant. Now he goes to the levee to sandbag 'cause everybody's afraid the river might come over the top or just break the levee altogether. He got back last night way past dark after Mama put Everett and me to bed. I didn't hear him come in. He says he has to stay on the levee tonight in a tent so they can keep on working.

Everett's been home all week on account the roads are too muddy to get to school. He's making a face, sticking his tongue out between his missing front teeth. It's aimed straight at me just when Mama and Dad aren't lookin'. I start to aim my tongue back but don't. I got in trouble for making faces yesterday. Mama made me scoot the stool into the bedroom and sit on it to think about the way I was acting. Everett is smiling now ear to ear, no front teeth.

"What's that?" Dad says, lookin' all panicked.

It's a deafening roar interrupted by *aawhroo, aawhroo*, the howls of Old Blue that stop immediately as the roar turns to rumble, water pounding our home, the door shaking and hinges coming loose as water gushes, sweeping me out from my chair out of the kitchen to Everett's and my room, as all of me goes under with my mouth wide open, throat and lungs filling with icy muddy water.

I can't see. I can't see! The water's muddy. Cold! I've hit the wall next to the door to Mama and Dad's room. Rushing water has me pinned to it as I struggle, my head coming up for air as I choke out the water, the grit remaining. With the light of the lantern, I see Dad coming toward me from the kitchen as I go under again, my feet touching the floor as I try to kick myself up but can't. The water is deeper than I am tall and I don't know how to swim—I'm only four! I'll paddle with my hands. Paddle with my hands! Paddle! My hands are in the air but my head isn't. I'm breathing water. It's all inside me!

Two huge hands grab me below my arms and lift me from the water, first to his chest, then to his shoulder, my face looking down at the muddy swirling liquid as Dad slaps my back forcing water from my lungs. I cough, then cough again as I gasp for air. He begins to wade to Everett, who is screaming, "Dad. Dad!"

"Tom, the boys!" Mama cries, top of her lungs from the kitchen, as Dad reaches and grabs Everett with his free arm, lifting him and slinging him to his other shoulder. Everett and I face each other no more than a half a foot apart, his eyes saucer-size, breathing through his mouth all the way to his lungs.

"Got 'em, Mary. Both of them. Now free yourself from that wall and wade to the door. We'll go from here to our room, then on to the ladder to the attic. I'm gonna follow you when you get here. "

"But, Tom."

"Don't argue, just come to me! There isn't time to talk."

Although I can't see, I know Mama's not moving.

"Mary!" Dad screams. "Get to the door and come this way."

I can sense Mama's heading toward us though she says nothing. I then hear, "Are my boys alive?" from a foot or two away.

"Yes," Everett and I say in unison before Dad says, "Can't hug 'em now, Mary. Might drop them."

He nods in the direction of their room and Mama wades ahead with Dad close behind, the water almost chest high on him, Everett's and my head bobbing just above water. I can tell he's struggling, breathing heavy, grunting with each movement toward the ladder, blocks of wood nailed to the wall in Mama and Dad's room back of the shack.

"I can hardly move, Tom," Mama says.

"You're gonna do fine," Dad says as he makes his way to her, Everett and me bobbing as he moves. "We've got to get to the attic and from there to the roof."

Dad's caught up with Mama and is nudging her on. In a moment we're to the ladder that leads to a covered square hole in the ceiling.

"You go first," Dad says to Mama. "I'll hand you the boys."

Mama's hesitating just like back in the kitchen.

"Go, Mary!" Dad hollers, and she begins to move up the ladder, pushing away the cover, then crawling into the attic.

"Tom, it's dark up here! I can hardly see."

"Nothing I can do about that. You grab ahold of each boy when he comes up," Dad says, then speaks to Everett. "I'm gonna turn around so you can put your hands firm on the ladder. When you've got a solid grip, let me know."

"But, I," Everett starts to object as Dad stops him.

"Not the time to dally, Son. You grab that ladder like I say. Next, I'll help balance you with my hand so you can get your feet on one of those rungs."

I feel Everett let loose as I turn my head to see him scoot to the attic, Mama reaching for him as he goes through the hole.

"Gunter, I'm gonna lift you," Dad says, grabbing me under my arms with hands that are the size of shovels, raising me as high as his arms will stretch as I reach for Mama, her hands taking mine, Dad pushing my body as I go upward. I enter the attic by simply reaching.

Pain shoots through my knees as they hit the boards, Mama dragging me a few feet, then reaching for me, her arms wrapping me. In her grasp I forget my pain.

The attic is dark but not pitch black. Dim rays of light come through the hole in the ceiling, the kerosene lantern at the other end of the shack providing it. Dad has come through the hole and Everett has run toward him. His arms are around Dad like mine are around Mama.

"We got to get a move on. That water's rising, so there's no time for any of us to sit around," Dad says as he nudges Everett away.

"What are we gonna do now?" Mama screams as she releases her grasp. "Are we all going to drown? Wanted to take the boys to the hills to stay with Mother. She's got room for all of us. But *nooo* . . . you wanted us all here. 'Need to stay together as a family.' Fine and dandy, we'll probably all die as a family!"

I'm scared.

"Mary," Dad says, not screaming. "Mary," he says again, coming toward her and reaching out as she turns and steps back.

Dad stops a couple of feet short of her, pauses then says, "Maybe I didn't make the perfect choice. Didn't see things happenin' this way. What's done is done and right now we gotta survive and that means getting to the roof."

Dad says nothing as he opens the big trunk that stores our spare blankets and change of clothes for the summer. Looking up he says, "Get some dry clothes for you and the boys, and set some aside for me. I gotta start choppin' away and I need the trunk to stand on."

"Summer clothes!"

"Mary, they're dry. We all need something dry. These boys are probably freezing as it is; I know I am. Get a move on. Now."

I am cold. I shiver, shake. Didn't notice till now.

Dad closes the trunk, setting it on end, then goes to the opening in the attic, picking up a rope that's on the floor, tying it to a board, securing the other end to his waist. He lifts the ax that leans against the wall and starts back our way saying, "Always have rope and an ax in the attic."

Mama turns to us as Dad stands on the trunk and swings the ax at the tin roof. It's metal on metal, the whole attic bonging.

"Put your hands up, Gunter, or I'll never pull this nightgown off," Mama says as she struggles with the wet cloth stuck to my skin.

My naked body is freezing, nothing on but a pair of wet socks. Mama turns me toward her and slips on short pants and a short-sleeved shirt, buttoning fast as she can, Everett dressing himself, quiet just like me. Dad's pounding the roof with the ax faster and faster. *Bong! Bong!* A little light comes through as he loosens a sheet of metal roof.

"Tom!" Mama hollers, and with it Dad stops. "The boys have no dry socks and no shoes. They have no shoes! No shoes! No shoes!" Mama keeps screaming.

"Mary get ahold of yourself. Nothing can be done about that now," he hollers back just before pounding the roof with more force than ever, the upper sheet prying loose from the lower as Dad keeps pounding and bending the metal till there's enough room for him to climb through. He lays down the ax and pulls himself through the opening.

A moment later Dad says from the roof, "Mary, go down to the end of the attic and untie the rope, then tie it around Everett's waist. Rope needs to be about five feet from the roof. Got the rope secured to the chimney and me. When you get through, set him on that trunk.

Mama says nothing to Dad, but speaks to Everett straight to his face. "I'm going to put a slipknot around you and make sure it's good and tight." She assists Everett to the top of the trunk, straining as she lifts. Dad pulls Everett up and gets him settled on the roof next to the chimney.

"Send Gunter next, and after you've handed me the blankets I'll help you up, Mary. Get all of you up here roped to the chimney and I'll come down and put something dry on and get the cigar box. Got to hold onto that box like it's gold."

Mama says nothing as she begins to tie the rope around my waist. She then looks me hard in the eyes. "I love you, Gunter."

Next thing, Dad's pulling me toward the tear. Just above the metal roof I feel mist and a hard cold wind straight in my face. Before me is gray sky and water as far as I can see.

TWO

The black sky is turning gray as waves splash over the low spot on the tin roof. Everett is leaned against the chimney, my body rested against his, both of us bundled close under the blanket. His stirring wakes me. We sat here all day yesterday and all last night. Dad led us in prayer at the times we normally eat, the only thing missing was food. I cried and cried yesterday afternoon when I thought of Old Blue, me tossing him a stick, him and me running up and down rows of cotton. My last drink of water was underwater. My hollow stomach gave up growling last night. I want a slice of ham as much as I want a pair of shoes for my naked aching feet. When I'm not thinking of my feet or stomach, I am thinking of my bottom, the crease of the roof painful as it can be. And now I got to go, just like Everett did last night.

"I gotta pee, gotta go bad."

"Gunter Wall, don't use that word!" Mama says soon as my words come out. "Where did you hear that?"

"Everett."

"Mary, let the boy be. He's probably hurting head to toe. Gun, you need to be real careful. Everett, he's gonna crawl over you so I can reach across the chimney and steady him. Come on, Gun." Dad motions with his head as he stands and leans over the chimney, securing me as I cross Everett.

As I stand, the crease of the roof pokes right into my arches. "Can I move up a little, Dad? The roof hurts my feet."

"Sure, Gun. I got both of your shoulders."

Dad's hands make me secure. I step forward a little and unzip in time to spray toward the edge of the roof, almost making it as the liquid splatters on the metal. It's the only fun I've had since I put the slice of ham in my mouth yesterday morning. I wish this could last all day.

"Better take your seat again, Gun," Dad says, and I obey, crawling back over Everett, taking my seat on the crease.

"I see somethin'. I see somethin' coming!" Everett screams.

Dad, who's still standing, looks where Everett points. "Sure is. I see two tiny dots on the horizon. Proud of you, Son."

I strain to look but the only dots I see are trees across the water.

"I hear the motor," Dad says, no yell in his voice as he stares in the direction of the dots. "They're boats, two of them. Somebody's coming this way, Mary."

Mama doesn't say a word, but I see light in her eyes. I can hear the motor now and see the boats coming straight at us. As the boats near, I see a man and a woman in the first and no one in the second. Just then Dad mumbles, "Jarvins," followed by a loud, "That you, Roy?"

"Yeah, it's me, Tom. Looks like you're stuck up on your roof. You go up there often?"

"Not recently."

"Looks like you could use a lift."

"Sure could," Dad says as the two men stare at each other. Mr. Jarvin has more creases on the half of his face than on all of Dad's. He has a beard, a thick one, coal black, and wears a cap with earmuffs that stand out halfway. Gone are his front teeth.

"I reckon we could find room. Just jostle the stuff in that boat back yonder. That is if you're not carrying much." The man is screaming over the roar of the outboard motor.

"All we got is ourselves, an ax, a rope, this little canvas bag with a few clothes in it, and a couple of blankets," Dad shouts over the noise of the motor.

"Sure that's all?" Mr. Jarvin says, cocking his eyes.

"That's about it. Where you goin'?"

Jarvin's eyes uncock. "Town. I reckon we'll go to town, and if the Mississippi's beat us there, we'll go to another place on the levee. We've been camped on the levee for about a month anyway. Our place got flooded long 'fore yours. We live on the wrong side of the levee. That's the way it is when you fish for a living. Problem is the levee broke, but I guess you done figured that one out. Weren't too far from here, from what I can tell."

"About that ride to town, we sure could use it."

"What do you say, Bonnie?" Mr. Jarvin says to the woman next to him.

"I suppose it would be proper," she replies.

"We would be appreciative, Bonnie," Mama says, picking up on her name. It's the second time this morning Mama's spoken.

Bonnie breaks a small smile without showing teeth, dimples breaking the many creases both sides of her mouth. She nods and Mama nods back.

"Gas is expensive," Mr. Jarvin says, breaking the nods, looking at Dad. "The extra weight's gonna put a dent in my gas."

"We can come up with two dollars when we get to town," Dad says.

"Where y'all wanta get on?"

"Straight down from the chimney." Dad points. "Water's all the way to the roof. We'll just slide down holding on to the rope. You'll need to pull that second boat right up next to the roof and toss us some of that extra rope where we can tether the front end to the chimney. Can you pull your boat up next to that one and hold on?"

Roy Jarvin studies the roof and the current, then begins to guide the boat, back boat in tow, to the spot Dad pointed. Next thing he's tossing rope, then holding the second boat right next to his.

It takes a while but we all make it down, Mr. Jarvin helping us into the boat, Mama scared as she can be. Dad comes last with the canvas bag and the ax.

"Roy, you suppose on the way we could ride by Mr. Wilson's? He sent his family off to the hills and stayed behind. Maybe check on some of the hands."

"Gas is expensive."

"Maybe I could come up with three dollars when we get to town to pay you for your troubles."

"Maybe?" Mr. Jarvin says, eyes cocked again.

"I'll pay you three dollars," Dad says without hesitating.

"Okay," he replies, smiling, the front teeth missing.

The moist air blows straight in my face as we head toward Mr. Wilson's, the boat bouncing with the waves, Everett and me bundled together under the blanket. I pull the blanket over my freezing ears, wrapping it as tight as I can, tugging on it as Everett tugs back. I guess we could turn the other way and have the breeze at our backs, but I want to see what's ahead and Everett's not saying anything. Mr. Wilson's home is the largest for miles around, but I can't see it yet, its view blocked by the massive gin two stories above water along a row of rooftops about the same size as ours.

The gin stands tall in the water. The houses don't, the roofs the only parts showing. Even over the roar of the outboard I hear cries and I see hands waving in the air.

I see Sweet Pea, Bo, Freddie Carl, and Lula huddled around their chimney. Freddie Carl and Lula are waving as Sweet Pea and Bo sit and stare. Freddie Carl works on the plantation and Dad likes him. I've played with Sweet Pea and Bo. Sweat Pea is my age. I hear cries coming from down a few houses and I cut my eyes that way. People are waving and screaming up and down the row of houses. Seems like a house is missing. I turn back and look at Sweet Pea and Bo.

"Can you slow it down, Roy?" Dad hollers above the roar of the motor and the cries for help.

Mr. Jarvin cuts the speed and the noises drop off some, the current still moving us toward Freddie Carl's house at a pretty good clip as he swings the boat, stopping just short of the tin roof, the waves from the outboard splashing well up the roof.

"Y'all made it," Dad hollers.

"Barely," Freddie Carl yells back. "Plenty didn't. Look around," he says, pointing to a row of houses that isn't a full row. "Water came down on us so fast I's afraid we wasn't gonna make it. Barely did. That house just washed away, right off the blocks it was standing on. Po' folks never knew what hit 'em. Can't no one swim 'cept for me. People scared to death, me included."

Dad nods. So do I. Sweet Pea and Bo are looking straight at me like they wish they could trade places. Kinda like me wishing I had a pair of shoes, except worse.

"I guess we're the first folks y'all have seen," Dad says.

"No," Freddie Carl replies.

"No?"

"Boat came through yesdiddy afternoon checking everything out, lookin' first for Mr. Wilson up in the big house. Mr. Wilson be drowned, had his body in the boat. Found him floatin' in his house on the second floor."

"Fred Wilson dead?"

"Dead. Dead as dead can be. Carried him on toward town. Said they would send somebody back for us, but I doubt it. That boat was little, two men in it—that is, in addition to Mr. Wilson. Didn't have room for us noways." Freddie Carl pauses then says, "So I wonder if we gon' sit here till summer comes or maybe just float our house to town like that one." He points to the missing house.

I look past the missing house at the people now silent on the other houses, then look back at Dad and he is silent too. I'm watching him hard. "What can we do?" he says.

"Nothin'," Mr. Jarvin says without hesitating. "These darkies gonna have to fend for themselves."

Dad pleads with his look.

"Couldn't help 'em even if I wanted to, which I don't. Don't have room for four extra. Gotta get to town and I done already rescued four of you today. I'd say that's 'bout enough. Mighty generous, that's what I'd say I've been. Mighty generous."

My eyes are on Dad, his look downward just beyond his right foot, which is moving backward and forward as if he wants to go someplace, but can't decide to get going. Suddenly, the foot stops. "Maybe I got a little more gas money."

Mama's face wakes up. I see her through the corner of my eye.

"Even if you got gas money, there's not enough room. We got a load already in this boat and you can't fit eight in yours, not with the gear we already got in it."

"You could squeeze my two between the lantern and that duffle bag in your boat," Dad says, pointing at a spot behind Mr. Jarvin. "The two of them don't weigh a hundred pounds." He pauses then says, "I got three more dollars."

Just as Dad finishes, I glimpse Mama starting to speak as Dad lays his hand on her shoulder. She says nothing and shrugs his hand away.

"Might cost me more gas than that with the extra weight."

"Roy, if I give you more than three dollars I might be spending our grocery money."

"Me and Bonnie gotta eat too. Need five more, take it or leave it— and I need half of it 'fore we leave, case we get separated when we get to town."

Dad hesitates then nods. Can't tell if he's happy or sick.

Mr. Jarvin's happy. "You find a place for those darkies in your boat and I'll scrounge a spot for your two in mine."

As Mr. Jarvin works us a spot for Everett and me, I see Dad pull money from the cigar box in the canvas bag, putting the box back quickly. A minute later Dad has us in the front boat squeezed between the duffle bag and the lantern. Mama and Dad are in the front of the boat behind us, with Sweet Pea, Bo, Freddie Carl, and Lula behind them. As Mr. Jarvin revs his motor, I look back at the houses and the people, black faces against a gray sky. There's a boy not much bigger than me, next to his dad on a rooftop, who follows me with his eyes, eyes that won't let go. I let go, look the other way.

THREE

Untying my shoestring, I stare at the worn black leather that's wrapped around my foot, a sock separating my skin from leather. Twelve years old, almost a teenager, and I still hesitate before taking a shoe off. Have ever since the flood, especially before swimming. Everett taught me to swim 'cause Dad made him. He also forced me to learn. I was scared of dipping my toes in anything deeper than a tub. Didn't want to get my head under. Did that when I was four and as far as I was concerned, that was enough for my lifetime. Everett finally got tired of arguing with me and instead started coaxing me along till I got my nerve up. Everett won't admit it 'cause he's fifteen and he's my brother, but I'm a better swimmer than he is. Won't even race me anymore.

Here I sit on the edge of Oak Leaf, Mississippi, staring across Lake Knox, hardly more than a big mud puddle a half mile across that's maybe ten feet deep in the middle. Walked here today with Everett to play water baseball. Didn't want me tagging along to play with guys his age, all a head taller than me, 'cause it might embarrass him. Mom made him. So here I sit waiting for enough to show up for a game.

Lake Knox is nothing like the Mississippi River. They finished a bridge across the river three years ago and we took the Ford over it to Arkansas. Looked the same as Mississippi. Flat. All my life except for the year and a half that we spent in the hills at Grandma's after the flood has been spent in the Mississippi Delta. I'm not twenty miles from the shack I was born in and twenty-five miles from Arkansas, the only other state I've been to and there only once. That's gonna be different someday. No telling where I'll go. For sure it'll be cooler than this place in August. I must have sweated away half my body today between working in the yard this morning and walking to the lake this afternoon. Don't work Saturdays, at least down at the cotton oil mill where Dad has worked his way up to foreman. Everett's done part-time odd jobs there for the past three summers, me starting this year. I get to watch Dad at work—"at work" meaning me watching him do his job. He gets people to do things without hollering and screaming at them. Just coaxes them along. I can tell the men respect him; so do I.

Anyway, today he had Everett and me pushin' the lawn mower and trimming Mom's bushes. "Gotta take pride in what we have." We moved into the house two years ago and it's our first home—at least the first we've not rented. Mom—started calling her Mom this year, Mama didn't sound right for age twelve—has always wanted things "looking right," but never more so than this house. It's not nearly as big as many in town, but it's bigger than that shack on the plantation—at least the way I remember it. I was so small then. Anyway, this one's got paint on the outside, white paint, bright as bright can be, with dark green shutters and a green roof. Yep, Mom insisted on shutters, green ones. Dad didn't see the point in shutters, but that time Mom won out. Matter of fact she does that a lot, Dad giving in when he can. I do miss the sound of rain falling on the tin roof. Water hitting shingles on wood just isn't the same.

I also miss Old Blue. Don't remember much of anything before that flood, but I do recall chasing that dog all the way down rows of cotton to the turnrow. Only time I ever caught him was when he wanted me to. That's when he was the happiest and so was I. Don't have a dog now and haven't since the shack. Dad said a dog competed for groceries and I guess for a long time he was right. We arrived here in Oak Leaf with little more than the promise of Dad's job, a manual one at the cotton oil mill that was just opening. All Dad wanted was "an opportunity." He worked his way up. Back to the dog. I don't think Mom wanted one anyway.

Took a year and a half to get to Oak Leaf. The day we left the shack in the boat we got to Franklin, the county seat. It's just this side of the levee and all the houses and stores had taken on water, just not near as much as the shack. Some folks camped on the levee, but we stayed on the second floor of a store, people crowded all around us. That was the last I saw of Mr. Jarvin and Bonnie. Sweet Pea, Bo, and their folks must have gone up north. So many did, I'm told. Haven't heard from them since.

We moved to Everett Crossroads, a place named for Mom's side of the family. It's nothing more than a general store, a church, and ten or fifteen houses, same size today as it was when I was four. Mom's family owned the general store and still does today. We arrived there with one dollar and some change in the cigar box. The reason I know it was one dollar is Dad saved it. "Gonna keep it till the day I die to remember that we and others were provided for and still had some left over."

Thinking of dogs, Aunt Martha, Mom's sister, treated Dad worse than some folks treat theirs. You know, the kind of folks that bully their dogs 'cause they're in control and they just enjoy doing it. Well, Aunt Martha treated her husband that way, but it was nothing like the way she dealt with Dad. Us moving to Everett Crossroads and living with Grandma, Mom's mother, was something Aunt Martha considered God's gift from heaven—at least Dad moving there and having to work in the general store. She ran the general store and seemed to run everything. Just loved to be in charge of everybody, especially Dad. She belittled him in front of others. He'd have died a young man if we had stayed there. I don't like Aunt Martha.

Mom loved Everett Crossroads. She was comfortable there with her mother in the home she grew up in, a big white two-story with a front and back porch. Dad almost had to drag Mom back to the Delta. All she could think about was that shack on the plantation, "a house we didn't own on land that wasn't ours." How many times have I heard her say that? Well, now she's got her house with green shutters on a paved street, not a dirt road. And we're doing fine, the cotton oil mill going twenty-four hours a day, six days a week, even in the midst of the Depression, Dad working his way up to foreman.

There's one other thing I remember in the shack before the flood, the summer before it came, hot as hot could be. Everett and I went up in the attic, just the two of us. Only time other than the flood I went there. Everett was pretending, telling me about faraway places: Egypt, China, India, and the picture show. We had never been to the picture show. Since then I have been to the picture show and to Arkansas.

"Gunter. Gunter Wall!" Everett awakens me from my thoughts. "You look like that statue that I saw in a book at the library, 'The Thinker.' You annoyed the Hades out of us to let you tag along and play with the big guys, and there you sit staring at your shoes. You wanta play water baseball with us? Or maybe we can just put a skirt on you and let you be our cheerleader. What do you think, guys?"

"Cheerleader, make him a cheerleader!"

"I want to play water baseball," I say. It riles me when Everett gets like this. Does it in a crowd and when it's just him and me. Did it this morning when I was going after one of Mom's bushes with a hedge clipper, telling me it would be after dark 'fore I was done.

I yank off my left sock, stand and unbutton a button, then peel off my shirt, take two steps, then right foot first into the water that's perfect temperature for a warm bath. It's August. Both feet in, I'm walking forward, the water knee-high my feet sinking two, three inches in silt that oozes between my toes, the trek slow, my calves straining as I move toward the crew of twelve, no, thirteen. I'm the youngest. Gonna be in the seventh grade and most of these guys are a head taller and heading to high school if they aren't already there. Tommy T., brother of R. C., has to be older, I mean really older. He's making his way back to the tenth grade while the others are making their way up. Seems like I remember him shaving five years ago.

We huddle, fourteen of us, Everett and R. C. picking teams, Everett going first and picking Rooster Murphy. Don't know Rooster's real name, but with one look at his pointed nose and chin, along with his long front teeth, he doesn't need further introduction. R. C. picks Freddie Parsons, then Everett, Marko Cellini, R. C., his brother Tommy T., and right on along till I'm the only one left. By default I make R. C.'s team and get sent to the outfield, Everett's team batting first.

They've set up three old oil drums half filled with water for the bases, home plate a cypress knee, the extension of a root that juts out eight or ten inches. We use a well-worn volleyball for the ball and our fists for bats. Home plate is knee-high in the water, first and third base waist high (for most), and second base chest high. I'm standing on my tiptoes, silt between each toe, chin tipping the water, in the outfield or outwater. Yep, that's the correct name: "outwater." My calves are straining.

Tommy T. winds up and heaves a side arm, the volleyball whistling through the air as Rooster steps back just before swinging his third miss. Rooster shakes his head as Willie Vaughan, the catcher, lobs the ball back to Tommy T.

"Baw, baw, baaaw. Baw, baw, baaw. Today you're a chicken, not a rooster," Tommy T. hollers at Rooster as he wades to shore. "You're afraid that ball's gonna hit you upside the head."

I would be, too. The inside of my head would be ringing for a week if that ball hit me. Glad I'm on Tommy T.'s team.

"Next," Tommy T. says, stretching the word for emphasis.

Marko Cellini steps up, no fear in his eyes. Got a determined look. Tommy T. sounds a loud growl as he heaves another side arm, the ball spiraling, spinning, then twisting to the inside just above the cypress knee. Marko stands solid, swinging his fist with all his might, missing. Still looking determined, he shakes his head as the catcher tosses the ball back to Tommy T., who for the moment is silent, no chicken sounds.

From my vantage point Tommy T.'s back is sturdy as a weathered board, his biceps the size of grapefruits. The biceps tighten, swell. He's holding the ball. Can't see his face. Can see Marko's, again the determined look, eyes right at Tommy T. The wind, the swing, and the ball goes spinning right at Marko before angling toward the cypress knee. Marko swings and the ball soars right toward me. No, over me.

I turn and put my arms and legs in motion swimming fifteen, no twenty feet, the direction of the center of the lake. Grabbing the ball, I dog paddle with my feet and throw in the direction of the infield, coming a good ten feet short. Roger Wallace standing at the second base barrel treads to the ball fast as he can, shoulder deep when he retrieves it. He turns, winds and tosses the ball the direction of the catcher, Willie Vaughan, the volleyball arriving after Marko.

I swim my way back to the spot where my tiptoes touch silt as Tommy T. hollers, "A shrimp can't make it in a lake. Shouldn't allow a shrimp in Lake Knox. No way he can make it."

His eyes are straight on me as I start to say something back just like I do with Everett, but I don't. No, don't wanta get crossed with that guy. His marbles roll the wrong way. So who's next? Bobby Stubbs. Been over to the house a few times with Everett. Nice guy, doesn't pick, poke fun. Tommy T.'s winding up, releasing, the ball is swirling straight at Bobby. Oops, he's turning but not getting out the way. Ouch! A red mark the size of a volleyball in the small of Bobby's back.

"Only way you'd ever get on base," Tommy T. taunts. "Bet you don't try it that way next time."

Bobby slowly treads to first.

Look, there's Everett. He's got an eye for the ball. Hate to admit it but he's better at this than me. Three more years and I still won't catch him. He has a God-given talent for hitting a ball.

Tommy T. waits and waits, then waits some more. Everett's not as big or strong, nor nearly as old as Tommy T., but when it comes to beating him at water baseball, Tommy T.'s no match, and he knows it. Wonder which way Tommy T.'s marbles are rolling this time. No telling.

Muscles tighten in Tommy T.'s back as his right bicep hardens. He hesitates, then winds and pitches, the spinning ball flying straight at Everett, then turning toward the cypress knee just before reaching Everett. His eyes are hard on the ball all the way. I can see all, clear as daylight. Next thing the volleyball is sailing full speed above me. I turn and see the ball hit the lake a full twenty feet behind me, then push off the silt bottom with my toes and take off swimming with every ounce of my energy, finally reaching the ball, grabbing it with both hands as I dog paddle with my legs.

What's that? It's my right calf, all tightened up. Got to reach for it. Now it's my thigh, legs all frozen up. Pain everywhere, my whole leg! It's a cramp. Been sweating all day and hardly had a drop of water. Happens on dry land, I'd just pull myself up and walk it off. No place to walk. Water's over my head! Nobody can see my face. I'm looking across the lake, not at them. Need to let go of my leg, tread with my arms. No, I can't! Got to grab my leg. I'm going under, mouth open 'cause I'm screaming with pain. Water's going to my lungs. Oh, I'm struggling! Paddle with my arms. Paddle with my arms! I can't. Got to grab my leg! I'm going under, now coming back up, choking out water to scream.

"Help! Help!" I'm yelling at the open lake. Can't see a soul. Can't see any of them. Blue sky above, no clouds, I'm going back under, reaching for my cramped leg. Nothing but silty water all around. I'm completely under.

Gotta get up. Gotta get up. Need air. Need air! What's that? I hear a voice, even underwater.

"Gonna get you, Gunter. Gonna get you." It's Everett's voice, calm as Dad's, almost to me. An arm comes around my chest just under my arms and lifts me up to air, the blue sky back in view. I'm coughing out water, now it's air through my mouth all the way to my lungs. I'm drinking air, gulping it, forgetting my leg pain for the moment as Everett swims toward shore, one arm around my chest, his other arm working the water with his feet. "You're gonna be fine, little brother."

I hear voices all around me, too many to make sense of it all. Everett's feet are now on bottom, I can tell. There's another pair of hands latching onto my right arm just about at my shoulder. Everett's got my other. They're pulling me, my face looking at sky, now lifting and carrying me onto the bank, my leg still cramped, shooting with pain.

Laying me on the ground, I'm able to match a face with the second set of hands. It's Marko Cellini. He's holding my shoulders down as I view the sky, Everett straightening my leg and massaging my calf, then my thigh, and finally bending my leg back and forth. The sky is now obstructed by eyes all around peering at me. The pain begins to subside, leaving behind a dull ache in my calf.

"You're gonna be okay," Everett reassures me. "Marko, sit him up," then back to me, "low on water?"

"Yes."

"I'll get my jug," Bobby Stubbs says as he retrieves his jug and hands it to me. I'm sitting up with only the faint ache remaining. I gulp water, my body craving it, then pause, gather some air, then go after the jug again. The water is lukewarm, but not full of grit like Lake Knox.

"I said we shouldn't put a shrimp in this lake," Tommy T. says. "A shrimp can't survive in that lake twenty minutes. Proof positive is on the ground right now. Now we're gonna have an uneven number for the game." Tommy T.'s counting on his fingers as he speaks.

He's counting on his fingers!

"If you're so tough why didn't you go after him when he was drowning? Chicken or just can't swim?" Marko Cellini says. Has the same look he had just before he hit his home run.

"Why, I oughta—"

R. C. steps in front of his brother. "Pipe down, Tommy T. There's been enough interruptions in the game without you startin' another one."

Tommy T. raises his hands like he's going to say something but can't think of anything to say.

"I'll sit out," Bobby Stubbs says.

Is Bobby caring for the group, or afraid of getting hit again? Doesn't matter to me. Anything that will shut Tommy T. up.

"Okay," Tommy T. says as he shrugs. "Let's play ball."

"You gonna be all right?" Everett asks.

"Yeah," I say as I smile at him. It's a smile I give, not a grin.

•   •   •

What a day. I'm worn out but not sleepy. Takes me longer to get to sleep than Everett. I can hear his breathing from the bed across the room. We used to sleep in the same bed at the shack and at Everett Crossroads. I'd wait till he got to breathing good then I'd yank his covers off; actually, I'd slip 'em off. Made sure he didn't wake up. Tonight just the thought of that makes me feel guilty. Might have drowned today. Probably would have. How did he get to me that quick? Must have been looking at me when he rounded the bases.

Been doing a pile of thinking lately. Hey, Everett called me "The Thinker," but he was just pokin' at me. I have been feeling more grownup, just not enough to die, not at age twelve. Not even a teenager yet.

Everett didn't even mention my mishap to Mom and Dad, didn't go to braggin' or to tattlin'. Dad would have been concerned, but would have probably said, "What'd you learn from it? Not all learnin' comes from a book." Mom would have gone crazy. She'd be walking the floor all night, even though I'm tucked in my own bed. Might have forbidden me from going near Lake Knox until I was twenty. No, Everett did all right. And there he sleeps. Need to start treating him better.

Back to me. All the other boys my age, at least those at church, have gone forward professing their faith in Jesus and gotten baptized. But not me. Haven't felt the urge just because everybody else is goin'. Not gonna do it that way. It's a matter of principle. Haven't got struck all at once like Paul was. Still, I've got the faith. God's not just "up there." He's right here listening, leading, forgiving. I know this. Need to start responding. This has all come on gradually, sort of like my daydreaming took me today when I was walking to Lake Knox. My mind tuned out about Third Street and the next thing I knew I was on the gravel road outside of town. Knew for a fact I was outside of town, but couldn't tell you exactly when I passed the sign. And that's where I am with my faith. Somewhere along I've passed over. Might not make sense to anybody else, but it does me. Long as I've got the faith, when or where it happened doesn't matter. Think I'll go forward at church tomorrow. Can't say my near drowning today hasn't motivated me a little, but that's not the reason. It's time.

FOUR

"Come on Robert!" I yell back, my leather soles hitting sidewalk fast, paper bag full of lunch and snacks hitting my leg every other step. Rays of early November sun peek over the rooftops and tree lines as the streetlights begin to flicker, then go out. "Streetlights"—a new addition to Oak Leaf, WPA put them up. Things change—gradually, it seems, until you open your eyes, awaken your mind, then notice your surroundings are different . . . like the plum tree in our backyard, a tiny seedling, not half the height of a nine-year-old, now three times my height, flowering each spring, plums green, then red, green leaves turning to brown . . . then loosened, falling to the ground.

Change, change, change. Ninth grade, top of junior high, and Everett a senior in high school, out on his own just next year. Me, fourteen, sort of like this early morning hour, caught between night and day, fast on the verge of grown up, height shooting up, me taller than five-foot-one-inch Mom and shorter than six-foot-one-inch Dad. Fuzz forming on my chin and above my lip, muscles shaping my biceps and chest. No longer a seedling, but not a full-grown tree. A sapling . . . yes, a sapling, physically, emotionally . . . a lot of growing done . . . plenty left to do.

Almost there, three whole blocks. Can't use the excuse, "train's on the tracks, had to wait on it." Not when we live on the right side of the tracks—at least as far as the school is concerned. I can hear the soles of Robert Rugetti's feet right behind mine, and the commotion of two school busloads of ninth-grade boys and girls ahead, each group competing to be the loudest.

Robert spent the night with me. Lives in the country, rides the bus to school. Today we're to be at school at six, two hours early. Those who live in the country spent the night with folks in town. Only way it could be done—that is, to get all the ninth-graders loaded up, on the road, then back again by night. Gonna go "live some history"—Mr. Reynolds, the history teacher's idea. Been doing it since Everett was in the ninth grade, becoming a "tradition." Anyway, no class today, 'cause we're going on a field trip to "live some history." Not going to class sounds fine to me.

Robert is one of my best friends. The other is Jimmy Street—son of the bank president, Mr. Street. He lives on the boulevard in a two-story house and doesn't have a cow or chickens behind his house. Does have a Chrysler. We've got a car now, too—a Ford. Had it two years, but it's older than that, and a little younger than me. Mom's been saying she's going to learn to drive ever since we got it, but beginning to have my doubts.

Anyway, Robert Rugetti lives in the country. His father came over turn of the century from Italy with the big wave of Italians that came to work the fields, pick cotton. His dad's too young to remember what it's like in Italy. He also never went to school, even one year. Grandparents still speak Italian. Don't have a clue what they're saying, but they get real excited about whatever they're talking about, hands moving faster than their mouths. And spaghetti—they eat it all the time. Folks over in the hills may have heard of spaghetti, but have never tasted it. Don't have a clue.

Well, the Rugettis farm cotton, and a few grapes. Couldn't figure out why anyone around here would be farming grapes. Last year I was out at Robert's just when they picked them. His dad and grandfather put them in a big wooden tub, then his grandfather took off his shoes, stepped in the tub, and started walking, "squishing" the grapes with each step. Later they bottled the grape juice, and Robert said it would be months before they opened it.

Well, it didn't take algebra to figure out they were making wine, simple as two plus two equals four. And alcohol is still illegal in Mississippi, repeal of Prohibition or not. I figured that if they got caught they'd simply say they were making it for communion. "Times are hard. Parish can't afford to pay for wine. We were just making it for the church." Anyway, I found out all the Italians were growing grapes, so communion is safe for many years to come. Financially, Robert's family is to ours what ours is to the Streets. He was one of seven: four brothers and two sisters, not including grandfather, grandmother, aunts, and uncles. I've finally figured out what Dad meant years ago when he said "too many horses eating out of the same trough." Robert's three older brothers didn't finish high school, and not because they weren't smart enough. They had to go to work.

"Hey, Wall, Rugetti, get a move on. They're saying if we don't leave soon, we won't have enough time for the trip. We'll have to go to class, and you know how much I love going to class." Otis "Hoppy" Pearson's voice bellows over the uproar of mostly fourteen-year-old hellions, his voice older, though not more mature, than those surrounding him. "Slow and Slower, come on!"

Where "Hoppy" got his nickname I don't know. Perhaps he didn't like the name Otis, or maybe he had hopped from class to class, his age at least two years beyond ours. Two girls in our class had "skipped a grade." Why couldn't Hoppy have just "hopped back a few?"

So here we are, thirty-six of us, I think—students that is, if all of us are here. And Mr. Reynolds—Doyle Reynolds—history/civics teacher fanatic, clipboard in hand, check a name here, check a name there, come on now, engine is running, bus is pulling out, gonna "live history today."

And there's Mr. Terry, principal for junior high and high school, decked out in buttoned sweater, all "buttoned up," hands crossed, fog of early November morning air flowing freely as he exhales, just like my own breath. Guess he's along to keep an eye on things—maybe both eyes—at least on the boys.

"Okay, Mr. Terry will see the girls aboard, while the boys wait up," Doyle Reynolds says, pointing the clipboard in the direction of the bus.

Shrill, inaudible sounds come from the direction of the girls as they load the bus, a unified swarm, as in bees heading to the hive. Mr. Terry, unfolding his arms, ambles through the swarm, the inaudible shrills muffled some as the bees enter the hive.

I catch my breath as clouds rise from my mouth, warm air meeting cold, as I view the sun edging above the housetops. Boys dash toward the bus, only to be slowed by Doyle Reynolds, gatekeeper and peacekeeper, with clipboard in hand, ready to pop one on the head for corrective measure. He spares them all . . . for the moment.

"We gonna get on board?" Robert says from behind me.

"Yeah, guess so," I say, as I move forward at a pace slower than those ahead. "Hope there's still room so we can sit together."

Onto the bus I go, noise all around, shrills from the beehive in the back, and voices between childhood and adult—somewhat low in pitch but high in volume—coming from the front. I take my seat, lay my sack lunch down, Robert right behind me, Jimmy Street and Hoppy Pearson just in front. Near the front of the bus, Mr. Reynolds stands, clipboard in hand. Mr. Terry next to him, arms crossed, eyes us all.

"May I have your attention?" Mr. Reynolds says. I hear him. Others don't. "May I have your attention? Listen up!"

The beehive gets quiet as activity stops, girls and boys looking to the front of the bus, "listening."

"Today's drive will take about four hours, one way. We'll stop for a break about halfway," Mr. Reynolds continues, his voice calm, deliberate. "Today we will learn and experience history. It will perhaps be a time on which you can look back someday and reflect. Now, you all appear to be seated, so let's keep our seats. I don't mind you talking, but I do mind you shouting—so keep things civil."

Doyle Reynolds stops talking with the word *civil*—a frequent word in his repertoire that he sings regularly, along with *civics*, *civilized*, and *civilization*. Laying down the clipboard, he takes his seat behind the wheel and pulls the lever, closing the door. Mr. Terry gives two approving nods, then takes the seat right behind the driver. The bus rolls forward, a turn into the street, one more turn two blocks down, then through the downtown, all the shops and offices closed for now, on past the cotton oil mill, the only place of current work activity, a place alive, thriving at a time when most say we are still in the thick of the Depression, on past some houses, then none. Now we are on a straight line of two-lane concrete, dead cotton stalks to the side with stretches of hardwoods here and there, the sun now fully round, glaring through my window as we roll south. I cup my hand to the side of my face to shield the sun.

"I think the guns are in the wooden box under Mr. Reynolds's seat. Got to be. That's why Mr. Terry is sitting behind him. Got to guard them." Hoppy Pearson turns so Robert and I can both hear. Jimmy listens in, too.

"Have y'all seen 'em before? The pistols are just alike, two of 'em with long barrels. Wonder who is gonna shoot 'em?" Hoppy pauses a moment before continuing. "Y'all ever shot a pistol before?"

Three heads shake in unison as Hoppy watches, then says, "I have." Hoppy pauses as the head shaking stops and mouths open, eyes widening. "Yeah, several times, actually. My dad's got one, for protection he says. Let me shoot it at some tin cans last year. I'm quite a shot."

"What good is shooting at tin cans?" Robert chimes in, sticking a pen in Hoppy's balloon—or, at least attempting to.

"If I can hit something as small as a tin can from forty yards, I can hit a deer, a rabbit, a robber, anything," Hoppy says, unaffected by Robert's comment.

Robert nods, nothing else to say—at least for the moment, as Jimmy and I look on.

"I've shot a shotgun," I say. "Twenty gauge. Dad got it year before last when his uncle died. Went rabbit hunting with Dad and my brother last year, and I hit a rabbit running at full speed, right before it finished running in a circle. Going again Saturday, all three of us."

"Well, people don't duel with shotguns. They duel with pistols," Hoppy says.

"People don't duel with anything, anymore," I reply. "Except us today. Besides, we ate the rabbit. Did you eat the tin can?"

Robert and Jimmy grin. Hoppy doesn't. Slowly, Hoppy and Jimmy turn back forward and things get quiet again, at least from our section of the bus. The shrill voices from the rear of the bus are now a light, intermittent hum, the sounds from the front not shouts of enthusiasm, but conversational, normal volume. I look out the window, across an open field a month or two earlier filled with cotton, now nothing but empty stalks, the sun slightly higher, but still a glare in my face. I cup my hand to the side of my face again to cover the glare and look forward, the bus engine now the loudest sound. Time to be quiet. Time to think. My mind wanders.

Screech . . . screech . . . Mr. Reynolds's foot goes heavy on the brake pedal as the bus slows, then turns in to the gravel. Animation fills the bus, the rolling motor vehicle filled with youthful people bursting with energy, others, such as myself, with a physical need to stop the bus. Yes, stop the bus so I can go pee. It's been almost two hours since we left and I'm about to pop. And look around, people going crazy. Noise deafening. The bus stops.

Mr. Reynolds rises, beat to his feet by thirty-six hellions ready to get out the door, open or not. "Okay, settle down . . . settle down!"

How can I? Where's the door? Out of my way! We're gonna stampede you, all thirty-six of us!

"We're going to take a fifteen-minute break to stretch our legs. There's a restroom inside the store. I want you all to be back in front of the bus in precisely fifteen minutes for a brief discussion of history." Mr. Reynolds eyes his watch with exactness, minutes not precise enough, seconds the real measurement.

Creaking door opens. Crowd down the aisle. Stampede! Stampede! On to the store. Place has something to do with a bear. Mr. Reynolds said so in class. Don't see any bears. Don't see a single bear. I run across loose gravel, on to the store, fourth in line. No girls in front of me, thank the Lord!

Minutes later, I'm back on the gravel, beside the bus. Boys are mingling near me, girls down the way, two drinking a Coca Cola or RC Cola, something in a glass bottle. Must be rich—or crazy; it's eight o'clock in the morning. And there's Mr. Terry, still on the bus, bladder of steel, legs that don't need stretching, guarding "the pistols."

"All right, gather close," Doyle Reynolds says, this time not shouting, as thirty-six former hellions gather like sheep, the chilly November air causing me to shiver, my coat on the bus, not on my body. Sheep gather closer together, huddle, warmth in numbers as the shepherd patiently waits for quiet, boys and girls now together.

"Thirty years ago President Theodore Roosevelt paid a visit to this area for a bear hunt. The expedition camped on this very spot." Doyle Reynolds gestures with his hand as he speaks.

"Bet he didn't come on a school bus," Hoppy says, just loud enough for Robert, Jimmy, and me to hear.

"President Roosevelt was quite a hunter, a real outdoorsman. He traveled the world to explore the great outdoors, and to hunt. This particular expedition brought him to the Mississippi Delta, at the time a vast flatlands, hardwoods outnumbering cotton fields—a wilderness." Mr. Reynolds pauses and nods, hoping that all are listening.

"Here we go again. Record's broke, same lines as last year. Heard this all before," Hoppy says, just above a whisper.

"Last year?" I say.

"Sure. Already been through this 'living history' routine before. Came last year. He's getting ready to tie the bear to a tree. Just wait and see," Hoppy says, completing his comments with total confidence.

"Well, at one time the black bear was plentiful in these parts, just like the hardwoods. However, by the turn of the century, the black bear was becoming scarce, perhaps from over-hunting, or loss of habitat. I don't know for sure. Anyway, the hosts wanted to ensure a successful trip for the president, *success* meaning he kills a bear." Doyle Reynolds pauses, nods, hopes the sheep are listening.

Hoppy stands, still quiet, confident.

"Man named Holt Collier, a Negro, best bear hunter in the state, corralled the bear, just like a steer. Tied it to a tree."

"Just like I told you," Hoppy says, this time not a whisper.

Doyle Reynolds looks up, eyes our direction. Someone is disturbing the flock. Is this someone trying to get his goat? Or perhaps just a ninth-grader being a ninth-grader. He continues, eyes now back to the total group. "Well, Collier guides the president and his entourage straight to the bear: a scraggly, puny creature, helplessly tied to a tree."

"Teddy bear, teddy bear, we're almost grown and standing in the cold, hearing a story about a teddy bear," Hoppy says, this time between a whisper and real talk.

Mr. Reynolds's eyes shoot our way, as if President Roosevelt had aimed and fired his gun. The shot misses. He looks at me. "Gentlemen, do you wish to tell the story, or should I?"

I shake my head, trying to communicate to Mr. Reynolds with my face that I wasn't talking, but he's not buying it. He thinks it's me.

Point made, Mr. Reynolds picks up with the puny, scraggy, creature tied to the tree. "Gun in hand, the president shakes his head. Won't even aim at the bear. No sport in shooting a bear tied to a tree. He went back to Washington without bagging any big game. The story of the barrel-chested, bespectacled president standing gun in hand in front of a scrawny bear tied to a tree appears in a cartoon. Hence, the 'teddy bear' is born. Soon, people are making small fortunes selling stuffed bears. And all of this because of a bear hunt a mile or two from where we now stand."

"So," Hoppy says.

So? I think.

Ninth-grade boys shrug while girls nod, smile, and engage in small chatter. "Neat." "Swell." "Swell and neat." "Really swell." "Really neat." I think I'm nauseated. Time to get aboard. Let's go shoot some pistols. I'm chilly. Open the door. Time to leave.

"Yes, a small part of our national history. Well, time to move on," Doyle Reynolds says, looking at his watch. "Oops, we're late. On board . . . ladies first, gentlemen second."

Onto the bus I go, right behind Robert, on past Mr. Terry, guard of the firearms, his arms folded, watching each student as they pass, granting a small nod here and there. Bees buzzing in the back of the bus, boys saying, "Hope I'm the one to shoot the pistol." "Hope, it's me." "Never shot a pistol before." "I have." Engine's running, brakes' creaking, door closes, bus onto the concrete as we all head south, hardwoods either side, the road flat and straight, hills ahead, pistol shooting to take place.

FIVE

The early morning November chill gives way to late morning warmth, the sun almost mid-sky. No need for a coat as we walk across the grounds, towering oaks amid ancient red brick buildings. The boarding school, although not boarded up, today has few boarders. After all, this is the Depression. Money is scarce, and so are students on grounds that once teemed with males, their ages a few years either side of mine. We enter the nearest red brick building, a two-story structure over a hundred years old, the massive ancient wood planks creaking as we cross the floor.

"History. History. We are walking on history. We are walking through history. Today is a day some of you will take note of, others not. It is my hope that by doing, not just hearing, you learn something. Learn to look around, make a mental note that the things that happen in the present will in the future be history. Things in this world happen unexpectedly, sometimes suddenly, sometimes gradually. The sudden everyone notices, the gradual, most don't. I don't know what the future holds. 'God knows,' as I say." Mr. Reynolds pauses, catching his breath before continuing. "Well, this school has been here since 1811. Students, usually of privilege, come to live and study here. Perhaps the school's most famous student was Jefferson Davis, the one president of the Confederacy. Perhaps one of you will someday be president. Nothing would please this teacher more; that is, if you are a good president, worthy of serving."

"Somehow, I feel like I'm the only one here who fully understands what he is saying," Jimmy whispers to me.

"What?" I say.

"Yeah, I understand. I mean, the part about one of us someday being the president of the United States. I figure it'll be me."

I smile a smirk, a "you're a comedian and this time you're really funny" smile.

Jimmy's face is serious, thoughtful, reflective. He says nothing. My gaze turns back to Mr. Reynolds.

"Well, this is the moment all of you boys have been waiting for. Your lone assignment was to bring the piece of paper I had you write your name on in class yesterday. I'm going to have each of you drop the piece of paper in this bag I'm holding, then I'll draw out two names." Doyle Reynolds extends the paper bag before himself, two hands firmly grasping the bag's edges, an open-ended receptacle for the opportunity of a lifetime.

Rectangular slips of paper float into the bag as each of us eagerly releases our clutch, hope riding sky-high as the slips land in the bottom of the bag. I briefly close my eyes as I let go, only to reopen them quickly to make sure that my ever-important slip didn't somehow miss the bag. I peer into it, arms somewhat extended, blocking those behind me, to see the slip of paper, *Gunter Wall,* front-side up. I smile facially, internally, then move on.

Mr. Reynolds seals the bag and shakes it once, twice, a third time, then reaches in, withdrawing the paper slip. "It is Pearson."

Otis Pearson! Hoppy? No way! Not fair! Well, maybe so . . . he didn't get to do it last year. Come back a second time, and you double your odds. Hey, it's a big deal, but it's not worth repeating ninth grade, is it?

"Can I be Aaron Burr? Let me be Aaron Burr! Can I be Aaron?" Hoppy is going mad, exuberantly so, as he hops up and down.

"We'll see, Otis. We'll see," Mr. Reynolds says in a calming fashion, hoping his demeanor is contagious.

Mr. Reynolds reaches into the bag a second time, his hand sifting through the slips of paper before grabbing hold firmly to one. "Gunter Wall. Yes, Gunter Wall. Well, I guess today you get to be Alexander Hamilton, our first secretary of the treasury. We'll let Otis be Aaron Burr, since he is quite anxious to play that role. Let's now proceed outside so we can relive a moment of history."

"Oh, how come Wall gets picked?" "Must have been rigged." "Some guys get lucky." Boy after boy makes a comment as we follow Mr. Reynolds out the door, down the steps, out into the grass toward a towering oak, leaves no longer green, now November brown, still holding firm to the limbs. A floating sensation fills my stomach, followed by the tightening of the muscles around it—sort of like the times I've jumped from a tree, freefalling toward the creek. Gonna be fine; think I will, but don't know for sure, like I've hit the water, gone under, and come back up to see the sky above. Never shot a pistol before. Never been shot at with a pistol . . . not a real one. Oh, I'll be all right, know I will.

How long have I been thinking? There's Mr. Terry standing at the foot of the tree, examining one of the pistols, placing a shell into it. Good, the shell has a flat top, no lead in it, just a casing filled with powder.

"Boys and girls, gather around." Mr. Reynolds calmly rallies the group. "Come in closer. Yes, closer. Okay, let's first go over some important facts. Alexander Hamilton served in the Revolutionary War, then later as secretary of the treasury during George Washington's first presidency, a position he later resigned. Prior to serving as secretary of the treasury, he was influential in establishing the Constitutional Convention and later its ratification. He believed in a strong federal government, a position greatly opposed by men such as Thomas Jefferson."

Come on, come on, you're rambling, Mr. Reynolds. I'm ready to shoot the pistol. Actually, I'm getting nervous, anxious. Let's get on with the show. Oh brother, look at Hoppy, bouncing up and down. Wonder what he's thinking?

"Now, Aaron Burr also fought in the Revolutionary War, starting as a private, later becoming a lieutenant colonel. In 1791, he defeated Alexander Hamilton's father-in-law for a post in the U.S. Senate representing the state of New York. He ran with Thomas Jefferson for the United States presidency twice, in 1796 and again in 1800. Because of a glitch in the United States Constitution, which was later corrected, he tied with Thomas Jefferson in 1800 in votes for the presidency. It took thirty-six ballots by the House of Representatives to solve this dilemma. You see, Burr was supposed to be vice president and Jefferson, president. In the end it all worked out, with Thomas Jefferson becoming president, and Aaron Burr vice president."

Why don't you just get to the point: Jefferson, president . . . and Burr, vice president?

"Alexander Hamilton was influential in helping see that Jefferson became president." Mr. Reynolds pauses, hoping to let this thought soak in. Girls appear to be listening, while all the boys stare at Mr. Terry, now holding two pistols. I attempt to listen and look at the pistols.

"Mr. Burr then served as vice president under Jefferson. Toward the end of his term, he ran for governor of New York. Hamilton supported his opponent, attacking Burr's character in the process. Burr challenged him to a duel. We take up at that point, July 11, 1804. Now, the duel actually took place in New Jersey. Not here."

"You mean it didn't take place under this tree?" Jimmy says. He, too, is listening, and watching guns at the same time.

"That is correct," Mr. Reynolds says, obviously pleased that at least one male soul is listening.

"Then why did we ride four hours in a bus for the duel?" Jimmy questions.

"I'll come back to that later, after the duel," Mr. Reynolds replies.

Jimmy's face reads, "Why not now?" but he doesn't speak.

"Dueling in the United States took place with pistols, not swords, as was sometimes the case in Europe. It was also legal—that is, in some places, while not in others. An important part of the duel was the presence of witnesses, of which today we have plenty. Now . . . let's see. Yes, Gunter and Otis, come with me, and we will proceed with the reenactment," Mr. Reynolds says, walking toward Mr. Terry just as he finishes speaking.

I hesitate, if only for a moment . . . no, longer than a moment, a tightening of muscles, stomach to groin, an airy sensation within, most notable in the lowest part of my groin. I squirm, weight on left foot, then on right, unable to put the left or right in forward motion. Frozen . . . gotta get going. Gotta get going. Hoppy and Mr. Reynolds are already at the tree trunk, Mr. Terry handing pistols to Mr. Reynolds, one now in each hand pointed straight into the air.

"Gunter . . . Gunter . . . what are you waiting on?" Mr. Reynolds's stare is direct.

"Nothing, sir." My feet now in forward motion.

"Now, Gunter, I'm sure you know to point the pistol into the air, not to aim it at anyone," Mr. Reynolds says, handing me the gun, my grasp now firm around the stock. "Otis, likewise."

Otis is smiling, no, smirking. People are staring at me, not all of them; some are looking at Hoppy.

"Now, come with me," Mr. Reynolds says as he begins to walk away from the base of the giant oak, out into an open area. "Now, here's the script. I'm going to have each of you step off fifty paces. Otis, you go that way." Mr. Reynolds nods. "And you the opposite, Gunter. The rest of you students gather around behind me. I said, gather around behind me!"

Students begin to move.

"At the time, neither man knew the outcome, live or die. Neither did the witnesses. Today we do. When I say 'fire' each of you will aim at the other and squeeze the trigger. Gunter, you will fall to the ground wounded. Do you understand? Gunter, do you understand?"

"Yes sir."

"Okay, now, once you've fallen to the ground, I'll have you, you, and you go check on Gunter," Mr. Reynolds says, randomly pointing at two girls and one boy. "Gunter, you remain on the ground until I tell you to get up. Do you understand?"

"Yes sir," I say before thinking. Now, let me get this in order. My mind is swimming in facts. Fifty steps and turn. Mr. Reynolds says "fire" and I pull the trigger. No, wait . . . wait . . . gotta aim at Hoppy first, then pull the trigger. Then fall to the ground. Do I scream? Do I go down gently or have my feet fly out from under me? Do I lie still, or wiggle, squirm? Mr. Reynolds is not much on details. He spent all his details on telling us "secretary of treasury, vice president, governor of New York." Now, who's the vice president? I'm confused.

"Gunter, are you with us?" Mr. Reynolds says, looking right in and through my eyes, straight to me.

"Yes sir."

"Well, let's get a move on. Back to back. Otis, you this way and Gunter the opposite."

My feet float. We're back to back, Hoppy and me. Don't even remember walking over. Now, one, two, three . . . forty-eight, forty-nine, fifty. I turn, air engulfing my stomach, flowing downward to my testicles. Can hardly stand still, weight on left foot, then right. I turn. Hoppy's hopping. I raise the pistol, weighty, unsteady, circling a small circle, up and down, left eye closed, right one open.

"Fire!"

I hesitate. Not long, only a moment, not even a second . . . yet, an eternity. I squeeze the trigger. Think I'm on target, right at Hoppy. This is weird. Shot at a tin can, shot at a rabbit . . . at a person? Didn't even hear a sound. Had to have gone off . . . smell the powder . . . strange sense of smell. Strong. All I can think about—oh yeah, I'm supposed to fall. I'm the one who got shot.

On the ground, I loosen my grip, let go of the pistol. Wasn't much of a fall, no theatrics, no melodrama, just sort of dropped to the ground with a thud. Now, look at the sky. Sun's right overhead, right in my eyes, better look someplace else. That's better, blue—clear sky, no clouds. What's that, a cloud? No, it's water, flowing water, pure, clear, never ending, unlike I've ever seen. I stare, with my eyes, my heart, my soul.

"I'm Aaron Burr! I'm Aaron Burr!" Hoppy's jumping up and down awakens me. "I'm Aaron Burr. I shot Alexander Hamilton."

"Settle down, Otis. I said, settle down!" Mr. Reynolds shouts with the second "settle down."

Hoppy stops.

Sally Roberson, Mary Smith, Jimmy Street looking down at me. "Jimmy, didn't see you get picked," I say.

"How's it going, Gunter?"

"Don't know. I guess weird, really weird. Glad I'm not really shot," I say.

Yeah, glad I'm not really shot. There's Jimmy and two girls looking me over head to toe. Never had two girls looking me over. Ever. That would be my luck. Two girls, not one, giving me the most attention I've had in my life just as I'm dying at age fourteen.

Jimmy lays a serious eyes-wide-open look at me as my mind drifts to the shore of Lake Knox summer before last, male eyes peering down on me, cramp wearing off as Everett massages my leg. Eerie thought. No, not really. I felt safe on dry land and even safer in Everett's hands, knew I was gonna make it, whereas two minutes earlier thought I was drowning—just the opposite of Alexander Hamilton. Two minutes—life can change fast. Look at Jimmy. He gets the most serious looks, but never one more serious than this. It's like he's traded places with me and he's the one on the ground. His eyes can't let go of me.

"Now class, let's gather around. Hoppy—I mean, Otis—give Mr. Terry the pistol. Now!" Mr. Reynolds says, waiting impatiently as Hoppy reluctantly hands Mr. Terry the pistol. I see all this from the corner of my eye.

"Good. Good," Mr. Reynolds continues. "Now, Alexander Hamilton didn't die immediately; he lingered for a day. Painfully, I'm sure."

Wow, I bet I'd really be hurting now . . . and wondering when I'm gonna die.

"Yes, Mr. Hamilton died the very next day. And Mr. Burr . . . yes, Mr. Burr. His life takes a path of great change. Here he is, vice president of the United States, having just shot and killed one of the country's leading figures. He continues to serve as vice president, but, for all practical purposes, his political career is over. So, why did we drive four hours in a bus to this spot? I believe you asked that, Jimmy," Mr. Reynolds says, turning toward Jimmy.

"Yes sir, that's what I've been wondering," Jimmy says.

"Mr. Burr came to the South, around these parts. He was suspected of recruiting a group to invade Mexico, maybe even an insurrection against this country. Who knows? He was a strange, shadowy man. Anyway, he was captured and brought here. There was a trial of sorts, as legend has it, under that tree," Mr. Reynolds says, pointing to the massive oak we had earlier stood under. "We are not sure that it was under that exact tree, but it was on these grounds."

"Was he convicted?" says Jimmy, ever the inquisitive one.

"No. No, he was released. He was, however, later tried for treason before Supreme Court Chief Justice James Marshall. He was acquitted. But, you see, there is a bit of history on these grounds, and I believe that by coming here to experience our little exercise, you will remember more. Yes, experience history. The events of the present become history. At your age, I never thought I would be a part of the World War, and yet I was. Never thought I'd go to France. I did. Didn't know what a depression was. Do now, twenty percent of our country not working. When your parents tell you there's not enough to go around, listen. Hey, I forgot to mention the flood. Any of y'all remember that?"

Nods come from all around; this I see from the corner of my eye. Do I remember the flood? Feet get cold just thinking about it. Gave me a shiver down my back just then, and here I am on the ground, supposed to be bleeding to death. Yeah, and they are all ignoring me. What if this were real? What if I were breathing my last breaths of life? Strange.

"Mr. Reynolds?"

"What, Gunter?"

"May I get up, sir?"

"Yes. Yes, Son. Hand the pistol to Mr. Terry."

I'm onto my knees, then to my feet, handing the pistol to Mr. Terry. It feels good to stand.

SIX

"Everett, you grab the shotgun," Dad says as he slams the door to the Ford. I pile out of the backseat, as Everett picks up the twenty gauge and places a shell in the single-shot shotgun, an inheritance to my Dad from an uncle. The shotgun is far older than Everett or me. I tend to set the age of most things according to my age, the Ford being five years younger than me, Everett three years older . . . so on and so forth. This is the third year in a row Dad has taken off a Saturday in November to take Everett and me rabbit hunting.

"Gun, you get the knapsack?" Dad says.

"Yes sir," I reply, knapsack containing precious cargo strung to my back. I'm carrying the cured ham and biscuits. Truth be, if I were alone, I'd been eating them right now.

"Let's walk on down a ways before we enter the woods," Dad says, field of dead cotton stalks to his right, woods to the left. "Last year, if I remember right, we had our best hunting down that way," Dad says, pointing.

Mr. Rugetti, Robert's dad, gave us permission to come on his land.

"Yes, this is the spot. Let's go lookin' for some briars," Dad says, turning into the woods with Everett and me in tow.

"Everett, you might want to get up here to the front. We're gonna let you start out shooting first, and let you try later, Gun. Heard you missed when you shot earlier this week," Dad says, a small smile crossing his face.

I know he's kidding, but he still gets my goat.

"Everett won't have any better luck than me if all he's got is powder in his shell. Can't kill a rabbit with just gunpowder."

I wait for a response, from either. None comes. Irritating.

"Everett, look at that thicket up yonder. I bet it's just teeming with rabbits. Probably get run over by the stampede. You be careful, Gun."

Dad's kidding is getting to me. He hardly ever kids. Always serious. Always working, or planning on working. Can't remember the last time he kidded me.

Dad takes a stick and throws it in the briars, the stick landing right in the middle.

Nothing.

"Well, boys, don't know what to think of that. Sure looks like the spot we stirred them out of last year. What do you think?"

"On to the next one," Everett says as I shrug.

Time passes, one more patch of briars, then another, and another, nothing but sparrows and killdeers scattering from the last two. No rabbits.

"Well, boys, don't know what to think," Dad says, the kidding gone from his voice, disappointment all over his face. Dad's usually not one to display his disappointment.

"Maybe if I were holding the gun," I say. "It would probably make all the difference in the world."

"If you can't hit a still Aaron Burr, how you gonna hit a running rabbit?" Everett says.

"Can't hit a rabbit if you don't see one," I say.

"All right, smarty britches, you take the gun. I'm tired of carrying it anyway," Everett says, handing me the gun just before we get to the next patch of briars.

I raise the shotgun to my shoulder to make sure I can do it with the knapsack on my back. No problem.

"Let's see what happens this time," Dad says, kissing the stick before heaving it into the briars.

Two rabbits shoot out the left side at the speed of light as I aim at the second and pull the trigger. Sounds so loud it about bursts my eardrums as two rabbits scamper on.

"Like I said, if you can't hit a still Aaron Burr, how you gonna hit a running rabbit?" Everett says, this time cocksure, confident, after the fact.

"Oh, I was just makin' sure the gun would fire. Nobody's shot it this year, and now we know it works. Those rabbits will be right back around after a while, and I'll probably get both of them with one shot," I say, thinking, how'd I miss it? Probably wouldn't have hit Aaron Burr even if there was lead in that bullet. Better buckle down, be ready for the rabbits when they circle back around. They don't return.

"You need to take a better shot next time, Gun. Best be patient, steady," Dad says, this time no kidding, just good advice.

Next briars, Dad tosses the stick, followed by the patter of paws on leaves quick as anything straight at me, one rabbit leading another. This time I take aim at the first rabbit, squeeze, and don't jerk as the first rabbit goes down, the other veering off in another direction. Second time is the charm. Sort of like Hoppy Pearson repeating the ninth grade. Not really; his second chance took a full year.

"Yep, gun works," I say. "One of y'all want to retrieve it for me?"

"I will," says Dad, without skipping a beat or making a comment.

Two briars later I shoot a second rabbit. Dad ties the hind feet of the rabbit to a leather thong strapped to his belt, just like the first one.

Just after tying the rabbit, Dad turns to Everett and me. "Don't know about y'all, but I'm about half hungry. Let's go find us a log to sit on and try some of those ham and biscuits."

The thrill of the hunt causes me to forget about my hunger, a hunger now reawakened by Dad. Yes, cured ham, salt upon salt on pork, placed within Mom's homemade biscuits. Rabbits are out of my mind, quick as they run.

"Let's find that log quickly," I say, as I follow Dad and Everett at the fastest pace we have walked all morning.

Just to the edge of the woods, in view of the empty cotton field, is a downed oak, uprooted, gnarled, tentacles extended in all directions. Twenty, twenty-five feet down is the first clear spot on the tree low enough for us to sit on. I lay the shotgun on the limb.

"Gunter, you might want to unload that thing 'fore you go to laying it down. That gun's got real lead in it, not like the one Hoppy Pearson was aiming at you earlier in the week."

Back to ribbing me again. Trying to make my blood boil.

"Gunter, this time I'm not kidding. I saw enough people shot and killed over in France, enough for a lifetime. Unload the gun," Dad says, serious as he ever gets.

"Yes sir," I say, shrugging before unloading.

"Now, reach in that knapsack and make sure the ham and biscuits didn't fall out while we were walking," Dad says, this time not so serious, a smile with dimples cracking the cracked skin.

I reach down, right hand in knapsack, grabbing the paper bag within, reaching again within that bag, then looking and collecting nine ham and biscuits, and three red apples. Mom loaded us up. "You boys are going to get hungry walking all day, so I'll fix three for each of you. I know they won't go to waste."

"Gunter, you gonna wait till Christmas to hand me mine?" Everett says. "You know it's November."

He always says that. Just substitutes the month. In January it will be "You know it's January." A dime for me each time he says it, and at fourteen I'm a millionaire.

"Here, Everett, your Christmas present. You get it early this year," I say, handing him a ham and biscuit just before I hand Dad his.

I open my mouth, teeth to attack biscuit, baked flour and grease hardened somewhat by air.

"Hold your horses, boys. Who's gonna bless this feast? People going hungry right here in these United States, and we got three ham and biscuits apiece," Dad says.

Everett looks at me, both hands on his ham and biscuit about chest high. I look at him, eye level, just above my ham and biscuit.

"Well, I guess I get to be the preacher today," Dad says. "Bow your heads." Dad pauses as eyes leave the feast, then continues, "Lord, we thank you for every morsel of this food: ham, biscuits, apples. May you bless it to the strength of our bodies. Now, there's lots of folks going hungry in this land, this very day, at this very hour, and here we are with an abundance. Thank you for giving me the job at the oil mill. A good job. Thank you for my boys. Good boys. Keep 'em safe. Keep 'em healthy . . . if you will. Thank you for this time we have together. Thank you for this day. In Jesus' name, amen."

I guess today he is the preacher. That was almost a full sermon. Now I'm gonna destroy this ham and biscuit . . . but, look at Dad. Is that a tear in his eye? Never seen one of those ever before, even after the flood. Why the tear?

"This sure is good," Dad says. "Y'all need to give your mom a hug, maybe even two when we get home tonight."

This ham and biscuit is just as good as the first. Better take a bite of apple to get the biscuit down. Can't remember the last time I was this hungry. Got two rabbits this morning. Everett got none, 'cause he didn't shoot. Not my fault he's got bad luck.

"Dad?"

"What's that, Everett?"

"Most folks go rabbit hunting with a dog. Beagles are the best, I hear. Why didn't we get another dog? I mean, after we lost Old Blue?"

Dad looks at the ground, studying a leaf, then looks back up, clearing his throat. "Lots of heartbreak losing Old Blue. Might seem strange, what I'm gonna tell you, Everett, but it's the truth. When we moved to town, we didn't have to have a dog. There were a lot of things we had to have, starting all over from scratch. I had to focus on the things we had to have, like food. Fact is, beginning all over, I was feeding all the mouths I could at the time. I guess since then we might could have swung it, but y'all weren't begging for one, so I just let it pass. Strange," Dad says.

Sure is. I'm fourteen and never bothered to ask why. Have to get us all sitting on a log together to bring it up.

"Boys, as blessed as we are, I sure wish I could do more. I'm really proud of both of you. Everett, in a few months you'll be graduating from high school, seven more years of education than I got." Dad pauses, looking to the ground a moment before raising his eyes back in the direction of Everett. "I wish I could pay to send you on to college. Never had a person in my family or Mom's either graduate from college. That would really be special."

"Don't want to go to college, anyway," Everett replies. "I want to get on with the railroad, become an engineer, see the country. That's what I want."

Railroad? Me, I don't have a clue. Haven't thought that far. Don't think the railroad's for me. I'm better with my head than my hands, second smartest in the class, behind Jimmy Street.

"Well, I think that would be just fine," Dad says, interrupting my thoughts. "Just do your best at whatever you get a chance to do. That's where most folks mess up."

What does he mean by that?

"Yes sir," Everett says, nodding his head as my mind drifts again, for a moment back to Old Blue, then to water near the roof of our house, finally to water on the roofs of other houses.

"Dad?" I ask.

"What's that, Gun?"

"Whatever happened to Bo and Sweet Pea? Wasn't that their names?"

"Yes it was, Son," Dad says pausing, perhaps wondering where my question came from. "Freddie Carl and Lula's two. Don't know for sure. Freddie Carl took 'em north, I think to Chicago. It was their chance to get away. Have no idea how they got the money to leave, but they did. Freddie Carl was always one to get things done. That was about a year after the flood, and I haven't heard a word since. That's the way things were. People got scattered everywhere, just like us. We ended up coming back to this part of the world, and others moved on. Why'd you ask?"

"Don't know. Guess I haven't thought of them in a long time. And what about that other family that gave us a ride in the boat?"

"Roy Jarvin and his wife. Last I heard, Jarvin was still running trotlines on the river. Folks like them just sort of hang to themselves. It was good they came along, wasn't it? We might have drowned or starved. Probably should go thank 'em, shouldn't we? Fact is, don't think I ever mentioned it, but I tried to look him up a couple of times after the flood, but they were too hard to track down. Never did catch up with 'em." Dad pauses reflectively, then says, "You 'bout finished with that last ham and biscuit, Gun?"

"Yes sir," I try to say, mouth half full.

"Everett, you grab the gun. Thought we might walk the dredge ditch this time," Dad says, standing as he speaks.

Everett held the gun the rest of the day. That afternoon we jumped a few rabbits, and Everett shot three, one more than me. Wasn't fair. Anyway, we cleaned them in the woods, as Mom wouldn't stand for us doing otherwise, then rode home in the dark, Everett talking about the three he shot all the way.

"Owwwee, let me see what you got," Mom says as we come in the door. "Take those shoes off. Take those shoes off, before you track all over the clean floor," she says before we can display the hunt.

I notice her graying hair, her wrinkles. Haven't looked at Mom of late. Not really. Life's been come-and-go. Growing up fast. Soon as we get our shoes off she smiles. It's good to see her smile.

SEVEN

"Man, it's cold." Robert Rugetti shivers as he speaks, the wind howling, biting, straight into our faces as we look across frozen Lake Knox, right on the edge of Oak Leaf, Mississippi, New Year's Eve, 1940, late afternoon.

Lake Knox is hardly a lake, more a big pond a half mile across and one mile long, five or six feet deep most places, maybe ten feet in the middle, almost drowned in it when I was twelve. It's never frozen one end to the other, at least not that anyone can recall; that is until this week. The temperature dropped into the teens two days before Christmas and has remained that way until the last three days when it dropped to near zero.

"Never been this cold before." "It's too cold to snow." I've heard it all from the old-timers over the past week, the last statement one I can't get a handle on because every picture I've seen of the North Pole has snow in it. People have been saying strange things and doing strange things—like standing in front of a lake at near zero with a twenty-mile-an-hour wind blowing in our faces.

"Why don't we do some ice fishing?" says Jimmy Street.

" 'Cause it'd take too long to put the boat in the water," I reply. "We'd be trying to break ice for hours just to get it in."

Jimmy, Robert, and Hoppy Pearson all stare at me with a "quit trying to be a comedian" look. At least, if only momentarily, it stops them from shivering.

Here we are, seniors in high school, almost ready to embark on the world—that is, with the exception of Hoppy Pearson. Hoppy embarked early, forgoing his senior year, which was actually his junior year, as he had drifted back a year once more—a habit he had begun in elementary school and repeated in junior high. Joined the army now and is in the air-something, a part of the army that deals with aircraft. He's here on three-day leave, stationed five hours away in Shreveport, Louisiana, and has learned to fix airplane engines. At first, the thought of someone flying a plane with an engine repaired by Hoppy Pearson is scary. Fact is, Hoppy's always been better with a wrench in his hands than a book. Actually, as I recall, he was always fixing things, or talking about fixing them.

"So, where'd you get that Ford, Hoppy?" I say.

"Shreveport. Wasn't running when I bought it. Couldn't afford to buy a runnin' car on soldier's pay. Paid forty dollars for it, and paid forty dollars for the parts to fix it. Took me two months to make it run, but run it will."

"What year is it?" Jimmy says.

"It's a 'twenty-seven. What's yours?" says Hoppy.

" 'Twenty-eight. Don't know that it matters with a Ford, 'twenty-seven or 'twenty-eight. They all look the same. Black."

"Maybe this will warm us up," Robert says, waving a bottle in the air as he speaks.

"Where'd you get that?" I say.

"Borrowed it from my folks. They won't miss it. Grape crop was good this year, and we got a room full of 'em, or we once did. Anyway, anybody got a pocketknife to get the cork out?"

"I do," I say, reaching in my pocket, nearly frozen hand meeting cold metal. I hand it to Robert.

"Yeah, this won't take long," Robert says, bottle in one hand, pocketknife in the other, digging in the cork, four pair of eyes fixed on the bottle.

"Let me make sure it's safe to drink," Robert says, left hand wrapped around the neck of the bottle, downing two quick gulps. "Ahh . . . now that's a vintage wine. June."

"Let me see," says Hoppy. "Probably weaker than hummingbird piss. I've drunk stuff over in Shreveport that'd take the paint off my Ford. Come on . . . come on. Hand it to me. Let me take a try."

"All right," Robert says, passing the bottle to Hoppy, the exchange like a baton pass between two sprinters, hand-to-hand-to-mouth.

"Not bad," says Hoppy. "In the army we'd call that a 'breakfast wine.' Let me take a couple more swigs to make sure," Hoppy says, taking two more gulps.

"Hey, what about me?"

"What about you, Street? This wine's not bad, but it's no banker boy's wine. Y'all drink champagne mainly, don't you?" Hoppy says, grinning wide.

"Only on the weekends," Jimmy says. "Now, let me make sure y'all know what you're doing. Let a man of good taste be the judge. Pass it to me."

Hoppy's grin spreads wider, creases touching his ears as he releases his grip and Jimmy gains his.

Two gulps, then a third followed by a cough. Jimmy obviously lacks the depth of Hoppy's experience. "A June wine is not a bad one. Personally, I prefer May." Jimmy coughs a second time after making his proclamation. He hands me the bottle, looking relieved as he makes the exchange, the glass cold against my hand.

What now? I've never tried this stuff. Ever. Had grape juice at the church plenty of times, but this can't be the same, though it looks just like it. Let's see. I'll use one hand, or two? Two. They all downed it like they were drinking water. Better do the same. Ooh . . . ooh . . . that burns down my throat through my chest, into my stomach. Now, can I do it again? I don't know . . . but they all did, so here I go again. Ooh . . . ooh . . . burns all the way down. Stomach's on fire.

"Now, that was good."

"Did you leave us any, Gunter?" Robert says.

Did I leave you any? Could have left you the whole thing. It's awful, I think, then say, "You're lucky it was so weak or I would have." I hand Robert the bottle, freeing me, if only for the moment, from further self affliction.

The bottle makes one more round, barely making it to me a second time. Sometimes in life we are fortunate.

We migrate to the front of Hoppy's car, Hoppy sitting on the hood. Why we are on the outside of the car, biting and bitter wind now to our backs as we face Hoppy? Making sense of one's actions at age seventeen is seldom logical, I'm learning.

"Yeah, they promised me I'd see the world when they signed me up. Spent the whole time so far in Shreveport. Been to two other states in my whole life—Arkansas and Louisiana—and they send me to one of 'em. Give me three days off and I got time to drive home and drive back." Hoppy is being as philosophical as I've ever seen him.

"I'm afraid that's gonna change," Jimmy says, "probably for all of us."

"What do you mean?" I say.

"I mean, we may all see the world. Maybe Germany. Maybe Japan. In a way, it would be better to go see them, then them come see us. Can't imagine what it would be like to have Japs or Germans here in Oak Leaf," Jimmy says thoughtfully. Jimmy gets this way: serious, philosophical, mature beyond seventeen. Gradewise, he is first in the class, while I am second—a distant second, the gap in our maturity and understanding far wider than the gap in our grades.

"Well, I don't think we've got any concerns there," Robert says.

"How's that?" says Jimmy. "You don't think war with Germany or Japan is imminent?"

"No, I don't think there's a reason for them to come to Oak Leaf. There'd be nothing for them to do. They'd all end up dying of boredom," Robert counters. "Speaking of boredom, I've got a quick cure for that," he says, heading toward Jimmy's car as all our eyes followed him.

Quickly, Robert emerges waving a second bottle of "vintage June wine" in the air. "I know my folks won't miss that first bottle. Not quite so sure about this one. Got that knife again, Gunter?"

"Yeah . . . yeah," I say, caught off guard, fumbling in one pocket, then in the other, before locating the knife.

I hand it to Robert as he repeats removing the cork, this time an "old pro," quick and to the point. Manners to the wind, he again goes first, bottle straight up, one gulp, two gulps, a third, then on to Hoppy, around to Jimmy, finally to me. This time I go slower, not like a sprinter trying to be first out of the starting block, but like a miler. Need to pace myself. Might collapse before the finish line. What would the crowd think? Doesn't burn as much this way. Not too bad. Not too good either. Oh well. I pass the bottle on.

The second time around (with the second bottle). I'm getting used to the taste as well as the routine. "Old hat."

"Another hour, and it'll be dark. Days are so short this time of year," Jimmy says, his words succinct as usual, but slurred.

"Uh-huh." "Uh-huh." Robert and Hoppy say in sequence.

To me, the cold is not as cold. And, although I'm not on the water, it seems that way, like I'm in a boat going up and down, kind of gentle, then a tad bit rougher, a little more unsteady. How's that? I'm standing on dry ground. The wine is making me strange.

Robert heads to Jimmy's car a third time and emerges with a third bottle of "vintage June wine," as the group begins to banter.

"Oh, this time I wanted May!"

"Mississippi wine. Don't you have any foreign wines . . . like from Arkansas or Louisiana?"

"Here's the knife, Robert. Sure you don't want to just pull it out with your teeth?"

"Don't you think your dad's gonna figure this out? Three bottles missing!"

"I'll worry about that next year," Robert calmly says, again going first.

"Robert, you got no couth," Jimmy says.

Hmm, *got no couth*, that's not like Jimmy, always grammatically proper. Never heard him butcher the English language before. Guard's down.

Once around, I take my turn, again the miler, not the sprinter, baton to Robert, on to Hoppy.

Hoppy pauses before partaking. "What year did you say your Ford is?"

Jimmy stares at Hoppy, like I-told-you-that-less-than-an-hour-ago-dimwit, before saying, " 'Twenty-eight."

Hoppy slides down the hood of the 'twenty-seven, walks down to Lake Knox, and keeps walking, unsteady at first, then more confidant, stopping to stomp, first right foot, then left, then both. Hopping. "Come on out, the water's fine!" he yells.

I look at Jimmy. Jimmy looks at Robert, then Robert and I look at each other. Robert walks toward Lake Knox, Jimmy and me in tow.

The ice is slick against the leather. I almost slip. Is it the ice or is it the wine? Both. The ice is firm, my legs are wobbly. The wind is hard in my face, stinging, unyielding. Oh, feels like the flood, riding in a boat on open water, wind in my face. I turn. Relief, back to the wind.

"Wonder how much weight this ice could take. Bet it's at least a foot thick, probably frozen halfway to the bottom," Hoppy speaks loudly, thinking the louder he speaks the better we'll listen. We all hear.

"What the point, Hoppy?" Jimmy says.

Ice or no ice, he's caught the lure. Hoppy's gone ice fishin' and caught a big one and gonna reel him in all the way.

"Well, the lake might not support a school bus, but a Ford . . . shoot, nothing to it. It'd be like gliding on glass."

"So, again, what's the point?" Jimmy says.

"Ford quit making the good ones in 'twenty-seven. Nothin' but sorry hunks of steel since, and I ought to know. I'm an expert on such things."

Jimmy looks at Hoppy, wanting to reply. Unable to counter, he says nothing.

"What I'm getting to is, a 'twenty-seven could easily beat a 'twenty-eight across this lake. Not even a race. Are you up to it, Jimmy?" Hoppy says with confidence.

Jimmy hesitates. I'm studying him, as are Hoppy and Robert. He looks perplexed, torn.

"Actually, I think that road around the lake would be a better test," Jimmy says, pointing back to shore.

"Naw, no sport in that," Hoppy says. "What we have before us is the opportunity of a lifetime. Lake's never been frozen before, leastways going back to the time of the Indians. Won't ever be frozen again, at least during our lifetimes. Opportunity beckons. What do y'all say?"

I shrug, Robert is quiet, Jimmy is contemplative. Hoppy is staring—confident, daring, tempting.

" 'Course, it needs to be fair," Hoppy continues. "Three of y'all in one car with just me in the other wouldn't be fair. Gunter, you ride with Jimmy, and Robert with me. Whatdoyasay?" Hoppy says, pausing then repeating "Whatdoyasay."

"Well, I guess that would work," Jimmy says sheepishly, devoid of normal confidence. He then braces himself, and replies from deep within, "Yeah, as long as it's two on two, I suppose that would be fair."

"Settles it," Hoppy says. "Robert, you come with me."

Robert's pale. Confused. Drunk. Hoppy's halfway to the shore when he wakes up and begins to follow, slowly at first, then a jog, trying to catch Hoppy before the shoreline.

I turn to Jimmy, a loss of words at first, then, "I can't believe we're doing this."

"Yeah, me neither," Jimmy says. Then, "If we're gonna do it, we had better get going."

On toward shore we march, slipping and sliding as we go, aided somewhat by the wind at our backs, as well as a faint glimmer of a setting sun peeking between the clouds, lighting the way, sunlight to our backs.

In no time we're in the Fords, Jimmy's on the left, me riding shotgun, open air to my right, setting sun through the clouds to my front, fifteen feet from the lake.

Just to my right, twenty-five feet, is Hoppy revving the engine, looking out the open air space of his door, a petrified Robert Rugetti to his right. Of all people, Hoppy has shown the wherewithal to separate the cars by twenty-five feet. "Might slide into one another, and ruin at least one good Ford."

"In order to be totally fair, I'll let you tell us when to go, Gunter," Hoppy yells over the engines.

I nod and think, what am I supposed to say? Been to track meets, but never a car race. At the track meets they use a gun, and last time I fired a gun with Hoppy Pearson around I didn't fare too well.

"Hmm . . . racers to your mark. Get set . . . go!"

Down the slight incline onto the ice, sliding and slipping, rear tires hit the ice, then ahead we go, tires spinning fast, car going slow. Out my window, Hoppy's Ford is half a car length ahead, his going straighter than ours, Hoppy's head straight ahead, tires spinning fast, car going slow, with Robert Rugetti grinning back at me the whole way. Robert's grinning! Lowlife.

"Come on, Jimmy, can't you keep us going straight?" I say, front of the car weaving one way, then the other.

"Hush up, Gunter! You got no idea what it's like driving on ice."

"Yeah, I really don't have any idea what it's like driving on ice after a bottle of wine," I say.

"Whoa . . . whoa . . ." Jimmy says, hitting the brake as the car swerves to the left . . . full circle.

Oh, my stomach . . . feel like I could throw up . . . dizzy like crazy . . . Oh boy, straight ahead again. There they are, two car lengths ahead with Robert looking back, grinning ear to ear, Hoppy all straight ahead.

"Come on, Jimmy! Come on, Jimmy!" I'm hollering.

Jimmy's looking, eyes forward, determined, serious, quiet . . . pale. Finally, "What's that?"

"What's what?" I say.

"Something doesn't feel right."

"Like what?" I say.

"Whoa . . . whoa . . . oh no!"

Front end of the Ford going downward, back end raised, then lowering slowly—the whole car. One foot, two feet, three feet, water coming up to the window. Water coming through the window.

"What's goin' on? What's goin' on!" I'm yelling at the top of my lungs.

"Better get out, Gunter, or we're gonna drown," Jimmy says with an air of calmness amid the mayhem.

Yeah . . . yeah, got to get out, I think, pausing a moment longer for my body to react to my mind, then placing both hands on the roof. I pull myself out, icy water on my back, then my legs, car slowly going down. I spy Jimmy across the rooftop. Our eyes meet and say "You've made it so far . . . what now?"

Car's going down.

"Gunter, gotta start swimming!" Jimmy yells a direct command like he knows just what to do.

I start swimming—or, at least try. Shoes on my feet feel like concrete, legs, stomach, chest numb with cold all the way to my lungs. Hard to breath. Hard to move. Got to move. Got to move! I swim with my arms, kick with my feet, then reach out for ice and try to lift up. Ice breaks. Ice breaks again.

"You there, Gunter?" Jimmy yells, his back now turned toward me.

"Yeah, yeah! Can't pull up! Ice keeps breaking," I say.

"Same here," Jimmy yells back.

I try again and again, and fail, total body numb. Finally, the ice quits breaking. Good. Good. Ice is thick again. I struggle to pull up. I try again. I can't. I can't! Don't have it in me. Eyes are closed, like that will give me more strength . . . conserve my energy. What's that on my arms just above my wrists? I feel a grasp through the numbness. I open my eyes. Hoppy Pearson.

"You're gonna make it, Gunter," Hoppy says calmly. "Just quit wiggling. Quit fightin' it."

Words hit me, like a brick. I go limp. Hoppy pulls me up, my knees now on the ice. He drags me a few feet and we stop. I collapse on my back, breathless, dizzyingly numb, head spinning, sky above me almost dark. My mind awakens. "Jimmy. Where's Jimmy?" Then a voice.

"Gunter, we made it," a panting Jimmy says. "At least for now . . . my dad's gonna kill me."

Relief. Reassurance. We're all alive. All safe. That is, until my dad kills me too. Oh, I'm cold, cold to my lungs; lungs feel like an ice pick is stuck right in the center. Last time I almost drowned here my lungs filled with warm water; this time it's cold air. Don't know which is worse.

"Better get a move on," Hoppy says. "Sun's almost down, and we got to get at least one car off the lake. If I don't get back to Shreveport in time, the army might really shoot me—or make me wish I was shot."

I go to my knees, dazed, numb, disoriented, peering toward the shore the direction of a sun that's disappeared, rays bouncing slightly against the dark clouds, old black Ford sits just before the shoreline. To my feet. We begin to walk. Sloshing in my shoes, slippery as slippery can be, leather on ice, wind down a little but still blowing at my face, at my body. Body's numb. No one says a word.

"Guys, car's not gonna make it on its own. Gotta have a push from the back, probably all three of you," Hoppy says.

I nod, as do Jimmy and Robert. No arguing. No one boasting. Hoppy slides into the Ford, no hopping from Hoppy. Third try, engine turns, exhaust fumes in my face, into my lungs, waking them up.

"Give a push!" Hoppy yells.

Spinning tires, slipping leather, we run, three of us with open hands on the back of the Ford. "Plunk," immediate resistance as the front tires hit the shoreline.

"Come on! Come on! Give it a shove," Hoppy yells over the roar of the engine.

Rear tires are spinning like crazy. Pushing with all my might, my feet slip every other push, Jimmy to one side, Robert to the other, nothing at first, then progress, half a car onto the ground, two thirds, then one final unified push and car's on terra firma.

We dash to the car, in through the passenger side, then pack inside tighter than canned green beans. Hoppy revs the engine as the Ford goes forward on frozen ground, first running over two wooden lawn chairs before heading toward a house.

"Watch out, Hoppy!"

A silhouette in front of us comes to life—Mr. Ruston, who owns the hardware store. Hoppy swerves to miss him—and the house . . . barely.

"What the hell's goin' on out here? What the hell's goin' on out here . . ."

Ruston's voice fades as we speed around the house, out onto the road, gravel flying everywhere.

EIGHT

"You boys are trying to put me in an early grave. First, your brother
has been home exactly four times in three years. I never see him. Moved
to Memphis because he wanted to work for the railroad. He could have
found a good job around here. I get a letter a month from him, if that,
and I write him twice a week. Now look at you, Gunter. Look at you!"

I'm sitting at the table, my body wrapped in two towels, both feet
crowded together in Mom's roasting pan full of warm water, and I'm
shivering, teeth rattling so loud as to be heard by Dad, who sits across
from me, and Mom, who is next to him. Her hands are shaking, tears
streaming down her cheeks as she speaks. Doesn't take much to get her
this way. Ignore her a day or two, she gets all pouty, stares at the wall.
Come in late two nights in a row and she's fit to be carried off in a
basket. Tonight I come in wet head to toe, icicles in my hair and on my
eyebrows. I'd thought about riding around in Hoppy's car for a while,
but I might have frozen to death. Literally. Hoppy dropped Jimmy off
first. Got no idea how the conversation with his folks is going right now.
Probably something like Jimmy saying, "I misplaced the car," Mr. Street
then inquiring, " 'Misplaced?' Where did you see it last, Son?" "Dad, I
think it was on Lake Knox?" "On Lake Knox!"

Guess I'm luckier than Jimmy. Maybe I'm not as lucky as Robert.
Hoppy was to take him home out in the country after he dropped me off.
Robert's all dry. "Lucky Robert," no immediate explanation necessary.
Wait a minute—three bottles of wine missing. "I'll worry about it next
year," he said. Well, January first is only five hours away. Mr. Rugetti, his
father, Italian to a T, gets animated when a leaf falls. "Three bottles of

wine missing!" And his grandfather—how does one holler, "Trimmed the vines, hoed the weeds, picked the grapes, squished them with my feet in a barrel, bottled them in the finest bottles!" all in Italian, top of his lungs, hands waving in the air?

"Gunter . . . Gunter! Where is your mind, Son? I've been asking you a question for the past minute, and you look like your mind's in another country. What gives?"

What gives? I know all right, but what do I say? Where do I start?

"Well, sir, Hoppy Pearson was back in town today. You know he's in the army now. Works on airplanes," I say, not knowing what to say next.

"Yes, I know Hoppy," Dad says, then stops, eyes on me . . . eyes through me.

Hoppy Pearson, lucky rat. Probably on his way out of town right now, while I'm facing the inquisition, just like Jimmy and Robert. He's a free man, a free man with a car. Wait—he did save my life. On the other hand, my life might not have needed saving if he hadn't showed up. We'll call it even.

"Gunter. Gunter!" Dad says, real loud the second time.

"Well, anyway, we went out to Lake Knox this afternoon: me, Jimmy, Robert, and of course Hoppy," I say.

"Lake Knox? May I ask why?" Dad says.

"Yes sir. Well, at first we thought about ice fishing."

"Ice fishing?" Dad says.

"Yes sir, ice fishing. We gave up on that though. Ice was too hard to crack. You know it's been cold quite awhile, already long enough for the lake to freeze all the way across. You remember that ever happening before?" I say.

Dad shakes his head. Says nothing. Mom . . . look at Mom, all pained in the face, like the next thing I'll tell her is that I died. Go ahead, get the basket to carry her out, not me.

"Well, anyway, we thought we would take the opportunity to drive Hoppy's car and Jimmy's car across the lake. After all, it might have been a once-in-a-lifetime opportunity. Hoppy's car made it."

"And Jimmy's car?" says Dad.

"Nope."

"Nope?"

"I mean, no sir. 'Bout middle of the lake, deepest part, it went through the ice, Jimmy and me in it," I say, finally getting it all out. (Although, I did leave out the part about the bottles of wine.)

"Oh, my God! Oh, my God, you went through the ice into the lake!" Mom stands up screaming like I'm still at the bottom of Lake Knox.

"What about Jimmy? What about Jimmy?"

"Hoppy dropped him off before he did me," I say.

Mom sits back down, Dad putting his hand on her knee to steady her. They both look at me. No, more than that—they scrutinize. We share a moment of silence before Dad says, "I lost a car once to water. Hurt losing that car. Thought we'd never make it up financially, but we did. Good we didn't lose you, Gunter."

"Yes sir," I say, feeling like I need to agree, at least verbally.

"Supper's still on the stove," Dad says, looking in the direction of the kitchen. "Why don't you help your mother put it on the plates."

I stand, wrapped in a blanket, socks on my feet, and hobble toward the kitchen, right behind Mom. We eat, few words said other than Dad's prayer thanking the Lord for having me with them. Even prayed for Everett's well-being. Must have done it 'cause we were on Mom's mind. No, the way Dad prayed, we must have been on his mind too.

Later, in my room, I sit wrapped in two blankets, feet again stuck in hot water in the pan Mom cooks the roast in. Can't seem to get fully warm, especially my feet. On my bed there's a letter, Everett's name and a Memphis address top left corner. I open it.

Dear Gunter,

Thought I would drop you a note and let you know I enjoyed seeing you Christmas. I wish I could have stayed longer, but my job with the railroad doesn't allow much time off. I hope to come down this summer. I've got some vacation time, and there would be nothing better I would like to do than see you all.

Life is not so easy. They work us pretty hard, but I'm lucky to have a decent paying job. Matter of fact, I'm lucky to have a job. Anyway, connecting the cars is hard work, but it is easier than loading them. What I really hope to be is an engineer. I guess you know that.

Anyway, I thought I'd encourage you to give college a try. I don't know how much money you or the folks have got, but I sure would go, no matter what it takes. You've got the brains for it, that's for sure, and it would be nice for a Wall to get a college degree. You would be the first.

Anyway, got to go. You take care of Mom.

By the way, home ain't so bad. It gets lonely here sometimes. The letters from Mom really do me good, so you encourage her to keep writing me. Matter of fact, if you get bored you can write me yourself.

Sincerely, Everett

I study the letter a minute longer, place it in the envelope, then get up and put it in my chest of drawers. It's a keeper. I cut off the light and head to bed, tonight with extra covers. It's been a quite a day and for right now it's my mind that's swimmin', thoughts of the day crowding it, like "why did I drink wine?" The answer is "I don't know," and there's got to be a better explanation than that. Like maybe it was just the time and the place. That's it! I'm seventeen. Be leaving here in a matter of months and I just felt like it was time. Yeah, that's it. No, it's not. Know myself better than that. I did it 'cause the others guys did. Just followed along and fell in. This time I really fell in, to a lake. Why did I get in that car? Drunk, acting crazy, or just following along? Nobody dragged me, did it on my own feet unassisted. This time my near drowning can't be blamed on something other than me. I've got to think about this. Almost drowned for the third time and I'm only seventeen. Couldn't have lasted another two minutes in that lake, and this time Hoppy Pearson of all people pulled me out! Hey, if it wasn't for Hoppy I wouldn't have been there to start with. Yeah, if it wasn't for Hoppy I wouldn't have been there to start with. Hoppy Pearson! No, it was me, and I don't know exactly why I did it.

God, other than the prayers at meals, church, and school it's been a month or two and I'm not paying attention to those half the time anyway, although I know I should be. No, it's been a good month since we've really talked. Please forgive me for what I did and help me figure out the steps I took this day. Don't need to repeat some of them. Also, thank you for sparing me from drowning. This was the third time. I'm old enough to understand there may not be a fourth.

NINE

M r. Street, Jimmy's father and president of Oak Leaf Bank is talking.
"So, Gunter, in less than five months you and Jimmy will be high school
graduates. I can't believe how fast you boys have grown up. In some
ways . . ."

Yeah, in some ways. Jimmy and I are currently the laughingstocks
of the whole town. If everybody in town didn't know about our mishap
by New Year's Day, then they did when the weekly newspaper came out,
headline saying "UNCONFIRMED REPORTS OF CAR GOING
THROUGH ICE IN LAKE KNOX." People saying, "Have to wait till
it gets real dry and the lake gets low, and we may be able to see the top of
it. Fishin' ought to be real good at that spot this spring. The bream'll be
bedding in it. Just drop your pole in the water and fill up the boat. Won't
even have to bait your hook! We sure are grateful to you boys for making
Lake Knox the best fishin' in the state of Mississippi. Wonder what you
two will think of next?" and on and on and on. My mind is swimming
like it does some nights before I go to sleep.

"Yes sir."

"Well, what would you like to discuss today, Gunter?" Mr. Street
says, wearing a deep red tie, starched cotton shirt the whitest of white,
pinstripe wool suit, looking through his reading glasses across the biggest
desk I've ever seen. Mahogany, I think.

"Well, sir, I came down to apologize for the car."

"Yes, the car," Mr. Street says. "Jimmy's going to miss that car. I
suspect he'll be walking for some time to come. Fortunately, it wasn't the

Chrysler," he says, eyes piercing through the spectacles, studying me like a balance sheet as I squirm, if only a little.

"Is there anything I can do, sir?" I say.

"Not really. You weren't the one driving," Mr. Street says, breaking eye contact for a moment before continuing. "Your father came to see me New Years Day. Offered to help pay, like it was his responsibility. Your father's one fine man, Gunter. You come from good stock." Mr. Street stops, letting what he says sink in, maybe waiting for a response.

"Yes sir," I say, a bit of pride filling my chest, a small smile crossing my face.

"A fine man indeed, your father," Mr. Street says. "He's taken all the opportunity in life he could have. Honest, industrious, a good people-person, a real asset to the oil mill I hear, and to the community. Yes, he's done well with life." Mr. Street pauses to collect his thoughts, then continues. "Not prying, Gunter, but do you know how far your father went in school?"

"Through the fifth grade, I think, sir," I say.

"I declare. Never would have thought. Would have guessed right off he'd have least graduated from high school. He carries himself well, as do you, Gunter. Where do you plan to be in a year?"

Where do I plan to be in a year? I wish I knew. Dad's been down to Mr. Street offering money for a car, and he's got nuthin'. Yeah, nuthin'. Sure, he's got a home and a car, but what I mean is, he has no money to send me to college, 'bout like everybody else in town.

"I don't know, sir," I say. "I plan on working at the grocery store again this summer, like I've done the last three. I've been able to save a little. I've got that savings account you helped me start a few years ago, so I think I'll have enough money saved up to go a year to junior college."

"That's excellent, Gunter. Excellent," Mr. Street says, pausing a moment as if shifting gears. "Well, as a banker I get to meet a few people here and there. You know, have a connection or two. Jimmy's debating between going to State College and the University. Hasn't quite decided yet, unless he's told you," Mr. Street says, in a statement that's really a question.

"No sir, he hasn't told me," I say.

"Would you be interested in either State College or the University?"

Would I be interested in State College or the University, Ole Miss? Who are you kidding? A Wall's never spent one minute in a college classroom, and you ask me if I'd be interested. But how? How? Last I heard my savings account was paying one percent, and what's one percent of almost nuthin'?

"Yes sir, I would," I say, suppressing myself, trying to act grown up, businesslike, in a banker's office. "But how?"

"Gunter, you're smart, really smart, Jimmy says. There might be some scholarship money available, even though the Depression hit all the colleges hard. When I attended the University, I worked three jobs, most of the years. It wasn't easy, but it sure beat the trenches in France," Mr. Street pauses as if he struck a chord within himself, a chord he quickly silences. "As I was saying, it wasn't easy, but—"

"Sir, I would really appreciate your checking around. I would work hard, hard as anybody you know," I say, cutting Mr. Street off before he finishes.

"Well." He pauses. "I'll start checking around."

"Great," I say, not holding back.

"Gunter, one more thing," says Mr. Street, eyes again piercing through his glasses, through me. "How can the two smartest people in the senior class of Oak Leaf High School think they can drive a car across a lake? Hoppy Pearson, I understand. But the two smartest in the class?"

Two smartest in the class . . . yeah, I felt that way thirty seconds ago, then he brings up the car one more time, reducing my opinion of my own intelligence to a level just above plant life. Wonder if Jimmy mentioned the three empty wine bottles? Surely he would have told me if he had. Naw, he hasn't mentioned it. And neither will I. Still, I owe some explanation. "Mr. Street, I've thought about that on more than one occasion. If you are looking for a rational reason, then I don't think I've found one yet."

"Hmm."

"Sir, it's been an honor," I say, rising to shake hands.

"Same here," Mr. Street says, rising to meet me, hand extended.

As the hands clasp, he peers one more time through the glasses saying, "Being smart and having good judgment are not the same. Wisdom."

TEN

Dense, damp, smoldering, the humidity just below a hundred, fixing to rain outside any minute, but hasn't. I sit covered in black robe, back row of students, waiting for the big moment as Mr. Terry speaks.

Mr. Terry, a scholarly sort, my principal for junior high school and one year of senior high (before becoming superintendent), stands before us, delivering one of his scholarly sermons, a pearl of wisdom, shaped and cultured from the finest grains of sand into a symmetrically round, smooth, brilliantly tinted, lustrous gem—a pearl for swine. Look in front of me at the backs of restless heads, all students probably thinking, "Come on, give us our diplomas, time to move on in life."

"Great times of changes you have experienced. Perhaps greater, even more turbulent times lie ahead. You, the class of 1941, entered school in the fall of the advent of the Great Depression. Little did any of us envision the travails that lay ahead at that time, financial difficulties beyond comprehension, right on the heels of the Flood of 1927. All this following a supposed age of prosperity. This very night all of Europe is engulfed in war; the Japanese battle the Chinese. Yet, this night, while we might not all abide in prosperity, we do abide in peace. I say the word *peace* with gratefulness, yet at the same time say it with apprehension, though not with fear. I believe you, with God's help, will respond to the challenges ahead, no matter on what front, or in what form. You will respond with courage, resolution, steadfastness, strengths you have acquired, not just as your own, or necessarily from within the halls of school, but through your parents, and from this community, and finally, from God above. From my observation point, in a school where all twelve grades reside on one plot of land, I've watched you grow physically from waist high. I've watched you mature emotionally, as well as mentally. Perhaps your greatest emotional growth will come in the next couple of years. It may be that you will be called upon to mature rapidly, as those did a generation before you. I wish you strength as you conquer the mountains before you."

"May I close in saying, while I hearten you to be steadfast in character and resolve, I encourage you to be adaptable to change. Our century, thus far, has been one of great change, as are all centuries. Yes, as are all." Mr. Terry pauses, repeating himself as if he needs to meditate on his statement, then suddenly continues. "Change today comes at an ever-accelerating pace, so you will be called upon to adapt quickly. Do so. Remember the dinosaurs. There are no more dinosaurs. They failed to adapt."

Mr. Terry stops abruptly. All said, now for us to do. Dinosaurs? "Remember the dinosaurs," sort of like, "Remember the Alamo." What do either have to do with me? I'm hot, dripping wet, trapped in this black canopy with a starched white shirt, tie around my neck. Probably lost five pounds just sitting here. It would take a sharp knife to cut this humidity. Now, we're standing, my eye catches Jimmy Street just down the aisle with the other S, Susan Smith. He looks so thoughtful, reflective. In a few minutes I'll be a high school graduate, last to get my diploma, a W. "Change" is what Mr. Terry was talking about. Standing in line alphabetically will never change and that's something I can count on. I'll spend my whole life trying to get from the back of the line.

As I reach the stage, I look out into the auditorium at Dad, white starched shirt with coat and tie, his "Sunday outfit." And there's Mom, smiling. It's nice to see her smile. Wish she would more often. And Everett. Yes, Everett. Took the train from Memphis. Took his vacation to see me graduate. I've written him three times since Christmas, three more than I've ever written him before. Probably would have never done it if he hadn't written me first. Saved that letter in my chest of drawers. Mr. Terry hands me my diploma and looks at me, saying without saying, "Use it well."

At the edge of the stage I turn to take the steps, first looking up before I embark. I'm stopped by the view in front of me of Mom, Dad, and Everett in the second row. They came early to get "good seats." Mom is smiling. Everett has the look that he is proud of me (a look a brother can tell, but no one else can). Dad is crying, wiping tears from under his cheeks with his massive right hand. For a man that only made it through the fifth grade, tonight is a bigger night for him than it is for me. I stand staring at the Walls, a family together tonight. The scene touches my heart. I wait a moment longer and soak it in. What the heck. I'll stand here another minute longer. I've been waiting in the back of the line for twelve years. Tonight, the crowd can wait on me as I gaze at my family, looking at them long enough to remember the details of their faces for as long as I live.

ELEVEN

Life magazine, November 17, 1941, top to bottom, two or three inches longer than any of my college textbooks. Strange, today is November fifteenth, Saturday. Never noticed that before, the date on the magazine yet to come. Probably never had time to read it this early before, working two jobs and trying to keep my scholarship. Hardly ever stop, seven days a week, but do on Saturday afternoon. Thanks to Jimmy Street, I'm reading *Life*, the subscription a special gift to him from his parents.

Well, here we both are at Mississippi State College, me 'cause I found a scholarship and two jobs, and Jimmy, I'm not sure exactly why. Might be because his father went to the University, Ole Miss, and Jimmy wanted to be his own man. Jimmy has an independent streak, a trait that's grown with age, almost to a state of rebellion with his dad over the last couple of years. "Dad went to the University; I'm going to State College." Jimmy never said that, but I could sense it, and still can.

Now, some of the freshmen are here because State College's football team was undefeated last year. Now, that's a reason to pick a college! Not a luxury I could afford. Dad gave me a ten-dollar bill the night I graduated from high school, and so did Everett. That was pretty much it. "Wish you well, Son. Going to college is something a Wall's never done. Sorry I don't have more to get you started, but it seems like I've been digging out of a hole my entire life."

So, here I am. Worked at the grocery store all summer. Lucky to have work. Lucky to have work here, at the library, and cleaning up buildings after hours. The job at the library allows me to study, when I'm not loading books on the shelves. It's served me well. The other job

. . . gotten good at moppin'. Have a whole new respect for Mom. I write her. Didn't at first, but Dad got word to me I needed to straighten up, so now I do.

Jimmy's got it better than me—not that he doesn't go hard, 'cause he does. He's conscientious about his studies, wants to be top in the class. Still, he doesn't have any jobs like me. He's in a fraternity though, and it's taken up a lot of his time, too much time. I can tell that's what Jimmy thinks. Serious-minded. Smart as anybody I know. For all I know, he could be president some day. Matter of fact, I remember him mentioning that years ago, the day of the duel with Hoppy Pearson. Hoppy . . . Hoppy Pearson, the army moved him on to Oklahoma, then to California last I heard. He might not see the world, but he's seeing the United States. Robert Rugetti's at junior college. Imagine that—first in his family to get a high school diploma, now he's in college. He was up to see us for a football game in October.

Speaking of football, look at these guys on the front of *Life*, fourteen of them, my age to three or four years older, members of the University of Texas football team. They look tough, tougher than me. Wouldn't want to go up against one of those guys. Three of them are smiling, and one more, kind of. The rest . . .

Past the cover, Ipana toothpaste, four- or five-year-old boy with perfect teeth, smiling, saying without words, "Buy Ipana and I'll be happy to brush my teeth. Matter of fact I'll even smile while I'm cleaning up my room. Buy Ipana. Buy Ipana." Watch out, Jimmy Street, that kid's gonna be president. You got no chance. Opposite page, tall, lean, elegant woman a bit older than me, dressed head to toe with Forstmann wool. Looks expensive. Mom never had an outfit like that. Never will.

I turn a couple of pages. A girl—no, a lady—wearing Vaseline hair products. A couple more pages, another real looker sporting a Hamilton watch and an outfit complete with fur coat and gloves, altogether worth what Dad makes in a month. I can't imagine. Wine advertisements. Fifteen more pages of mostly advertisements, then another wine we've all got to buy that will be perfect with the Thanksgiving turkey. I turn a few more pages. Wow! Two whole pages of shiny, sleek Pontiacs: red, silver, blue, champagne, two-tone of champagne and blue, then a silver and blue two-tone. Rich! Rich-looking, got to be rich to buy. Then a sudden thought through my mind like a bolt of lightning. They don't put the wine and car advertisements on the same pages. Wise magazine, *Life*. "Good judgment," what Jimmy's dad would probably say.

Would you look at that mud? Looks like a Delta cotton field, mid-March, cars and trucks stuck up to their axles in deep, thick mud, puddles all around. Some woman correspondent's been to Russia. Look at the next page, some place called Yelna, a dismal photograph of stark, treeless terrain ravaged by war months before, now left vacant, lifeless against a gloomy overcast. I turn the page. Trenches, dugouts—like what I heard Dad mention (though only once or twice, and then in no great detail). I turn the page again. A dead girl and her grandmother on the ground, killed by a German bomb. Below, a separate picture, the mother sitting on a bench, a distant gaze sort of like Mom's from years ago as we sat on our rooftop, this gaze more distant, more despondent. I turn the page quickly.

An aerial picture of merchant ships in the North Atlantic stretching as far as the eye can see, soon to be armed, the Senate having authorized, the American public having demanded. The picture below, an American patrol officer viewing the flotilla from the air. Enough of this, been working all week, need something lighter. Where's that article about the Texas football team? I leaf through the magazine, almost to the end.

Students with torches stand in front of a lighted tower, a night picture. Fans in the stands. There's the coach kneeling in front of the team. Players going to class. Guy with a letter jacket in front of that tower again, a girl on either side! Page after page says "Undefeated, we're the best. Famous. Winners." Hey, about time for State's kickoff.

"Jimmy, kickoff's in eight minutes," I say, looking at my watch.

Jimmy reaches for the radio next to his bed, turns it on. "Opera." Jimmy turns the knob, "Some guy is talking about something serious . . . static."

"Today we're broadcasting from Pittsburg, Pennsylvania, home of Duquesne. Mississippi State College enters this game riding a two-year non-loss record, marred only by a tie to LSU last month. Today we've ventured far from the South, a cool, no, cold November day."

"Do Cane," I say. "What kind of name is that for a college?"

"Do who?" Jimmy says.

"No, boo who. That's what they're gonna do when it's over. Bulldogs are going to chew 'em up like a bone, then bury them," I counter.

"North versus South. Appomattox is no more! Yankees won't know what hit 'em. Wasn't Pickett's charge in Pennsylvania? This time Pickett leads them to victory!" Jimmy says, pumped.

I smile and nod. "Bulldogs are gonna run over 'em."

"The kickoff. We're under way," the radio announcer says enthusiastically, his familiar voice traveling over a thousand miles to our dorm room.

I lay my head on the pillow and prop my legs on a pile of books at the other end of the bed and get ready for the trouncing.

• • •

Two hours later the trouncing is complete. "Today's final, Duquesne—nineteen, Mississippi State—zero. It will be a long trip back for our Bulldogs. First loss since 1939. Almost forgot what losing was like. That's it for today from Pittsburg."

"Cut that thing off, Jimmy," I say, a pit in my stomach, not like a loss of life, but a pain nonetheless.

Jimmy doesn't budge, a paralyzed body with an unbelieving gaze.

"Football scores from around the country," blares from the radio. "The Saturday the giants fell, that's the story of the day. Word just in from Austin, Texas. With two minutes to go, Texas Christian drove seventy-three yards, with a scoring strike of nineteen yards with eight seconds remaining. Today's final, the Texas Christian Horned Frogs—fourteen, the University of Texas Longhorns—seven. The mighty, undefeated Longhorns go down in defeat before a packed home crowd. If that's not enough, the Mississippi State College Bulldogs, until today, a tie the only blemish on their record, are shut out by Duquesne in Pittsburg, nineteen to nothing."

"Cut that thing off," I repeat.

Jimmy obliges, and I pick up *Life*, looking at the fourteen faces on the front cover, dated November 17, 1941. Let's see, three are smiling, and another one kind of. Bet none of them are smiling right now. Imagine. Couldn't stay undefeated till the date of the magazine.

Glancing across the room at the magazine, Jimmy says, "Life changes quickly."

TWELVE

Placing my fingers on the laces, I raise the football to just behind my shoulder, bending my arm back, then release it forward, the wounded duck flying to a spot well to the left of the intended target, Jimmy Street. Jimmy darts, grabbing the ball with outstretched arms, extended hands, his fingers reaching around the leather, securing the ball just above the ground.

"You're making me work, Gunter," Jimmy says, tossing the ball back to me, the pigskin landing perfectly in my breadbasket, my only effort guiding the ball to the midsection with my hands.

"You need the exercise," I say. "I get mine mopping floors and emptying trash baskets. The only exercise you get all week is going up and down the dorm stairs. You're out of shape, Street."

Idle talk on a lazy December Sunday afternoon, the weather neither sunny nor cloudy, hot nor cold. Nothing distinct about the day, one that runs together in one's memory, a forgettable blur devoid of distinction. It's quiet out, not the bustle of the week with people dashing to class last minute, preoccupied with their responsibilities. No, today is Sunday, a day of rest, an afternoon of leisure before hitting the books tonight.

I hold the ball, my mind drifts aimlessly, no task at hand other than to pass the ball back in Jimmy's general direction when I get ready. I raise the ball to just behind my shoulder, but stop, my efforts interrupted by an extended honking horn from a red Pontiac, newer model, speeding toward us, swerving parallel, then coming to a stop, motor still running, four guys in the car. I've seen them before but don't know their names. Upperclassmen. The one in the passenger seat hollers out through the open window, "Japanese have bombed Pearl Harbor! Japanese have bombed Pearl Harbor! It's all over the radio." The Pontiac speeds off, tires spinning.

"Pearl Harbor?" I say. My mind's blank. I've heard of it, but can't place it at this moment.

"Hawaii," Jimmy says.

I don't know what to say, so I say nothing. I feel nothing. I have no anger, excitement, rage, pain, happiness, or joy. Nothing.

I look at Jimmy, twenty-five yards away and motionless. I look at his face, the face of a person deep in thought, his mind well beyond the moment to events ahead, as if he has foreknowledge of things to come, his thought, his understanding, well beyond mine.

These are things I can sense but cannot explain. The football is back in both hands near my midsection. I feel the lace, the grains of the pigskin. At this moment I have no other thoughts. I say nothing. Jimmy says nothing in return.

THIRTEEN

The mammoth switch engine screeches to a halt, a thousand tons—no, more—in tow, connection pounding against connection, sounds and cars as far as I can hear and see. Two men move slowly to detach a coal-laden car from a boxcar, their backs turned to me as they disconnect, freeing the coal car and the switch engine.

Here I stand, marine private dressed in uniform on a June morning, 1944, waiting. It's 9:00 a.m.—no, zero nine hundred, three hours till we pull out, all two hundred of us heading for Parris Island. Dad said he'd been to Paris once during the last war, but he didn't remember seeing an island. "Just guess I wasn't paying attention," he said, kidding me the whole time, nervously. Everett's long since joined the Army and has been fighting in northern Africa. If Mom were a nervous wreck before this war, her emotions are now wrecked to the equivalent of every locomotive in the switchyard colliding simultaneously. Her clasp around my midsection when I last saw her two weeks ago was rib-crushing, a mighty grip from a tiny woman that left me gasping for air and tears rolling down her cheeks.

Now, here I am in the very switchyard in Memphis that Everett labored in prior to joining the Army, two years of college behind me, that number of years greater than any Wall to come before me, two years short of a degree. I joined the Marine Corps and was chosen to be with their "best and the brightest" for the V12 Program, then grouped together with others of like talent, all of us destined to become commissioned officers (or so we were told). We've spent the past year studying together, living together, coming together to enter the Marine Corps as privates with the hope of later becoming a second lieutenant, one who would lead a platoon into battle. During the past year we've read of marine involvement, the wounded and dead in the thousands. More lieutenants are needed.

"Hey, Marine, what you lookin' at?" comes a booming voice from inside the switch engine, over the roar of the burning coal and running engine. The voice awakens me as I walk closer to the switch engine.

"Heading to a place called Parris Island," I holler back, hoping to be heard above the roar. "Me and two hundred others. They're gonna put us through the ropes when we get there," I say, now almost to the engine, my eyes upon the engineer, a man about my dad's age, give or take, with weathered skin, creases running everywhere, cap on head—not a farmer's cap, not a hat, the cap of an engineer. The man has rank, has some authority, pulls a train, kind of. Probably longs to be engineering cross country, maybe across the Great Plains, the Rockies, stopped only by the Pacific. Today he'll go one mile, maybe two, then come back. Still, he's "driving the train."

"Yeah, we've been seeing a lot 'bout your age come through, mostly Army. 'Stack 'em and pack 'em,' we say. Put 'em in converted boxcars, bunk beds floor to ceiling. Send 'em east, send 'em west, then put 'em on a boat so they can go farther east or west. Me, I go east and west too— mile and a half at the most. Too old to send overseas, and too young to fire. Been working more hours than I can count. Trains are haulin' troops, tanks, guns, jeeps, as well as what we used to. Don't sit around idle anymore. So, where's this Parris Island, east or west?"

"East," I say. "Somewhere in South Carolina. Been getting in shape for a year, or trying to. 'Bout a third of the guys I've been with are college football players. I mean, used to be. Big, strong, and tough. Took me a while to get up to speed with most of them, but I'm holding my own. Tell us we got no idea what's ahead, although I've got plenty of ideas. It's gonna be tough," I say, not ten feet from the engineer.

He nods.

"So, how long you been an engineer?" I say, no longer having to shout.

" 'Bout fifteen years. Worked for the railroad for twenty-five. Used to think I'd be hauling boxcars all over the country. Gave up on that idea years ago."

I nod back, then say, "What's it like inside there?"

"Step on up," he says, not the answer I expect.

I hesitate. Step on up? Then, why not? "How do I get up?" I say.

"Step up right here," he says, pointing as he talks.

I do as instructed, no hesitancy, never noticing that the two men earlier on the ground have beat me on board.

"Never been in one of these, have you?" he says, then, "Name's J. D.," the other two men grinning as he speaks.

"No, sir," I say.

"Then you've never engineered a locomotive." J. D. adds his grin to the others as he speaks.

I shake my head. Dazed.

"Let's trade places," J. D. says, rising slowly.

I hesitate again.

"Come on, Marine, they're expecting us on the other side of the yard. Got troops, tanks, groceries, and who knows whatever else to get goin'," J. D. directs.

I place myself in J. D.'s seat, at first uncomfortable, physically and emotionally. Where's the steering wheel? I think. Then, how do you stop this thing?

"Times a wastin', Marine. You gonna get us in more trouble than we can get in ourselves," one of the two brakemen says, a burly man with unkempt beard, gray and red, halfway to his chest. He takes a swig from a half-pint bottle, its contents not clear, but brownish red. The other brakeman and the engineer join him, and although the shape of their half-pints are slightly different, the color of the contents is not.

"Fella can get real thirsty working on trains," J. D. says. "Real thirsty," he says again, this time followed by a gulp, not a swig.

I again hesitate, then say, "So, where's the steering wheel?" realizing my absurdity, my awkwardness, as soon as the words come out. I then say, "I mean . . ." then can't say what I mean.

"Don't know, haven't seen it all week," J. D. says as the trio laughs, lifting their half-pints upward, then downward.

"Naw, doesn't come with a steering wheel," J. D. continues. "All you got to do is push that throttle on the right forward. Just don't push it too fast. I'll let you know how to stop it when we get to that point."

I reach for the throttle with my right hand, grabbing it firmly, pushing it forward slightly, no hesitancy, the butterflies arriving in my stomach as the switch engine edges forward, dense steel weighted on steel, a different feel than rubber on concrete. I edge the throttle forward a bit more, glancing out the side window as we move past one boxcar, on past the next. Our pace is slow, steady, comfortable. I've found my pace, my groove; for the moment the butterflies have "flown away."

"Doin' all right, Marine." J. D. says. Nothing more.

I keep my eyes straight ahead, boxcars now on either side. I can see them through the corners of my eyes without looking out the side windows. I'm at ease . . . for the moment. We've gone a half mile, three-quarters, maybe more? Don't know. If this thing has an odometer, I couldn't find it if I wanted to. So, when do we stop? No, *how* do I stop this contraption? Didn't ask that question, did I? I look for the brake pedal, attempting to look at the track ahead and the floorboard simultaneously. It doesn't work. Floorboard wins. Butterflies return to my stomach, this time in droves. They've invited their friends.

"Hey, J. D., how do you stop this thing?"

"Well, we haven't quite figured that one out yet," he says, a serious look on his face, his cohorts offering no additional explanation.

What if I wreck? Court-martialed before basic training? Headline reads, "MARINE HIJACKS LOCOMOTIVE, CAUGHT WHILE TRYING TO FLEE BEFORE BASIC TRAINING." Basic training? I thought this is what "basic training" meant! My mind is going haywire.

"Best you let me trade places, Son, before you get us all in trouble," J. D. says, this time meaning business.

I hop quickly out of the way, and J. D. eases in to the seat. I glance ahead, to the end of the track—not far, tracks from all directions converging at one spot. J. D. grabs ahold of a lever on the upper left, works with it, and the switch engine begins to slow, easing to a perfect stop, my heart rate slowing as the train slows, fortunately not coming to a complete stop as does the train.

"Well, Marine," J. D. says. "It's the end of the line, at least for you. We've got most of a day's work still ahead. Best you be headin' on back to meet up with your group."

He stands and holds out his hand, catching me off guard. I extend mine, our hands clasping firmly, J. D.'s eyes upon mine, a serious look in them—not the look of a moment before when he regained control of the switch engine, but a serious look of sincerity. "Wish you well, Son. Whatever happens, at least you drove a locomotive. How old are you?"

"Twenty-one," I reply.

"Not many twenty-one-year-olds have had their hands on the throttle of a locomotive." J. D. pauses without releasing my hand, then says, "I guess, you being a marine, you'll be going after Japs. Get plenty of 'em."

J. D. squeezes my hand tight after he completes his words, then releases. "The best way back is the way you came. Might want to get a move on."

I turn. The two brakemen nod, and I make my way back down to the ground. I begin to walk, a mile and a half of track ahead, my mind confused, dazed. It drifts, then settles. Everett, my brother. Three and a half years in these yards. Didn't even ask J. D. and the other two if they knew him. It all happened so fast. Always think of stuff later. Well, not going back now. Going ahead, don't need to dally. But Everett, three and a half years here. Did he ever "put his hand on the throttle?" I mean, had he ever experienced a locomotive? That's what he was gonna do before this war started. I pause my thoughts.

Wait, if ever he'd driven one of these, he would have written me. Haven't gotten many letters from him. Only if he had something really important to say. This would have been really important. Yeah, he would have written. Sure, he would have. I've spent less than two hours in a rail yard and have already engineered a locomotive! Everett, three and a half years and not a word from him on it. Ha-ha! I guess I'll have to be the one to write. Yeah, I'll write *I'll show you how, after the war's over. Always having to teach you stuff.*

No—I catch myself, humor leaving my body, competiveness gone, if only for a moment, mind drifting to northern Africa, tanks in a desert. Never even seen a desert, only pictures. Mortar shells? Again, only pictures. What do they sound like? For now, I'll keep my engineering experience to myself—that is, until after the war. That's when I'll tell him. Do it in person. Yeah, that's the way. Hey, just about back to where I met up with J. D. and the brakemen. Might want to mosey on over to where I'm supposed to be. Don't need to miss the train.

FOURTEEN

"Back up, I said, back up! All of you but Wall! Out here, Wall," drill sergeant's screaming at the top of his lungs.

The others back up, forming a big circle, leaving just me and the drill sergeant staring at each other, his the sternest, harshest look I've ever seen, his eyes piercing at and through me. "I saw a smile on your face, like there's something funny or fun going on. Fun or Funny—no, 'Smiley,' that's what we'll start calling you. So, Smiley, take the sheath off your bayonet—I said, take the sheath off your bayonet!"

I reach quickly and remove the sheath.

"Now, come at me. Come straight at me! Try to stab me!"

I pause, not for long, only a second or two.

"I said, come at me!" He yells at the top of his lungs.

I hesitate.

"I'll see to it you're locked up in solitary till the war's over. You'll forget what sunshine is. Come at me 'fore I come at you!"

I run, bayonet aimed straight at him, fifteen feet away at most, then wood on wood, rifle against rifle. I'm on the ground, weight of his foot on my midsection, point of his sheath-covered bayonet touching lightly against my heart. He rubs the bayonet, almost a tickle. Didn't catch what happened. Too instantaneous.

"Okay, hop up, Smiley," he says, no smile on his face, no yelling, no screaming, just matter-of-fact, one last tickle of sheath against the heart before removing it and his foot. "On your feet, let's go again."

I get to my feet, back up ten paces, and charge again, adrenaline flowing, anger swelling within me. Wood on wood, body against body,

I'm on the ground again. Foot and bayonet are on me again, his eyes staring at and through me sharper than the bayonet without the sheath.

"Smiley's dead," he says, the eyes now aimed around the circle. "Japs have been doing this for years. Been practicing on the Chinese, so they can get really good for you. Your life may come down to what you learn today . . . and tomorrow. We're gonna get this down right. Gonna drill you on it every day this week. Maybe every night. Jap'll come after you at night. Gonna have to learn to fight when you can't see. On your feet, Smiley!"

I get up quickly as I can, then pick up my rifle three or four feet away.

"Line up single file right here!" the sergeant yells.

We rush to line up, me in the middle of the pack staring at the straw-stuffed enemy ahead: fake soldiers filled with straw, targets on their chests.

"We're gonna start you young ladies out on soldiers that can't fight back. Still, some of you are gonna lose. For the moment, I'm betting against Smiley. You're gonna tumble and stab, tumble and stab . . . those dummies, that is. Not yourself. We've had some clumsies come through here that did more damage to themselves than they did to the dummies. Tumble and stab. Tumble and stab. Now, watch me."

He takes off running, a few feet before the dummy hitting the ground with a somersault, then up just before the dummy, stabbing it with the bayonet, all in one fluid motion. On to the next dummy. Then to the next, straight down the row.

My turn—somersault, then up. Then fall to my left. I hop up, run at the dummy, bayonet on the bull's-eye.

"What's the matter, Smiley? Forget to take your high heels off?"

Next one. I don't fall this time. Bayonet in the straw, pull it out. Strange feeling, really strange. Then on to the next. Dizzy, real dizzy, head swimming, body off balance, breathing hard, out of breath.

"Head back the other way. Head back the other way! They said you college boys were in shape. Bunch of you played football. Must have been powder-puff! All the while marines fightin' Japs at Tarawa and Guadalcanal, and you guys playing football with the skirts. Did they ever take their high heels off? Get a move on! Back the other way!"

I'm dizzy. My lungs hurt. Somersaults . . . somersaults, stab with the bayonet while my brother's in a tank. Why are we doing this? Must just want to abuse us. Makes no sense. Abuse, that's all it is.

FIFTEEN

"Well, Mississippi, better enjoy it while we can. Don't know when or if we're coming back through California, Hollywood and Beverly Hills, girls like we've never seen before, all decked out, fit to kill for. Tomorrow night, it's back to Camp Pendleton, and next week out to sea."

"Missouri, I can't believe you're doing this. How much did you say you borrowed?"

"Three hundred dollars—and my goal tonight is to get rid of all of it. Hey, Mississippi, if I make my goal, will you help me pay my way back to Camp Pendleton?"

"Sure, Missouri, I'd be glad to pay your way back. I'm also hoping to help you spend your three hundred dollars. I'd do more than my part. Explain to me again how you got it."

"There's a bank out here in California loaning it to marines. Came by Camp Pendleton two weeks ago. Marine Corps pays me sixty-five dollars a month for being a second lieutenant, and the bank withholds between twenty-five and thirty, can't remember the exact amount. Where we're going we won't have much of a chance to spend money anyway. Bank's betting I'm gonna make it at least a year. I kind of like the thought of that. Live or die, I've got the three hundred dollars right now, and I'm making good use of it. Brought twelve of you here, rented out the rooms, and rented out this corner of the bar. I figure we can catch up on our sleep on the trip over to Hawaii."

Missouri's making a lot of sense, I think. How did I miss out on my three hundred dollars? Nobody told me about it until after the fact. This sure is a fancy place. "High rent," and Missouri's renting. Rich and famous come here all the time, and guys from Oak Leaf, Mississippi, don't. I'm probably the first.

"So, Missouri, how does it work? I tell the bartender I'm thirsty, and he gives me choices, most of which I've never heard."

"That's about it. You'll get the routine down pretty quick. You're a smart guy, one of the smartest I've ever met."

"This time you're blowing smoke at me," I say on the way to the bar.

I met Missouri at Quantico, officers' training; that was a barrel of fun. Just started calling him Missouri after he called me Mississippi, both of us small-town boys among a bunch of city guys. Got a lot in common, background-wise. In some ways, we are different though. Missouri's bolder than me, maybe 'cause he's six feet four and I'm six feet. Bold. Got to be to borrow three hundred dollars to spend at a place like this. If it was up to me, I'd have probably never set foot in here. "Too rich for my blood," I'd say. Anyway, we both showed up at Camp Pendleton together, where they've had us on hold till enough second lieutenants die so they can ship us over. We ship out Tuesday for Hawaii, but not the one I've always heard about. At this Hawaii, they put us up on the side of a volcano, with scorched trees for scenery and dry ash to walk on. Only time we'll see the beach is when the boat lands.

"So, what will it be, Lieutenant?" the bartender says. He's older, probably in his fifties, too old for fighting, although, from his not-so-straight nose looks like he's been in a fight or two. Might could still step in if things get a little out of hand.

"Oh, I don't know. Not much of a drinker."

"From down South—what part?"

"Yeah, Mississippi."

"Would have never guessed. So, what can I serve you?"

"Like I said, I'm not much of a drinker. Just for curiosity, since I'm not the one paying, how much is a Coca Cola?"

"One dollar."

"One dollar—for a Coca Cola!"

"How much is a 7-UP?"

"Same."

"You've got to be kiddin'!"

"What's that fellow at the table over there drinking?" I say, nodding my head toward a civilian across the bar with a tall cylinder-shaped glass with a cherry in it.

"Singapore Sling. Used to only get it in Singapore, now you can get it here. Don't suppose you see too many of those down in Mississippi. Got gin in it."

"How much does it cost?"

"One dollar, a buck, four bits, whatever you want to call it." He shrugs.

"Same as a Coca Cola! You can't be serious. Well, since it won't put my friend out any more money, I'll try one." I say.

A moment later he hands me the cylinder-shaped glass, cherry and all, and I begin to gulp. "Not bad," I say.

"No, it's not bad, but you might want to slow down. It might look like water, but it's not," the bartender says, a look of concern on his face.

"It's okay," I say. "If I survived Marine Corps basic training, I can survive a Singapore Sling. Probably several of them."

"Whatever," he says, turning to the next marine. "So what will it be, Lieutenant?"

I walk to a table, our section of the bar, and take a seat, working on the Singapore Sling as I go, repeating the process twice more.

"I promised not to let you guys down," a voice comes from across the bar.

I look up. There stands Robinson, ripe for the cover of *Life*, full uniform, granite-chiseled handsome, the kind of guy girls flock after, surrounded by a flock, six to be exact: three blondes, two brunettes, and one girl with auburn hair—all about our age.

"I've died and gone to heaven," Missouri says just loud enough for me to hear, as he stands and heads toward the flock. "Let me help you with your chairs," he says in the plural, halfway to the girls.

They smile. Look at those smiles, soft, inviting. Look at those shapes. Never seen anything like this in one room in my whole life. Not before. Maybe never again. Now they're walking toward me, Missouri directing them the whole way. Hey, he left the chair next to me vacant. So maybe, just maybe . . .

I stand. "Let me get your chair," I say to the girl with the auburn hair, pale-skin face, no blemishes, tall, five seven, maybe five eight, all legs.

"Where y'all from?" she says to me.

"Camp Pendleton," I say.

"No, silly, I said 'where y'all from?' I was just talking to you."

"Oh. Mississippi. I'm from Mississippi. Guess I've got an accent."

She takes a seat, and I take mine. I stare.

"So, what can I get you to drink?" I say, the only words I can think of.

"A daiquiri."

"Yes, a daiquiri. I like those. Have them all the time back home. Been missing 'em," I say. "I'll get both of us one, if you don't let my seat go."

"I won't," she says smiling, perfect teeth to go with everything else.

A what? A daiquiri? Never had one of those in my life. Never even heard of it. Hope I don't forget how to pronounce it. What if the bartender asks me to spell it?

"You want that Coca Cola now?" the bartender says.

"Not gonna let you charge my friend a dollar for a Coca Cola," I say, momentarily forgetting the word I'm supposed to have on the tip of my tongue.

"So what's it gonna be this time?

"A . . . uh . . . a daiquiri . . . I mean, two daiquiris."

"Light or dark?"

"It comes in colors?"

"No, Son, but the rum does. Are you getting one of these for a young lady? May I suggest the light rum?"

"Yes, light will be fine," I say, hoping that she's a "light rum" person. Yes, she . . . what's her name? Gunter, you idiot. You fool!

"You be careful, Son," the bartender says, handing me the daiquiris. "These are different than Coca Colas."

A moment later I place both daiquiris on the table, hers first. "Where I come from, we take care of basic needs first, even before we introduce ourselves. Needs like getting a drink," I continue saying as I seat myself. "Now that we've taken care of that, I'm Gunter Wall, from Oak Leaf, Mississippi, currently stationed at Camp Pendleton. And yourself?"

"Vivian Lemur, Los Angeles, California, currently stationed at the table." She smiles.

Now what do I say? What do I say? "Are you in college?" I ask, thinking immediately, oh brother, what if she is twenty-three or twenty-four? What are you trying to do, insult her?

"No, tried that for a year or two, but got bored. Never been too fond of the books. I'm an actress . . . or, least I'm trying to be. Lately I've worked part-time at a ladies' clothing store in Beverly Hills. Hope to get signed on with one of the studios, maybe MGM. Things are looking pretty good, in spite of the war. By that I mean, there have been some cutbacks. But, I'm really encouraged. Supposed to hear Monday about a movie. Not a big role, just a line or two, but a start. So, tonight I'm just out with my friends. Sally—" She nods to the blonde at the end of the table. "—turned twenty-one today, so we came here to celebrate. What brought you up from Camp Pendleton?"

I wait a moment, looking at her soft, smooth skin, green eyes, auburn hair, her smile disappearing as she waits for my reply. "I guess we came up to celebrate, too. One of my buddies, Missouri, recently came into some money. Wants us all to share it. Heading back to Pendleton tomorrow evening. We're staying here tonight."

"Wow, this place is expensive," she says, a serious look on her face. "I've only set foot here once before. So, do they have anything like this where you come from?"

What difference would it have made? I think. Only way I could have got in would have been to work there. "No. Hometown does have a hotel, but nothing like this."

"You have any brothers or sisters?" she asks.

"One brother, Everett, somewhere the other side of the world in the Army, probably riding in a tank. Yourself?"

"One brother four years younger than me, a spoiled brat. Six more months and he'll be wearing a uniform. It will be good for him."

"Wouldn't it be nice if he didn't?" I say. "I mean, wear a uniform. The war would be over, 'cause we won. It's gonna happen someday, just a matter of when."

"So, when do you leave?" she asks, a thoughtful look.

Tuesday morning, zero six hundred, more than fifty, less than sixty hours—not long,

I think. "Next week," I say. "I guess you'll be in front of a camera, and I'll be on a boat. We've both got pretty exciting weeks."

"Yeah," she says, the smile returning to her face.

I stare. Can't help it. She's beautiful. Six months looking at marines, and God knows how much longer I'll be looking at them. Freeze this moment!

"Gunter, are you all right?" Vivian says.

"Yes . . . yes, I'm fine," I say waking from my dream world. "Are you okay with that daiquiri?"

She smiles, a soft smile, looks at the glass, shaking it slightly. "I could probably use another one," she says, the smile broadening.

"One condition," I say.

"What's that?"

"Guard my seat with your life."

"Done," she says, winking at me as I almost trip getting up.

"Two daiquiris, light rum," I say, or at least think I do. Did I say rum or run? Had to have been rum. Feeling a bit dizzy . . .

"If you prefer, I could give you a Pepsi rather than a Coca Cola," the bartender says, smirking.

Wonder how he got that crooked nose, I think, before assessing his build. Hmm . . . might have gotten it in a boxing ring. I cool a bit and say, "No, two daiquiris."

A moment later, I'm back with Vivian. "Oh, look," she says, giggling. "Look at Sally, silly Sally."

I look to the end of the table, blonde-haired Sally, just turned twenty-one, balancing a bowl on her head, a marine either side clapping. She's obviously been drinking. So have I. My head's spinning. "Singapore Slung." Hickory daiquiri doc, the mouse ran up the . . .

"She really is silly, don't you think?" Vivian says, drawing close to me, her hand on my thigh.

A rush of blood up my leg, lower abdomen, upper abdomen, chest, arms, head, back down both legs to my feet, blood pumping wildly throughout my body, almost through my skin.

Vivian leans forward, whispers in my ear, a slight tickle on the edge of the ear with her lips as she speaks. "It's fun being silly every once in a while, don't you think?" She backs away a bit, smiling her smile, perfect white teeth separated by red lips, deep red, coated by expensive lipstick.

"Oh, look what I've gone and done," she says, removing the cloth napkin from around the daiquiri, dipping it, applying it to my ear. "Lipstick. Everybody would wonder."

"Yeah."

"Gunter, you sure are smiling," she says.

I bet I am.

"So, enough silliness. I'm gonna be an actress. What are you gonna do when you get back? If the war were over today, what would you do?" She says, her look not silly.

What would I do? Don't have a clue. War comes along three months into college, and all I can think about is which branch of the service I join. What will I do?

"I'm going back to college. Gonna finish college," I say.

"Then what?"

"Don't know," I say, quick as a reflex, not even thinking, then thinking, may not be coming back. Marines are dropping like flies, most of the fighting still ahead, and I head out Tuesday. "It'll be something good," I say, "No, great."

"You smiled again," she says. "You were frowning for a moment. I don't like it when you frown."

"Yeah," I say, forcing a big smile, my mind on the trip ahead. Will I come back?

"So, how do you like California?" she says.

"I've decided I like Hollywood and Beverly Hills better than Camp Pendleton. Like I was saying earlier, we don't have hotels like this where

I come from, nor shops and restaurants. But, as for living here, I don't know. Where all have you been?"

"California. Never been to another state," she says, saying without saying that she wished she had traveled east, or north, or south, or somewhere. "I'm going to do it someday. Gonna make it big. Make lots of money so I can see the whole country . . . maybe even Europe."

I look at her, mesmerized by her beauty, her gracefulness, boldness, tempered slightly by vulnerability, a girl who wants to go everywhere and has never left home.

"I bet you will," I say.

The night moves on. We talk about this and that. I tell her a lot about the flood, rabbit hunting, Everett, college, and driving a locomotive. She talks about acting, her friends she's with. Doesn't talk much about her family, only about her "spoiled brat" younger brother, nothing about her mother or father, almost as if she doesn't want to.

"It's almost midnight," I say. "Would you like another daiquiri?"

She shakes her head.

"I'm gonna get one more," I say. "That is, if you don't mind."

She shakes her head as I head to the bar for one more free drink, not wanting Missouri to fail on his goal. The bartender is no longer giving advice. Looks like he's given up. He hands me the daiquiri, and I head back to Vivian, "on top of the world." What an evening. Never had one better, I think.

We talk a bit longer, Vivian saying, "Gunter, you sure are smiling a lot."

Her saying this only makes me smile more. I look at her: auburn hair; pale light skin; red, red lips; white, straight teeth to go with the perfect smile. I lean forward toward Vivian and keep leaning, my face, my body continuing to lean, straight toward the table . . .

•　•　•

I open my eyes once, twice, a third time, room spinning slightly, head pounding, queasy stomach—no, my full abdomen, groin to chest. I reach to my chest, T-shirt snug to it, marine shirt off. I look down under the sheets, pants off, underwear on. I look up, head throbbing, nausea extending now beyond my abdomen, as if I could experience it in my arms and legs.

"You alive?" Missouri says. "Thought at first you might be the first in the group to go. 'How and where did he die,' they'd say. 'In a bar in Beverly Hills,' I'd tell them. 'True hero right to the end. Only one in our group to lose his life on American soil. He sure died happy,' I'd tell 'em. Never ever seen a marine smiling that much."

"Where's Vivian?" I ask alarmed, heart pumping wildly.

"Well, I can't exactly say, but she didn't look too pleased the last time we saw her. Matter-of-fact, that's an understatement. That was when me and two others carried your passed-out body out of the bar."

"Got to get ahold of her," I say with urgency.

"And how exactly do you propose to do that?" Missouri says. "Can I help you look for her address and phone number in your pants pockets?"

"No," I say. "Didn't write those down."

"Well, the way I understand it, Casanova always carried a pen and pad. He also made sure the ladies didn't have a pen and pad. All this to say, you and I are both just bumpkins from Mississippi and Missouri, and we've got a long way to go in a lot of ways."

"I'll find her," I say.

"Sure. We're due back at Camp Pendleton in less than six hours. Got to check all of you hangovers out of here, before they start charging me another night's rate—which I don't have. Might have enough money left over for hamburgers, if you guys will pay for the transportation back."

I rise out of bed. Painfully. I cross the room to the desk, phone on top, next to it a phone directory, four to five hundred times thicker than the one in Oak Leaf. I open it and thumb to the L's, searching for "Lemur." None.

"I can't believe it," I say.

"What's that?" says Missouri.

"There is not a single Lemur in the directory. She didn't talk much about her parents. Matter of fact, exactly nothing. I'd think at least her parents would be listed. Vivian's living together with a couple of those other girls at some boarding house. What are the other girls' last names? What's Silly Sally's last name?"

"Who?"

"Never mind," I say, my disappointment currently more painful than the headache.

"Mississippi. Bet her last name's not really Lemur. That sounds like a fox or something. Probably a made-up name. You know that's what they do out here with movie stars. None of 'em use their real name. Wonder what hers is."

"Vivian Lemur," I say, almost angry at Missouri this time. "Vivian Lemur."

SIXTEEN

"So, you've been up here once before, Sarge," I say, shifting gears on the jeep as we continue up the mountain, open space with occasional volcanic ash and intermittent charred trees to either side, far as we can see.

"Yeah, pretty desolate," Sarge says.

Still, it's seventy-two hours of R and R with no colonels looking over our shoulders.

"Not the Hawaii I envisioned," I say. "When I think of R and R in Hawaii, my imagination carries me to the beach, volcanic rock ten, fifteen feet high just ahead, with a girl in a grass shirt, lei around her neck, dancing to a ukulele, waves of the Pacific roaring behind her, spray going high into the air. One time she's a blonde, next a brunette, then a redhead—finally, a native. Whatever."

"Saw that several years ago," Sarge says, grabbing my attention. "Not exactly like you described it. Actually better. Then again, a true marine never talks, so I'm not talking. That was all before Pearl Harbor. Hawaii was a different place. Marine Corps was different . . . everything was different. Only beach I've seen recently was Tarawa. Rather not see it ever again. Only trouble is, I do see it at night . . . see it in my dreams," Sarge says, eyes and mind now miles away.

I look ahead. Missouri's jeep thirty, forty yards in front. Then behind, a caravan of covered trucks, loaded with two platoons. Finally, over my shoulder, two feet behind me, Brooklyn, a private with an accent too thick to cut with a steak knife. Obvious communication barrier, me with my Southern drawl. Still, I like him. Don't know exactly why. He's young.

Don't know exactly how young, just young . . . young in age, young in maturity.

I turn to him, "Brooklyn, if I get tired of driving, I'll let you take over."

"Can't do that, Lieutenant," he says.

"Don't disobey orders, Private," I say, halfway seriously.

"No sir, I can't, Lieutenant," he says. "I can't drive. Or at least I've never tried. Not much use for a car in Brooklyn. Family doesn't own one."

"Doesn't own one?" I say, startled. Then, "We didn't either for a while. So, you've never been behind the wheel of anything?"

"No, sir."

"Well, I've never been ram or wild pig hunting, but I am this weekend. Maybe we can work in a little driving lesson while we're up here," I say, looking over my shoulder, a broad youthful smile covering his face.

"I'd like that, sir."

I look ahead, Missouri's jeep thirty yards in front, the road (if one could call the tracks a road) winding gradually up the mountain. Ahead in the distance is our "hotel," four concrete block buildings with no lawn, no bushes, only a few volcanic charred, leafless trees well beyond in the distance.

The caravan comes to a halt, screeching brakes almost in unison. The marines pile out from under the canvas canopy, their first view of "Shangri-la."

My mind awakens as I jump from the jeep, thinking I'd better get control before the mutiny. "Line up single file," I yell.

Slowly, marines line up, bedding gear in hand, low inaudible grumbling coming from their general direction. From next to me Missouri stares at the line, saying without saying, "What will you say next?" Asking myself the same question.

"First, we'll unload our gear. My platoon in these two buildings," I say, pointing. "There are supposed to be rations—not just the canned stuff, but real groceries, even steaks, but those are for tonight or tomorrow night." I say this based upon what I was told, wondering if the captain was playing a cruel trick. "Mutiny," I think.

I start to say, "there's beer stacked to the ceiling" (as the captain had also said). I, however, refrain, not even saying there's supposed to be a reasonable amount of beer here for us, then actually saying, "If any of you are going ram or wild pig hunting, then you'll have to wait to consume any beer that you might find on the premises. You are now dismissed."

Marines dash to the concrete buildings, their motivation enhanced by the word *beer*.

Brooklyn lags behind. "I guess that remark applies to driving lessons also," he says.

"Yes, maybe you'll also get a ram or a wild pig to go along with your driving lesson," I say before turning to Sarge. "Let's grab a quick bite. A fellow could get hungry tracking down a ram."

Missouri walks up long-faced, saying, "Can't get a guy in my platoon to go hunting."

"Total, complete lack of leadership," I say. "If you're lucky, I'll let Sarge go along with you to show you how to hold a rifle."

Missouri gives me an "I'll best you yet" look and heads toward a concrete building saying, "Meet you back here in thirty minutes for *your* rifle shooting lesson."

No time later, up the mountain we go, food barely settled, Missouri in the lead, his jeep twenty yards ahead with no clue as to where he's going. He just had to be the first to leave. Wouldn't have it any other way, Sarge with him, Brooklyn with me, up the side of the mountain, no trail, just "up the mountain."

Missouri brings his jeep to a halt next to a charred tree, barbed wire extended from its side fifty, sixty feet to the next charred tree. He signals us forward, and I oblige, pulling up next to him.

"Meet back here at sixteen hundred," Missouri barks, letting us all know he's in charge. "I think we'll go right," he says, signaling.

"I'll probably be back here at twelve hundred with a couple of rams and a pig," I say. "I'd bring more, but we can only carry so much in a jeep."

Missouri shrugs, driving his jeep right as we head left, winding about three hundred yards. I stop the jeep.

"Brooklyn, load your rifle. We're hunting for what walks in our path," I say.

"Lieutenant, I've never shot anything but a target."

"Well, don't shoot a ram or a pig smaller than a target," I say, smiling. "When they're that size they don't have much meat on 'em."

He smiles.

We walk for about forty-five minutes, whispering occasionally, hoping not to be heard. The flat-surfaced volcanic-ash-soil gives way to ravine, a hard rocky surface, just the terrain I would envision a ram standing on. So far, no ram. We walk another fifteen minutes with no sign of life other than our own.

"What's that?" Brooklyn whispers.

Two, three hundred yards away, at an elevation a couple of hundred feet above us, stands a white statuesque creature, miniature at this distance, yet imposing, its figure to the forefront of the sun. The white statue glistens.

"Who's it gonna be?" I ask.

"You, Lieutenant. You go ahead."

I raise my rifle, set the bead on the ram, straight within my peep sight . . . steady. I slowly squeeze.

The statue moved! It moved before I shot. How can that be? I think these thoughts and say nothing.

"Can you believe that, Lieutenant?"

I say nothing. Nothing to say.

"Do you suppose we're not the first marines to try to kill him?" Brooklyn says.

"Perhaps."

"Do you think we should stay put, or move on to a new spot?" Brooklyn again questions.

"Let's move on," I say. Intuition.

Another fifteen minutes, we're on a ledge, like a ram, the view ahead as far as I can see. Behind: more ledges, highest place I've ever stood. I take one last view in front, tempted to continue. Alas, there are no flying rams. I turn to face the ledges, this spot the best I've been for seeing a ram.

Twenty minutes, thirty minutes, an hour we sit, Brooklyn occasionally fidgeting, anxious for a driving lesson, myself intent on not being bested by that bumpkin from Missouri. We had heard two shots separated by ten minutes. Then again, I had shot and hit nothing but Hawaiian sky.

"Lieutenant, look," Brooklyn whispers, nodding to a ledge as a bird flies a hundred yards away. "You got your chance."

I raise the rifle slowly, peep sight on the bead, bead just below the neck of the ram. I squeeze slowly, this followed by a reverberation in the ravines below. The ram falls, no staggering, a quick drop on the ledge.

"Nice job, Lieutenant. Now, how are we going to get it?"

"Haven't figured that out," I say. "But we will." I eye the fallen ram, marking the ledge with a charred tree twenty to thirty yards from it.

The walk to the ram is strenuous, my calves and thighs taut, few words said on the way.

"Decision time," I say. "Clean it here, or when we get to camp?"

"Don't know," Brooklyn says with a "how would I know what to do with a ram?" look on his face.

"I say we clean it here. Any weight we can shed will make a difference. This high altitude is about to do me in."

Brooklyn looks at me, saying without saying, "Fine with me, as long as you do the cleaning."

I remove my knife and go to work, doing it the same way I did the only deer I've cleaned, that four years ago. Clumsily at first, I get the hang of it, thirty minutes later finishing.

"Brooklyn, let's both grab a leg," I say, "right above the shoulder. We'll drag it."

He nods.

On the way down we talk. It makes the trip easier. Things like, "Where have you been before you joined the marines?"

"New Jersey."

"Got brothers and sisters?"

"Two of each. We're Catholic. I'm middle of the pack."

"How long your family been in America?"

"Grandparents came over from Lebanon, turn of the century."

"Parents?"

"Father works for a laundry. Mother takes care of the family." Then, "I remember being hungry, real hungry when I was six or seven, a couple of cold winters, not much coal for the furnace. Remember huddling, wrapped in a blanket with two brothers. Remember it like yesterday."

I nod and listen. He's likeable. He's young, just like most of them back at camp, eighteen. We get to the jeep, winded, exhausted. With one last effort, we heave the ram in the back of it.

"Driving time," I say, handing him the keys.

He smiles, heads to the driver's seat, nervously placing the key in the ignition on the third try. He tries to turn the key toward himself, twice, then finally forward. The engine cranks.

"That pedal on the left is the clutch, the one on the right the brake. You push the clutch in to shift gears. This is your first gear." I point. "That's where you start. Don't worry about running into anything, 'cause the closest tree is sixty yards off."

We begin to buck down the mountain.

• • •

"Nope. Never seen a ram in a grocery store back where I come from," Missouri says. "Sell lots of pork, though. Fellow's got to know what to go hunting for, something edible."

"Only go for the rare, the exotic," I say. "At least in Hawaii. It's a wonder you didn't shoot a cow, then brag about it. Two point. Look, I shot a two point!"

"I miss beef," hollers Big Tex, all six foot five inches—almost too tall for the Marine Corps, a kid from somewhere in the state that he never quits talking about. I start to reply, but decide that would be futile. Next thing, he'd be arguing that the Pacific Ocean is nothing more than a big lake in west Texas. I stay quiet and look at the simmering coals.

It's been quite an evening. Lots of commotion at first when Missouri showed up with a wild pig in the back of his jeep, Brooklyn and I with a ram in the back of mine. Guys gathered around and did some real talking. Most had consumed a "reasonable" amount of beer—at least, that was the word I heard a couple of them from Missouri's platoon say. We didn't have a bit of trouble getting two pits dug. The guys in my platoon sort of made a race out of it. "You guys are too weak to dig in a sand pile." "At least we're smart enough to know which end of the shovel to put in the ground," came the chorus from the other pit. Lots of back and forth.

Missouri had come up with the idea of "borrowing" some barbwire from the volcanic-charred trees, and a few of the guys wove it together to make a grill. Another group gathered up a pile of charred trees. A little gas on the charred trees and with one match we had an instant barbeque pit. The cooking isn't so instant: fifteen to twenty hours. When we put the meat on, comments come from all directions. "Can't let the fire die down. Meat might sour." "If a flame starts, could burn the whole thing up in ten minutes." "Yeah, got to keep a water bucket and lots of wood on hand at all times." "Somebody's got to keep an eye on it."

Right now, all eyes are on it. Guys, mostly standing, some sitting, all gathered around staring at the fire, most drinking beer and talking. With the exception of no girls, it's a perfect setting. Still, in a sense it is perfect in its own way, a moment in time when our only responsibility is to keep our eyes on a pig and a ram.

I look around. I'm one of the "old men"—twenty-one. Lots of eighteen- and nineteen-year-olds. When I was their age, I was a freshman in college—a long way from a mountaintop in Hawaii. Smiling faces. Youthful. Enthusiastic. Girls or no girls, a great moment in time, the type of moment to freeze, to can, to preserve . . . to savor. I smile, not just facially, but deep inside. I sit quietly watching, smiling. The hours pass. Gradually, the group tires, then retires—not all at once, but gradually. It's on toward dawn, no flames, just simmering coals with a faint glow. Just add a charred log every hour or two and keep an eye on the meat.

We're down to four: me, Missouri, Sarge, and Brooklyn, the ones who scaled the mountain, shot, cleaned, carried and carted the meat. The ram, the pig, they mean more to us than the others. Can't let anything happen to them.

"Lieutenant."

"What's that, Brooklyn?" I say.

"One of the best times of my life."

SEVENTEEN

Forever at sea, queasy most of the time, partly due to the Pacific, the rest to uncertainty. Three months on Hawaii and February finds me headed the opposite direction from America—somewhere for battle. They haven't told us where yet, but they will. They'll school us, have on everything else. We sleep, stacked five, floor to ceiling. We're privileged. Most of the noncoms down below are stacked seven to ten. We all hope and pray the guy at the top doesn't throw up. Seas haven't been too rough. Fortunate.

"What's this?"

"Happy birthday to you. Happy birthday to you. Happy birthday, Mississippi. Happy birthday to you." They're all singing, the "singing lieutenants," Missouri carrying the cake, no icing, just a big biscuit with a bunch of candles—twenty-two, I guess.

"Make a wish," Missouri says, six-foot-four-inch beanpole, holding a big lighted biscuit, smiling ear to ear.

Make a wish? Caught me off guard. What's my wish? Hard question. Let's see? Not so hard. I want to live. I want to live through what's ahead and go home. Oh, I'll never let these guys know that. Just tell 'em "No Japs gonna get me. No way." I'll show them my confidence. But no, I'm scared. I blow at the candles with every ounce of air I've got, constant and long, emptying my lungs until there's nothing but smoke.

"Probably wishing to be with some girl. Wishing he was back in California with some movie star," Missouri says.

Hadn't thought of that, I reflect quickly, thinking of Vivian Lemur. Alas, no address, no telephone number.

"Colonel wants to see all of you right now," the messenger says, breaking up the party, a serious look on his face.

The smiles disappear, replaced by serious looks, as if the messenger is deadly contagious. We look at each other, as if perhaps one had some forewarning and had kept a secret. If that's the case, it's still a secret. We begin to follow the messenger.

A moment later we encircle a table with an island model on top, a plaster mound the size of a large anthill at the tip of one end.

"Iwo Jima," says the colonel.

I stare at the island model, concentrating on the anthill at its top.

"Japs, thousands of them are dug in there. They're in caves, foxholes, bunkers, whatever, according to our intelligence. We'll see to it they're bombed good before we make landfall. They won't just be standing out in the open when we get there," says the colonel.

Lieutenant (can't remember his name) says, "What's this hill on the top of the island?"

"Mt. Suribachi," says the colonel. "They call it a mountain, although it's only five hundred and fifty feet high. The island's only four and a half miles long and two and a half miles wide." The colonel gets quiet, like he's waiting on a question, or a batch of them. None come. "We'll be preparing you with the details over the next day or so; you'll be ready. Your men will be ready. We will inform them tonight. You are dismissed," says the colonel with no hesitancy, no lack of confidence.

We stand like statues, eying the model. No one says a word. No one moves.

•   •   •

Seven, eight miles ahead, I guess—smaller on the horizon than the model on the table—is Iwo Jima, with Mt. Suribachi standing at its south end, the early morning sun edging upward as I stare just as I've done for two or three miles. "Keep your head down," they told us. Good advice that no one is following, even the lieutenants. How can we? Our planes are flying overhead bombarding the island in front of us, smoke reaching into the sky from the bombs hitting the island, rumbling sounds reverberating from the distance. The ride is rough in the LST, a ship smaller than the carrier that we loaded on to reach the shore. I sit in an amtrac with my platoon, ready to plunge into the sea, then onto the beach.

We've prepared for everything. Back in December while in Hawaii, they let us "go to the beach." First, they put us on tiny boats in horrendous waves, so we knew what it was like to throw up (which most of us did).

We then slept on the beach with the wind blowing furiously. Got us used to the cold, as well as wet, gritty sand that stuck to everything. "Just a taste of things to come," they told us.

The day after they showed us the model of the island, the colonel started preparing the captains, captains the lieutenants, the lieutenants their platoons. "Zig and zag, don't run straight. Harder to hit you with a bullet. Don't forget how we told you to handle a grenade. Flank to the left, flank to right. Flame throwers, steady with your aim. Repeat in your mind how to handle the demolition. Corpsmen, you're going to be busy . . . maybe too busy." All these things part of classic training to which Sarge, seasoned like petrified wood, says, "At Tarawa it all went to hell in a hand basket anyway, but we improvised and kept going. In the end, we took it. I'm one of the fortunate ones who lived to tell about it. I plan on doing it again."

The island is getting larger, the bombs louder, the sea rougher—or, at least I'm noticing it more. I'm quiet; we all are. There's a hollow spot in the pit of my stomach. It's been there before, but never this large, never so deep. I keep my eyes ahead to the island.

The beach is straight before us, Mt. Suribachi imposing, to the left. The sounds of our planes overhead and bombs hitting Suribachi are deafening. The amtrac is in the water, now hitting sand. I run out yelling, "Let's go," water to my waist, carbine in hand, pack on back. I run, or try, my feet sinking in a soggy mixture of sand and volcanic ash, water weighted against my thighs and calves. I press forward, hard as I can, carbine in hand, shoulders and arms working as hard as my legs.

I'm out of the ocean, water still in my shoes, moving a little faster, but not much, the black sand and volcanic ash no more stable than finely ground flour. I zig and zag. That's been drilled into me. Ahead are craters formed from our bombs dropped earlier. They slow my trek.

To my right, corner of my eye, ten or twenty yards, a marine falls with a thud. Reminds me of a pecan dropping out of a tree. Not in my platoon.

Mortar shells are coming down from the direction of the mountain, hitting the beach, marines flying in the air, in pieces. Rifle fire is coming more than going, Japs in their bunkers, or at least concealed from sight, shooting at marines, over six thousand of us. I drop into a gritty sand and ash crater just as a mortar shell soars over my head, exploding thirty to forty feet behind me. The ground rumbles.

I rest a moment, looking at a high terrace in front of me, unable to see beyond it. I dash ahead twenty feet and jump into a hole, following in the path of a fellow marine who has now gone over the ridge. On all fours I crawl up the terrace, my knees sinking in the sand and ash clear to my thighs, my elbows deep in powdery grit. I peer over the terrace to open space ahead, a blessing and a curse. For now, no more uphill crawl. We are now open targets, no terrace to aim over, just a clean shot from inside a well-protected bunker. Ahead, two marines are blown into midair, having stepped on land mines simultaneously. The land mines are more plentiful now, like a bumper crop of sweet potatoes back home. If I dug just below the surface I'd find them everywhere. I squelch the thought, realizing if I stop to rationalize then fear will overcome me and I won't move forward, do my job.

From the left corner of my eye I spot Frenchie, a young kid in my platoon from south Louisiana who speaks better French than English. He dashes ahead, not zigging or zagging, getting struck and falling into a crater twenty yards ahead of me. I pause briefly, dumbfounded, my heart and mind confused, before I dash ahead zigging and zagging, my feet and ankles sinking now up to my calves in the sand and ash with each step. I dive in the crater, landing on Frenchie's blood-soaked body, as he screams from my impact.

Guilt robs me of my senses. I look at his eyes, five to six inches from mine, then back away, his blood now soaking me.

"I hurt," he says in English before beginning to mumble in French.

"Corpsmen will make their way up," I say, offering no more than comforting words. "Can I give you some water?"

He nods, and I reach for my canteen. I screw off the cap and begin to pour slowly. His eyes close. His mouth closes. His body shakes, then all movement leaves it.

For a moment my thoughts are lost, my mind is blank. I don't know how to respond. I'm holding his head in my left hand. I lay it slowly to the ground and stare, realizing there is nothing I can do. I look up. I must move on.

EIGHTEEN

It's the third day, early morning, sun's been up for an hour or so. The cold rain of yesterday has stopped. Word is out that more than four thousand marines have been wounded, more than six hundred dead. Rumor or truth, I don't know. I do know I've seen and heard more than enough blood and cries of pain than one should for a lifetime. Should have gotten a night's sleep. Didn't. Down a ways—thirty or forty yards—flares were flying at one or two in the morning, followed by an explosion of rifle fire. Japs were trying to sneak up on us. Thank God somebody was awake. Looked that way at daybreak, and must have seen fifteen or twenty Japs dead on the ground. Anyway, I never returned to sleep. Couldn't.

Suribachi's still in front of us, maybe two football fields. Under normal circumstances I could run to it in thirty seconds, even with a rifle and pack. Have no idea how long it will take to go those two hundred yards, and then take the mountain. Days? We'll do it. I say we, meaning the U.S. Marine Corps. Hey, I'm a part of it . . . and my platoon. My platoon, thirty-nine—no, thirty-five. Two days of fighting and four dead, plus six too wounded to keep going, moved back and being tended to. Some of them won't make it. Said a prayer for each of them by name. Also said prayers for the twenty-nine remaining—no, thirty. I have prayed for myself. Out here I could go any minute.

"So, we've got to deal with that bunker," Sarge says. "Won't ever get to the mountain till we get past it. They're all around the mountain's base. This one is ours."

Sarge is egging me on, pushing me without saying so directly. Men need other men.

"Don't know exactly how big it is, do we?" I say.

"Nope. Probably connected to something else underground. No telling how far it may go."

"Got to load it up with TNT," I say, turning to Ralph Thompson, a farm boy from the Midwest and one of my three squad leaders; rather, one of the two still alive. He's spent the night in the hole with Sarge and me. I knew we'd need to be close together first thing. First thing has come.

"We'll get the bazookas and flamethrowers to hit it first," Ralph says as a mortar shell hits twenty yards in front of us, exploding.

"Wake-up call," Sarge says, as another mortar shell flies overhead, rumbling the ground forty yards behind us.

Too far back to hit my platoon, I think, still reeling from the shock of the one that hit in front of us. "Ralph, crawl on over to the next foxhole and tell them it's time to start moving forward. It's another thirty or forty yards before we can do any damage with a flamethrower. Get 'em to spread the word down the line."

"Yes sir," he says as he begins to crawl.

The day passes slowly, progress marked by inches. Two more in my platoon die today. At least that I know of; we're not lining up for roll call to take count. I keep them organized as best I can, but the rifle fire is constant, the mortar shells startling, the situation chaotic.

I ought to be used to mortar shells. But mortar shells aren't routine, they come when I'm not looking, not really looking. At moments I'm lulled to listlessness by lack of rest, adrenaline asleep, suddenly reawakened if a shell hits really close, sometimes bodies flying in the air, in pieces. The black sand and ash is blood red in many places.

"Start firing," I holler one direction, then the other. It's a slight break in the fighting, slight defined as less than a minute. It's those with real firepower I'm directing, privates with bazookas down the way either side, as well as a flamethrower. They're anxious, almost like kids waiting to open their Christmas gifts. Booms come from either side, flames from one, all this aimed fifty to sixty yards out to our bunker or pillbox, don't know exactly what to call it. Don't know how big it is, or how many Japs are in it. Just know it's one of many manned caves full of them. My platoon can't take them all, but we can and will take at least one. The bazooka's booms and the flames are followed by shots from M-1s and carbines, a rotation set in motion and repeated.

It's well past mid-afternoon, darkness just a ways away, still time to take the bunker before we can't see. Maybe. Who knows? Could be a bunch of them holed up in there, ready to come out at night and shoot us, or stab us with their bayonets just when we doze off in the early morning hours. It happened last night, shots lighting the moonless, starless night, cries and screams of pain and death interrupting my hopes (and needs) for sleep. Got to take that bunker. Got to get them first—all of them.

"It's time to move forward," I yell, and the platoon moves forward, zig and zag, thirty yards to a new set of holes created by our bombing. It's the most progress at one time we've made all day. This time no one goes down. I can't believe it.

We resume the routine. I can see the rifles pointing out of the bunkers, out twenty or thirty yards, and ten feet up. Could hit 'em with a rock if I had one. And there aren't that many. Counted five or six the last time I poked my head up. Still, no way of telling. Could be connected by a tunnel to another bunker. Could be they're just laying low for the moment.

Flamethrower Mills, young kid from Alabama, fires right on target, at and beyond a protruding rifle. Flames and screams come from the bunker, followed by a moment of silence, almost as if both sides are pondering the events. Private First Class Johnson, young kid from Kansas, breaks the silence, firing his bazooka, hitting two targets holding rifles on the left side of the bunker.

I think, strangely enough, from the perspective of the other side, that they should have been farther apart. Then . . . no, they're huddling closer together. Men need other men.

We continue to peek up and take quick shots with M-1s, carbines, bazookas, and flames, all aimed where we see rifles, or movement. Finally, there are no rifles. There is no movement. Time to move forward.

I send Privates Watson right and Thurston left, fast. No shots are fired at either side, as they edge past the visible parts of the bunker, each dropping low in a hole to either side.

I turn to Ben Hodge, trained in explosives, three days waiting to apply his skills. He's anxious. I look to see if I can spy any movement, any rifles, any hint of human life in the bunker. I see none. "Go to the left, next to Thurston," I say.

He runs, not as fast as Thurston, bangalore and explosives in hand, and makes it as far as Thurston, dropping in a hole at or near him. No shots are fired from the bunker. None come from the mountain just beyond. Our singular attention is focused on our task.

Hodge and Thurston edge across the bunker a ways and begin their task of using C-4 to explode successfully, creating a crack in the top of the bunker. Hodge begins to work with the bangalore, the metal tube with his guidance working its way through the top of the bunker, his objective to make sure the explosive-laden metal tube goes all the way to the interior of the bunker.

I tell the platoon to keep their eyes open for any sign of enemy, not just within the bunker, but on beyond, up the mountain. Still, I know their eyes are on Hodge, orders or no orders. Can't help but be. I look up the mountain, then back in the bunker, my focus for the moment not on Ben Hodge. I have to obey my own orders.

Hodge, with Thurston's help, completes the task of getting the bangalore into the bunker. Hodge nods to Thurston and Watson and all three start coming toward us at a gallop, not a sprint, Hodge with the wires for the explosion in hands. I'm looking straight at Ben Hodge, my eyes on his every step.

A rifle shot comes from inside the bunker. Just from the corner of my right eye I catch the light of rifle fire amid the oncoming dusk. Hodge hits the sandy ash, his body now motionless in the approaching darkness. My platoon is stunned, silent, just as I am. I collect my thoughts. It takes a moment.

"Mills, hit it left side," I holler.

He scorches the bunker, right on target, his flame throwing followed by a bazooka blast and shots from M-1s. No orders given, just action, or reactions from my platoon.

"Thurston, get the wire. Watson, get Hodge," I direct.

Neither hesitate. They dash to their assignments, Thurston grabbing the wire from under Ben Hodge's body, and Watson lifting the lifeless marine to his shoulder, much as one would a potato sack. Thurston dashes back, Watson behind him, slowed by the weight of the body. No shots are fired.

Now back in the bunker, I stare at Ben Hodge. Lifeless. I look up to eye my platoon. It's almost dark, but I can see their eyes (or in my mind I can) staring at Ben Hodge, all life gone.

"Can you detonate that bunker?" I say to Thurston.

He doesn't move. No acknowledgement of my question.

"Thurston, do you know how to set that thing off?" I say, this time loud and firm.

His eyes awaken from their focus on Ben Hodge, and he nods. Slowly, he reaches for the detonator, connecting it with the wire.

I look at the bunker, then quickly glance left, then right. All the platoon is looking ahead. A moment's wait, then the explosion, horrendous noise and lightning light interrupt the darkness. The bunker caves in. Ben Hodge's dead body lies still.

NINETEEN

It's mid-morning, fifth day on the island, a third of the way up the mountain. Yesterday, the fighting was light—for my platoon. I could hear battles raging to the north, a mile or so—heavy. Today it's quiet on the mountain. Strange, like the eye of a hurricane. Never been in one of those, but the eye is supposed to be the calm between either side of the destruction. I catch my breath, look out toward the Pacific.

"Wow! Hurrah! Hey! Yahoo!" Cheers of all types awaken me. Cheers, from my platoon. Cheers from around the mountain. I look up, top of the mountain, can't be a hundred and fifty yards, at a tiny flag whipping in the wind, an American flag, top of the mountain. Can't see the stars and stripes, but I know it's American. We all do. My heart pumps hard. A tide of blood swells within my body—energy, exhaustion, joy, and hope all mixed into one strange concoction inside my skin. I smile. It's a deep smile, not shallow. I say nothing. I smile.

"Now, that's something, isn't it?"

I look downward to answer.

"Yeah, Brooklyn, that is something. Never seen anything like it."

He smiles back. He still looks young, but not youthful. I return my focus to the whipping flag.

The morning passes. One series of rifle shots breaks the quiet from around Suribachi, as we hear rumbles in the not-too-distant north, the fighting there still constant. Volunteers are asked to gather and carry bodies to the beach, and several from my platoon oblige. "Watch out for booby traps," they're told. "Jap'll do anything to get you."

I stay put. Don't know when or how I'll be needed.

A new wave of cheers comes from around the mountain. I look upward, the tiny flag replaced by one much larger, the stars and stripes identifiable. American. The wind whips the flag against a sky that is clear—red, white, and blue against light blue. Again, I feel a swelling within my body, exhilaration filling me.

"Lieutenant . . . Lieutenant Wall." Two Marines, unfamiliar, stand before me. I don't notice rank. I'm off guard.

"Colonel wants to see you," the one on the left says.

"Colonel?"

"Yes, the colonel."

"Where?"

"Down by the beach."

"But, I've got my platoon," I say.

"Can't speak for that. Colonel says he wants to see you, and wants you to come now. Right now."

I turn to Sarge. "Can you keep an eye on things?"

"Yes," he says, leaving no question in my mind.

We begin our trek. It's short. Downhill. No resistance. Simple. I say "simple." No, it's not. As I near the beach the bodies are piled high, marines on one side and Japs on the other. Can't even count them—and look, they're bringing more, stretchers with the wounded. Too many to get to all at one time. Some will die as they wait. Pain.

I near a tent, one of my cohorts in front, one behind. I've not even bothered to ask their names. I'm numb, disoriented. Why does the colonel want to see me?

The marine in front leads me to a spot before a tent, the Pacific to the backside, waves rolling in against a clear blue sky. A man, older than my father perhaps, turns toward me. I salute, a reflex.

"Lieutenant Wall . . . Gunter Wall?" he says.

"Yes sir."

"Have a seat," he says, gesturing to a chair.

I obey.

He seats himself three feet away. I look at his face, tired eyes set within hard-earned creases focus on me, giving me the sense he has turned off the world. All is shut out, all but me.

"Want a Hershey bar?" he says, reaching in his pocket, handing it to me.

I accept it, realizing I've hardly eaten a bite for five days, hunger striking my stomach.

"Go ahead, eat it," he says. "I've already had mine."

I obey, unwrapping the bar halfway, biting off a third of it without giving any thought. I begin to chew and slowly swallow. Never had chocolate this good. Never had food this good.

"You're from Mississippi," he says.

"Yes sir."

"Been to college?"

"Couple of years," I say. "First in my family to go."

"Really?" he says. "You'll get to finish up when you get back. Your first battle?"

"Yes sir."

"How are your men doing?" he says.

"Fine," I say, a reflex, no thought required, pride within me. I then stop, think a bit, then say, "Seven dead. Nine wounded, seven of them too injured to fight, for the present. We made it to the base of the mountain night before last. Took a bunker, pillbox . . . whatever. We were one of the first to get there. Really proud of my men."

"Good," he says.

My thoughts return to my trek down to the beach, when I asked myself a dozen times, "Why does the colonel want to see me?"

"Parents still alive?" he asks.

"Yes sir. Also got a brother someplace in Europe."

"Yes," he says, nodding as he speaks, removing a telegram from his pocket. "Everett . . . brace yourself, Son," he says, handing me the telegram, folded.

I grab and unfold. *Private Everett C. Wall. Died in combat. February 22, 1945.*

I go numb. No feeling. No pain. Devoid of emotion. I stare at the telegram. I read. I reread, and it remains the same, my tired eyes to the depth of soul in disbelief. Can't be. Thoughts flash. He never engineered a train. It was his dream. Now it's Everett and me on Lake Knox, his arm around my chest, swimming me to safety. My graduation night, Mom, Dad, Everett, the look of pride for me on Everett's face, the Walls all together at a moment in time . . . rabbit hunting, sitting on a log . . . little-boy dreams of faraway places: Egypt, India, China.

Neither of us made it to those places, did we? But we both ended up far away—Everett in northern Africa not far from Egypt, then in Europe. And me, at a place that to this point no one's heard of: Iwo Jima. Two brothers, apart at opposite ends of the world. Apart. One dead and one alive. And now, a thought of rabbit hunting again—Everett, Dad, me together. Remember it like yesterday. I smile, then catch myself. How can I do that? No time to smile. No place. I brace myself. Face goes serious. I feel hard as a stone from the surface of my skin to my innermost being.

I look up.

"I thought it best to deliver it in person," he says, his eyes tired as eyes get. "This war's not of our making. It's not something anyone in his right mind would wish for. But for now, winning it is our responsibility, as it was your brother's. As much as I hate to say it, we've still got three quarters of an island of ravines, pillboxes, and bunkers, all filled with the enemy. Up that mountain you've got your platoon to lead. As hard as you might hurt, those eighteen- and nineteen-year-olds need you to lead them. Today, try to get some rest. You're gonna need it for what's ahead."

I look him in his eyes, eyes reawakened from tiredness, his having searched deep and found strength submerged . . . somewhere . . . now resurfacing. I know why he is a colonel, why he is on this speck in the Pacific at this moment in time, leading.

"One more thing, Lieutenant," he says, pausing as we both stare. Say a prayer for your mother and father. Say it today. As much as you might hurt, you have no idea."

As I turn to head back to the mountain, past the dead and the wounded along the way, he says, "You'll be accompanied back, just as you came."

"That's not necessary, sir," I say, as I turn back toward the colonel. He says, "Oh, but it is. Men need men."

•   •   •

Better get some sleep. They say tonight might be our best chance for some time to come. Gonna be going the other direction on the island starting tomorrow and we'll have to be alert around the clock. Got to get sleep. Got to get sleep. But I can't—not with Everett on my mind on top of all else. Today, when the colonel broke the news to me, I went numb, then had a dull emotional pain in my chest. Next thing, I'm thinking pleasant memories of Everett, Dad, and me, and I'm smiling. Smiling! That's when I blocked it all out, got tough and marched on back up to my men. Never run that emotional gauntlet before—never had a brother die. Right now the emotional pain in my chest is not dull; it's piercing like nothing I've ever felt. Slept in the same bed with him the first five years of my life, his body next to mine. Even slipped the covers off him. Makes me so guilty to think of that. Wouldn't be here tonight if not for him. Nobody, other than Everett, was paying attention to me that day in the lake. Couldn't see it clearly then, but looking back later I knew. Just one of those things you can't prove in life, but you know.

And what the colonel said today about Mom and Dad is true. I may only be twenty-two, but I can figure that one out. Much as I hurt, it can't be like Mom. I cuddled with Everett, but Mom carried him in her body and nursed him with her breasts. Dad held him in his hands. Dad's gonna have to hold Mom in his hands now. She's fragile.

What's that, a tear in my eye? Much as I've hurt for my men who have died and are wounded, I've held my composure, haven't shed a one of those. Right now I don't feel so composed. I hurt.

Deep inside I believe Everett's in the place of peace. I do. But it just doesn't seem natural, him not being alive. I'm struggling. I know Mom is. Know Dad is too. *God, please grant all us comfort, let us see beyond this night.*

TWENTY

Three weeks on Iwo, and my platoon's not made it three miles. My platoon? Thirteen dead and nineteen wounded, some twice. "Sew him up and put him back out there. Patch his body together with baling wire." That's what the conversation is. Nine of the wounded are fighting. Some have no business being out here, but we press on. Thought about Everett several times, always at night when I couldn't sleep, which has been most nights. Japs come out of nowhere, crazed. Get you when you try to sleep. Yeah, "crazed" twenty-four hours a day. Their fighting makes no sense, at least not to my way of thinking. Some have said, "Well, they think if they die for the emperor, they'll come back again. Reincarnate, or something." Must be. Haven't come upon one yet that has surrendered.

Never seen land like this either. Ravines everywhere. Couldn't drive a tank or a jeep through one of them if your life depended on it, which at this moment it might. A northward yard, foot, inch, anything is progress. Problem is, there are caves everywhere, many of them natural. And if there isn't a cave on the side of a ravine, they've made one, and tunnels connecting them. Heck, for all I know there could be three Japs under me right now just waiting for the right time to come out. That's why I can't ever rest. It's the element of surprise, minute by minute, day and night. Don't sleep. Hardly eat. Just shoot first, and don't miss.

Brooklyn and Thurston, loaded with ammo, head to toe, crawl toward me from behind. It's midday and they've been back to restock. Can't believe the amount of shells we've been through.

"Shells for your carbine, Lieutenant," Brooklyn says.

"Thanks," I say, nodding, looking at Brooklyn. Half-inch black peach fuzz covers his face, not the thick beard that many have. Interesting. Haven't taken note till this point. They all look older, I think, as I glance both ways, if only for a moment, at bearded eighteen- and nineteen-year-olds, some with peach fuzz and some heavy-bearded. Brooklyn takes the prize for peach fuzz. Still has a youthful look, but dirty—unshaven or not.

I add the shells to my nearly depleted stockpile.

Brooklyn stands to remove ammo from multiple knapsacks weighted upon his back. Machine gunfire opens, shells coming in succession far faster than I can count, cutting Brooklyn open chest to waist, knocking him back three, four feet. This, followed by flames from our side, hitting the mark forty yards out, just to the side of a scrubby tree, a Jap soldier up in flames. He screams. Human pain.

I turn. Brooklyn's entire midsection is opened wide, blood flowing freely as his limbs writhe, his eyes open for a second as I look at them. They close.

I fall on him, grab, put my arms around him. I raise up, making fists in both hands and begin to pound his chest, blood on my hands, on my sleeves, blood splattering in all directions. "Don't die! Don't die! Don't die, Brooklyn! Don't let him die, God!" I collapse, arms around him again, blood everywhere. I cry, floodgates opening. Save the one tear shed for Everett, I haven't cried since I set foot on this island. Didn't cry in basic training. Haven't cried in years. But I cry—and I can't stop, my living body against Brooklyn's dead one.

Don't know how long my body has been on his. Seconds? A minute? Minutes? I look up. The whole platoon is staring at me, and it feels like the whole world. Brace yourself, Gunter! Snap to; you're the lieutenant.

I raise up and start to stand, suddenly stopping myself. "Wait! I can't do what Brooklyn did!" flashes suddenly through my mind. On my knees, I look around at the stares. The men are dazed, bewildered, pained? I don't know. They are motionless.

"There's nothing we can do for him right now," I say. My tears have quit flowing. "It's time to press forward. They'll be along later today to carry his body down with the rest."

TWENTY-ONE

Four weeks and three days . . . twenty-four hours a day. Platoon's not a platoon—at least, nowhere near forty of us. I'm alive, against the odds for a second lieutenant. They've been replacing lieutenants like flat tires on jeeps. "I think we can patch that one up. Nope, need a new one, that one's a goner. Need to replace it. Need to replace him. What's the difference?"

It's night. Not seeing that many Japs as we edge forward, only a short distance now to the north tip of the island. Mostly snipers that appear out of nowhere. They come out from under the ground and pick off a marine or two before we fill 'em with shells. They know they're gonna die, no question about it. I guess they think maybe they can go two for one: "Lose my life and take out two marines."

I'm tired, all the time. Only chance I had for a good night's sleep was on the day I found out Everett died. My mind's all muddied up, thicker than floodwater, nothing clear. Got no idea how much sleep I've gotten. Doze off and on. Rustle of the wind . . . marine turns the other way in his sleep . . . any noise, any movement—no matter how slight—my eyes open wide, my adrenaline flows. Then, I lie awake, sometimes till sunup. Like right now. I'm as alert as I'll be at oh-eight-hundred, adrenaline at its peak. Far as I can tell, everybody else is asleep. Then again, how would I know? It's dark.

Nobody's mentioned the day Brooklyn died—that is, except Sarge, about three days later when nobody was around. Told me he was glad to see I was still human and cared about the men. Said "I bounced back and put my head back on my shoulders." Said he noticed the guys were "a little wary for a day or so, but after keeping an eye on me, were now ready to let me lead them against hell."

Don't know whether Sarge was just trying to pump me up or not, but the guys are still pressing north, foot by foot. And they've never questioned my commands.

Sarge—I'd be dead, if it weren't for him. He's been here before, so to speak. Not for quite as long an uninterrupted stretch, but he's been here. And he's survived. He's told me to start sleeping with an M-1, in addition to my carbine. "Lieutenant ought to have both—a perk of being a lieutenant. M-1's got a bayonet." So, I've got a carbine and an M-1 as my bed partners tonight.

A sound! Can't tell what it is . . . human movement? Don't just hear it; I sense it in front of me. What to do? I wait. I look. I listen. If I speak, I may get shot, even in this hole. If I fail to speak, my men might die—if it's the Japs.

"Wake up," I say, in a voice above a whisper.

I hear stirring in the trenches and nothing from in front of me. Makes no sense, does it? To wake them up. Disturb what little rest they might get. And yet, I must. "Get your guns ready," I say, firmly, boldly.

I can hear them moving, grabbing guns as I say, "Keep your heads low. Stay down in the trenches."

I sense a presence in front of us, yet I see nothing. Then, a shot from the trench down a ways lights the night, showing human forms, all in front, now running directly at us in numbers that seem like the entire remaining Japanese army. Shots come from trenches. A flare goes up from our side, turning the night to day. Screams, screams of the crazed advancing right at us, at me, twenty yards, ten yards. I fire my M-1 and a Jap is blown back. I hear his scream above the others.

I look, right upon me, a soldier with object in hand, my finger no longer upon the trigger of the M-1, my right hand on the front end of the stock. I thrust the gun forward, just like at a target stuffed with straw. It's different. Harder, firmer, nothing like I've felt. Strange.

Hard metal strikes against my left shoulders, pain flying down my arm. I pull the trigger, my finger having found it, a reflex. A shot goes off, in and through the human form now slouched in front of me.

Shots continue, more from our side than the other. They slow down, then stop. "Shoot a flare," I holler, and two go up almost in unison. No one is charging. Bodies lie before us, a moan, a groan, slight movement.

Moans, groans, also from our side, one or two, in English. Sounds of pain. I feel pain. Left shoulder. I raise my arm up. It hurts, but nothing's broken, I guess. With my left hand I reach for my enemy's weapon: a shovel.

Stunned. Perplexed. I lie motionless for a moment, then become the lieutenant. "First, nobody stand up. Any flares left?"

"I've got four," says Johnson.

"Two," says Mills.

"Fire one out there, Johnson," I say.

Bodies, dead bodies, all but two with no movement, just moans of pain. We'll tend to them at daybreak if they're alive.

"For now, don't shoot unless one of them advances," I say. "Any movement this direction, then let 'em have it. Who's shot on our side?"

"Lowery," hollers Watson, at the same time that Ruffin says, "Thurston." I hear them both.

"Watson, where's Lowery hit?" I say.

"Left arm."

"Put some sulfa powder on it and check the bleeding. Can't let him lose blood. Can you hear me, Joe?" I say to Lowery.

"Yes," he says, pain gripping his voice.

"You're gonna make it. Just hold on till sunrise, probably three hours. We'll get you where you need to go."

"Ted, can you hear me?" I say to Thurston.

Silence.

"Ted, can you hear me?"

"Yes, Lieutenant," Ted's words spoken hastily with gut-driven effort through pain and heavy breathing.

"Where are you hit?"

"Side. Left side, just under my ribs."

"Ruffin, apply pressure. Slow the bleeding, and give him water. We're gonna hold tight till daybreak."

"But, Lieutenant, Ted might not make it. We need to get him to a doctor right now," Ruffin says.

"Ruffin, neither of you might make it if you try. Stay put. That's an order, do you understand?"

"Yes."

"Ted, you're gonna make it," I say. "Do you understand?"

"Yes."

"That's an order," I say.

"Any one else hit?" I say.

"Lieutenant . . . sir."

"What's that, Thompson?"

"Sarge ain't moving."

"Sarge ain't moving? What do you mean?"

"No sir. He's . . . dead."

Silence.

Sarge . . . can't be. My mind's all muddied up again, thicker than ever. Numb. I'm numb, just like the colonel handing me the telegram about Everett. Motionless. Speechless. Just like everybody.

I snap to. "Any Japs alive in a trench?"

"Got one here I stabbed in the side with a bayonet. Already pulled the bayonet out. He's bleeding like crazy, but still alive," says Creighton.

What to do? What to say? Feel like I ought to order him shot. I hate these Japs. I pause. I think. I say, "Creighton, put pressure on his wound to slow his bleeding. Give him some water."

"But . . . sir?"

"That's an order."

"Yes."

"Cranford, you in the same hole as the wounded Jap and Creighton, aren't you?"

"Yes."

"Keep your M-1 aimed at that Jap. If he so much as makes a move at you, shoot him."

"Yes sir."

"Creighton?"

"What, Lieutenant?"

"First, search that Jap. Make sure he doesn't have a knife—or a spoon or a fork. Make sure there's no grenade."

"Yes sir."

"Then, attend to his wound. Rest of y'all, if you've got any dead Japs in your trench, toss 'em out. Just make sure there's no grenades on them before you do. After that, all the rest of you keep your rifles aimed forward . . . that is, with the exception of Thompson and Mills. I want the two of you aimed the other way."

"Why's that?" says Thompson. "We've already defeated them to the south."

" 'Cause they'll come out of nowhere and come at you with anything," I say as I grab the shovel.

TWENTY-TWO

"That you, Missouri?" I say. Would never have recognized him if he weren't six foot four and lean as a rail—no, leaner, now gaunt to the point that a stiff wind might blow him into the Pacific. His beard's like steel wool, right out of the box. Tired eyes make him look ten years older.

"Mississippi, you're uglier than a mule's ass. If it weren't for that silly accent, I wouldn't know it was you," Missouri says, none of his alertness, none of his wit lost—or, at least on the surface it seems that way.

"Yeah, we made it," he goes on, a smile, a twinkle in his eye as he speaks. The smile abruptly disappears, replaced by a serious look, more serious than any I've ever seen on Missouri. "Mississippi, we made it. A lot of my group didn't. And second lieutenants . . . for a while there someone said they were replacing us like tent pegs. Imagine that."

"Yeah," is all I say. Can't think of much to say. I'm worn down with exhaustion, physically and emotionally. It's good to see Missouri, good to be standing on the northern tip of Iwo. It's good to be alive. Victory. Yes, that's what it is—victory. Still, at this moment, I'm so spent I can't feel it. We're supposed to be leaving, today perhaps. If not today, then tomorrow. Yet, in a way, when I leave, not all of me will. So much has happened in such a short time, not quite forty days.

Forty days? Forty days of rain, and you've flooded the world. Forty days of resurrection, and you've changed the world. Almost forty days of fighting, and you've changed me. What am I telling myself? My mind's getting all muddy again.

"Mississippi, wake up, you're elsewhere," Missouri says.

I wake up.

"I guess we've both got a mountain on our minds," Missouri goes on. "Maybe some day we'll sort it out. Today, I'm just grateful to be alive. Yeah, they tell us in a while they're gonna walk us back to the spot where we set foot on this place, then ship us back to Hawaii. They say if we go along the beach, it'll take us two or three hours. Think of that. It took us thirty-six days to get here, and it'll take us two or three hours to get back. It almost doesn't make sense, does it?"

"No," I say as I soak in Missouri's profound thought.

"How'd your platoon come out?" Missouri says, switching my mind again.

"Too many died. Too many were wounded. Fifteen dead, eighteen wounded."

"Had eleven die," Missouri says. "Plenty more are held together with baling wire; they'll be limping and hurting the rest of their lives. And here we are, hardly a scratch on either one of us. Fortunate."

"Yeah."

"Well, there's the call to line us up and march us back. Let's go stand in line." Missouri nods as he heads forward, then stops and turns back. "Mississippi, word's out they're gonna let us spend some time at the cemetery before we board ship."

Missouri's words grab at my heart, producing guilt. Why? Maybe 'cause the only scratch on me is from the shovel on my shoulder. It's sore, but nothing's broken. A few more days and I probably won't feel a thing. Got men all over the island that will hurt the rest of their days. And the dead—fifteen in my platoon.

"Don't know whether I can handle it," I say.

"What do you mean?" Missouri says back sternly.

"Don't know whether I got it in me right now."

"Don't know whether you got it in you? You're going up to that cemetery if I have to drag your ass up there. I got no plans for coming back here, and I know you don't. You've got but one chance in your lifetime, and this is it. We're going through the entire Fifth Division till we find all eleven of mine and fifteen of yours. Heck, the ship may go off and leave us, but we're gonna pay our respects to every last one of them."

Missouri's the most persuasive guy I've ever met. And, most of the time, he's trying to talk me in to doing what's best. It's just . . . I don't know. I feel kind of dead on the inside.

I say nothing as we begin to march side by side, me on the inside, Missouri on the Pacific side. Yeah, he's between me and the ship; he planned it that way. Gonna drag my . . . we march. Time passes. I reflect—Frenchie, Ben Hodge . . . not Ted Thurston—or at least he was alive last I heard, but barely hanging on. Bynum, Brooklyn . . . Brooklyn, so young . . . peach fuzz for a beard, and only drove one time in his life. Gramatti . . . Kopernak . . . we're getting near, white crosses everywhere, more than I've ever seen.

We've walked, almost as long across the cemetery as our trek to it. Missouri's found all of his men, each buried below ash and sand and a cross, at one of the farthest spots from the place each called home. A life given, so others could still call the place they live "home."

I hate to admit it, but that six-foot-four-inch beanpole from Missouri was right. Again. I've found fourteen crosses, but none with the name Paul Jones on it. Even Missouri's getting anxious.

"Ship's gonna leave and I'll be left here to starve to death with a redneck from Mississippi. Gunter, don't you think we had better start heading on?"

"Go on, Missouri. Head to the beach if you're afraid you're gonna get left. I've got to find his grave. If I don't, it will worry me to my own grave."

"Might not be buried yet. There's still some they've not got to," Missouri says, this time with no smartness in his tone.

We wander five minutes, ten minutes, stop at the end of a row. Paul Jones.

Tears come to my eyes. My voice cracks as I speak. "I wouldn't be standing here alive today if it wasn't for him. I'd have died several times." I try to continue, but it's harder. "He was an uncommon man with a common name. Nobody knew him by Paul Jones, only as Sarge. Iwo Jima was just one too many islands in the Pacific," I say, finally getting the words out.

•   •   •

"We're the only two guys on the back of the ship looking the opposite way from Hawaii," Missouri says, the sun almost down as we stare across the Pacific water as far as we can see. We've stood gazing for over an hour with not a word spoken. It's been a full day. We've walked the length of Iwo Jima, paid our respects, and boarded a ship now a couple of hours out to sea. The sea is calm. All is calm; first time I can say that for well over a month. For the past hour it's been the two of us gazing in silence.

"Iwo is four to five miles long and two and a half miles wide," Missouri says, as we continue to gaze. "A two by four."

"It really isn't that large, is it?"

"Nope. When we were fighting for Suribachi, it seemed like Everest."

"So, what are we staring at?" I say.

"Japan . . . can't see it, but we both know it's over yonder—four big islands, one of them over eight hundred miles long. Got more Suribachis than you and I can comprehend. Tons of little islands bigger than Iwo. Also, a few million crazy people."

I gaze harder at the setting sun as I ponder Missouri's words. Right now I don't have an ounce of positive emotion left in my body. I should. Hey, we took the island. Planes can now refuel and make it to Japan. It's one of our greatest victories of the war so far. But I've hardly slept in over a month, and every time I've thought about that island today it was about the dead. I survived and so many didn't.

I *survived*? What about Sarge? Brooklyn? My brother Everett, the other side of the world?

No, I was spared. That's what the folks say where I come from. It's at this very moment I've come to sense what it means. I was spared.

The final rays of sun disappear from the horizon.

TWENTY-THREE

Mail call is the definition of anticipation. A letter comes. A letter doesn't come. Either way it can make your day, or break your day. You don't have to read a letter to tell what's in it—not really. Just look at the guy's face. Might bring a serious look. Might bring a smile. Might make a man cry, even when battle didn't.

Fellow over there tore his open before he got out of the line. Everybody else is waiting while he's reading. Now he's smiling. Come on, buddy, move on, the war might actually end before the rest of us get to fulfill our expectations. Good. He's moving.

"Wall," mail guy hollers, and I edge forward to retrieve my one letter. I say "letter." It's larger than the normal letter: manila, containing more than a page or two. Unlike the fellow a moment ago, I like to take my mail back to the tent and read it in private.

Only mail I get is from my folks. Used to be (before Iwo, and before Everett died) I'd get a letter from Mom every two days, three at maximum. Could tell she missed me, really missed me. She'd give me the news about town. So-and-so's been sick, but they're getting better. This person or that had a baby (big news, 'cause with all the young men gone, a birth was a "headline"). She'd tell me what the other ladies said about "their boys," some in Europe, others in the Pacific, some stationed at home. I say "at home," not meaning Oak Leaf, but the United States. Funny how one's definition changes, isn't it? Mostly Mom picks up her news from ladies at church, or down at the grocery store. She's not really social, I mean society-type social. But gradually, she's gotten to know more people in Oak Leaf. Went from going to the grocery store "just to pick up groceries" to making it a meeting place. As a child I overheard the women say, "So, how is Gunter doing in Mrs. So-and-so's class? I hear she's difficult." (There are a lot of so-and-so's in Oak Leaf). "Gunter's doing fine, I guess. He hasn't said much," Mom would reply. Small talk.

All sorts meet at the grocery store—all sorts meaning everybody shops there: rich, poor, mostly white, though there are a few Negroes. Most of the Negroes shop the other end of downtown, different foodstuffs on the shelves. Conversations go on at those stores, too—more lively. I know because I had a paper route for a while. Folks would always nod and smile when I delivered, pausing their conversation just long enough to acknowledge me.

Mom only took one sabbatical from grocery shopping that I can remember, early part of forty-one, immediately following the car-in-the-lake incident. She had Dad do the shopping for a while. That lasted about three weeks, till Dad lost patience. Only time I can remember him doing that. He finally put his foot down.

Anyway, Mom would pick up other "news" at the drugstore—or *stores* (Oak Leaf has two drugstores, both with soda fountains). Really, the drugstores are more the places where the junior high and high school students go for their "news," much like the picture show.

Church is the other place Mom got to know people. At first it was just worship. She went there for worship every Sunday, come rain, shine, healthy or sick, along with Dad, Everett, and me. She got to know the other women at church, first in her Sunday school class (women her age), then preparing food for "those in hard times," where she got to meet women of all ages. Anyway, not downplaying worship, but church has been good for Mom. It got her to meet people and to do for others.

When I left home for college, I had a lot of time to think about these things. Wait—I didn't have a "lot of time," 'cause I was working, going to class, or studying most of the time. But, when I did have a free moment to think, let my mind drift, I did think about Mom, how she was doing. I wondered how she would have done had the flood not come, had we stayed on the plantation, miles from a grocery or drugstore, church perhaps just worship. I could see her becoming withdrawn, a tendency she's always been on the verge of: right to the bank of the river, but not quite in the water. No, Oak Leaf was the best thing for her. Then again, what if we had stayed at Everett Crossroads, Dad working at the store? Talk about being on the edge of the river. Aunt Martha would have just pushed him in, and the man would have drowned. Funny how you see things, having reached some semblance of adulthood.

No, Dad's job at the oil mill gave him an opportunity. Gave us an opportunity. And Oak Leaf, well . . . I miss it, now that I've had a little free time on my hands back on Hawaii, Camp Tarawa.

I enter the tent, seat myself on the cot. Back in college I'd have plopped on it. Things change. I tear the seal, now in a hurry. Got to quench my anticipation. Mom didn't write when I was on Iwo, and hasn't since. Dad's written a total of four times. He's never been one to write. Don't know whether it's lack of schooling or whether he's just reserved in that way (like most men). Anyway, he wrote the four letters, and reserved or not, I could feel his pain like a knife stuck in my own flesh. Said Mom was staring at the wall, worse than right after the flood. He wrote in the second letter that he'd got her "out of the house to attend a worship service," and that "it was her first time out of the house since the funeral over two weeks earlier." Then he said, "Time will help, but won't heal—never fully." I couldn't tell if he was talking about Mom . . . or himself.

There's a cutting from a newspaper, folded, its message concealed by the front of a letter, four pages. I start to read the letter first, but am compelled, driven (don't know why) to unfold the clipping. Jimmy Street's picture, in uniform, chest up, army cap on, handsome, daring, a lead-the-group, lead-the-world look on his face, front page *Oak Leaf Gazette*. "Local Army Captain Dies Leading Troops in Germany."

My heart stops. I go numb, then tears in my eyes, no conscious effort to create them.

Army Captain James Halcomb Street Jr. was killed in combat April 16 in the Ruhr, a region in Germany, where two days later over 300,000 German troops surrendered. "Jimmy," as he was known, was a native of Oak Leaf, having graduated from Oak Leaf High School as valedictorian of the Class of 1941. He attended Mississippi State College prior to entering the army, where he rose to the rank of captain. He fought in the D-Day invasion and the Battle of the Bulge. He is the sixth from our town to have died in the war.

Jimmy is survived by James Halcomb Street Sr., father, and Thelma Street, mother, both longtime residents of Oak Leaf. A memorial service is to be held Friday at 2:00 p.m. at Oak Leaf Presbyterian Church.

With grateful appreciation, the Oak Leaf community mourns the loss of Jimmy.

Can't be. It can't be. I met Jimmy in the first grade, first day of school. Twelve years of growing up, then two years of college before we went separate ways, Jimmy to the army, me to the marines, a half-world apart.

Smartest guy I'd ever known, with looks to go with brains. Could have been anything. Could have done anything. Only person I ever knew of whom I could say, "He could be president." Probably didn't have to die. Probably went charging, leading troops at the enemy, headstrong. Yeah, headstrong. That's Jimmy. No, that *was* Jimmy.

I look at the picture: young, handsome, confident, Jimmy Street, dead at age twenty-two. I move the newspaper to behind the four-page letter and begin to read. The handwriting is Mom's, the first time I've seen it since the day before Iwo. I'm caught off guard. Tears have stopped, my heart is pumping to the maximum.

Dear Gunter,

Before you read my letter, please read the newspaper clipping.

I'm sorry I haven't written since Everett died. This is the first time I've written those words. I've started to write that down, just to myself, but I couldn't. I've tried to write you, but each time the pen froze in my hand. In many ways that describes me. Your father has been most patient. He has had to deal with his own sorrow, as well as mine. He's a strong man who has endured a lot, but nothing compared with Everett's death (those words again). It's an odd experience, your son going first, not as a child but as a full adult. No matter how I think of it, I can't come to full reconciliation, and perhaps never will.

I did, however, take a step in that direction when your father and I went by and dropped a pound cake off at the Streets'. It's the first time, except for drives to church, that I've ventured out the front door since the memorial service for Everett. Folks turned out from all over for the service. Not an empty seat in church. After that, I locked myself in the house. I wouldn't even answer the phone.

Your father made me go to church. He said it was what the Lord wanted, something I tried to argue about, but couldn't come up with an answer. We went, but I made him slip in the back late, and leave before the final hymn.

Night before last I cooked supper for your father and baked a pound cake for the Streets. It was the first time I had done for anyone else since I got the message about Everett. I was preparing supper, something I hadn't done in almost two months. Your father came home from work early that afternoon to bring me the news about Jimmy. We sat quietly in the living room for the longest time. About dark, I went in the kitchen and started peeling potatoes. Then I opened some canned vegetables. After a while I felt like making biscuits, so I did. The moist flour felt so good in my hands. For the first time in weeks I felt useful. I couldn't stop with the biscuits.

I was thinking about Thelma, what she was going through. I started on the pound cake. It wasn't much, but it was something, and I had to do something. Oh, I know all she and I have in common is that we've both lost a son to war. But, that's much more in common than most people will ever have.

Tom and I went yesterday to deliver the cake. It was the first time I had been in their home (so large, two-story with antiques). And there was so much food that my pound cake seemed lost, insignificant. She was visiting with some of the wealthier women—plantation owner's wives and such—when her eyes caught mine. She excused herself and walked to me, putting her arm around me. It was like station in life didn't matter, not for the moment. We shared grief, something in common far greater than wealth or social status. She then looked in my eyes. I've never had a woman look me in the eyes like that, if only for a moment. I'll never forget it as long as I live.

I didn't sleep much last night. My mind was on many things, not the least of them you. I thought about Everett's death, then about Jimmy's, finally about you. Jimmy was Thelma's only child. I have you. I apologize for not writing. I also apologize for not praying for you, something I'm more ashamed about than not writing. For a while I stopped praying for everyone except myself. All I could think and pray about was my own pain and sorrow. That changed night before last.

I love you, Gunter.

With love, Mother

My tears return. They're not tears of pain or sorrow. No, they are unexplainable, neither sorrowful, nor joyous, maybe somewhere in between—if there is such a thing. I put the newspaper clipping inside the four-page letter, then open my trunk, placing the letter carefully inside a box within the trunk. I stare at the box for a moment, then close the trunk before drying away my tears.

TWENTY-FOUR

Tracers soar from all directions, leaving trails of smoke against the blue, the machine-gun fire coming from all directions. The shooting began an hour ago. It stopped for about fifteen minutes, started again, quit, and now has resumed for about a minute.

"I guess the troops are taking orders," I say sarcastically.

"Heck, Mississippi, the captains and lieutenants may actually be giving the orders to fire. Right now I feel like getting my carbine and taking a little target practice on some clouds—if I can find any. Today there are no clouds!" Missouri yells exuberantly over the noise of machine-gun shots.

I nod, agreeing. It's been a couple of hours since we got the word we had dropped a bomb in Japan, an atomic one. Yeah, an atomic bomb, something they said couldn't be done. We dropped it on some place called Hiroshima; I think that's the name. Never heard of it before. Anyway, not long after we got the news, word started going around that the Japs are going to surrender, or already have—one or the other. Then the shooting started. Never seen people so excited in all my life.

"Duck, Mississippi!" Missouri hollers. "Those tracers are flying a bit low."

They are, and I duck.

"So, you think it's really over, Missouri?"

"You bet. Not even the Japs are crazy enough to keep going now. I bet the bank in California that loaned me money is celebrating, even though I only owe one more month on my note. Mississippi, we're gonna live. That is, if our own troops don't shoot us today."

The machine-gun fire continues, although it is again headed in a more heavenly direction.

"There goes another one," Missouri says above the explosion, as another latrine flies into the air in countless pieces. I hope no one was sitting in it," he continues, then, "Just think—some of these guys are gonna be going to college. Yep, college campuses will never be the same."

"So, what should we do right now?" I ask.

"Well, it doesn't look like our guys are the ones who are trigger-happy. All the shooting is coming from over yonder. As for me, I've already done enough shooting for this year," Missouri says.

"You didn't answer my question," I reply.

"I know . . . I know. I was just thinking," Missouri says.

"Trouble happens every time you do that."

"That's true," says Missouri with a smile that says, "I'm mischievous," followed by, "You remember that night we went to Hilo?"

"Sure do."

"I've still got some vodka left in my trunk, and I say it's time for a little celebration," says Missouri, his smile turning from mischievous to devilish.

"Oh, no," I say, objecting verbally, at the same time knowing I'm fixing to get in trouble.

"Relax, Mississippi. No way they're gonna do anything to us. If there's ever been a time in our lives to let go, this is it."

I can't tell Missouri no; nobody can. When he gets it in his mind something's gonna be done, it's just as well as done.

"Now, Mississippi, I bet you haven't finished off your bottle of vodka since we got back," Missouri goes on.

Finished it off? I haven't even broken the seal. Seems like every time I have "one or two," something unintended happens. Well, this time there's no Vivian Lemur around to disappear on me. Wait . . . I'm the one who disappeared, right? And this time there's no frozen lake, no vehicle I'm riding in. Hey, the war's over. Why not?

"Oh, all right. I'll try to scrounge for it," I say, all the while knowing exactly where it is in my trunk.

"Good. Now, go round up that bottle and come meet me at my tent," Missouri says. "But first, better put it in your canteen. Wouldn't want anybody to get the wrong impression."

I nod, then head to my tent.

Moments later I'm seated in a folding chair in front of Missouri's tent, sipping from my canteen, the burn of cheap vodka searing my chest cavity. The tracers have stopped, but the cheering hasn't. It picks up down the ways to the left, then simmers down, only to ignite again with another crowd from a different direction.

"Yep, this is the life," Missouri says, just before taking another sip from his canteen.

I take another sip, just a trickle this time, the ride down my chest cavity a bit smoother than the first. I nod to acknowledge Missouri.

"So, what you gonna do when we get home?" Missouri says.

What am I gonna do? I think. Quit getting up before daybreak is the first thought that crosses my mind.

"Mississippi, you there?" Missouri says, letting me know he's waiting for an answer, even if it takes until dark.

"If I can scrape together the funds, I guess go back to college," I say. "You know, I haven't taken out any loans, like other people I know. Been saving my money."

Yeah, saving my money, sixty-five dollars a month. Only reason why is because I haven't had anything to spend it on, except one bottle of cheap vodka. What does one spend his money on, on top of a mountain in Hawaii with no stores?

"Then what? What are you gonna do with your life?" Missouri comes back, quick as a bullet.

"Don't have a clue," I say. "Nobody in my family has ever been to college, much less graduated. So, ever since I was knee high, it's been 'you've got the brains in the family, Gunter. It would be a shame if you let that go to waste. You're destined for college.' All the while, nobody, including myself, has a clue what I'm supposed to do after that. In some ways my brother, Everett, had it better than me. Sorry, I meant to say had it figured out better than me. He knew he wanted to engineer a train— even though obviously it didn't work out that way; war changes things. Lately, I've thought it would be a gift if I lived to see age twenty-three."

"Well, I'm going to be a lawyer," Missouri replies, quickly. "Going to be a great one," he says, before going quiet again to take another sip from his canteen.

I sip with him and say nothing. Don't have a clue what I'm going to do other than finish college.

• • •

"Wake up, Mississippi," Missouri says, like he's said it for the fourth or fifth time, sort of like Mom back home. "Wake up, Mississippi!"

"Missouri, it's pitch dark and . . . my head's killing me," I say. "Where am I?"

"For the moment, safe on your cot. But that could change quickly."

Oh . . . oh, my head's throbbing, my body's spinning, my stomach's filled with nausea, and, with the exception of Missouri's flashlight he just pointed in my face, my surroundings are the definition of dark.

"How did I get here?"

"Took three of us to carry you," Missouri says. "Truth is, none of us were in great shape to do the job. It's a miracle we didn't all roll down the mountain and float off in the Pacific."

"So, why are you harassing me? Why disturb my bliss?" I say, realizing, just as I say it, that *bliss* is the wrong word to describe my current state.

" 'Cause the war ain't over. Right now we both got a hangover, and we still got the crazy Japs to fight. No surrender has taken place, and the word is circulating that the top brass will be around to inspect things at oh-six-hundred. Gonna make a point!"

"What's the point?" I say, almost throwing up the words.

"Point is, you had better get your scrawny redneck butt out off that cot or the higher-ups are gonna be on to it for the duration of your stay in the Marine Corps. The rest of us will be taking a ship to Japan, while you'll be swimming. Not that it will matter in the long run, because we'll all probably end up dead. Nevertheless, *our* ride over will be a lot more comfortable."

Again, when Missouri wants to get me to do something, "no" is not an option. I rise . . . slowly, queasily, painfully, and begin to search for my uniform. I stumble back onto the cot, as it almost collapses.

"And to think that in a little more than an hour you're gonna be trying to stand at attention. Better try again." Missouri places his hand on my bicep, assisting me up.

This time I'm more seaworthy. I reach for my pants with success, placing my left leg through the trouser without stumbling, followed then by the right.

"Well, I think I had better go check on my own troops now," Missouri says.

I sense a tinge of guilt in his voice.

"Yeah, I remember that wild-hair story you told me about Hoppy Pearson." Missouri begins to ramble. "Told me how he'd saved your life, after he almost cost it. Well, I don't want you saying someday Old Missouri got you booted out of the Marine Corps. No, you'll live to tell the story of how he saved your hide. That is, if you ever get your scrawny redneck butt out of here soon enough to get your guys to clean up their mess. See you," Missouri says as he exits my tent, just as I put a hustle on.

My guys are as enthusiastic about arising today as I was. They've never been harder to prod, but prod I do. I push, pull, yank, and cajole until our area is spotless, right at oh-five-fifty-nine . . . when up walks the colonel with his entourage. I stand at perfect attention (or so I think) and salute him.

"Lt. Wall, we are here for inspection," he says with authority.

From the corner of my eye I catch a glimpse of my men. Can't get a full read. What do they know? Was Missouri mistaken? A rumor? I stare at the colonel, who is eyeing my men one at a time. More than appearing dejected, he looks to be reaching deep in his gut to do what has to be done, although he doesn't want to. Even through my stupor I can see this.

"Gentlemen, the war is not over. We will continue to prepare."

TWENTY-FIVE

"I will not surrender to a child," the interpreter says for the third time.

I've rephrased the question slightly each time, questioning the ability of the interpreter—at least, within my mind. I got to Japan less than a month after the surrender and have been here over two months. Only twenty-two and I'm in charge of an area a quarter the size of my county back home in Mississippi, just more people. Japan's a crowded place— I'm the mayor, sheriff and judge all at once. I feel like Moses before Jethro sat him down, people coming to me with issues constantly. Woke up this morning wishing I was going rabbit hunting, free at least for one day from my seven-day responsibilities. This is the time of November we would always go.

Across the table I stare at the admiral, two, perhaps two–and-a-half times my age, in full dress. He stares, no . . . glares back through his spectacles. It's the most defiant look I've ever seen. No two-year-old, having recently learned the meaning of disobedience, has ever given a greater look of defiance. And although I'm not a parent, I have seen that look.

"Tell him again we're going to search the whole compound, including his desk, for weapons," I say, looking across the mahogany desk that is so lavish, stately, that it makes Mr. Street's desk back at Bank of Oak Leaf look like a desk from grade school.

The glare intensifies as he says, "A child!"

I know what he's said before the interpreter translates. A child? I'm almost twenty-three, and I spent thirty-six days fighting inch by inch across an island, trudging through as much blood as ash and sand, followed by a gut-puking ship ride from Hawaii to this spot, where I sit on the visitor's side of the desk. This yahoo still thinks he's got home field advantage. Thinks he can bully me. What to say?

"General MacArthur's orders," I say directly, as I seek to go ahead in the staring contest.

"MacArthur," he says with contempt, just as the interpreter begins to speak.

"Today we will remove all semblance of anything military from this office, from this school, from these grounds: quotes on the walls, military books, the shirt on your back, as well as your pants. I didn't plan to be abrupt, but you are so obstinate," I say, trying to remain calm.

The interpreter tries to keep up until he reaches the word I assume is "obstinate," when he shrugs politely.

"Belligerent," I say, to which the interpreter again shrugs.

"Stubborn," I say.

This time the interpreter says a word in Japanese, and the admiral gives a sneer, then crosses his arms, saying without saying, "I'm not going to do a single word you say."

"These two men will escort you to the vacant room at the end of the hall," I say.

This time the interpreter translates my words with no difficulty—at least, I assume. For all I know, he is saying, "Your mother is a pig, and you're the ugliest of the litter." If so, that explains the admiral's obstinacy. For now I'll go with my gut, that the translator is pretty much on target.

The admiral resists. I nod, and the marines to either side grab an arm to "assist the admiral to his feet," while Private First Class Johnson just to my left aims an M-1 at him to "further assist."

"I had hoped this conversation would have been more peaceable," I say. "The first two meetings of this type I've had with others were far more amicable. We drank tea like gentlemen."

The translator seems to do fine for a while, then stumbles. I assume he is stumped on the word "amicable." Whatever. It won't make a bit of difference with this guy. The lowdown was he had some success early in the war, before his fortune turned—like it did for a lot of the early heroes. They "placed him out to pasture." Stuck him here to run a propaganda school for sixteen- and seventeen-year-olds. Quite a step down.

His escorts are at first a bit forcible, out of necessity. However, his resistance becomes more relaxed after he stands.

"There are several choices of civilians' clothes in that room down the hall," I say. "Take his uniform and put it with the rest. We'll burn them all together later today."

The admiral begins his trek down the hall, a marine on either side, with Private First Class Johnson, M-1 in hand, traveling right behind. My translator remains with me as I circle the desk and begin to open drawers. No guns, just pens and pencils. Pretty boring.

I walk to the wall across the room from his desk, to two expensively framed photographs: Tojo, and the emperor. I remove each and place them in a box. Kindling. I begin to search the bookshelves, and though plentiful—with the exception of one book that seems to glorify Tojo, (which I add to the kindling box)—the rest seem harmless, nondescript. But then, how would I know? The words are Japanese and the books are written backward. I leave them on the shelf.

"Lieutenant! Lieutenant!" Johnson hollers as he enters the room. "The admiral has locked himself up in that vacant room and won't come out."

"He's done what?" I say.

"Locked himself up."

"Johnson, what in the world was he doing in that room by himself?"

"Changing clothes."

"Changing clothes! By himself?"

"Yes sir."

"While the three of you were outside the door picking your noses."

"Yes sir . . . I mean, we were outside the door . . . not picking our noses. We wanted to give him some privacy. I mean, we're not supposed to watch an admiral change clothes."

"Johnson, you're not supposed to watch OUR admirals change clothes. This guy is not our admiral." Then I think, I've covered a lot in boot camp and on Hawaii, but never instructions regarding enemy admirals undressing. We are going to add that one to the list. "Come on," I say as I head down the hallway, translator behind me, Johnson behind him.

"Holler in there, and ask him when he'll be out," I instruct the translator.

"What?" he replies, probably not having a clue what "holler" means.

"Ask him when he'll be out," I say slowly, clearly.

He speaks in Japanese, loudly enough to be heard through the door. Then repeats himself twice before shrugging.

"I can shoot the knob off the door," Johnson says.

"You most certainly will not," I say. "You must have seen one too many westerns or gangster movies. Sure as sunrise tomorrow morning, your bullet would ricochet off that doorknob and kill one of us. Next thing, 'Well, how did he die?' 'Took a bullet off a doorknob.' 'Came from his own gun?' 'Really?' 'Yeah, really!' Now, where's that ax we confiscated this morning?"

"In a pile out back," Private Johnson says.

"Go get it," I say, noticing a bit of lethargy in his step. "Now!"

He takes off running.

Minutes later I start on the door, weathered wood hard as iron, wondering if I'll ever get through it.

"I can do this, Lieutenant," Johnson says.

"So can I," I say, wondering how Dad pounded open that metal roof so fast when the flood came.

"Ever done it before?" Johnson says, noticing my clumsiness.

"No, but I've watched someone do it."

"When was that?"

"Right before I peed off the roof of my home," I say.

"Whaaaat?"

"Never mind. Just be ready with that M-1 as soon as we've got a hole."

I keep chopping, my heart pumping wildly, my breathing heavy. The wood begins to split. I keep striking with the ax, my speed picking up as I gain confidence. Another minute, and I reach through the door, quickly unlocking it, then pulling my hand back, moving the door, hiding behind it as I say, "Johnson, go first. Shoot to kill if he comes at you."

"Oh . . . ugh," says Johnson as he stands immobile in the doorway.

I come from behind the door and peer into the room.

On the floor lies the admiral, motionless, a small dagger to his side, a larger one lodged below his chest, blood everywhere.

"Hara-kiri," says the translator from behind me, the words the same in Japanese as in English.

I stand in shock. Is there anything I could have done differently?

TWENTY-SIX

Two more days to wake up on board this ship. The ride so far has been smooth in every way. My eight months in Japan were something. For the whole time, I never stopped to rest. I was always in charge. Decide this, decide that. When I get back to Oak Leaf, I won't even be in charge of my home. That's okay. For now I'll take the trade. Two more days! Midday, we should be home. Hey, never thought I would call California home, but I'll be back in the United States again, and that's home. Then, a week or so left in the Marine Corps and I'll really be heading to Mississippi.

Can't wait to see Mom and Dad. Lately, Mom's been writing almost as fast as I can read. She's been letting me know all the "news." However, there was one letter Dad wrote. It was about a young man who drove all the way from Missouri to "pay his respects." Dad wrote: "He was a tall, lean young man about your age, and of all things, he called himself Missouri. It was not his real name, but he said that's what you called him. His real name is on the address he left. Said you might want to write or even come see him sometime. He said there aren't many people he would drive five hundred miles one way just to deliver an address to. 'Actually, I'm only doin' it for one guy, Gunter Wall,' he said. He came to see us because he wanted to let us know you were going to be fine, and that we needed to quit worrying about you. Said he got to feeling guilty 'cause he had been home a couple of months and you were still in Japan."

Dad said Missouri's visit meant even more to him than it did to Mom. Said it helped him quit worrying about me.

"That white-suited wimp will be around any minute," someone from across the room says, interrupting my pleasant thoughts.

"Yeah. Don't think I'll ever make up another bed for the rest of my life," someone else says.

"Amen."

"Amen."

"Gonna sleep till noon."

"Hurry up! He's coming."

We all move to attention in front of the bunks, bunks stacked floor to the ceiling. We're one ship in the middle of a line far as the eye can see in both directions, each filled floor to the ceiling with bunks, bunks filled at night with marines or navy, ours with marines on a naval boat.

The ensign enters in crisp white apparel, his gait fluid, elegant. We stand erect, shoulder to shoulder, lieutenants. He stops and starts, pausing long enough to eye the perfectly smooth bunks, those within eyesight. (Some of the bunks are too high to observe from floor level, and he chooses not to go higher.) He stops abruptly two feet from me, a look of strong displeasure covering his face as he shakes his head. He points to a candy wrapper on the floor under the bunk. "Pick that up."

Who is he talking to?

"You, Lieutenant." He looks straight at me. "Pick that candy wrapper up," he says, like a parent to a child.

What? Get on my knees and crawl under a bunk for a candy wrapper I didn't put there? And this guy is no higher rank than anyone in the room, just another branch of service. He's only in charge (or thinks he is) because we're on a naval ship, and he's Navy.

"No."

"What's your name?" he snaps.

"Lt. Gunter Wall, United States Marine Corps," I say firmly, shooting him with my eyes.

"And what did you say?"

"Hell, no," I say.

Why did I say that? Have I gone loony? He's just the kind of jerk who would try to get me dishonorably discharged two days from shore, two weeks from Oak Leaf, over a candy wrapper. I look to my left to see a clenched fist, then to my right, two. In front of me I see two marines, jaws tight, eyes ready for battle. The room is filled to the brim with men who've fought, led troops at Okinawa, Iwo, Tarawa, Guadalcanal, Peleliu, and on and on. Men who've seen more blood and death than any human should in a lifetime, many wounded (more than once), patched back together like baling wire wrapped around hay, then sent back into battle to fight, to lead, take the beach, take the mountain, take the island . . . And today this guy walks in, dressed in starched white, top to bottom.

If one drop of blood got on his outfit, he'd have it immediately sent to laundry. I'm not going to pick it up. No way. Not just for me, but every man in the room. We deserve respect, not demeaning.

"Ensign, if you feel that it is *so* important to remove that candy wrapper from the floor, then perhaps you should do it yourself. To me, it's not that big an issue," I say.

What am I doing? All the time in the marines, less than two weeks from home. This guy could make my life miserable. Might do anything, get me labeled "dishonorable." Almost there—and I blow it.

"Lt. Wall, I'm afraid you'll have to come with me," he says, trying to be authoritative, but falling short, like a basketball in a free throw that doesn't make it to the rim, the ball sailing through air, only hitting hardwood.

"Now, why would you want to go and do a thing like that?" says Lt. Ferrell, a guy from somewhere in the Midwest, I think. Only spoken to him once or twice. Met him onboard this ship. Understand he fought in a bunch of battles. Came into the marines early on in the war.

"No one asked for your comments," the ensign fires back.

"No, but since I saw you throw that candy wrapper on the floor, I thought I had to speak up," Ferrell comes back.

"I threw the candy wrapper on the floor? What are you talking about?" ensign says, caught off guard, completely startled.

"Yep, threw it on the floor, then tried to get a marine on his knees to pick it up. I'll get through to the fellow running this ship and explain it all to him. If I made it across the beach at Tarawa, then I can surely make it up to the top of the ship."

"Yeah, I saw you do it, too," comes from down the row, to the left.

"Me, too," says the lieutenant next to him.

"So did I."

"Me, too."

"And me."

"And me."

"I saw it, too!"

"Ensign, I'd hate to see the stuff sewed on that pretty white suit get torn off. No, come to think of it, I wouldn't. I actually think it would be nice. However, if you'll just run along like a nice little boy, we'll spare you that indignity," Lt. Ferrell says, this time with even greater authority than the first time he spoke.

Ensign hesitates, his eyes are the only ones in the room not staring at himself.

"Better run along, or you'll be late for tea," Lt. Ferrell says.

This time there's movement as the ensign begins to retreat backward, almost tripping. He then turns and exits, in silence.

Moments later, after the ensign has left, Lt. Ferrell extends his hand for a handshake. First name's Bob," he says. "Sorry, I've not had a chance to shake your hand before."

"Gunter. Gunter Wall," I say, our hands clasped firmly as we speak.

TWENTY-SEVEN

"No, Brooklyn, don't stand. That's an order. That's an order!"

"No problem, Lieutenant. Nothing's going to happen to me. I'll be going back to Brooklyn. Can't wait to show my parents how to drive. Really looking forward to seeing them." Accent thick as ever.

"Don't stand!" I yell, as he stands and I leap to grab him.

Too late. Just before my hands can grab Brooklyn, the bullets begin to tear his body, blood going everywhere as he falls to the ground, flames hitting the Jap I see through the corner of my eye, shrieking coming from that direction as I fall on Brooklyn's body, pounding him, pounding the ground with my fists . . .

Where am I now? Oh, that's Private Johnson, part of my group on Japan.

"Ever done it before?" Johnson says.

"No, but I've watched someone do it."

I begin to chop again, metal against wood, difficult, exhausting. I'm making headway. Wood is beginning to splinter, just a little, now a little more. I've got to keep going, pick up the pace, swing harder, give it my all. Good, good, I think. Now I can open the door. I do. I see blood—blood everywhere. Japanese admiral, on the floor, one knife to the side, another lodged in his body, all motionless.

"Hara-kiri, same in English as in Japanese. Hara-kiri, same in English as in Japanese. Hara-kiri, same . . ."

He's coming at me, middle of the night . . . predawn hours . . . whatever. It's dark; I should be sleeping. No . . . no, I shouldn't, or I'd be dead. We'd all be dead. He's coming at me . . . coming at . . . He's got a weapon. I've got mine. I thrust the bayonet as he strikes me on the shoulder. Pain! Pain . . .

What's next? I'm on Iwo, then Japan, then back on Iwo. Still on Iwo now, just another day and place, the colonel handing me a piece of paper, *Everett O. Wall* on it. What's going on? Everett's dead!

"Can't be, Colonel. Must be a mistake, misreported, mistranscribed, telegraph malfunction, or a cruel joke," I say.

"None of those, Lt. Wall. It is the truth," the colonel says firmly. "Now, it's time for you to go back up the mountain to your platoon."

"Yes sir," I say, numb inside, as I stand, turn, begin to walk.

"Wait, Lieutenant," the colonel says.

I turn and look at him.

"Don't go alone. These two men will go with you," he says.

"I can do it alone."

"Not on my watch," the colonel says. Then, "Men need men."

"Is that all I need?" I say, wanting, needing more explanation.

"No," says the colonel.

•   •   •

I open my eyes, body under bedcovers, wringing wet with sweat head to toe, heart pounding furiously, adrenaline flowing wildly. My body shakes with fear.

Where am I? I think. The room is pitch-black. Where am I? Where am I?

Dormitory. Starkville, Mississippi.

War ended over three years ago. No, it hasn't. This is the third night I've fought in it this week. This war could go on forever.

What night is this?

Thursday . . . yeah, Thursday. There's something . . . ?

Yes, I'm going home to Oak Leaf tomorrow afternoon, going home for the weekend. Haven't seen the folks since September, and it's only two weeks till Thanksgiving. Catching a ride home. Dad's gonna take me rabbit hunting. Haven't done that since high school, a long time ago. So much has happened since high school. I'm supposed to graduate from college in two months.

Had three goals the past two and a half years. First goal was to make it to the next morning—just make it through the night, overcome the legions of nightmares that invade me. They've become more frequent, not less. Can't control them coming. Fight them off as best I can, half-afraid that when I fall asleep the next one will be worse.

Next goal was to each day put one foot in front of the other. Oh, life's not that bad. Government's picking up most of the tab. Eat three times a day, tuition's taken care of, and nobody's shot at me in over three years. Yeah, "being taken care of." And while my soul cries out for more than that; it's like I'm dead inside, all the fight removed. Where is the man who led his platoon, oversaw a region in Japan, and stood up to that naval ensign? The man regressed when he got to Oak Leaf—though not immediately. It was like a leaky faucet, the gradual drip to drizzle to constant flow that can't be turned off by the simple turning of a knob, two months in the making. I slept late, no reveille in the Wall home, then lay in bed staring at the ceiling, and at Everett's empty bed, knowing he would never sleep there again. Time on my hands spent in self-imposed solitude, thinking of the war, though for the most part not the good times—like that of sitting around a couple of pits cooking a pig and a ram surrounded by smiling youthful faces. Every thought of that evening skips me forward to an imaginary moment at the same spot one year later where a third of the faces are missing. It's times like that I have guilt—for being here, me no more deserving of life than those guys—or Everett—or Jimmy Street.

Fortunately, those thoughts don't come often, but when they do, they pierce me. Maybe if when I came back to Oak Leaf I'd have gotten busy and not sat around letting Mom do everything for me while I waited for my paperwork for college to come through . . . yeah, if my time had been occupied, then I wouldn't have drifted to my lethargic state. Maybe.

Third goal was to finish college, a first for a Wall. Then what? I've crammed two years of college into two and a half, never reaching my potential or even coming close. No social life. No girl. Aren't many of those here at State anyway, but there's the W, a girls' college no more than a stone's throw from here, and I've made little or no effort to venture that way. I'm a turtle, feet and legs tucked within my shell. In two months I'll have a general business degree, my only interviews so far to be a salesman. A turtle in a shell as a salesman! Who am I kidding?

Now, can I go back to sleep? Did three nights ago. Couldn't last night. Heart's slowed down a bit. I've quit sweating. Maybe . . .

TWENTY-EIGHT

" 'Bout time to take a break, don't you think, Gun?" Dad says, looking like he needs one.

"Don't get much exercise at college. Everything but my trigger finger needs a rest. Fortunately, I did make it count the one time I used it: one shot and one rabbit. Problem is, I think you, me and Mom won't be satisfied with just one. We'll have to do better this afternoon," I say.

"May not be as many rabbits out here as there used to be. Don't know. It's been years, Gun. Think we can find us a log to sit on? That one we sat on in the past is probably long since decayed."

"Yeah," I say, switching my attention from the red and yellow leaves of a sweet gum tree set against the sunny November sky to the floor of the woods, searching for a log. "Let's go back to the edge of the woods, out near the field. That's where we've always sat before."

Dad nods, and we walk, me with the shotgun, Dad with the knapsack and the rabbit, its feet tied with a leather throng to his belt. We circle around two briars, hoping to see a downed log or a stump. None yet.

This patch of woods is lowland. Floods in the winter and spring, so much so it's not worth clearing to raise cotton. It looks like it's been select cut in the past couple of years, the Rugettis maybe putting up a little cash from the sale of timber. I say that because of a few stumps I've seen as we've walked. Maybe we can find two stumps near each other, one for each of us.

Up ahead I see a stump and a saw-cut log, maybe five feet long, right near it. "Let's try those out," I say.

Dad nods, a smile breaking the creases on his face.

A moment later I've laid the shotgun down and found my spot on the stump. It's not the most comfortable seat I've ever sat on, but it will do to rest my tired legs. I let Dad have the saw-cut log maybe ten feet away. It looks more restful.

Dad reaches in the knapsack with one of his coal-shovel-size hands and retrieves a paper sack, then stands and walks toward me before I can get up. "Mom's biscuits, cured ham in 'em just like you like them."

Mom's biscuits. Cured ham. Don't get those at college. Surely didn't get those in the Marine Corps. I can taste them in my mind before I try them with my mouth. "Thank you, Dad," I say as he hands me three, along with an apple, all with one hand. (It takes me two hands).

I start to take a bite before he gets back to his log, the movement toward me, hand to mouth, stopped by Dad's voice. "Why don't we take a second and bless it," Dad says. "I'll do the blessing if you like."

"Yes . . . yes, of course," I say, the ham-filled biscuit no more than six inches from my mouth.

We close our eyes and Dad begins, "Dear Lord, first, thank you for this food. Bless it to our bodies." Then a pause, a lengthy one. "Thank you for this day," followed by another pause, longer this time. Then, "I appreciate this time with Gunter. Wish I had it more often . . . He's gone through a lot . . . and is right now. I can tell . . . If you will, help him." Pause. "In Jesus' name, amen."

I open my eyes to see Dad, creased weathered face, eyes locked on mine. I hesitate, then move the biscuit to my mouth, almost a reflex. I begin to chew, salty-cured ham between biscuit, tasting it slightly, my mind going multiple directions at once. I say nothing. I simply chew, following this by another bite of ham and biscuit, then another . . . and another.

"Mom and I were talking the other day about all the exciting things going on. First, this rabbit hunt, followed by Thanksgiving and Christmas. Then, you'll be graduating from Mississippi State College in January. Gunter, we can't tell you how proud we are of you. Yeah, proud and excited."

Proud? Excited? I've spent two and a half years doing what I could have done in two, and I have no idea what I'll be doing come January. I've interviewed a time or two, but what to do? Nothing definite. And he said, "Going through a lot right now . . . I can tell." How can you tell? Haven't said a word. Does it show? My mind's racing. I continue to chew, relieving the biscuit with a bite of apple.

"Had a hard time myself when I came back from war," Dad says, waiting a moment to see if I want to comment.

I don't.

"Gunter, I grew up poor. Even in a land of poverty, we were poorer than most. Didn't fully realize how poor till I got away, got a perspective when I went to war. Strange way to get a perspective, don't you agree?"

I nod.

"But, I tell you what. I had a good upbringing. That was something else I got a perspective on while I was away. My folks gave me a lot more than fine clothes and a steak to eat. They gave me an upright upbringing and handed me a faith to go with that. I say, 'handed it to me'; I meant to say, 'guided me along.' Meant a lot when I was in those trenches in France. Meant a lot when I got back. Saw some pretty awful stuff over there in France." Dad stops talking, like he's come to a fork in the road and is trying to decide which way to go. Or, maybe he knows which way he's going and wants a comment from me. He continues to wait.

"Yeah," I say. "I've seen some pretty awful stuff . . . no, I've lived it." I pause, pondering what I've said, how I went from "saw" to "lived," then say, "Can't get it off my mind, especially at night."

"I know about that," Dad says, nodding.

"You do?"

"Oh, sure. A trench in France is nothing like a ditch in the Mississippi Delta," he says. "Lots of memories I'd rather not have."

"Do you still have them?" I rifle back.

"Not near as often. Occasionally."

"Ever question what you did?"

"Depends on what you mean," Dad says. "I had a lot of down time and sleepless nights when I got back. Didn't want to get up and tend to the fields, so to speak. Was living with my mom and dad at that time. Strange, coming home, living out in the country, having been to war, then to Paris. Oh, I'm rambling now. Ever question what I did? Sure."

I hesitate a moment, not sure where the path is headed, then say, "At night I dream. Guilt for not saving lives, and guilt for taking them. Seems like I have guilt both ways. It's three, four nights a week. Started a month or two after I got back." I pause to think, then, "Strange, I've never mentioned it to anyone. Just kept it bottled up within me, and I've gone about my day."

Dad sits on the log, arms folded, nodding, listening. We sit a moment in silence, then he says, "Gun, you no more started that war than the one I was in. You were asked to serve, and you did." Dad pauses again. "I had the benefit of seeing something most unusual in France after the fighting was over, right before I came home. Up on the side of a mountain was a big castle built centuries ago. Obviously nothing like that in Mississippi," he says, nodding, then, "Bigger than anything you can imagine. Over on the cliff, near the edge, was a big hole, going down thirty or forty feet to open air below. All the way down that hole were swords and knives, embedded on the sides. Wasn't enough just to toss somebody off a cliff. Had to make them suffer along the way."

I listen.

"Here's the noble, king, count, whatever, living in a big castle, who cares no more about his fellow man than to torture him as he kills him. Probably had no jury, just him as the judge of some poor guy he had a run-in with. So here he was, some old noble, king, or count of no account, all the money and power in the world, putting it to his own use, no matter what he put his fellow man through." Dad pauses, clears his throat.

I continue to sit on the stump listening, wanting to bite, eyes on Dad.

"Awhile after I got back, I came to reason that although I didn't have things perfect, I was fortunate, not having a man like that ruling me, my family, my neighbors. Came to realize that I was glad to live where I live, and when I live, poor or not. Now, as far as I'm concerned, in this last war we fought the likes of Hitler, Tojo, Mussolini. Doesn't matter whether it was centuries ago or today—in my eyes they were all sorta like that fellow with the castle. We don't need any of them ruling over our families, or our neighbor's families. If ever there was a reason to fight, this time we had one." Dad takes a long pause. "Do you know how hard it is for me to say that, losing Everett?"

Dad stops, his face like the sky in that brief moment just before rain, his creases deep, more pronounced than ever. His eyes moisten.

For some reason I begin to speak. "Dad, I don't want you to take this wrong, having lost Everett, but there've been times when I've felt that part of me died at Iwo Jima, like I left much of myself on that island. There've been times I've felt guilty for living, like, why am I alive, when men all around me died? I've thought that more times than I can count. Even had guilt about killing a Japanese admiral that I didn't kill. He killed himself, wouldn't surrender to a lieutenant."

Dad stares, the moisture in eyes dried, his face now a face of certainty. Reminds me of the reawakened look I saw on the colonel's face just before he sent me back to my platoon at Iwo. "Gun, you didn't kill that admiral. He was killed by his own pride. You, however, might be killing yourself a little bit each day, and that's got to stop. God spared me in France, spared me to marry your mother, spared me to survive a flood, spared me to raise two fine boys, spared me to tend to people every day. The Lord's left you alive, he didn't Everett, and he didn't a lot of young men. But you, you've got the gift of life."

Dad looks at me like he's got many things to say, saying without saying, "It's time to talk. Should have done this long ago."

"I finally gave in," Dad says. "Figured I couldn't make it on my own. Kind of a joint effort, you might call it. At first I asked God to forgive me for some stuff, then I wouldn't forgive myself. That doesn't work. Then, there was stuff that I wouldn't ask forgiveness for, and that doesn't work either. Finally figured out we'd better get together. Been through a war, a flood, no money, the Depression, the death of a son, and more nights than I can count fretting over you. Just mentioning all that makes me tired—tired, but not worn out. I'm not done for. Got things to tend to most every day. No, not done for . . . and you're not either. This time doing what's right means forgiving yourself, most of all for being alive. Gunter, you've got a lot of tending to left to do—the rest of your life. You don't need to squander it." Dad comes to a halt, looks up in the sky, at the one or two clouds of the sunny midday November sky. He's left me to think, speak if I want.

I chose not to speak, to chew on my ham and biscuit, moisten my mouth between bites with juice from the apple, process what Dad's said. He's never been one for small talk. When he speaks, it matters, perhaps never more so than today. He's reaching out, trying to lift me. Worn out is what I've felt like, a struggle some days to just put one foot in front of the other. I guess if there's anything I've done right, it's that I've kept putting one foot in front of the other, never come to a complete halt. Get up. Go to class. Study—no, put a book in front of my face, that's closer to the truth, my mind twelve thousand miles away, if not further, off into space, off into eternity, never quite stopping anywhere, just drifting. But here and now, Dad's reaching for me with his heart, it bigger than his massive hands. He's reaching and tugging; I need to grab hold of my life while I've still got the strength. I've not drowned yet.

I could be doing worse—a whole lot worse. Folks vent their demons different ways. Some guys came to college and couldn't put their foot in front of the other. Couldn't get up, go to class, even if the government paid for it. Others fell in love . . . with the bottle, some to celebrate (nightly), others to forget. Guess I'm fortunate. My drinking career never really got off the ground. Nothing good ever happened when I drank. Nothing. But me, I've become a recluse, though not totally. Get up, eat, go to class. Book in front of my face as my mind wanders. Go to sleep. Fight the war. Don't sleep. Get up. Repeat the previous day. Where to from here? Where to for me?

Dad's giving me advice. Never steered me wrong before. Actually, he doesn't steer much. He just goes about his day doing what's right, leading by example, doing the things that need to be done, pointing a direction here, pointing a direction there, not really giving orders, just comments. He's a whole lot smarter than the fifth grade. He has wisdom—that's the word, the word Mr. Street gave me down at the bank following the "car in Lake Knox" incident.

"Gun . . . Gun, you there, Son? Gun?" Dad looks at me, concerned.

"Yeah," I say, a reflex.

"You gonna eat another ham and biscuit? A sparrow could eat what you have."

"Yeah," I take a bite from the second one and begin to chew. I want to say, "I've been chewing on other things," but don't.

My mind shifts from myself to Dad, his life. "Tell me about Mom."

"What do you mean?" Dad says with a nervous look.

"How did you meet?" I say as a smile steals the serious look from Dad's face. It's a warm smile.

"Well," he says, the smile widening. "I would go to their store at Everett Crossroads on Saturdays from time to time. She caught my eye right off. Eventually, I caught hers, not long after she graduated from high school. Finally, I got up the courage to ask if I could come by. I knew the answer before she spoke; the look on her face said yes. Anyway, could tell right off that I didn't exactly meet everybody's approval, coming from way out in the county with only a fifth-grade education. I think her folks were expecting a whole lot more. Well, we started meeting in secret. Wasn't easy, but we made ways. Anyway, we eloped." Dad stops.

Eloped, a word I've never heard Dad say. Nor Mom. "Yeah, I know," I reply.

"How'd you know that?" Dad says, startled. "Did your mother tell you?"

"Nope. Overheard Aunt Martha saying it back when we were staying at Everett Crossroads when I was five. At the time I had no idea what eloped meant, but it sounded important, so I made a mental note."

"Yeah, Aunt Martha," Dad says, shaking his head.

"How'd you get over to the Delta?" I say.

"Heard of an opportunity through a friend I grew up with. You know, somebody knows somebody, usually the way things work out. Had that nailed down before we ran off together. Let me tell you, it was quite an adjustment for both of us. Your mother was used to finer things, and her folks sent us nothing, and I had nothing. It was just the two of us and the good Lord above out there on that plantation. Mr. Wilson put me to overseeing a few hands, and the rest of it was sharecropping. He let me oversee 'cause I served in the war, and must have gained some valuable experience."

I'm soaking this in. Stuff Dad's never told me, nor has Mom.

"Well, *lonely's* one word for it," Dad says. "Especially in the winter when the cotton was all picked. Yeah, nothing but a howling wind blowing across vacant fields. *Tough* is another word for it, although I don't really know a word to truly describe it. A couple of years into it, her folks offered for me to come work at the store for a small wage. Your mom wanted to go back. I didn't. I was finally getting a little self-worth. We were making do, and the carrot of getting a more responsible position on the plantation was dangling in front of me. I got to figuring we were gonna move up in the world one way or another. I was sort of getting my confidence up, even though I'd still have an occasional dream about France—not the good parts. They'd seem to come in the winter, dead of night, the fields vacant, the wind howling. Crazy, seldom have them anymore, couple of times a year. They're different, not exactly something that happened, but I know that my experiences in France are at the root of them. Enough of life has come and gone where they don't really affect me like they once did. Like I said earlier, or alluded to, I've been taken care of pretty good through some difficult times . . . Now, how in the world did I get off on this? You were asking about your mother."

"Yes," I say, nodding, listening to every word.

"Gun, all in all, your mother has been pretty patient, long-suffering in some ways. She's more fragile than I am. Good Lord just made all of us different; we all got our strengths and weaknesses. At the core of her heart, she's a loving person. Got an abundance there that spills over on me. Can't tell you how that's groomed me through the years." Dad pauses.

I nod, adjust my seat on the stump.

"I've made some good decisions, and I've made mistakes," Dad says, switching directions a little, his comments shifting away from Mom. "I think that staying on that plantation was a good idea. Made us stronger, more independent. On the other hand, keeping y'all there till when the levee broke wasn't. I should have listened to Mary. I was wrong, almost dead wrong as far as my family was concerned. I could have stayed behind, sent y'all on, spared all of you a lot of grief. You could have left the Delta with a pair of shoes on. Mary fought me tooth and nail for almost a month about y'all's safety, and I blindly kept saying, 'It'll be fine. Levee's not gonna break. Never has before.' Yeah, well, it did, and that's the most upset Mary's ever been in her life. And you know what, Gun?"

"What's that?" I say.

"Although she was mighty scared, the frustration she vented wasn't over herself, it was over you and Everett. The fact that my poor decision put the two of you through what it did was something that set her to boiling like never before or since." Dad pauses.

"You shouldn't be too hard on yourself. Everything turned out okay."

"Not because of me," Dad says. "I think the good Lord saw us through that one. Sent Roy Jarvin along with a boat to pick us up. Could have either starved to death, or floated off somewhere and drowned."

"Yeah, well I could live to eighty and not forget you rescuing Everett and me from the water and getting us all up on the roof. And, you had that cigar box of money set back to help us through."

"Yeah, maybe it was a joint effort in getting us out of that fix. But, I was the one to get us into it to start with. Believe it or not, that's been the hardest thing in my life to forgive myself of."

I ponder what Dad's said, then change the conversation back to Mom. "So, how's Mom been doing? She writes me all the time. Keeps me up to date on the goings-on around Oak Leaf. Then, always, 'I really love you, Gunter,' every letter. You must be spending every dime you make on stamps and paper."

"Gun, to the core of her heart, she's a loving person," Dad repeats himself, smiling a little before his face turns serious. "Loving hearts can be the most seriously wounded. Didn't know whether she would heal for the first month or two after Everett's death. Had my doubts. Going to see Thelma Street after Jimmy died woke her up, made her realize she wasn't the only one on this planet grieving. Oh, she had her moments. Still does. Sort of like my dreams of war that still come back on occasion. But hers are different. They come on in the daytime, when she's awake. Gun, know what?"

"What's that, Dad?"

"They come on me, too," Dad says. "I think in some way they always will. Maybe like those dreams of war, my thoughts about Everett will become less frequent, as they have so far. Maybe they'll be different, like my dreams. But, Gun," Dad says, taking a long pause," they'll always be with me."

We both sit in the quietness of the woods, right on the edge of the cotton field, a field covered in naked stalks, yet to be plowed under. I note my surroundings, my mind drifting on what Dad's said, and on my own unshared thoughts.

"Gun, back to your mom," Dad says. "All in all, she's doing fine. She does a lot of serving, helping others. Cooks meals when church folk and neighbors get sick, helps out teaching young children at the church. I think those things give her a sense of worth."

I nod.

"Gun, we'll go to bed hungry tonight with only one rabbit," Dad kids. "Better get back to work. By the way, James Street down at the bank asked about you earlier this week. Actually, he called me at the house one night. Wanted to know when you'd be graduating from State College. Told him January. Anyway, he wanted to know what plans you had after that, and I told him I didn't know. He then asked me if you'd be home for Thanksgiving. Said he wanted to see you that Friday, if you were available. Told him I didn't know, but you'd call him. Might want to spend a little on a long-distance call first of next week."

"Mr. Street? Give him a call? I think I'll call him Monday," I say.

"Well, let's go get some more rabbits," Dad says, standing.

We do—two, to be exact. Skin them in the woods and get home just before dark.

"Mom, this is delicious," I say between bites of rabbit and rice smothered in gravy. I have no idea what Mom would have cooked had we not returned with rabbits, this perhaps a sign of faith in Dad and me. I look at Mom and then at Dad, their faces aged from my years of high school when I ate at this table every night. I take note of their faces, their smiles, the types that go far beyond the face, deep to the heart. It's a moment to remember.

I take my fork, scooping some snap beans, raising them, placing them within my mouth, chewing, savoring a taste I haven't had in years. They don't serve snap beans at the school cafeteria. Didn't serve them in the Marine Corps. I pause to think of a time years ago at Everett Crossroads when I adamantly stared at snap beans and refused to eat them, denying myself dessert.

It's strange the things you miss when you've been away from home.

•   •   •

Everett Wall, clearly typed on the paper.

"Can't be, Colonel. Must be a mistake, misreported, mistranscribed, telegraph malfunction, or a cruel joke," I say.

"None of those, Lt. Wall. It is the truth," the colonel says, firmly. Now, it's time for you to go back up the mountain to your platoon."

"Yes sir," I say, numb inside, as I stand, turn, begin to walk.

"Wait, Lieutenant," the colonel says.

I turn and look at him.

"Don't go alone, Son. These two men will go with you," he says.

"I can go alone."

"Not on my watch," the colonel says. Then, "Men need men."

"Is that all I need?" I say, waiting, needing more explanation.

"No," says the colonel.

I open my eyes to darkness, knowing exactly where I am: my bedroom in Oak Leaf. Just spent the day hunting rabbits with Dad. Had supper with Mom and Dad. I'm wringing wet with sweat head to toe, my heart's pounding furiously, adrenaline's flowing wildly. I have fear.

The pounding of my heart begins to slow. My breathing returns to normal, steady. I stare into the darkness, my eyes opened wide. I close them.

God, help me end the war! I can't go on reliving it night after night. I'm not up to it. I beg you. I beg you! I lived it once in real life; isn't that enough? Isn't that enough! Please! Please help me quit dreaming it . . . and help me move on. Help me forgive myself. Let me be grateful for my life. I need to live it. In Jesus' name! In Jesus' name!

TWENTY-NINE

"Mr. Street, I appreciate you seeing me today," I say, dressed in a starched white shirt, collar a bit too tight, tie snuggled within my dark blue suit.

"Gunter, it's good to see you. I enjoyed talking with you on the phone earlier this week. That was the first time we've spoken since I saw you when you came home from the war. And just imagine, in another six weeks you'll have a diploma from Mississippi State College. That will feel nice—first in your family to graduate from college, I presume, unless another relative has beaten you to the draw."

"No," I say, surveying the office as I speak. It's been almost seven years since I sat here the last time (my only time), that visit following my "swim" in Lake Knox. My mind goes into high gear, thoughts flashing. It seems like a lifetime has happened since then, although at this moment I'm looking at my lifetime ahead. I stare across the massive desk at Mr. Street, President of Bank of Oak Leaf.

"Banking in a small town is an interesting business," he says, pausing before continuing. "I guess I've got about as good a pulse of what goes on in Oak Leaf as anyone. Came to Oak Leaf in the early twenties, right after I graduated from the university. Times were booming, although we didn't notice it quite as much here as in the big cities, particularly up north. Still, times were good—that is, until the 1927 flood. Quite a setback, even though we fared better than many parts of the Delta. About the time the town really got back on its feet, the Great Depression came upon us. We were later to receive it than most parts of the country, but came it did. We almost closed. Were you aware of that?"

"No sir," I say, thinking that wasn't exactly what I had on my mind at age nine or ten.

"Anyway, we didn't. We kept our commitment of stewardship both to our stockholders and the community, although I do think the stress took its toll on Mr. Withers. He died of a heart attack in 1936, sitting at this very desk. He was working late one night . . . Anyway, the board saw fit to name me president at the ripe old age of thirty-eight. Rather incredible, don't you think?"

I nod.

"Gunter, I didn't grow up with a life of privilege; in retrospect, perhaps it's a blessing. Family didn't own land, nor bricks and mortar. Just had a good family, good upbringing. In my mind that's worth more than land and buildings. By the way, I think I can say the same for you. Well, I always thought I had to go the extra mile, go a little harder. Anyway, the board saw something in me and granted me this richly rewarding opportunity. I feel like I've been a part of helping grow this town, helping bestow jobs, helping give wise advice, helping steer things in the right direction. Wouldn't trade where I am for the throne of the king of England."

Mr. Street is speaking with the zeal of a Baptist preacher. I've always thought of him as starched-collared, reserved. Oh, I guess he is most of the time, but not right now. He said he wanted to visit with me about my career opportunities, when he spoke with me on the phone. So, where are we going? I'm listening. I'm thinking.

"Gunter, I watched you growing up. First grade on, I was impressed. I remember you coming over to the house from grade school right on through high school. With the lone exception of your and Jimmy's youthful indiscretion on Lake Knox, your record here in Oak Leaf is stellar. You served as an officer in the Marine Corps and soon will be a college graduate. All that to say, at the start of the year we will have an opening for a starting position at the bank—for somebody." James Street pauses.

What do I know about banking? I ask myself, and answer "nothing." Then again, what did I know about leading troops into battle? Nothing, until I did it. "Tell me about it," I say.

"You would work as a teller for the first six months. Then, we'll allow you to open accounts: checking, savings, certificates of deposit. Lending money comes later, probably two to three years out, if things go according to schedule. Lending money is an art, as well as a science. My hope is that you would learn the basics, one step at a time, and someday become an officer."

I listen. Never thought about being a banker. Not until this week. Never thought about coming home to Oak Leaf. Fact is, I'm starting to get in a panic trying figure out where I'll be come January.

"Now, of course any hiring must go past the board. We would need your college transcript, resume, references, and so forth. What I want you to do is think about it, then get back to me in the next week or two. We'll go from there," James Street says, peering through his glasses from behind his big mahogany desk, suited in gray pinstripe, buttoned-down white-starched shirt with red tie. "Any questions?" he says.

"So, the game plan is to end up an officer, not a teller?"

"Precisely," James Street replies, his nonblinking eyes peering through his glasses.

"Good," I say. "The Marine Corps gave me a chance to become an officer, and an officer I became, in the end a good one. I'll be in touch."

"Good," he says. "Now, I've got work to get on with. We were closed yesterday for Thanksgiving."

He starts to rise but I remain seated as James Street slowly lowers himself back into the big chair. Now is the time to say what's on my mind. "Growing up, I had a lot of friends. Among them I had no higher opinion of anyone than Jimmy. I don't know whether this is the time and place, or if there is any such thing, but I wanted to tell you that I miss him. The world misses him. I always thought he would go on to greatness, more so than anyone I grew up with, met in college, or the Marines. I've wanted to tell you that ever since I got back after the war . . . I thought it best now."

Mr. Street peers though the glasses at me, then blinks, tears coming from each eye as they open. "Thank you, Gunter," he says, pausing, then slowly rising to his feet.

We shake hands as he says, "Give me a call."

I walk out of his office feeling strong for the first time in over two and a half years, like the day aboard the ship, coming back on the "magic carpet ride," when I refused to pick up the candy wrapper. I walk past James Street's assistant, Mary Marbury, a fixture here forever, the only female employed by Bank of Oak Leaf, on past the desks filled with men in suits, past the tellers, out through the front door.

THIRTY

"Yes, Mr. Williamson, the interest rate for certificates of deposits is down considerably from two years ago. Interest rates at that time were the highest of either of our lifetimes. The economy heated up after the war, followed by those excessively high rates. They didn't last forever, as they never do. This is good if you are borrowing money," I say, pausing, not knowing what else to say.

"Young man, I didn't come here today to borrow money," Mr. Williamson counters. "I've had my savings here at Bank of Oak Leaf since the 1920s. Haven't borrowed a dime since the 1930s. What I want is a good return on my money."

I look at Mr. Williamson as he shakes his head, his face an amalgamation of displeasure, fear, frustration, bewilderment, a tinge of anger. The shaking stops, his eyes peering through the round wire-rim spectacles, eyes straight on mine, set against a background of aged skin, a scalp of thin strands of gray. Looks a bit like President Truman.

"Shoe sales, that's what I did: male, female, boys, girls, all sizes. Had a route all over the Delta, retail stores in every nook and cranny. Did it since the mid twenties. Weathered the Depression and rationing of leather during the war. Made the company good money—that is, up until last year, when some young Turk decided to put me out to pasture. 'Now that you're sixty-five, don't you think it's time you started slowing down?' Then, 'We think the company would be better served by someone more energetic . . . also, one who can better relate to people in changing, expanding times.' Basic cow manure. Now, here I am with a monthly Social Security check and a paltry pension, and my wife and I need the interest on the money to get by." Mr. Williamson stops abruptly, the eyes through the spectacles seeking, almost pleading for different news.

What to do? We are currently charging less for interest on loans than he's been earning in his certificate of deposit. Rates have dropped somewhere back to near normal. It's a fifteen-thousand-dollar CD. The bank offers a higher rate for those of twenty-five thousand or greater, albeit still a far cry short of the rate he is currently earning. I can't offer that rate for fifteen thousand, not without an officer's approval. Speaking of "young Turks," I don't qualify. At least, not like that fellow who sent Mr. Williamson "out to pasture." Don't have the authority.

"Young man, you just don't understand, do you?" he says, heading shaking in frustration.

No, I don't. Not really. Today he's not selling the shoes, he's walking in them. Shoes . . . shoes . . . don't know why it is, just the thought of having them, or not having them, still sends a chill over my body. That night, that next day, on the roof . . .

"You don't understand," Mr. Williamson repeats, his head now still, eyes pleading through the wire-rim spectacles, straight on mine.

No, I really don't understand. No one ever really does, do they? Just guess I can try.

"Tell you what—we've got ten days till it automatically renews. Let me check to see if there's anything more that can be done," I say. "Give me three days and I'll check with an officer."

"Well, I'll be looking around in the meantime. Had my money here, all of it, since the 1920s. The bank was good for a dollar during the Depression. I'd like to keep my money here," he says. "I'll drop back by Friday to see what you can come up with." With that he stands, as do I, making a point to shake his hand firmly.

"I'll look forward to seeing you Friday," I say, thinking perhaps one of the officers can make an exception for a higher rate. Or perhaps Mr. Williamson will come to understand by Friday that this is just the way it is with interest rates.

I look as Mr. Williamson heads out the door, my thoughts shifting from him as I turn my eyes across the room to the desk of Bradford Martin, nice enough of a man, mid thirties, married. Went to war, never had the benefit of college, currently at my station with the bank. Wears a bow tie (everyday). Who is that young lady sitting across his desk? Slender, dark brown hair, pale white skin, five feet five or six . . . I'd guess. Never laid eyes on her before. Know that for a fact, or I'd remember. Got a serious look right now, like she's listening intently. He's handing her some papers to sign. Now she's returning them. She's smiling—look at that smile. Beautiful, and not just the smile. Wow. Now she's getting up, nodding, smiling, turning, walking (gracefully), and now out the door, leaving me with my thoughts.

Got to find out who she is—got to. I hesitate, thinking she's probably married. Then again, maybe not. Still, she's probably dating someone seriously. I mean, anybody that attractive would have to be. Then again, if she just moved to town? What if somebody beats me to her?

I jump up, head toward Bradford Martin. Got to catch him before he leaves. One o'clock and the bank closes for an hour, and he'll be heading home for lunch. I reach him just as he finishes tidying his desk.

"Bradford, the young lady who was just here?"

"Yes," he says, saying without saying, "I've had a full morning. Now I'm starving, so get out of my way, and quickly."

"She looks familiar," I say, lying.

"Familiar? How can that be—she just moved here this week. Just finished at Mississippi College for Women, and starts teaching here in three weeks—elementary school, I think. She's staying at that boarding house where all the young single female teachers usually stay. You know, they must have some special arrangement with the school." Bradford finishes, looks impatiently at me.

"Yes, that must be it. She went to the W, as in 'women.' That's what we called her school at State College, too long a name to say the whole thing every time. Must have had a friend at State College dating her a few years ago. You know, the schools are only twenty miles apart and . . ."

"Gunter, Martha has fixed me a delightful hot dinner . . . which is currently getting cold even in this dreadful August heat. Now, if you don't mind—"

"Just curious if my friend said she got engaged."

"Now, Gunter, official bank policy—"

I cut him off. "Bradford, is she getting married?"

"No. At least that never came up."

"And I was trying to remember her name . . ."

"It would be highly irregular."

"Bradford, if you don't make dinner today, Martha will just serve it to you tomorrow—cold. Her name?"

"Oh, all right. All right! Gunter, sometimes you can be such a pest. Her name is Betty— Betty Penrod. From over in the hills somewhere. And now, if you don't mind," Bradford says, giving me a "if you don't let me get to my house, then Martha may never cook a meal for me again" look.

"It's been a pleasure doing business," I say as Bradford scurries out the front door, leaving me behind to think. Betty Penrod . . . Betty Penrod . . . went to the W . . . just moved to town . . . going to teach elementary school . . . not married.

I head out the front door, out into the August heat, cross the street to the right of the bank, then cross Main St. to the drugstore on the corner for my usual meal: an egg and olive sandwich. Oh, I don't eat it everyday. Some days a hamburger and a Coca Cola, other days ham and cheese. But today, the usual. I seat myself on the counter stool.

"Egg and olive, with a Coca Cola?" comes from across the counter.

"Yes," I say.

"Egg and olive?" comes from the female voice, stool to my right.

I turn, caught off guard. Soft pale skin, dark brown hair, young female, Betty Penrod! My heart pounds. I turn forward, frightened, then turn back, regain my courage. "Yes, egg and olive sandwich."

"Oh, forgive me," she says, blushing, embarrassed. "I didn't mean to blurt. It's just, it's just . . ."

"You've never heard of an egg and olive sandwich," I say. "This place is known for them. You must be new."

"Yes . . . yes, I am," she says, blushing again, a tinge of redness on pale white skin, teeth whitest of white. All this followed by a smile, a soft beautiful smile.

My heart is pounding . . . thoughts racing . . . nervousness flowing from chest to my knees. Tongue seems like it's stuck in drying cement.

"Name's Gunter Wall."

She hesitates before replying, first examining my left hand. "Betty Penrod," she says, smiling again.

Inward I go, all of me to the depth of my abdomen. I push as though it's my last chance, last one of my lifetime to find the energy to break the cement encasing my tongue. One final surge from the depth of me . . .

"So, how recently did you move to Oak Leaf?" I say, this time a little easier than "Name's Gunter Wall."

"Yesterday," she says. "My father and mother brought me over."

"I would say that's just moved here. What brings you to Oak Leaf?"

"I came here to teach first grade. Just graduated this spring from Mississippi State College for Women. It's my first job and I'm nervous, really nervous about it. Also, nervous about being on my own, although I'm not really on my own. I moved into the apartments up near the school, where there are a number of female teachers. Sort of like the dormitory."

"Will there be anything else, ma'am?" comes from across the counter. I don't take my eyes off Betty's face, this time studying chocolate eyes,

eyes and deep dark brown brows keen against the pale white skin, yet matched with it, as if by nature.

"No," Betty says, turning away from me to reply.

"So, are you from here?" she says, still looking away, pale white skin of cheek and neck her background for the silhouette of dark brown hair.

"Kind of," I say as Betty turns back toward me, her chocolate eyes gazing straight at mine, her right brow slightly arched. I pause momentarily, as if the eyes have gone to my soul, then say, "moved here when I was five, and except for the war and college, I've been here ever since. I work at the Bank of Oak Leaf."

"Bank of Oak Leaf," she says. "I just came from there. Opened an account."

"Really?" I say, acting surprised, feeling a tinge of guilt for my false act. I struggle to say something and don't.

"Well, I've got to get going." Betty stands and lays the exact change on the counter.

"Hope to see you around," I say as I stand, wishing I could keep the conversation going . . . spend more time with Betty . . . not let her leave!

"Yes," she says, the tone of her voice leaving me to question, "yes?" or, "yes!"

Betty walks toward the door, her slender body and her hip movement graceful, gait the perfect pace. Leaves me in midair.

"Will that be all, Mr. Wall?" comes from across the counter.

"Yes," I say, fumbling as I reach for my wallet, handing over a dollar bill as I turn to look for Betty. She is gone . . . and I am left with my thoughts. Gunter, you dummy—how awkward are you! Where are the words, the right words, when you need them? Now, she's gone. Good thing Oak Leaf is a small town. I'll find her. Better do it fast. Every bachelor in town will be tripping over himself trying to catch her.

THIRTY-ONE

"Ten minutes," I say aloud as I glance at my watch. That's how long I've stared at this chunk of metal in front of me. It's standard black, same as my Ford, the weight of the receiver atop seemingly heavier than that of my Ford, the thought of lifting it almost unbearable. I tried multiple times last night, the line busy the whole evening. Then, "She can't come to the phone right now. May I tell her who called?" "No, I'll just call back later." "Better not be much later. Nobody likes getting woke up around here," came the female voice.

Oh, they wouldn't mind if it's the right man, I think, then say, "Okay," before hanging up. Yes, I hung up, but I didn't give up. Yet, here tonight I sit, supper finished, nothing to do in particular, staring at the phone receiver as if the entire weight of the world rested upon it. I nervously extend my left hand to grab the receiver as "the weight of the world" leaves it and leaves me holding a heavy-enough telephone receiver.

"Number please."

"Yes, uh, 655J."

"I'll put you through," then "line's busy."

"Uh, I'll try back later."

"You have a nice evening, sir."

Do those women talk on the phone all the time? Place must have a dozen of them living there, all single, mostly teachers—and one phone. First of the school year and a few new girls come in each year, most fresh out of college, including Betty. Somebody's probably beat me to her, some old snake-in-the-grass that she's too good for. By "too good for" I mean she's not the type girl to be taken advantage of . . . needs proper respect, a lady in the pure sense. I mean . . . what do I know? Only met her once. Yeah, but I can tell. I hastily grab the receiver.

"655J," I say before the operator speaks.

"Yes sir, I'll put you through."

Three rings later, "Hello," says a voice that says without saying "I've been picking this up for years, and I've given up hope it's for me."

"Betty Penrod, please."

"Again!"

"Yes," I say, not knowing what else to say.

"Can I tell her who's calling?"

"Uh . . . Gunter Wall."

"Well, it took you long enough to spit that out. Did you forget your name?"

"Uh . . . no."

"I'll check and see if she is available. Phone's downstairs, she's upstairs. This young girl's a lot of work," she says, laying down the receiver, then, I hear footsteps on a creaking staircase trail off, followed by a knock on a door in the far background.

"Betty, sweetheart, telephone." Her words followed by a muffled sound.

"Who is it? Some guy with a funny first name. Gunter."

After a lengthy pause, I again hear inaudible background conversation.

"I'll tell him you'll be down," I hear, followed by footsteps on the creaking staircase.

"She'll be down directly," come the words, followed by, "I need to get a room upstairs next year—away from this phone. Never had to take so many calls in all my life. New crop of sweeties with men ready for the harvest," she says, laying the receiver down with a thud.

I wait . . . and wait. Finally, "Hello," the voice immediately evoking thoughts of chocolate brown eyes, dark brown eyebrows against pale white skin, followed by the thought of her slender body and graceful hip movement as she walks.

"Hello, Gunter?"

"Yes . . . yes . . . it's me . . . Gunter. You know, from the drugstore. I—"

"Yes, I know."

I pause. What now? Then, "I understand school has started. How is your first-grade class?"

"Oh, they're the cutest little ones," she says, animated. In my mind I can see her smiling at the other end of the line. "They're such babies at the start of the year. Only a handful went to kindergarten, so for the most part they are just adjusting to sitting in a desk."

"I see. Uh . . . there's a nice restaurant, Oak Leaf Cafe. Believe it or not—great Italian food. I'd love to take you there Friday night."

"Sorry, have plans."

"Saturday?"

"Booked."

Gunter, you dummy . . . waited over two weeks to call. She's probably engaged by now! Wedding's Saturday. What do I say? I scramble, think. "Does this mean no for this weekend, or no forever?"

"No for this weekend. Call me Sunday night."

I hang up encouraged, knowing I'll call the minute the sun sets on Sunday.

THIRTY-TWO

The mugginess of August nights has turned to more temperate, bearable late-September warmth, almost pleasant, Oak Leaf abandoned for the high school football game fifteen miles to the east. Betty and I walk the two and a half blocks, no more than eight houses, to Oak Leaf Cafe, a chance to visit. She suggested we walk, not ride: "Let's take a walk. I've been cooped in the classroom all week. Tell me about your week."

"Oh, don't know. I'm still learning the banking business, a lot to learn. James Street, bank president, has been a great guide. Taught me more than I could have ever learned on my own. Recently, let me start making loans, small ones. Made two this week." Talking is easy.

We walk, I slower than usual, Betty in semi–high heels. (I notice the heels less than her slender legs exposed, half her shin covered by hose— that, and her slender arms in the sleeveless dress, early autumn green). I keep talking as we walk, right up to the door of the Oak Leaf Cafe, realizing I've done most of the talking, and just now realizing it. I open the door, and Betty goes ahead with a graceful gait.

Oak Leaf Cafe doesn't look like some of the places I saw out in California. Not fancy, not formal, just good food.

"Gunter, tonight pick your seat. Everybody's left town. Gone to the football game. Team won the first game big, really big. First loss, we'll fill back up. So what are you doin' in town?" Marita says, half Southern drawl, half Italian accent, as she lays the menus on the table.

"More important priorities than a football game," I say, smiling at Betty.

She smiles back, exposing her teeth in subdued fashion, as I pull out her chair, seat her.

Moments later Marita returns, places down two waters. "Coca-Cola or tea?" she says, assuming we must want one of the two.

"What would you like?" I say.

"Coca Cola," Betty says, smiling again.

"I'll take the same."

"So, you know what you want?" Marita says, pen poised on pad, eyes aimed at mine, "ready for business."

"Not yet," I say, hinting, *you can go now . . . you can go now . . . you can . . .*

Slowly, Marita lowers the pen and pad, gives me an "I was ready to take your order" look, then ambles behind the counter where Frank, dressed in a white cook's outfit—apron and hat included—is leaning against the wall, arms crossed, staring at his only customers, Betty and me. I nod and Frank nods back . . . kind of. The eyes are still on the two customers. I cut my look back to Betty, upgrade the scenery, just as Marita places both the Coca Colas down with a thud, ever so quickly retrieving the pen and pad and her dedicated focus on me.

"Not yet," I say to Marita's disappointment. She turns, rounds the bar, leans on the wall next to Frank, the two a crossed-arm duo.

Great, I think, Frank and Marita have gone to the theater tonight, and Betty and I are the stars.

"Is it always this crowded?" Betty says.

I can immediately tell she is kidding, making me feel at ease.

"So, what do you suggest?" Betty says, looking at the menu. "They have hamburgers, but I can have one of those any old time."

"Veal cutlets."

"What? Never tried that before."

"It's time, tonight. They're breaded, fried. Comes with a salad topped with Italian olive oil, and an anchovy."

"A what?"

"An anchovy, a little small fish, salty as can be."

"Well, I—"

"Trust me. Give it all a try. And if you don't like it, don't spit any of it out. They're watching your every move," I say, winking.

"Okay," Betty says with a fearful look given in jest, her body wiggling in fright as she gives me a full smile.

Inside I feel warm.

"I feel guilty if we don't go ahead and order," Betty says.

One look to behind the counter and Marita pushes her torso from the wall and ambles around the counter toward us, retrieving the pen and pad as she comes.

Minutes later, Betty and I sit, salad before us, an anchovy on top of each, Betty's eyes the size of saucers.

"Don't worry, it didn't come from Lake Knox. It's probably from the Mediterranean," I say, grinning.

Betty reaches for her fork and knife, the sliver of fish too much to attempt in one bite. Cutting it in half, she bites and chews slowly. "Hmmmm," she says, chewing some more, then, "not bad," as she goes for the other half.

Across the room I glance at Marita and Frank, leaned against the wall, arms crossed, both nodding.

We eat salad, then breaded veal cutlets, Betty commenting more than once that the food is different than anything she's had before, and she likes it. I talk, more than I should. But, I have so much to say, and she's listening. Marita comes and goes, cleans the table. I guess. Don't really notice much. I'm focused on Betty: eyes, smile that says as much as the words, her upper body movement speaking to me as she talks or listens. Her slender arms, her ankles (I notice them again when she cuts her eyes away). I absorb it all and want to know more.

"That be all," Marita says, having walked up unnoticed, her words a statement, not a question.

"Yes," I say, a reflex, then realize I don't want my time with Betty to end. Want to talk some more—and just look, observe. Alas, it's out the door, onto the sidewalk, temperature neither hot nor cold. No wait, a touch of coolness, ever so slight, a hint of season change, the type that rejuvenates, causes me to note the moment, want it to last.

Down the sidewalk we walk, past the drugstore where we met, the bank across the street, where I first saw her, the brick buildings turning into homes, with small lawns, then a large lawn, lush grass, the two-story home of James Street, bank president.

"These new shoes are killing my feet," Betty says, slowing down, stepping onto the grass, coming to a halt as she extends a hand for me to hold, my grabbing it a natural reaction, no thought required. It's my first touch of Betty, as she balances her body, me her steady strength, her balance for the moment, Betty dependent upon my strength, me holding strong. She removes the semi-high-heel shoe. "How about the other foot?" she says, releasing her grip, extending her other hand. I grab.

This time I feel a rush of blood coming from my hand, flowing like floodwater from a break in a levee, up my arm, through my chest, down my loins. She removes the other shoe.

"Oh, do you have any idea what it's like wearing high heels?"

"No."

"It's so uncomfortable, so unlike the shoes I wore as a child. And even then, when the weather was warm, in the summer, school out, I wanted to shed those. It made me feel free. And it still does," Betty says, standing on James Street's lawn, the grass soft enough to not tear her hose. "What about you?"

I pause, jolted. About me? I want to be agreeable. I mean, at this moment, anything to be agreeable—but I can't. My shoes are bound to my feet: security, comfort.

"I like shoes," I say.

Betty looks me straight on, puzzled. I can see her face, the streetlight across the street just enough light.

"I mean. I—" I pause. What to say? Don't want to appear strange, peculiar. First date. But there's something about shoes on my feet. Can't take them off till I crawl in bed. Can't explain—even to myself. This time I've got to try, at least to Betty. But how? She's looking right at me.

"Shoes and beaches," I say, before thinking, Gunter, you make no sense.

"Shoes and beaches?"

I look to the sidewalk, catching a glimpse of Betty's shins and feet. I'm sinking. Feels just like my feet in the ash on Iwo. Don't want her to think me strange. Don't want her to perceive me weak. What do I reveal?

"There was a time," I say, "when I was four. Dad, Mom, Everett—my big brother who died in the war—" I pause, clear my throat. "It was the Great Flood, 1927. We spent a day and a night on our roof, surrounded by water far as the eye could see, cold as cold could be, wind blowing. Everett and me, no shoes on any of our feet, my feet the coldest part of my body. I can feel it to this day. I like shoes. Don't ever want to be without them again."

I stop with that, then think. Never told that to a soul. Thought it a thousand times. No, ten thousand times. But, I've said it to no one. Not until tonight, my first date with Betty.

I look up, her puzzled look gone, her gaze no longer perplexed. Betty's eyes meet mine. She's listening. This I can see, even in dim light.

"And beaches. Haven't seen a beach since the war. May never see another one the rest of my life unless I'm with the right person—someone who can cause me to look at a beach a different way."

Betty slowly raises her arm, extends her hand, reaches out for me, our hands meeting. This time there is no rush of blood throughout my body, no sudden surge of exhilaration. I am immersed in calm.

•　•　•

"Remember this spot?"

"Yes, I took my shoes off here on our first date, then walked on the lawn. That was in September, and it made me feel so free, just like when I was a child. But, I don't think I'll try that on damp grass three nights before Christmas," Betty says, the warm moist air of her breath against the cold night air visible by the light of the streetlight across the street. She's smiling, not a grin, but a subdued pleasant one, the corners of her mouth curved upward ever so slightly.

It's the curves at the corners of her mouth that for the present I can't resist as I pull her body to mine and kiss her as she kisses me back—but only for a moment. Betty moves her head back from mine shaking it slightly, giving me the same subdued pleasant smile as before the kiss. She then pushes back, not forcibly, but cleverly until we are holding hands, looking at each other's eyes, the streetlight providing just enough light. "Gunter, do you know where we are standing?"

"On the sidewalk."

"Yes, the sidewalk in front of your boss's home," Betty says, knowing I've answered her question in half-truth.

"Well, we've got to change that," I say, releasing my hands from Betty's, as I place my left arm behind her back and right arm under her knees, sweeping her off her feet.

"Where are you taking me?"

"To the sidewalk next door where there's less light and where we're not standing in front of James Street's home."

"But, Gunter—"

"I'll have you there in no time; just relax and enjoy the ride." Hey, this is easy, Betty's light as feather. Almost there and coming in for the landing. I'll stand her right here and kiss her before she objects. There. Did it. She's not pushing me away, just like normal. This is nice. This is my chance! I release and drop to my left knee and begin to take my right shoe and sock off.

"Gunter, what are you doing!"

"I'm undressing—my feet. Here, I'm working on my left foot now, had to change positions to do that. I've never gone foot-naked with a woman before—at least, not outdoors in December. I'd only do this with you Betty, no one else. You hinted at me doing this on our first date."

"I think you've taken leave of your senses."

"No, I know exactly what I'm doing," I say, my weight now resting on my right knee as I reach out and grab Betty's right hand with both of mine, my grasp firm on the outside, but gentle on her hand as I look at her barely visible face.

"Betty, although it may not seem this way, I've never opened up to anyone like I have with you. It's not my nature. Mostly I keep my thoughts and feelings to myself. Always been that way and probably always will be. I want to share more with you, so much more—like my life, the rest of it, however long it lasts. Will you marry me?"

"Gunter, I . . . I . . . don't know. I wasn't expecting this—at least, not tonight."

"Maybe it's the Christmas lights or the feel of the night or the fact that you are going home to your folks for the holidays and I won't see you for two weeks—or it's that inviting smile of yours. Whatever. I've had special feelings toward you since the time I first laid eyes on you and they have only grown more since I've gotten to know you. These past few weeks my heart has almost burst yearning for you. Betty, I want be with you till the day I die."

"I don't know. I . . ."

My hands go limp and Betty slides her hand from my clasp and steps back, the light from the streetlight blocked by a tree limb to where I simply see an outline of her face, the limpness now contagious, spreading through my entire body. Can't get a read, can't see her face. My insides are caving. It's the uncertainty of the moment. Did I spring it too quickly, maybe should have been doing some hinting along the way? Might should have waited longer; our first date was only three months ago. Maybe none of this matters, 'cause the answer would always be no, simply a question of when, not if.

"Gunter."

"What?" Oh, it's a struggle to get a word out.

"I need to give this some time. We've only dated three months and exclusively for only two. What we are talking about is the rest of my life, too. We've talked of my engagement that my fiancé called off in March. I was supposed to marry six months ago, and be living in Memphis, not Oak Leaf. This has been quite a year, the biggest roller coaster ride of my life. When you first asked me to go on a date and I had to decline, you asked me if it was no for that weekend or no forever. Do you remember what I said?"

"No for the weekend."

"Remember that. Starting tomorrow we've got two weeks apart, time to think about each other." Betty steps forward, reaching for and grabbing my hands, lifting them to around her waist as she edges closer, giving a gentle kiss to my lips.

What now? I'm confused—part of me feeling like I died, the other filled with hope. For now I'll chose hope.

THIRTY-THREE

I stand erect, no slouch, dressed in white tux, my once-in-a-lifetime experience, Mississippi August heat sealed inside the layers of tux, shirt, T-shirt—then, deeper inside my skin, heart pounding just above the butterflies in droves that fly feverishly, almost landing before soaring upward, then downward again, not quite landing.

"We gather here today before God . . ."

Wow—one year, almost to the week since the day we met. This happened fast, but why not? I'm twenty-seven, my only concern, am I going to get the call for Korea? Would it be right to marry Betty if I'm called, or do we speed it up? Maybe this time they're going in alphabetical order. *Wall*. Hope so. This time I'm not fired up about going.

Our backs to the crowd, small-town church where Betty grew up packed, minister robed in black standing before us, my Dad all starched-up next to him. Look at Dad, salt-and-pepper hair turned to salt atop weathered skin, creases running like canyons in all directions, his look serious, solemn, reverent. There is no displeasure in his eyes. Can't see Mom, but I did when I came down the aisle. Most excited I've seen her since I came home from the war. She smiles when Betty's around, not jealous like some mothers. Betty's always gone out of her way with Mom and Dad both.

My eye catches Missouri to my left, and Robert Rugetti just beyond. Missouri has come all the way down from Missouri just to see what kind of a lady would marry me. "Must have tricked her. Is she of sound mind? Anything to get out of Korea." He had all sorts of things to say, but in the end he and I are both glad he came down (and that I'm marrying Betty).

Missouri's fortune at present isn't faring as well. He graduated from law school in the spring, and the United States Marine Corps now wants him to "apply his many talents in Korea," none of which have anything to do with the practice of law. He flies out in nine days.

Robert Rugetti and I have gotten back together, renewed our friendship. He's farming cotton. Served in Europe in the war and got two years of junior college—more than anyone to date in his family. He's not only farming with his family, but has started expanding, buying his own land. I think he's going to make it big.

I look at the minister. "Marriage is an institution ordained by God " My eyes turn to Betty, dressed in white head to toe, soft white pale skin, tanned ever so lightly by the summer sun. She's trembling a bit. Guess she's nervous. Hope it's about the event, not me. I've wanted to see her every day since we met. Took me two tries to get her to go out with me and that same number to get her to marry me. Her love must not have been at first sight like mine.

Found out she loves movies, so I've gotten to like them again myself, just as I did when I was a boy. We don't miss a one. Although I've got a car, unless it's been rainy or cold, we've walked most places. Small town, three blocks to eat, three blocks to the movie, so different than a city.

She's great with children, loves her first grade class. She'll be teaching first grade again this fall. We talk a lot. Talked about everything except battle. Don't talk with anyone about that, although I almost did with Missouri. I guess it was seeing him, and the fact he was heading out again that made me start to mention it, only to have Missouri say, "No need to put any damper on the best day of your life. I'm real excited for the two of you." That was that.

Yes, today we start our lives together, Betty Penrod and Gunter Wall. One. Can't imagine what it would be like without her. Look at her. All that I could hope for. In a moment, we're committed for life.

"Do you, Gunter Wall . . . in sickness and in health . . . love, honor, and cherish until death do you part?"

"I do."

"Do you, Betty Lee Penrod . . . until death do you part?"

"I do."

The ring goes on my finger. I place the small gold band on hers, her hand smooth, young, no wrinkles. We kiss, a soft and simple one, her smile infectious, a trait I've come to love, though this time it's more radiant than ever.

We turn, the organ's playing up-tempo. I'm in a daze. There's Mom, smiling. Down the aisle we go, people either side. Don't notice who they are; my mind and eyes are now all on Betty. She's still smiling, no longer trembling.

THIRTY-FOUR

We look westward, half the sun peeking over the peak, rays splintering upward in all directions against a Blue Ridge haze. It's cool, almost jacket weather, a total contrast from the Mississippi August heat three days back, the day I married Betty. We've sat for over an hour on this porch high atop a North Carolina mountain, watching the sun sink from quarter sky. Another fifteen minutes the rays will be gone, replaced by countless other suns called stars dotting the sky in all directions. We sat yesterday, same spot, watching it all, sun to rays to stars, our conversation intermittent.

It's strange—the process of a man getting to know a woman. When you first meet, one feels the compulsion to speak, not let the conversation die, afraid that if the fire goes out, it might not be rekindled. So, one keeps on talking small talk out of fear—fear that if the conversation dies, so will the process. Don't know why I was so worried. Yes, I do. Romeo I never was, shy with girls in high school and my first round of college. Came back after the war and withdrew gradually into a shell, not planning to go that way, just ending up there, not socializing with girls . . . not socializing with anyone.

Thank God, I reemerged. Still can't believe I met Betty when I did. I'd have never met her a couple of years earlier. She could have walked right in front of me and I would have never spoken, might not have even looked up. Looking back, at that time I was a sad soul, a lonely soul. Not lonely now. Got Betty.

I learned with her I didn't have to talk all the time (although that took a while). I was afraid she was going to give up on me the first two months we dated. Finally got comfortable with being quiet, realized she wouldn't walk off and leave me if we quit talking.

Betty's not shy around people. She can carry on a conversation with a six-year-old or a seventy-year-old, and can be comfortable either way. Best thing is, she can carry on a conversation with me, get me to open up beyond the small talk. Never know ahead of time she's doing it, just realize it sometime later.

"Want to go inside?" Betty says, temptingly, suggestiveness in her voice and on her face. The starlight and rising moon allow me to see her raised eyebrows and almost devilish look, her eyes saying, "I'm up to it, are you?"

I hesitate, caught by surprise—again. I thought she would want to hold hands, maybe cuddle. Female stuff. Maybe I've got this marriage thing figured wrong. Is it anything like conversation? I mean, I was afraid that if I ever quit talking, she would lose interest. Is this anything like that? What if I say, "Not right now?" Does that send the wrong signal, like I'm just a hand-holder, a cuddler, or worse yet, "I know you're older, Gunter, but I didn't realize you were that much older"?

"Yeah, let's go inside," I say, obviously the right words, said without passion.

"Well, if you don't really want to," Betty says, almost before I get the words out. "What's the matter, you don't find me desirable?"

Uh-oh, this isn't heading in the right direction. Might get sentenced to solitary confinement—life sentence. Yeah, monks live on mountaintops, like right where I'm sitting at this very moment. Better start talking. Better start acting. Yeah, "acting."

I place my arm around Betty's shoulder and move toward her, my lips posed to meet hers, my eyes momentarily closed, only to immediately reopen like a flash of lightning as she abruptly turns her head.

"Well, if you don't want to," Betty says, expecting me to complete the sentence.

I sit in stunned silence, thinking—which can sometimes be the wrong thing. Seconds pass like mini-millenniums. Where are the words when I really need them? It's time to act. Yeah, "act." Don't do so, and if I live, I'll live to regret. Been trying to follow James Street's advice he keeps preaching to me at the bank. "Wisdom."

I abruptly stand, lean toward Betty, scooping her bottom with my right arm, her upper back with my left.

"Whoa!" Betty says. "What's going on? What are you doing?"

"Thought you said you wanted to go inside," I reply, the same vigor in my voice as in my body. "Say you want to go inside, then you just sit there."

I've now got her up, one hundred and twenty pounds of the most beautiful woman anywhere, in my arms, then one foot in front of the other, like I've learned in life, applies to everything. Ten feet to the door, hold her with one arm, her arms around my neck as I turn the doorknob, open it with my hand, close it with my bottom, and lean Betty on the bed, tumbling on top of her.

"Wow!" she says before kissing me, then retracting her head to smile, to look me in the eyes, the room lit by the lamp at the side of the bed.

I lean forward to kiss as she reaches to unbutton my shirt, starting at the top, working downward, backing up her body again to help me with my shirt, this starting a chain reaction that leaves us covered only by a cover. It's two bodies in embrace, husband and wife, Gunter and Betty, man hardened by life's experiences, softened by the embrace of his wife. I tighten my embrace.

THIRTY-FIVE

"Are you sure you are up to it?" I say to Betty, her once one-hundred-and-twenty-pound body ballooned to a number I'm afraid to ask, eight months, three weeks pregnant.

"Yes, I need out of the house," Betty says as she strains to stand. "Another week and I'll be homebound forever, nothing to do but read, tend a baby, and listen to radio. You may have to buy me a television."

"Not sure we've got the money for one of those," I say. "Particularly with your quitting work."

"Oh well," Betty says as she struggles toward the door, stopping for me to open it.

It's then down the steps, out to the car, open the door, then wait . . . and wait as Betty finagles her body into the seat, completing the event with a sigh as I close the door.

It's August, hottest month of the year, two years married, almost. Anniversary coming up in ten days and I don't think we'll be going out. I crank the car and ease out the driveway, down the street. It's been a busy week. Stayed at the bank late a couple of times, trying to get ahead before the baby comes.

"So, what's the name of this picture show?" I say.

"*Cat on the Prowl*," Betty replies, her eyes lighting up, definitely glad she's getting to go. "Yes, *Cat on the Prowl* and air conditioning. I think we may need one of those before we get a television."

"Yeah," I say, doing banker's math in my head. Let's see, television, air conditioning, and one income. No way. "So tell me about this movie," I say after dashing those thoughts.

"Can't believe you haven't heard of it."

"Nope."

"The actress starring in it was on the cover of both *Look* and *Life* last week. She's the rage of Hollywood. Probably about your age."

"Who's that?" I say.

"Vivian Lemur."

I hit the brake, a reflex.

"Gunter, something wrong?" Betty says. "Are you trying to jolt the baby out right now?"

"No," I say, speeding up the car.

"Now what are you trying to do, set a new speed record?"

"No," I say, slowing the car back to a snail's pace, thinking about Vivian Lemur. Haven't seen her in eight, no, nine years. Haven't seen her but once.

"Gunter, you look pale," Betty says. "Are you okay?"

"Fine."

"Have I said something wrong?"

"No."

"Done anything wrong?"

"No," I say, pulling up in front of the picture show. "I'm going to let you out while I park the car," I dash around to open the door.

I wait . . . and wait.

"Ugh . . . ugh," Betty says as I assist, Betty tugging, weighting my arm as she stands.

"Why don't you go inside to the air conditioning while I park," I suggest as Betty struggles through the thick August air toward the door.

Moments later we sit, darkness broken by light, projector to screen, air conditioning chilling the auditorium, the coolest place in Oak Leaf, with Betty eating popcorn, a large box. "Sure you don't want some?" she says, the words muddled as they flow through kernels of popcorn.

"No, thank you," I say, wondering what's gotten into Betty. She hasn't wanted to eat a bite the past three weeks.

"Oh boy, movie's starting," Betty says, this time clear, no obstruction by popcorn.

Music blares several decibels higher than the trailers. The words *Cat on the Prowl* flash across the mammoth screen, followed by *Vivian Lemur*, almost as large, female star before male, as a gentleman allows the lady to go first when entering a room. Other smaller names come and go quickly on the screen as the picture fades then returns to the side view of a slender yet shapely lady, nicely dressed before the makeup counter in a department store. She turns, the camera focusing on her face: pale white blemish-free skin, straight white teeth between expensive lipstick, the smile fresh but not totally wholesome, right eyebrow arched slightly, medium length auburn hair waving as she turns her head toward the camera. The camera freezes, as it makes the visual statement, "Stop, look, America."

She hasn't changed much, has she? May have even matured in perfection with aging—like some say (but I wouldn't know), "a ten-year-old wine versus a one-year." I'm the wrong guy to be watching this movie tonight. *God, what am I doing here?*

I turn to view Betty as she stuffs a handful of butter-drenched popcorn in her mouth, her eyes intently fixed to the screen, mine on her face. Strange—wonderfully strange, that is—her face is not swollen, but lean, fresh, youthful, clean, radiant. Haven't noticed this lately. I've been fixed on the rest of Betty. And yet, here with only the aid of projector light, I see. I look at her face, don't know how long, but long enough to lose track of the goings-on on the screen.

I eventually get back to the screen, a showcase for Vivian, those words describing the movie. Not much else to it. Don't need to worry about Vivian's future, for a while at least. Hollywood will keep promoting her until the wrinkles come.

In no time, it seems I'm pulling up in front of the picture show with the car, Betty struggling out into the unchanged August heat, my opening the door, assisting her in, then down the street we go, the short drive to the house.

"Did you look at her?" Betty says.

"Look at who?"

"Vivian Lemur."

"Oh, her," I say. "Of course I did; she was the whole movie."

"That's not what I meant," Betty says. "Did you look at her, like you wished you were with her, not me. I mean, I'm all . . ."

What to say? Yeah, I looked, but hey, I didn't do too badly. Didn't let my mind ride too far down that trail. Did wonder more than once what would have happened if I hadn't passed out back at that Beverly Hills hotel. Would I have written her? Would she have written back? Would she have seen me when I returned from overseas?

"Well, I guess your silence answers that," Betty says, her tone saying, "sentenced, guilty."

"No, it's not that at all. My mind was just drifting."

"Sure. You just think I'm all big and fat, not desirable. Not like . . . like Vivian Lemur."

Betty's about to cry. What gives? I'm just riding down the road and fail to reply with the speed of lightning, and now I'm in the doghouse and I don't even own one. I need to start getting better at action instead of reaction—or retreat, or whatever. What do I say? Do?

I wheel in to the drive, park the car, remove the keys, then hesitate ever so briefly before I lean across the seat, placing my arm around Betty's shoulder, and kiss her cheek.

"It's just . . . I look in the mirror, and . . ." Betty's sobbing brings her words to a halt, momentarily. "I don't know what it is this evening. I looked in the mirror today, naked. Then I started wondering what kind of mother I'm gonna be." The downpour starts.

What am I supposed to do? This is nothing like making a loan at the bank. Nothing like leading troops.

I lean closer, hold tighter, squeeze. I squeeze some more. Betty squeezes back and eventually the downpour stops, with Betty saying, "I don't know what's gotten in to me today."

We make our way into the house, Betty heading straight to the bedroom and collapsing on the bed, then immediately begging, "Water, got to have ice-cold water. I'm burning up! Can you get the windows? Turn on the ceiling fan."

What first? Bound to be wrong any way I go. I hurriedly cut on the ceiling fan and open the windows before retrieving glasses filled with ice and water from the kitchen. Betty is fanning herself, head propped on a pillow when I return. She keeps the fan going in one hand as she takes the glass in the other and begins to gulp the water, not saying a word in the process. Never seen her this way before.

"Would you take my skirt and shoes off?" Betty says as she lays the glass now containing two ice cubes on the table next to the bed. "Couldn't reach my shoes if I had to."

I oblige, wondering how anyone pregnant or not could get around in heels that high. I assist Betty with undressing, then redressing in her nightgown, the whole event taking several minutes. I dress for bed and it's lights out and on to sleep, at least myself. I'm exhausted. It's sleep—it's sleep.

"Gunter, wake up. Gunter, wake up . . . *Gunter.*"

"What honey?" I say, caught between a dream and reality.

"I just had a contraction."

"A what?" I say, still half-asleep.

"A contraction!"

"Oh, one of those. Okay."

"Okay? Wake up. I'm going into labor!"

"You are," I say, leaping up, cutting on the lamp. "What should we do?"

"Call Doctor Whitehead. Call Doctor Whitehead!"

"But it's after eleven."

"I don't care if it's after midnight. Call Doctor Whitehead!"

I walk to the living room in the dark and pick up the telephone, the operator answering immediately. "Dr. Luke Whitehead, home number," I say, expecting the operator to know what to do.

Fourth ring, Luke Whitehead, the doctor who's delivered half of Oak Leak over the past thirty years, answers, "Ye*esss*."

"Dr. Whitehead, Gunter Wall, Betty's husband."

"Ye*esss*."

"I think we're going to have a baby!"

"Ye*esss*. I would call that an accurate assessment."

"What I meant to say is, Betty had a contraction."

"How far apart are they?" Dr. Whitehead says in a deliberate manner.

"How far apart? Don't know, she's only had one."

"One?"

"Yes, one. She had it just a minute ago."

"Get your watch and start timing them. When they get to ten minutes apart, either call me or drop by the office," Dr. Whitehead says in monotone.

"Drop by the office?"

"Yes, if it's during business hours. We can walk across the street to the hospital. I'll be talking to you," Dr. Whitehead says, meaning, "run along now, while I go back to sleep."

I return to the bedroom, Betty sprawled across the bed, both her hands just to the foot of the mountain.

"It's cramping down here," she says, rubbing a spot in her lower abdomen. "And my lower back is starting to hurt. Think you better get me to the hospital?"

"No, he says we need to start timing the contractions, and to either call or come by when they get to be ten minutes apart."

"Yeah, that's the instructions he gave me a month ago. Just guess I got excited," Betty says.

I look at my watch, the time 11:17, thinking Dr. Whitehead had wished Betty had not gotten "so excited." I seat myself at the foot of the bed, viewing Betty, her expression anxious. We wait . . . and wait. Suddenly, anxiousness turns again to excitement, Betty's eyes wide as saucers, "Oh, oh, oh, it's coming again."

I look at my watch, noting the short hand is between the three and the four, the long hand just beyond the nine, thinking "oh, oh" is right, that wasn't anywhere near ten minutes.

"This one's hurting a little more than the first," Betty says, her face fearful as well as excited.

I stand and walk from the foot of the bed to my normal spot and crawl in, Betty scooting over as I seat myself, my left hand clasping her right. The contraction is subsiding, and the clasp of our hands brings comfort to her face, as well as a radiant smile.

The night is long. My back gets stiff. I stand from time to time and stretch, packing Betty's bag around four, eventually making a pot of coffee at five. The contractions become more frequent, deeper, more painful, the pain in Betty's lower back more constant. There have been four contractions the past hour, not six. Betty is looking tired. I am tired. Fifteen minutes begins to feel like an hour. I drink a cup of coffee. Then another, and another. Time passes.

"Oh, oh, oh! This one hurt more. Oh, it hurts. How long has it been? I said. How long has it been?"

"Just over eleven minutes." I reach to hold Betty's hand, and she shoves it away abruptly.

"Help me up!" Betty shouts.

Whoa, never seen her this way before. I think before acting.

"I said, 'help me up!' Have you gone deaf?" Betty says, this time grabbing my left arm with a vise grip just above my hand.

I act quickly, reaching for her other arm and trying to lift it as she moves her legs to the side of the bed, then onto the floor.

"Help me change," Betty says. "I said, 'help me change!' "

I walk to the dresser where I laid Betty's clothes earlier and bring them to her, then stand before her, offering more a concerned look than any physical assistance as Betty switches clothes.

Minutes later, around nine, I park the car in front of Dr. Whitehead's, saying to Betty, "Wait here a minute as I run to his office."

A moment later I'm back. "He said just go on across the street and check in."

"I'm really, really hurting," Betty says, no longer shouting, a combination of pain and "I'm ready to get this done" on her face.

I crank the car and wheel across the street to the hospital, a small building the sum total of an admissions desk, nurses' station, an operating room, a waiting room, and six patients' rooms, and I have Betty in one in no time. I hold her hand, or rather she holds mine, her clasp grip-tight. The nurse has come and gone, timing the last contractions at six minutes.

"When is he going to get here?" Betty says, tightening the grip.

"Any minute now," I say. "He said he had a couple of patients to finish up with."

"Well, he had better hurry up! Oh, oh, oh!" Betty says, back to shouting again.

The door opens and in walks Dr. Whitehead, probably late fifties, but hard to tell. He's a man who has lived on little sleep year after year. I look and can tell.

Just seeing him walk in reassures Betty, as she releases her grip, a calm coming over her, if only for a moment. I've watched her facial expressions change more times than I can count. For the first time, I think I see a well-hidden smile just below the look of pain. A smile of relief? Hope? I think hope.

"Well, I think we'll be having a baby today," Dr. Whitehead says.

Can't tell whether he's trying to be funny or serious. He smiles a little. I'm still not sure.

"You might want to head on down the hall," he says to me, gesturing to the door with his head as he speaks. "Actually, you can step across the street and call any future grandparents, if you would like."

I reach and gently clasp her hand. "Next time I see you, you'll be a mother," I say, smiling.

Betty smiles back as I turn and leave, down the hall, across the street, two phone calls, one to Mom, another to Betty's mom (long distance, nice of Dr. Whitehead's office), then back across the street to wait.

Time passes. I don't notice my lack of sleep, must be nervous energy. I reach in the stack of magazines, *Look* on top. Vivian Lemur is on the cover, but I don't go under the cover. I turn it over, stand and walk. Mom shows up, becoming effervescent, talking.

"Didn't have a hospital when I delivered you," Mom says. "Delivered both you and Everett out on the plantation, midwife both times, up all night."

Odd, I knew I was born on the plantation. Didn't know it was by a midwife.

"Has to be so much safer here at a hospital with a doctor and nurse. I didn't even have my temperature checked." Mom pauses. "Your father was in the other room the whole time. Midwife didn't want him 'messin' with anything.' Guess that's no different today, is it?"

I nod, listen.

"In retrospect, there are a lot of things I wish could have been done differently, but not having you and Everett, not marrying your father."

I keep listening, my mind and body caught between lack of sleep and nervous energy, confused. I'm quiet. I let Mom do the talking.

"Oh, that plantation. I don't miss it at all. I do, however, miss the moments with both you and Everett. I had you both pretty much to myself every day. I felt needed, wanted. In some ways, even though we were poor—and I mean really poor—those times are some of my best memories. Your brother helped me tend to you, called you 'my brother.' He wasn't jealous the least bit like some siblings are. He wanted to look after you, protect you. I can remember those times like they were yesterday. Do you remember helping me make cornbread? You must have been three or four."

I think, dig deep, can't remember. I start to say no, then yes, but go for the middle ground. "Maybe," I say.

"You would help me in the kitchen with everything. It was so much fun. Such good memories, Gunter." Mom stops with the mention of my name and looks me straight in the eye, her face older than I've noticed to this point. First time I've really looked her in the face—I mean really looked—since my walk down the wedding aisle. My mind is affixed to Mom's face.

"Gunter . . . Gunter." Mom's lips are moving and I'm watching but not listening. "Gunter."

"Yes," I say.

"The last few days I've had a bushel basket full of memories of when you boys were born, when you were little. I guess it's the coming of this child that's brought it on. Until the past few days, those days seemed distant, faraway. This past week they've come alive, completely resurrected. Seems like they just happened. In my mind the thoughts are all pleasant, except for one." Mom stops, as if to struggle with her next words.

She has my full attention. "What's that, Mom?"

"The day of the flood, the months following," she says, her statement unfinished, her look serious, eyes to floor, then straight back at mine with the speed of a rabbit.

"Well, that wasn't pleasant for anyone. Every time my feet get cold, that's all I can think about," I say.

"That's not what I meant," Mom comes back, my words barely out of my mouth. "It was the way I behaved." Mom stops. "Oh, maybe I shouldn't take your time with this today, with the baby coming. But, it doesn't seem like I'm ever alone with you. Your Dad and Betty are always around, which is fine. But, life hasn't granted us any time alone for a long time. So . . . what I am trying to say is I didn't treat your father right. I blamed him for almost causing us to drown, for nearly freezing us to death, for neither of you boys having a pair of shoes on your feet—all because I was 'right.' All because I told your father that we should have headed to my family in the hills—at least, you two boys and me. I had tried to talk him into it for almost a month, but he wanted to keep the family together. Wanted to take care of us. When the flood came, all I could think about was that I was right and he was wrong, and he'd put us all through a mountain-high stack of misery. I took it out on him the day of the flood, the next day, and almost every day for three years."

I'm listening, low on sleep, first child due anytime now, and Mom pouring out her memories from a quarter of a century ago.

"Never once did I stop and give him and the good Lord credit for bringing us all out alive, including himself. Poor Mrs. Wilson's husband who owned the plantation died, and between the Twenty-seven Flood and the Great Depression she never got on her feet again. Died broke. You know what, Gunter?"

"What?" I say, quick reflex, intently listening.

"Your father never once lashed out at me. The only time he got firm with me was when he got his mind set on taking this oil mill job in Oak Leaf. That time he was right. The Depression took its toll on the family store in Everett Crossroads, then 'the crossroads moved,' so to speak. As we both know, the store ending up closing during the war. My sister and her family took it hard. None of them have starved to death, but things certainly didn't turn out as well for them as they did for us. Your Dad was firm, but he did look out for me. Gunter . . ." Mom stops again midstream.

"What's that, Mom?"

"Your father is a good man, a strong man. To say his beginnings were humble would be as great an understatement as I could make. He and the good Lord have helped me through my deep valleys. Well, today I wanted to tell you I apologized to your father years ago for the way I behaved in the flood and times following. I might have been right for trying to get you boys out before the flood, but I was wrong for how I treated your father, and I was wrong for how I treated you and Everett."

I pause, not knowing what to say, totally unscripted for Mom. "There's no need to do that."

"Hush up, Gunter. Yes, there is. I was more concerned with my fears and for faulting your father than I was with being helpful. At the time, all I offered was blame and fear. The fear was one thing, the blaming another . . ." Mom stops, solemn face, her eyes hard on mine. Suddenly, her face turns to a smile. "Enough of the past. Today is one of the big days of your life. So, is it going to be a boy or a girl?"

My mind is swimming, the water full of thoughts of Betty, a baby, Mom talking about events of a quarter century ago, all muddied by lack of sleep. Boy or a girl? I smile and say, "How would I know?"

"But, you are bound to have a hunch," Mom says.

"A girl."

"Oh my, that would be something, first girl in four generations of Walls. The odds are against it. What are you going to name her? I mean, if it's a girl."

"Anna Elizabeth. Betty's choice."

"And if it's a boy?"

"Won't say. I'll surprise you if it is."

Mom smiles, starts to press harder, then doesn't. She gets quiet. I get quiet. We wait.

About eleven, the nurse—past middle age, stoic, unanimated, matter-of-fact and monotone—says, "We'll be delivering shortly. Dr. Whitehead wanted you to know," her voice trailing off as she heads back toward delivery.

She reawakens me. I sit up straight, adrenaline flowing, blood pumping, a small flight of butterflies in my stomach. Mom sits up straight too. Betty's mother is not here. Won't be here till late afternoon or evening. Had to make preparations for a four-hour drive. Her dad has to work, pay the bills. I'll call him this afternoon. He'll know before her mom.

A bit after noon, Dad shows up. "I figure they won't close the oil mill down if I don't make it back by one," Dad says. We wait, a threesome.

Soon Dr. Whitehead emerges, white gown head to toe, subdued smile (his maximum, I surmise). "You have a healthy baby and wife. Everything went smoothly, very smoothly for a firstborn."

Oh, boy! I think, grateful that Betty is fine, and so is the baby. The baby? Yes, the baby?

"Well, what is it?" Mom says.

"A boy."

Mom's eyes open wide. I have no idea what that means. She then says, "Time is up. What are you going to name this young Wall, Gunter?"

"Not so fast," I say. "Is he ready for us to see him, Doctor Whitehead?"

"Will be in just a couple of minutes. We've got a glass window right down that way. They'll place him out. Only baby here, so you can't miss him. Congratulations. And now, I have to check on your wife," Dr. Whitehead says as he heads back down the hall.

We go to the window to wait.

"What are you going to name him, Gunter? Gunter, talk to me. What are you going to name him, Gunter?" Mom's like a cuckoo clock.

I hold my ground until a softer, gentler nurse than the one I met a moment ago comes out holding a boy, head full of brown hair, bundled in blue. She lays him in the tiny bed and unveils him, head and arms moving in rapid motion.

I look, admire, marvel, then say, "Thomas Everett . . . Thomas Everett Wall. Thomas, for you, Dad. Everett, well . . . for my brother."

Dad's smile sends wrinkles across wrinkles, tears in his eyes, like rain in the midst of sunshine. I turn to Mom, quiet now, her whole being focused on Thomas Everett Wall.

THIRTY-SIX

I stand next to the bed, Betty holding Thomas Everett, less than five hours out of the womb, and already we call him "Tommy" or "Little Tom." Betty's still groggy from the anesthetic, but livelier than a couple of hours earlier. I've been here that long. Betty's only complaint, the pain in her thigh, pale by comparison to labor, but painful still. She's complained to the nurse, three trips down, who gives her the same reply, "Your body has been through a lot."

"Gunter, will you hold Tom for a minute? My leg is really beginning to hurt." Pain overshadows the smile on Betty's face as she speaks.

I bend over and take Tom, holding him securely against my chest, fearful of dropping him. Betty throws back the sheet and reaches for her thigh, now swollen, enlarged to the point it's noticeable from halfway across the room.

"Well, how are we doing?" Dr. Whitehead says as he walks through the door, smiling.

"Fine," I say without thinking, then start to elaborate, until I see Dr. Whitehead's attitude and conversation directed at Betty. He had said "we" to be social, courteous.

"My thigh is really beginning to hurt," Betty says, her hand rubbing the top of the thigh.

"Let me see," Dr. Whitehead says, crossing the room, observing the leg from the left, the right, the top, comparing it to Betty's other thigh, running his hand across it, the smile leaving his face instantaneously. "How long have you noticed this?"

"A couple of hours," Betty replies.

"Have you made the nurse aware of it?"

"Yes, more than once."

Dr. Whitehead shakes his head, then backs up so he can see us both. "There appears to be a blood clot in your leg."

"How do we work it out?" I say, alarmed.

"We don't 'work it out.' As a matter of fact, that's the last thing we want to have happen. We don't want it moving upward toward your chest cavity. If that happens, it can become quite serious. Yes, quite serious."

"What do we do?" Betty says, concern and worry on her face.

Worry penetrates my mind, my heart. I start to repeat Betty, but wait.

"Normally, we try to stop it from going upward toward the lungs."

"How?" I say, thinking he is not explaining fast enough.

"A surgeon goes in below the chest cavity to the artery. It's a major procedure, a relatively new one at that."

"There has to be a simpler way," I say, thinking of what Betty has already been through today.

"No," Dr. Whitehead says abruptly. "Young man, young lady, this is quite serious. I'm calling an ambulance and we're heading to Franklin. I'm also calling ahead for a surgeon to be there as soon as possible. Is your car still here?"

"Yes," I say.

"Good, I want you to follow in case I need a ride back tonight. I don't normally ride in the ambulance, but your wife needs to be attended. Pull your car around back." Dr. Whitehead speaks with the authority of a superior in the Marine Corps. "Walk with me, and we'll leave your son in his bed down the hall. I hope they take better care of him than they have your wife."

My son? I think. Strange. Forgot he was in my arms. How can that be? All my attention on Betty.

Dr. Whitehead walks close to Betty, reaching, gently grabbing her hand, saying, "You're going to do fine. I'm sorry you've got to be put back in an operating room again today, but it's necessary. We've got to get you to Franklin General Hospital in a hurry and get the surgeon there. Okay?" he says nodding convincingly.

Betty nods back, agreeing, then says, "What about Tom? What about my child?"

"I'll have a discussion with both nurses, you can be certain. I repeat, 'certain.' He will receive the attention of the heir to the throne of England. Now, come with me, Gunter."

Betty interrupts, "What about my mother? She's to arrive any minute. She'll come and . . ."

"I'll call my folks from the desk. Tell them to come down this minute. Dad and Mom will take good care of her. Besides, she really didn't come here to see us anyway. She'll get to see Tom treated like the heir to the throne of England," I say, smiling.

The smile is infectious.

Halfway down the hall, Dr. Whitehead stops me. "Gunter, this is quite serious. We won't be wasting any time on our trip to Franklin." With that he heads for the nurses.

Minutes later they wheel Betty out, placing her in the back of the ambulance, Dr. Whitehead crawling in with her. The ambulance driver, Fred, says, "When was the last time you drove ninety?—'cause that's what you're gonna have to do to keep up with us."

"Never," I say.

"Tomorrow, you'll answer, 'last night,'" he says before running to the driver's seat, turning on the revolving red light and siren, closing the door, then off, all before I can close my car door, my engine already running.

Hope my car will go ninety, I think. The drive is usually twenty, twenty-five minutes. Tonight? Both hands are glued to the steering wheel, my foot to the floor. Good thing he didn't say "a hundred." He'd leave me high and dry. Oh, but what's going on up there? Has Betty's pain got worse? Is she okay? *God, she's only twenty-three. Yes, God. God let her live. Yes, God, please let her live. Please let her live.* Strange day. Strange night. Women used to die in childbirth all the time. But this is 1953: hospitals, doctors, surgeons, anesthesiologists, antibiotics. This time we'll need at least one of each. I bet he can go a hundred. I'm probably slowing the ambulance down. Go on ahead. Go on ahead! Leave me! It's all right to leave me. *God, let Betty be all right.*

I pull in behind the ambulance, back of Franklin General, brakes screeching. Ambulance driver has the hatch up, and people are scurrying out to put Betty on a gurney before I can get my car door open. One of them yells to me, "Can't leave your car there. Park over there," he says, pointing.

I hesitate, wanting to argue, but get back in my car and obey, tapping on the glass window a moment later, seeking entry. Then down the hall. "My wife, Betty Wall, just came in with Dr. Whitehead."

"She's already gone to the operating room. She's in luck, all right, or has been living right. Dr. Perkins, a surgeon, was here making rounds. He's as good as they come. Nobody better anywhere. Knows all the latest procedures."

"Can I meet with him for a minute?"

"Nope. Don't believe you can go in the operating room. Go find you a seat down the hall in the waiting room. Might want to get you some coffee. Could be a long evening."

"I already know about long evenings," I say, thinking about my thirty minutes of sleep last night. But that was different, wasn't it? Long in a different way. Wasn't worried a bit about Betty. It was just a new experience, my first with childbirth, lack of sleep. Somehow, I wasn't really worried. Tonight I am. She's only twenty-three, two years younger than Everett when he died, a year older than Jimmy Street, four older than Brooklyn. But, this is Betty, my wife, and there's no war, nobody firing shots. *God, please don't let her die. Let her live a long life. Please let us live long lives together.*

"Sir, did you hear me?" the lady behind the counter says. "There's a waiting room down the hall with coffee."

"Yes," I say as I walk down the hall to the coffee pot, pouring coffee in a paper cup, then sit down to wait, adrenaline mixed with fatigue. Hey, I ought to be able to handle this. Lived on not much else than adrenaline for over a month on Iwo. I'm out of shape. Yeah, but I'd rather not get in that shape ever again. I sit, my mind racing a hundred thoughts, but always coming back to Betty. How is the surgery going? How is she doing? Then to God: asking, pleading, begging. Time passes.

A door opens and in walks Dr. Whitehead, followed by another doctor dressed head to toe in white mixed with blood. My first look is to Dr. Whitehead's face, a tired smile on it, as he gestures me to remain seated, which I don't.

"How's Betty?" I say, standing awkwardly.

"She's come through fine," says Dr. Whitehead. She is going to be in bed for a while, both here and when she gets home. She'll of course need some help with your son."

"Oh, she'll have too much of that," I say, thinking Mom and Betty's mother are probably fighting over him at this very moment.

"Thought you might like to meet Dr. Perkins. He did the surgery."

"Robert Perkins," he says, a man somewhere between my age and Dr. Whitehead's, holding out his hand, a slender hand, I note, one of dexterity. He smiles and nods, but says nothing else.

"Gunter, have a seat," Dr. Whitehead says as Dr. Perkins seats himself in a chair adjacent to mine, and Dr. Whitehead seats himself in one to the other side. I follow suit.

"Dr. Perkins and I were talking, and we agree that your wife doesn't need to go through this again."

"Oh, I agree," I say. "This blood clot thing was a bit much."

"That's not exactly what I'm saying," Dr. Whitehead says, pausing. "I'm referring to getting pregnant. The risk is too great. We don't ever need to run this risk again. Ever. Am I clear?" His eyes are straight on mine, leaving no question of misunderstanding.

I nod, not in agreement but to collect my thoughts, the past twenty-four hours almost more than I can absorb.

"We'll go over that with her together in a few days if you like," Dr. Whitehead says. "That might be best. Your young wife has been through quite an ordeal, so we might not need to pile anything else on at this time."

I nod again, my tired mind trying to filter my thoughts as to what is most important at this moment. "What are my options tonight?" I say.

"Well, you can either go on home and get a good night's rest, or you can sleep on a cot here and have a poor night's rest. Betty will be in recovery all night. We hope to put her in a room in the morning. Isn't that your game plan, Bob?" Dr. Whitehead says, turning to Dr. Perkins.

"That's it exactly," Dr. Perkins says. "She'll have careful eyes on her all night, and I'll probably put her in her own room midmorning."

"I'm staying here," I say.

"Whatever," Dr. Whitehead says, as a puzzled look covers his face.

"I don't expect you want to walk back to Oak Leaf, do you?" I say. "Especially in the dark. Why don't you take these?" I say, removing the ignition and door keys from my key ring. It's the Ford about thirty yards behind where the ambulance pulled up. It's blue, not black. I upgraded this time."

Dr. Whitehead hesitates.

"It's the least I can do for you saving Betty's life. I thank both of you," I say, momentarily acknowledging Dr. Perkins. "Why don't you just park it in front of your office and leave the keys at the front desk. I'll be by sometime to pick them up."

"Okay," Dr. Whitehead says, then, "Bob, do they have a phone around here anyplace? I need to call Elizabeth and tell her I'm in Franklin. She was expecting me for supper hours ago."

"Follow me," Dr. Perkins says, as they head down the hall.

I collapse in my chair, thinking I can worry about the cot later. What a night. What a day. What a night again. Never could have seen all this coming a day ago. Sometimes life changes fast, and it changes when I least expect it. Betty is alive. *Yeah, God, that's what I asked you for. I also asked for a long life together, Betty and me.*

THIRTY-SEVEN

"So, you think you can put it all in one loan?" Hoppy says.

"I could if it was just our bank, but we're going to have to package this deal with another. That other bank doesn't know you're good for a dollar like I know you are. You're going to have to get your accountant to get us a current balance sheet, as well as the last two years profit and loss statements. If we put it all together in right form on the front end, it should fly on through. Send them bits and pieces they start questioning things, thinking you're trying to cover something up."

"You know how much I like dealing with accountants and numbers, don't you?" Hoppy says, rolling his eyes. "What I know is building crop dusters. Give my group any single engine plane from World War II or Korea, and we can take it apart and put it back together flight-ready with our eyes closed. Gunter, we're selling them all over Mississippi, Louisiana, and Texas. Far as I know there's only two guys in the United States putting more of them out there than my company—one in the panhandle of Texas and another in the Imperial Valley out in California. The way I see it, there's no reason either of those fellows should be in front of me. I'm ready to step to the front of the line. Just need a little cash to see old Hoppy Pearson through."

"Hoppy, even though it's 1960, four million dollars is still more than a little cash."

"Who's the second largest employer in this town?" Hoppy says.

"Hoppy Pearson's Airplanes of America."

"And it should be the largest. Just need a little more cash. I'm always thinking ahead," Hoppy says. "You once asked me why *crop dusting* wasn't in the name of my business. 'Cause like we discussed today, I'm gonna start selling World War II Classics to rich guys up east. Status symbols, that's what I'm gonna be selling. They got a house and a yacht out on Long Island—or some such place—to go with their penthouse in New York City. Now they need, I repeat, *need* a World War II Classic. We'll take our planes and put a more expensive coat of paint on them and charge three times as much. Do you reckon those fellows at that big bank you deal with will comprehend all this?"

"They will if you'll get me the numbers. Do you need me to call Fred so he knows what I am asking for?"

"Gunter, I know exactly what you want. It just reminds me of that little rodent that Khrushchev tried to recently socialize with out in California, Mickey Mouse. This whole procedure is 'Mickey Mouse.'"

"I understand what you're saying, but I still need the numbers to put the package together. Get them to me this week."

Hoppy stands, grease on his pants, shoes, and hands, one of which I shake as he exits. My secretary was recently complaining about some grease we had to clean out of the chair he'd sat in. I told her for what he brings in to the bank we could afford to get him a new chair every time he comes in.

I was fortunate that Hoppy latched on to me. "Any banker that was crazy enough to ride on a lake in a car is the kind of banker I want to deal with," he said. Worked at plane manufacturing up in St. Louis for a few years after the war and saved every dime he made. Came back here and started buying broken-down planes and parts. Needed to borrow a little cash about the time I started lending money. He came to me, now he's the richest man in Oak Leaf. For all I know, he's the richest man in America with a tenth-grade education. And now I'm a vice president at the bank, one of three. Make loans left and right and seldom get questioned by the board. Hoppy's deal this time is unique. It needs to be sold to the board with part of the deal farmed out to a bigger bank. I can do it—if he gets me the numbers, not just for the board of another bank, but for myself.

Hoppy's long on ideas and energy, but short on details. Kind of likes to fly blindfolded and low on flight fuel. I need to keep tabs on the details—for Hoppy, the bank . . . and for myself. "Keep tabs on the details," James Street says, one of his many words of advice. He's still the bank president, been for twenty-something years. Speaking of details, he's schooled me on about every detail I could dream of in a lifetime. "You don't have enough time in life to make all the mistakes yourself," he's reminded me in a nice way on more than one occasion when I was about to step in a ditch. "Always do the right thing," he'll say, with an emphasis on the word "always." Next thing he'll come back to the word "however," "However, this . . . however, that." "Got to sometimes walk the tightrope—bank's interest on one end, customer's on the other. Got to keep your balance."

Next appointment, Aaron Johnson, a Negro who's got a small grocery store couple of blocks off of downtown that looks busy every time I pass. Had no reason to go in. Don't shop there, and he's not a customer of mine—yet. Got a call yesterday from Bob Cellini, Marko's grandfather. "Getting too old to keep all my money tied up in real estate," he says. "Need for you to talk to Aaron Johnson; he's solid as an oak tree and needs a loan to buy a piece of my real estate. Don't need to owner finance 'cause I want cash, not a note." He's due here at three.

I open his file. Nothing to it but four statements, all at our bank. A small certificate of deposit, savings account and two checking accounts: one personal and one under "Handy Grocery," the name of his store. Let's see, they total about . . . fifteen thousand! Why isn't he a customer already? Hmm . . . Don't see any loans. Guess he's just fallen through the cracks. I glance at the big clock on the wall just above the entry door that you can see from any spot in the bank, small hand on the three, large one edging toward the twelve as the front door opens and a Negro enters, dark black, medium height and weight, glasses, nothing distinguished about his features, dressed in short white shirt with tie, dark pants, steady gait, small leather briefcase in hand.

He nears my desk and I stand to greet, first saying his name (to make sure it's him), he saying mine, followed by a handshake. He seats himself in the chair recently vacated by Hoppy, my only concern his white shirt and the grease.

"Aaron," I say. "Can't believe we've never met," which I really can't. Oak Leaf is not that big.

"I reckon it's 'cause running a grocery store is six days a week, sun up till dark, even in August. Most of the time when I come in the bank, it's to make a deposit. Never thought a bank officer would want to take his time to count nickels and quarters, so I just deal with the tellers."

"I see," I say, nodding, my hands held together, elbows lightly touching the chair arms, posture erect, for the moment my leaning backward slightly, listening with my body as well as my ears. "I don't see any loans you have with us. Where do you do your borrowing?"

"Borrow or pay interest?" Aaron says, peering through his glasses, glass as thick as an empty six ounce Coca Cola bottle, studious looking, exacting, the type man who could tell two pennies are missing from a five-pound sack of coins.

"What do you mean?" I say.

"Suppliers deliver the goods; you pay in thirty days, there's no interest. Wait sixty days, you pay an arm and a leg's interest. Ninety days, two arms and two legs. When I first got started, right after the war, I was paying two arms and two legs, and I almost ran out of arms and legs. Now, I make sure they got the money by the twenty-ninth day." Aaron stops talking. All said.

"Well, we certainly appreciate your using the bank. Bob Cellini said you have an interest in a piece of property of his, and he wanted you to see me."

"I came to Mr. Cellini 'bout two months ago. You can only stack so many cans and chickens in that little place of mine up on Sixth Street. Folks get packed in there like sardines in a can. Can't hardly move around on Fridays and Saturdays, much less get 'em checked out. Got to have more space." Aaron stops. All said, again.

"So, what building are y'all talking about," I say, thinking I know the answer.

"Building where Hammonds Clothing Store was," he says, giving no more than the answer to my question.

Hammonds Clothing Store, I think. Dale Hammond, got cancer and died about a year and a half ago. No one in his family to run it, no buyer to be found. Bank got most of its money—but not all of it. Wasn't my customer, thank goodness. So, the building has sat vacant for a year and a half, only empty one on north Main Street, right between a hardware and an auto parts store. Not good to have an empty building downtown; not good for Bob Cellini.

"So, what's he asking for it?" I say.

"Sixty-five thousand," Aaron says, unblinking eyes peering through the empty Coca Cola bottles.

"Well, for starters I'll need a current balance sheet and two years profit and loss statements," I say.

"Mr. Cellini said you would need those." Aaron opens the briefcase and hands me a stack of papers. "The balance sheet is on top, and I've got three-year 'profit statements' beneath them. I don't have no 'loss statements.' "

"I see," I say, grabbing the stack, looking briefly at the balance sheet, the number 0 boldly showing under the word "liabilities," the plural word incongruent with the singular 0.

"I also brought these," he says, grabbing a bigger stack, handing it to me, two hands required, as I reach across my desk. "Those are statements for the past five years from the folks I buy from. As you can see, I live up to my motto, 'always paid by the twenty-ninth day.' "

I glance at the first two or three pages, the number 0 appearing below both sixty and ninety days.

"Why do you feel your customer base would follow you?" I say.

"Why wouldn't they?" Aaron comes back, not an ounce of doubt in his voice. "Folks'll walk an extra two blocks if you treat 'em right and deliver the goods at a good price. And I won't be messin' with the price just to get a building paid for. Didn't do it with the one I got now. Not gonna do it with this one."

I lean back in my chair. Haven't had anybody this prepared in a while. Old man Cellini's coached him like a national championship coach. Cellini wants the cash, Aaron Johnson wants the building, one that's been sitting vacant, and might continue to do so, not good for downtown Oak Leaf. Only thing—two guys on the board, big stockholders, Tom Hallman, Frank Haywood, are opposed to anything progressive. First, it will be, "Hoppy Pearson, four million dollars?" And, "He doesn't even grow cotton." Then, "Can't let a Negro get too close to the center of downtown. Next thing, you got no downtown."

It's Tuesday afternoon, Tom's seventh birthday. Promised I'd come home early today, let someone else close this place down. The board's executive committee meeting is Monday at nine, second and fourth Monday of the month, and next week is the second Monday. Am I gonna take those guys on twice Monday morning? One or two more questions.

"Aaron, we've never lent you money before. Tell me about yourself."

"What's there to tell?" he says.

"Where are you from? How'd you get started? I see by your hand you're married. Tell me about your family."

"I'm from Oak Leaf, graduated from the other high school," he says, nodding to the opposite side of town from Oak Leaf High. "1942. Good thing, you know, 'cause a couple of years later they were grabbing you when you hit eighteen, still in high school or not. Anyway, I was in the Army and they sent me to England, then France and Germany."

"France and Germany," I say the words that catch my attention. "What parts?"

"Normandy, Battle of the Bulge," he says, shrugging.

"You were there D-Day and Battle of the Bulge?"

"Yes sir," he says, energy in his voice. "I guess you might say I'm lucky to be sitting here today. Mighty lucky."

Battle of the Bulge? Normandy? Probably a lot of fighting in between . . . and afterward. "Were you wounded?" I say, completely forgetting I'm a banker. Don't know why I ask.

"No sir," he says. "Mighty lucky. Only thing was the frostbite. Thought my toes were gonna fall off. Don't never think about that in August, like I do long about December. Oh, my feet hurt every winter. Guess they will till the day I die. Try not to think about it this time of year. You know, want to push it out of my mind . . . just like those battles. Wouldn't have brought it up today, but then, you asked."

Yes I did, I think, for the moment my mind miles away from lending money. Had a dream the other night. Have them about twice a year now. Different, not vivid or exactly like the dreams when I came back from the war. These dreams are disguised, but I know where they have their roots. The other night, of all things, it's a farmer coming after me with a shovel, striking me on the shoulder—pain! I woke up two o'clock sweating and couldn't go back to sleep. Fortunately, it's only a couple of times a year. Very fortunate.

"Well, I saved my pay, came back from the war and started working for Mr. Rawlings at that store I own now. Worked there in high school for him, and he took a liking to me. I'd like to tell you I started on my own two feet, but that ain't the gospel. Mr. Rawlings set up a way for me to buy and for him to ease on out. Wouldn't be here today if it wasn't for him." Aaron pauses to catch his breath. "I guess at this stage I need a couple of more Mr. Rawlings. Mr. Cellini's offering at a fair price, and I'm asking for a loan at a fair rate, that's all. Been working at the store fourteen years, and married to the same woman for thirteen. We got two children." He pauses again. "When can you let me know?"

I pause to collect my composure, sifting through what Aaron has told me, then say, "What about your present building?"

"Already got a renter that wants to start a sewing shop. The rent will be two-fifty a month. He can't move in till I move out."

"We will need it as collateral," I say, then, "Life insurance?"

"Got two twenty-fives, two ten thousands, and a five," he says, starting to reach in the briefcase.

"Don't need them today," I say, "but we will if we set up a loan."

"When will I know something?"

"Probably next week. Do I have your phone numbers?"

"No, I'll give you both, although I don't know why you need the home number."

"Why's that?" I say.

" 'Cause I'll never be there when you'll call, less it's on Sunday—then, less than half a day."

I nod, thinking of the statement he has made as I jot down two numbers.

He closes the briefcase, we stand, shake hands, and he exits as I look at the big clock above the door, now a quarter of four. I look at the file that earlier had four statements in it, that now looks as thick as a dictionary. I file his file and Hoppy's in my desk. It's time to leave; it's Tom's seventh birthday, and I've got a special gift to pick up.

THIRTY-EIGHT

A Ford and two Chevrolets remain parked in front or near the front of our home, each separated by space, a sign that others have come and gone, and a few remain for Tom's seventh birthday party. He'd been anticipating the event for two weeks, and now it's winding down. I park the car, then exit the carport, rounding the house where card tables are up along with streamers, balloons, a birthday cake that's half missing, and Dixie Cups, most a third to a quarter full of vanilla ice cream. The crowd has come and gone, and three ladies, two young boys, and one young girl with ponytails and glasses remain. They're exchanging pleasantries, small talk, and my entry speeds their exit.

"Tell Tom and Mrs. Wall you had a good time, Sarah," Jenny Smith says to her daughter, as Sarah obliges with, "I had a good time."

We all nod, smile, speak, followed by three choruses of "You take care" as the guests round the house, the children with some small favor in hand, all disappearing, leaving the three of us, Tom viewing gifts galore, a pile on the side of the house next to the carnage (shredded boxes, torn wrapping paper, and discarded ribbon). The event is over—same time, same place next year. Tom will joyously play with his gifts a week or two, then forget about them, the newness gone, their fate eventually to be added to the carnage, "another addition to the city dump."

Betty smiles. It's a tired smile but not an aged one, her face clear, smooth pale white, unwrinkled, thirty. Thirty? An age I used to think old, but now before me a woman as beautiful as ever. No, more so, her maturing adding extra dimensions to her facial features: color, clarity, distinctiveness, substance.

"So, how was it?" I ask Betty, Tom ignoring me, rummaging the gift pile.

"Whew! I'm about to fall over. Even these shade trees don't offer much relief. Let's see, I've baked a cake, blown up balloons, set up tables, mixed Kool-Aid, and told Tom six hundred and three times, 'No, it's not time yet; doesn't start till three.' "

I walk over and give a hug, a muggy one, my white cotton shirt and tie against Betty's party dress, moisture saturating the cloth somewhat, our bodies close. I give her a peck on the lips, then back away, needing relief. It's hot.

"I've got something for Tom," I say, a puzzled look on Betty's face.

"I thought his gifts were the party and a fall church outfit," Betty says. "Remember, budget."

"Yeah," I say backing away sheepishly. "Just wait here and I'll be back in a minute."

I turn, walk away, round the house, enter the carport, and look through the car window I've left rolled down to a tiny object on the seat that now stands to its feet and barks a "child's bark." It's a beagle, male (thought about the future), a two-month-old—a surprise for Tom, as well as for Betty. I reach down with both hands, short hair and wiggling body in my hands, so light that I feel the wiggling more than the weight. "Yip yip" comes from its mouth, high-pitched, no weight behind it. I breathe deeply, thinking what I will say to Tom, then to Betty, the latter thought overshadowing the first.

I round the corner of the house, wiggling beagle in hands, Betty stuffing garbage in the can, Tom running about in circles with one of the toys, as the tiny beagle barks, "Yip . . . yip."

Human motion to the front of me stops instantaneously, followed by the turning of two heads toward me, Tom's eyes opened wide as Betty's mouth. Elation, shock. Tom runs toward me. Betty doesn't move. "It's a dog! It's a puppy! I've got a dog!"

The wiggling intensifies as Tom nears, the puppy's attention turned directly on him. Tom reaches out as I say, "Be careful," the beagle leaving my hands to his, then hugged to his chest, an immediate bond.

"You might want to put him down for a minute," I say. "He's been in the car awhile."

Tom continues to hug a moment longer, then places the beagle on the ground, a tiny stream of liquid hitting the ground just seconds after he lands. I look up. Betty has yet to speak— with her mouth.

"It's not coming in the house." Betty has spoken.

"No. No, of course not," I say. "What's that thing we used to put up when Tom was a baby to keep him from getting on the floor furnace? Can't think of the name of it, but I found it in the closet the other night. I've already figured out how to put it in front of the closet in the carport, where he can't get out tonight. First thing Saturday morning, Tom and I are gonna build a dog house—put in right over there out of sight." I talk fast, not letting Betty get a word in edgewise.

She says nothing.

"I bet he's thirsty," I say.

"What do you have to serve him with?" says Betty.

"I got a little tied up at the bank. Meant to run by the hardware store and pick up two bowls, one for food, one for water. I can get those tomorrow." I pause to let Betty ponder my good intentions.

"Tonight we'll just use one of those paper plates for his food: leftovers, scraps, and such. For water . . . perhaps a cereal bowl. Yes, a cereal bowl— that is, until tomorrow."

Betty stares.

What gives? Thought she would be tickled pink. A dog for Tom! Wow! Didn't consult, didn't discuss. Do I need to get twice as much lumber? Two doghouses?

"Betty, honey," I say, moving toward her, putting my arm around her shoulder, turning back toward Tom as I do. He's running in circles, ribbon in hand, with beagle chasing, tiny legs moving fast as they can.

From the corner of my eye I see a thaw in the ice, a smile, not a grin, coming from Betty, the rest of her body relaxing at the same time.

"What are you gonna call him?" I say.

"Pistol Pete," Tom hollers back.

How did he arrive at that name? I have no clue. Cowboy? Gunslinger? "Sounds fine to me," I say.

Betty smiles. Still doesn't grin.

"Tom, go grab your least favorite cereal bowl and come fill it up with water at the hydrant. Got to learn some responsibility if you're old enough to have a dog," I say.

Tom nods and takes off for the back door, Pistol Pete's tiny head cocked to the side, perplexed.

"Gunter, I just don't know," Betty says, shaking her head.

"Honey, I had so much fun with a dog when I was a little boy. Lost him in the flood and always wished I had another one. The boy needs a dog," I say, pausing, then, "Sorry I didn't talk with you about it, really sorry."

"I think it will be all right as long as he stays in the yard," Betty says in the affirmative while still shaking her head. "I don't think we currently have the funds to refinish the hardwood floors or replace the rugs, much less the furniture. Daddy was forced to put Gene Autry out in the yard after he gnawed on most of the dining room chairs."

"Gene Autry, the Singing Cowboy, gnawed on the dining room chairs?" I ask.

"No, Gene Autry, my little brother's dog."

"Was he a beagle?" I ask, pressing my luck.

"A little of this and that," Betty says.

I don't respond. Tom has returned, bowl in hand (cowboys all over it), hydrant running, water spilling everywhere, Pistol Pete lapping the water, his head soaking wet.

Later that night, I lie in bed with Betty, arm around the same shoulder, thinking I've smoothed it all over, window unit blowing cold air (our home addition for the summer), the hum of the motor and sound of blowing air drowning all sounds, save one.

"Yip . . . yip . . . yip . . ." comes from the carport.

THIRTY-NINE

Monday, 8:58. I sit surrounded by six executive board members, James Street and two other vice presidents, all seated around the oak table, turn-of-the-century, big enough to seat several more, two large files in front of me. I've shaken hands, my right hand and arm sore from Saturday's doghouse construction, exchanged pleasantries, and seated myself. Today, unlike most of these meetings, I'm prepared to talk. Normally, my loans (unless someone is well behind on payments) are cut-and-dry, nothing to discuss.

James Street does most of the talking, and lately it's been mundane; the bank's prospering, town's growing, farmers are expanding, times are good. There's a presidential election ahead, but either way, things will be fine.

James Street seats himself, head of the table. "Since we're all here, let's go ahead and get started."

James Street, bank president, man who hired me, my business mentor, counseled me more times than I can count, purveyor of wisdom, passes typed papers left and right, papers filled with numbers black on white—reality. I say "reality"; they don't tell the future, only the present or the past. I watch him orchestrate, the maestro at work, rest of the orchestra for the moment just tuning their instruments. So, how will he handle what I'm about to do? Let's see, he says, "Always do the right thing." Yeah, sometimes that's the walk on the tightrope, bank on one end, customer on the other. And there's always politics. Always. Oh, not like the election in November, or the primaries just held. With those it's all or nothing, win or lose. No, it's like the politics between the elections, compromise here and there, when the politician decides where to stand his ground, not to budge, and why not to budge? To get reelected, or because he committed to "doing the right thing?" Politics . . . politics.

"As you can see, with the exception of two major loans that are over 120 days past due, loan payments are punctual, deposits are up, profits are good. Unless a hurricane comes along and sends us bad weather, the cotton and soybean crops are excellent," James Street says, half jokingly.

"What about these two loans?" Tom Hallman interrupts.

Tom Hallman, only thing he sees in a green pasture is cow manure. He just wants to take in deposits, doesn't want to loan. Fortunate for me, these aren't my loans.

James Street steps in. Doesn't have to, he didn't make the loans. Could first let each of my fellow vice presidents offer an explanation, but this time he chooses to do the explaining. "Tom, as I've oftentimes said, 'If we don't have a few loans go delinquent, then we're not making enough loans.' Even if there were no assets to back these two loans, our current profits would make these losses almost unnoticeable. Fortunately, we've got enough collateral on each of these where the losses to the bank would be minimal. Besides, both of the businesses are seasonal. I think we need to give each at least three more months before we begin to think of any drastic action."

James Street answers smoothly, directly, to the point, and although I haven't studied these numbers, I know he has. I also know that while he might play politics, he wouldn't mislead the executive committee, or anybody.

"In other words, you're comfortable with it for the moment," Tom Hallman says, nodding.

"Yes," says James Street as Tom Hallman leans back in his chair, arms folded, continuing to nod.

"I think Gunter has a couple of potential loans he'd like to go over with us this morning," James Street says, gesturing toward me with his hand.

This is tougher than usual. Traditionally, if I'm presenting to the committee, I've gotten positive feedback from James Street. Last Thursday, Hoppy delivered the numbers and I carried them, as well as Aaron Johnson's file to James. He listened, looked at the files, then said, "Do what you think," no feedback. I mean, going from three to four million on a loan: "Do what you think." Negro wants to buy a building, some might raise their eyebrows because of location, and he said the same thing.

"Yes, I've got two loans I recommend we need to move forward on," I say as I pass a company balance sheet, two profit and loss statements, as well as a summary of Hoppy's current loan around the table. "Hoppy

Pearson is wanting to expand his business in two ways. First, he thinks he can expand his Texas market for crop dusters. There's an expansion potential in the Panhandle. Also, he's got an idea for selling his rebuilt World War II planes to wealthy folks up east as status symbols—sort of like yachts in the air. The only increase in cost would be in marketing, travel expenses, and paint. Hoppy would put a different paint job on the planes and charge a significantly higher price. Basically, if they sell, the main thing that will increase is the profits. Any questions, so far?"

"Status symbols? Who in their right mind would want to go and do a thing like that?" Tom Hallman says, searching for the manure in the green pasture, just knowing that if this loan is approved, somebody other than the plane buyer will step in it.

"Don't know anything about the rightness of these people's minds, but if their pocketbooks are right, it won't matter," I say lightheartedly, smiling.

The group, save Tom Hallman, smiles back, chuckles, even James Street.

"Hoppy hasn't missed yet. The man's got a knack for marketing that I've never seen in anyone else. Besides that, he builds a quality plane. He markets like heck initially, then it's word of mouth and repeat business. Bottom line, at the present he's at maximum production for his building and equipment. To move forward, he has to expand his facilities. Two reasons to move forward. One look at the numbers, they're impressive to say the least. Second, look at Hoppy's track record." I quit talking.

Roy Windham, board member, quiet, studious, judicious, says, "But, you're recommending we farm some of this out to a larger bank?"

"Yes," I say. "Same as last time. We've got him down for three million right now. One million shared with another institution. What we need to do is increase the amount of the loan to four million, a proportional share farmed out elsewhere, at the interest rate I have listed."

"Why?" Roy counters.

"Why farm part of it out?" I say.

"Yes."

Why? I looked at the numbers, and they look excellent, fast growing, no problem to get an approval here or elsewhere. But . . . gut feeling, art versus science. Hoppy's on the edge, always will be. Times are good right now, economy growing, folks are looking for a real airplane instead of a model airplane for a hobby. Times can change. Gut feeling.

"Exposure," I say. "I suggest we lend the money at this rate, but limit our exposure."

"James?" Roy says.

James Street leans back, hands folded in lap, pauses, then says, "Gunter has a knack for making a good call." He says nothing more.

"Any more questions?" I say.

Heads shake, seven vote, James and the executive committee, the vote unanimous for my recommendation.

"One more recommendation," I say, passing around the papers for Aaron Johnson, looking at faces left, right, and straight as they peruse the facts. "Bob Cellini's building on north end of Main, vacant for a year and a half. Aaron Johnson, one of our customers with $15,000 in the bank, was referred to me by Bob. Aaron has more than enough assets and income to back the loan. It's a good risk, if I've ever seen one," I say, then get quiet.

Things remain quiet for a moment, then Frank Haywood says, "Looks like a bad risk to me, plain as the nose on my face," nodding as he looks around the table for affirmation. Tom Hallman nodding in agreement, James Street and Roy Windham staring at the nodding heads, the rest of the eyes, save mine, staring at the table.

"Why's that?" I say, staring at Frank Haywood.

"Well . . . uh, you know," he says, grinning.

"Frank, must be I haven't fully woken up yet, this being Monday morning," I say, smiling. "But let me take time and try. First, this is north Main, not central or south. We're not talking about changing the complexion of the whole downtown."

"We're not required to accept the loan," Frank interrupts.

"Oh, I agree. Of course Bob Cellini sent him down. I didn't take the time to pull Bob's information today, but between his deposits and loans with our bank, we could probably have a morning-long discussion. Bob's been holding this empty building for over a year and a half, and an empty building doesn't sell our downtown, even on the north end."

"It's just like one domino in a line. Tip one down and they all start falling, one at a time till they're all down," Frank comes back, waving his hands in the air.

What to say? Don't know exactly where Frank's coming from. He's opposed to a lot of loans that have nothing to do with race, just his conservative nature. Maybe he's genuinely concerned about the future of Oak Leaf. On the other hand, perhaps he's blinded by racial prejudice. I guess I could draw that out of him. Matter-of-fact, I know I could, but we're in a group and we all need to work together in the future. But, Aaron Johnson? Man's worked six days a week, umpteen hours a day building a business, being thrifty. Done so since he got back from the war. The war? Normandy . . . Battle of the Bulge . . . fighting in between

. . . fighting afterward. Still fighting? In a few months he'll be dealing with frostbite. Yeah, every winter for the rest of his life. Because of guys like him we are breathing free air. Who are "we?" Politics . . . politics. What to say? Why to say it?

"Y'all, the world's changing. In some places, California, large cities in the Midwest, the trend is to the suburbs, shopping centers. Buildings like Bob Cellini's are being vacated by choice. Got to get to the hot spots."

"You think that will happen here? This isn't exactly Los Angeles," Frank says, serious look on his face.

"Eventually," I reply. "Construction of the four-lane on the south side of town starts next spring. First thing, somebody will open a filling station. Cars need gas. Next, somebody will build a retail store, then another. I'd say that during this decade we'll need to open a branch of this bank out there—a small one, mind you. Change is inevitable. This bank does not need to become a dinosaur. You know there are no more dinosaurs because they failed to adapt."

"What does all this have to do with us?" Frank comes back.

"Aaron Johnson's financial numbers are as solid as this oak table. If we don't make the loan—and at a reasonable rate, I might add—one of the banks in Franklin will. Bob Cellini will see to that. He might also seek more suitable financial arrangements for himself." I pause, then continue. "No, the way I see it, the upside of us taking on this loan far outweighs the small downside of a Negro-owned store on the north end of Main. Two years down the road the only people who will remember the deal will be Aaron Johnson and Bob Cellini, both in a positive way. I say we need to move on with the loan. Any questions?"

Silence.

I look around the table and most heads are nodding.

"Well, do we have any objections to the loan?" James Street says, his eyes behind the glasses surveying the table.

Frank Haywood starts to speak, then doesn't, his head shaking slightly.

"Well, I think that's about it for today. I've got a busy Monday ahead, and I'm sure you all do too," James Street says, standing energetically, rounding the table, making a point to shake hands with all six members of the executive committee. I do likewise.

Small talk follows, most of mine with Frank Haywood. The room empties and James and I walk out together, him saying, "Why don't you swing on by my office for a minute, Gunter."

We cross the lobby, James in front, nodding, waving, waking up those physically here but whose minds have yet to arrive—all part of a role called "presence," his presence vast, having become bank president during the latter part of the Great Depression, the presence growing, blossoming, through a world war, the Korean War, the fifties, and the first year of the decade of the sixties. Past Mary Marbury we go, her presence also immense, ancient when I came here, more ancient today, "keeper of the door." She nods—no smile, no frown, no comment, just watchful eyes. Into his office we go, James rounding the massive mahogany desk, saying, "Catch the door," just as I'm about to sit.

I oblige.

James adjusts himself in the big leather chair, clears his throat, folds his hands, looks briefly at me, then off in the distance, somewhere beyond the walls of the bank, the outskirts of town, on past the state line, out of the country, and on and on as if to another world. Suddenly, the eyes come back.

"As you are aware, I've recently made a trip or two to Memphis."

"Yes," I say, assuming the trips are bank related.

"The last one was not good," he continues.

I stare, no clue as to what he means.

"Probably two months, three at maximum—that's what both specialists gave me. Cancer's in both lungs. They may try some heroics, which I'm not opposed to. But I could tell by their eyes, tone of voice, my chances are about zero." James hesitates, clears his throat again, a faint smile across his face as he continues, "This is not public knowledge. As a matter of fact, at this moment you're the only person with any affiliation with the bank that has a clue. I trust that, for the present, you will keep it that way," he says, his eyes widening.

"Yes," I say, trying to respond with something more profound, but I can't. For the moment I'm numb, gone blank.

"Seems such a short time ago, we were sitting in this same room following the drowning of my car. Yes, such a short time ago," he says, his head shaking, repeating himself. "Gunter, recently you might wonder why I've nodded at you, thrown it back in your lap when you've come to me for advice."

"Yes, I've noticed," I answer truthfully.

"I've been weaning you. I knew something was wrong with me months ago, not knowing exactly what. It's just something one can tell. You've shown maturity and wisdom well beyond your age of thirty-seven."

He becomes quiet, nodding his head, letting this sink in, perhaps for both of us. "Curious," he continues, shifting gears. "I understand why you put Hoppy Pearson's loan before the committee today—and, by the way, I agree on upping his loan . . . and on farming some of it out. Hoppy sort of got the two of us together when you were a senior in high school when my Ford went through the ice. Just in case he tries to land an airplane on Lake Knox when it freezes next time, we're better protected the way you've structured his loan, aren't we?" he says, smiling.

"I think so," I say, smiling back, my mind drifting for a moment, wanting to console, comfort, encourage, but assessing that direction is not his intention for the moment.

"No, it was the Aaron Johnson loan. You could have gone ahead, made the loan or declined it without coming to the committee. So, why?"

I pause, collect my thoughts. Politics or the truth? The truth. James Street is laying it on the line, so will I.

"First, the day he came by, knowing the sale might create some friction, I was tempted to find a good reason to turn his loan down, but there were no 'good reasons,' only bad. The man has traits of character anyone would admire, a strong thread in the fabric of society." I pause, think judiciously before proceeding. "Well, I could have gone ahead, approved the loan, and had some members of the executive committee in your office questioning what kind of bank you're running. Just their nature, for whatever reason. I thought I'd just nip that future discussion in the bud today. I was convinced I could get it both ways—a fair loan for Aaron Johnson and the tacit approval of everyone on the committee. That's what happened, didn't it? Regardless of what happens in the future, I've limited the 'I told you so's.' "

James nods, gives a smile, not a surface one, but a smile that goes to the depth of one's being, mostly unseen, yet conveyed. We sit in silence for a moment.

"Gunter, a moment ago I mentioned our meeting when you were a high school senior. There was also the one just before graduation from college."

My thoughts flash, don't drift, to that moment. It's like I'm there, not just my mind, dressed in my suit, looking great, insides torn between hope and despair, two or three years back from the war, almost not able to put one foot in front of the other, but wanting to go forward, needing a steady arm to help me, not letting me fall to the ground. Just hold me a little now, and I can walk, then I'll pick up the pace, run forward. Just need someone to help me rekindle the flame, remind me it's there, stoke it a little. James's voice brings me back to the present.

"Earlier, when you were a little boy, I saw something special in you. Even saw it the day you came to talk to me about the car in the lake. You were the only one to own up to it. That said something to me. I knew

I wanted to talk to you when you were wrapping up your education. Thought you could be a driving force—if you just had the opportunity. I thought you could lead. I was right.

I nod, listen.

"I think you're the man to take over the reins of this bank." James stops abruptly.

President of the bank? Thirty-seven? The other two vice presidents a decade older. Could bring somebody in from elsewhere. Me? Now?

"I thought from the beginning you could lead this institution; now I know."

I sit silent for a moment, then say, "Can you sell the board?"

"Did you sell the executive committee today?"

"Yes," I say.

"And you believed ahead of time you could?"

"Yes."

"I can sell the board. For now, keep all this under the lid. I'll work out the details and get them done," James says.

"Betty?" I say. "This affects her."

"Only if she won't tell . . . anyone. The whole process could go up in flames. Remember, this affects a lot more lives than just yours and mine."

I nod. "Anything else I need to know?"

"Yes. I'm sad to say, it's time for Mary Marbury to retire. She was here some time when I arrived, devoted her adult life to the workings of this institution. We'll have to have a special event for her retirement. A gold watch won't do. Maybe we give her the bank clock; she's been here almost as long as it," he says, smiling. "I'll work through that. I'd suggest we elevate Maggie Stewart or Lynette Garrett, hire from within. Do you have a preference?"

"Lynette Garrett," I say.

"I agree." James nods. "Remember, I hired both of them about five years ago. You always have to think ahead, at least two or three steps. Might want to hire another woman to fill Lynette's spot."

I nod again, just listening.

"Gunter." A lengthy pause, then, "Always do the right thing."

How many times has he said that? I think, my mind fixed on that comment as he begins to stand. I start to stand, a reflex, then get caught halfway up, confused. What to say? All my attention at the present on myself, and the man before me is dying of cancer. Finally, on my feet. "James, the cancer, I . . . I thought I came to the office today as well-prepared as ever for a day, but I wasn't . . . for this. The pain?"

"At the present, tolerable. It's more on my mind than in my chest. When you know your time is limited, you can't imagine all the things that go through it: serious, silly, meaningful. All coming and going, converging sometimes all at once. Events from my childhood, youth, things I haven't thought of in years. I can't imagine all the ground my thoughts will cover during what time I have left."

I nod, listen.

"Doesn't matter how many memories my mind has covered in the past couple of weeks, my thoughts keep coming back to a handful of things—the same ones."

"A handful?"

"That's about it. Thelma, we're one year shy of forty; we were looking forward to that one. Yet, better at this point to look backward, thirty-nine years—more memories and experiences than I can count. Need to recall those, and enjoy every minute we've got left. Looking toward heaven, been learning about it since I was a child. Looks like I'm going to get there ahead of some others." James takes a lengthy pause. "Hope to see my folks and Jimmy. Haven't seen him in years, although I've thought about him every day—no, several times every day. He was our only, Gunter. Can't explain the pain . . . or the hope." Another lengthy pause, then, "There are a few others, some still here like yourself, those who have gone on, people whose presence has been of value to me . . . others that I have been of value to. Gunter, it's important to believe you have been of value to others."

Moisture forms behind the glasses—minute, condensed, almost undetectable, but I see it. He's fighting, holding back, not a man to wear his emotions, emotions at the present a wellspring within, dammed by self-control.

"I'm here when you need to talk," I say, our eyes locked. "I'll say more than one prayer for you and Thelma. A miracle might happen, and I won't need to change desks."

"I would appreciate that," James says.

Our eyes release. I turn, open the door, nod at Mary Marbury, walk across the bank lobby, my mind on James Street. No man other than my father has done more to shape me to be a better man. It's strange—at this moment I'm numb inside the same way I was when I first learned of Everett's death. It hit me later like a spear in my chest, straight through my heart and soul. That will happen. I know it. James Street believed in me at a time when I had almost lost hope. He's helped keep me there—even to this day.

FORTY

A bit uncomfortable, I adjust my bottom on the concrete, Betty's hand in mine, the two of us on the seawall, the sand and Gulf of Mexico in front, tide coming in, full moon, a tad larger than last night when we sat on this same spot. It's our fourth night, final evening, our second getaway—that is, just the two of us—since Tom was born; this our first trip to the beach. As much as we've enjoyed this time alone together, I'm afraid we're going to have to bring Tom on the next trip to a beach. That's what Betty has said more times than I can count, and she was the one who insisted we get away alone!

She was right . . . this time. Strange . . . day-to-day life . . . marriage, with a child. Go to work, come home, work stays with you, on your mind even when you sleep. Betty's been home most of the day tending things, seeing to Tom when he's not in school, or after school when he is. Eat supper together, spend a little time with Tom, watch television, go to bed, repeat the day. Oh, there's nothing wrong with any of this. Got air conditioning in our bedroom, television in the living room. Don't have to worry if there's food to eat, only what to pick from. So different from the poverty of my early childhood. I take so much for granted, including Betty. Certainly can't let the mundane take over when it cones to the two of us.

We've had four days together, and it will be five counting the drive back. Talked more on the way down than we have all year—or, it seemed that way: Tom, our parents, movie we saw last weekend, and Pistol Pete—ours for three and a half weeks, currently spending time with my folks, along with Tom. Found him a place in their carport . . . confused little dog. Then it was James Street and what he and Thelma must be going through. Finally, my future: bank president to be, at least we think so. Discussed that and James with her the first time three weeks ago this upcoming Monday, the same day he told me. My emotions had set in when I told Betty that evening, my voice cracking as I spoke. This is not the way I would choose to become president of the bank.

Betty listened, patient, calm, no hysteria, no elation, knew something was on my mind the second I walked in the house. "What's wrong?" first words out of her mouth. "Nothing," the first out of mine, her being wise enough not to press the issue. Tom was standing there wanting to take me outside and show me a trick Pistol Pete had learned.

No, she went about preparing supper, putting it on the table. Had me pray a prayer, eat, whisked Tom out to play with Pistol Pete before the dishes were cleared.

"Let's talk," she said, and so we did. Her intuitiveness about me is incredible. Sees things about me I don't, like I'm the player on the field about to get tackled from behind, and she's viewing the game halfway up the stands on the fifty-yard line. "Speed left, turn right, slow down and he'll miss you," advice that's right on track, almost every time. I'm beginning to learn to listen. She's a strong woman, also headstrong at times. Didn't see that at all when she was twenty-one, twenty-two. All I saw was a "gorgeous little schoolteacher." Love struck me; I had no clue. I do now.

That night Betty listened, sympathetic for James and Thelma, as well as me, my relationship with James what it is. Then, "Why do you think he wants you to be the president of the bank?" I explained, rehashed what James said, what I thought, to which she replied, "I think you will be an excellent bank president." Then, "Let's not count the chickens; just go about your day. Stay your course, and if things blow up, you're still you and I'm still me. I'm behind you regardless."

She stood, rounded the table, rubbed me on the shoulders, kissed me on the forehead, then left me to think. I offered with the dishes, but it was, "No, you've had a full enough day; just sit here awhile." I did.

I look down the beach, lights dotting the shoreline, the lighthouse standing tall, beaming brightly, then out in the Gulf, four, five shrimp boats, just getting started, a night's work to be done. Just in front of us are two young boys searching for flounder, their lights also beaming, they the only others on the beach. I turn, look toward Betty as she turns toward me. We kiss. No, not the peck in the morning, this one prolonged. We were married nine years ago today. "Need to go some place other than the picture show on our anniversary," Betty said, headstrong, the Monday night I came home with the news from the bank, just before we turned out the lights. I started to raise a fuss, saying, "Better not leave town, something might happen at the bank."

"Lots of things will happen at the bank, whether you're there or not," Betty countered. Then, "Looking back at his life, I know what James Street would have done; he'd have left town with Thelma."

FORTY-ONE

I look across the massive mahogany desk, through the glass, the glass that separates me from the rest of the bank yet allows me to view the goings-on and people to view me. Over the past decade, as the bank has grown, we acquired the lot behind us, added an extension to the building for accounting and record keeping, as well as more parking. The "real banking," however, still goes on in this lobby, all within my view. My first day on this side of the desk, I thought I would need back surgery by three o'clock. Had to get a new chair. For sure, the one James had was behind the desk before he arrived at the bank and perhaps before Mary Marbury came.

Mary Marbury took retirement better than I thought. James handled it almost seamlessly, a delightful affair at the Garden Club. Presented her with a silver tray with silver coffee pot, tea pot, and various other pieces of silver that seemed to equal all the silver dollars in the bank vault. The bank clock is still on the wall. Truth is, she saw her retirement coming, had for a while. Took it in stride. Still unmarried, whole adult life spent here, now retired. Need to pay her a visit soon. Would be the right thing.

My own transition, at least behind the scene, did not move as smoothly. Took longer than James thought, his health deteriorating rapidly as he politicked. Had a special board meeting the first week in October and I was voted in. I think a lot of it was my age, to which James said, "Gentlemen, in November you will have two choices for president, not of this bank, but for the United States; one is forty-seven, the other forty-three. If the whole nation's not too hung up on age, this bank board shouldn't be either."

Anyway, here I sit, late October, and James is at home, but not for much longer. Went by to visit him yesterday afternoon, afraid that might be our last. No miracle yet. At this point it's day to day. I'll give him a day of rest, go tomorrow. Thelma's taking it hard.

Robert Ruggetti ought to be here any minute. Clock on the wall says almost four. Hardly see him anymore, and when I do it's mostly business. I'm the banker and he's the farmer who's constantly trying to expand, try something new. He's building a small empire of cotton and soybean fields. Was even reading me a scientific journal on how to farm catfish last time he was in. A "fish farmer"? I don't know about that. Still, that shouldn't surprise me. While Robert's bold, he's more calculated than Hoppy Pearson. Keeps an eye on the numbers. Today he's coming to pay off the crop loans—a good year, an easy meeting.

It's strange though, twelve years of school together, a groomsman in my wedding, and we seldom get together. Lives go different directions, even when you're in the same small town. And yet, to this day I feel that I could ask him for a favor and he would honor it and I likewise. Today, I have a favor to ask.

Front door opens and Robert enters, dressed in khaki head to toe, already bald on top, just like his father and grandfather. He crosses the lobby, his gait steady, course direct, just like his life, always moving forward. Time for me to move forward too. Out of my seat, to the door, smiling first, speaking first, "Well, where you been?"

"For five months I was out in the heat while you were sitting here in air-conditioned comfort. Got two choices in this town to keep cool, the bank and the picture show, and nobody sits all day at the picture show. If I'd had any common sense, I'd have come seen you in August. But no, I'm out in the fields, paying for your air-conditioned comfort."

I nod. Don't disagree. He's right. "Yes, I sat here so you could have the opportunity to be out in the sun. That's what we're about here. Opportunity. Even furnish chairs for our best customers," I say, gesturing to one as we both sit.

"Many more years like this one and you won't have to farm," I say.

"Not so," Robert says. "My grandfather, mid eighties, is still piddlin' with it. Same will be true with me. Me, I go out and make a pot of money one year, and the next thing you know I'm looking for more land. My grandfather just worked on the land when he got here. I not only like farming it, I like owning it."

"Well, buy land you have," I say, thinking of how Robert has expanded.

"Think I'm gonna take a breather this time, pay down on some of the land after I pay off the crop debt. Just a hunch, like much of life is," Robert says, a faint hint of his grandfather's Italian accent in his voice.

"Just like we discussed on the phone," I say.

"Yes. You got the papers for me to sign to do the transfers?"

"All right here," I say sliding two sheets across the mahogany. "The transfer is for the crop loan, the other to lower the debt on that piece of property you bought two years ago."

Robert studies meticulously, signs slowly (always slowly), and slides the papers back.

Not a lot of small talk today. Had that on the phone yesterday for thirty minutes. Got all caught up on family, that type of thing. Today, mainly business.

"Robert," I say, leaning back in my chair, "remember that stretch of woods I used to go rabbit hunting in with my dad?"

"Yeah, some of the worst cropland in the Delta. Floods easy, and there's more clay than dirt under those trees. Won't grow nothin' but hardwoods. Came with the land when my grandfather bought the place. Trees on it when I was born, and there'll be trees on it till the day I die. Why do you ask?"

"Bought Tom a beagle a couple of months ago and thought we might go rabbit hunting. Haven't done that but once since I was in high school."

"So, you want to go rabbit hunting on that land?"

"Yes, I do," I say, smiling.

"Why sure. Anytime. From now on. Like I said, 'there'll be trees on it till the day I die.' So, I give you permission to go on it till the day you die."

FORTY-TWO

We walk, Tom beside me, Pistol Pete in front, Ranger—Pistol's father—in front of him. Fred Baxter, who sold me Pistol Pete, lent us Ranger for the day—nice, understanding of him. Midmorning and no rabbits. Rabbits might have migrated elsewhere, like folks did years ago after the flood. It's been years since I set foot on this land. Times change.

As we near a thicket, Ranger runs ahead, Pistol Pete behind, perplexed, as Ranger walks in the thicket, nose to the ground, zigging, zagging, sniffing. Both dogs disappear, the only sign of their existence the rustling of the thicket . . . suddenly the bark, noticeably beagle, followed by a shrill, miniature bark, a confused echo as the rustling halts and scamper ensues, beagle barks rapid now.

I stand, poised, shotgun in hand.

"It's rabbit, isn't it?" Tom says, eyes big as saucers.

"Yes," I say, adrenaline flowing.

"Don't we need to run after it?"

"No, we stay put; a rabbit always runs in a circle."

"Why's that?"

"Don't know," I say. "It's just the way it is."

The barking continues, more distant now, adult followed by pup.

"So, we're just gonna stand here?"

"That's right," I say. "They'll all be coming back this way—that is, if Pistol Pete can keep up."

"What do you mean, keep up? He's probably out in front of Ranger. Might even catch the rabbit," Tom says.

I say nothing.

The barks are getting closer, aimed at Tom and me, louder, then, in front of us, the scamper of feet, so rapid that if I blink, the object is lost. I raise the shotgun, bead on the rabbit, straight on it—rabbit straight at me. I pull the trigger, a roar in the woods. I miss, and the rabbit veers to the left. I swing the gun, Tom behind me, Ranger right behind the rabbit barking wildly, tiny yips from a distance behind Ranger. I place the bead on the rabbit, easier this time from a side view. I squeeze, followed by a second roar in the woods. The rabbit falls, instantly. Ranger stops as he reaches the rabbit, sniffing it. Little barks continue, Pistol Pete finally reaching the rabbit, sniffing it, backing off, observing Ranger, again moving forward, sniffing, then backing off, observing Ranger.

I walk forward toward the rabbit as Tom speeds past me, stopping just in front of it. He picks it up, examines it. "Where do we put it?" he says.

I reach to my belt and retrieve a leather throng, tie the rabbit's feet to the loose end, Pistol Pete jumping at the rabbit, pawing it as he jumps. "Get back," I say, brushing Pistol Pete with my hand.

"Do you think they're any more rabbits in the woods?" Tom says.

"Got to be."

"Well, let's go get them," he says, walking ahead.

Ranger looks at me for directions, and I say, "Come on, boy."

He takes off for the next thicket.

Later, almost noon, Tom and I sit on a log, Pistol Pete and Ranger resting on the ground. I've brought biscuits, ham, apples. Tom and I both munch on an apple.

"Do you think we'll get more than one?" Tom says.

"Hard to say, but I think so."

"How many did you get when you were a boy?" Tom says, full of questions.

"Different amounts, different times. I was older than you the first time I came. I actually shot the gun."

"Can I shoot the gun?" Tom says.

"Not yet."

"Why not?"

"It would kick so hard, it would knock you off your feet. It's a twelve gauge."

"A what?"

"A powerful shotgun. Bit much for a seven-year-old. Someday."

"Do you think Pistol Pete will ever be able to chase a rabbit on his own?" Tom says, disappointed.

"Sure. He's just a puppy, less than five months. In human terms, that would make him about three and a half. Dog years happen seven times as fast as human's. Dog your age would be about forty-nine. Just don't live as long as we do. Anyway, another year and Pistol Pete will know more of what's going on. Two years, he'll be a great hunter—that is, if there are any rabbits."

"So, you had a dog?"

"Old Blue," I say. "Disappeared in a flood when I was four, so I never took him hunting."

"Disappeared in a flood?"

"Yeah, a big one. Lots of people lost their lives. Rode in a boat with some folks, and I never saw or heard from them since. Some people just disappeared, others moved far away and never came back; they got a new life, I guess, and tried to forget the old. We moved here."

"You, Grandma, Pappaw, and Everett?" Tom says, then, "Was Everett older or younger than you?"

Everett was older, I say in my mind . . . strange, I've never really discussed Everett with Tom. He is only seven. "He was older," I say.

"Since he was older, was he a better shot than you?"

A better shot than me? No way! I think. Then, think more . . . yeah, he probably was. "Everett was a better shot," I say. "We had one shotgun given to us by an uncle of Pappaw. Shared it with Everett, just like we shared a lot of things."

"And he died in the war?" Tom says.

"Yes. He, and a lot of people."

"Were you with him when he died?"

With him, no. I was a quarter of the way around the world from him. We were both so far from home. Tom's questions are taking me back to that day, the colonel breaking the news, fighting all around me.

"Dad? Dad?" Tom says, trying to get my attention.

"No, I was in Iwo Jima," I say, pausing before continuing, now urged to say more about Everett. "He was a good big brother. Took up for me more than once, the first time when he was only a year older than you." I look at Tom, so small, and at that time Everett seemed so large, so grown up.

"Anything else he did?"

"Oh, plenty. Saved me from drowning when I was twelve. But there was so much he didn't get to do," I say, emotion now in my soul, in my voice (I can hear it). "He always wanted to be the engineer of a train, to travel the railroad tracks all over America. That was his dream. He knew what he wanted to do before he got to high school. Went to work in a railroad yard in Memphis as soon as he graduated and he worked around trains till he went to war. But as far as I know, he never engineered a locomotive. I think he would have told me if he had. Everett wouldn't have kept quiet about something like that." I pause, then keep talking because Tom is listening, looking at me straight on. "If being a good big brother was any indicator, he would have would have been a good father."

Tom looks at me, then asks, "Why didn't Pappaw come with us today and hunt like he used to with you and Everett?"

"Well, Pappaw's in his sixties now and has been on his feet for a good part of the day most of the years of his life. Walking as far as we will today would have been hard on his feet and legs. You may not realize it, but your legs are gonna be sore tomorrow. Mine too."

"What about Pistol Pete's legs?"

"Don't know," I say, smiling. "I don't know how to ask a dog."

"I bet he will be, 'cause he's been running, not walking."

"Well, we better get a move on if we're going to get some more rabbits. If we get two more we'll have enough for Pappaw and Grandma. Matter-of-fact, we better get enough for all of us. Your mom to the best of my recollection has never cooked a rabbit, but Grandma has cooked plenty. We need two more.'

Tom jumps off the log. "What are we waiting on?"

Pistol Pete and Ranger both come to their feet, tails wagging.

FORTY-THREE

"So, you're not willing to expand the loan at this rate?"

I lean back in the leather chair, look across the mahogany desk at Hoppy Pearson thinking, "tightrope." Hoppy's on one end, bank's on the other, me on the tightrope. Then, "Always do the right thing," the last adage oftentimes easy to discern, other times not. This is an "other time." Hoppy is flying high—maybe too much so; the oxygen's getting thin, so to speak. Call it intuition, God-given common sense, whatever. I don't feel right about him expanding. Here's Hoppy, known him since grade school. Pulled me out of a frozen lake. Aside from the oil mill, biggest client we've got. I'll play hell with half the board if we lose him. Still . . .

"Hoppy, you've got a great business going. Have you thought about letting the assets catch up with the debt before you expand further?"

"Nope."

"Have you thought about succession planning? You know, organizing the corporation so that if something happened, you would have the lieutenants in place to keep the business going. You know, you've got over two hundred—"

"Employees," Hoppy says, cutting me off. "We've been over these things how many times?"

"A bunch," I say, smiling, now realizing my comments are to no avail.

"Got life insurance assigned to y'all, case I die. For now, that's good enough for me. All I know is that I want to expand, and a bank out of Memphis has been beating down my door trying to get me to go with them. Say they'll loan me that amount of money at the rate I mentioned."

Thoughts flash of *what if?* No, can't do it no matter what my emotions say. Got to do the right thing. Can't make the offer; it's too great a risk. Got other people's money to keep in mind.

"Hoppy, we'd love to keep you as a customer, but we can't enlarge the loans. For now, that's the bottom line."

We talk a minute longer, shake hands, Hoppy leaves, I sit at my desk staring at another file, pretend I'm working, my mind still on Hoppy. Not all things last forever: businesses, customers, marriages (Hoppy's been through two). I'm old enough to know this, but it doesn't make it easy. It would have been less painful with a stranger. Known him most of my life. Today I "made the call." Next executive meeting, I'll be questioned, not just with questions, but on my judgment, because "I made the call."

"Mr. Wall," Lynette, my assistant, says over the intercom, "There's a most unusual man on the phone calling from Kansas City."

I only know one "most unusual man from Kansas City." Calls me every couple of years out of the clear blue: an attorney, got his own firm, has another child every other time he calls.

"Put the call through," I say.

"Just wanted to check and make sure that bank hasn't fired you yet," coming from the other end of the line, voice as familiar as yesterday, no introduction needed. Missouri.

"No, but I was working on that this afternoon. Maybe if you call back in a couple of weeks," I say.

"Sounds like you might need some good advice. I've always pointed you in the right direction."

"Yeah, let's see, I recall the last time I got drunk, you were the one that helped get me there."

"Then bailed your sorry rump out the next morning. Probably saved your hide from a court martial. Oh, how little credit I am given—at least from Oak Leaf, Mississippi. Here in Kansas City, people pay me top dollar for advice. Can you imagine?"

"Scary," I say. "Me handling most of the money in this town and people paying you for advice. Who would have thought that twenty-something years ago."

"I would have," Missouri says, no joking in his voice. "We grew up fast . . . took on responsibility early."

Silence at both ends.

"Tell me, any more children?" I say.

"Heavens, I hope not! You know something I don't? Five in ten years. Whew! Law school, then Korea; Marge and I got a late start with marriage but we've made up for lost time. We both agree, five's a great place to retire. How's Betty? Tom?"

"Betty's fine. Tom's in the ninth grade, got big hands like my dad, and big feet. He's gonna do some growing someday; he hasn't yet."

We pause again.

"Gunter," Missouri's dead serious. "I was reading an article the other day about the Marines Corps transporting the bodies of those who died from Iwo back to the United States . . . bringing them home."

"I hadn't read that."

"Anyway, I had a dream last night." Missouri stops. "Do you have dreams?"

No one's asked me that except Betty. I've never described them to even her—my wife.

They're infrequent now. Disguised, masked in representation, not graphic. Can't remember them when I wake. God's been merciful.

"Not like I used to," I say.

"Last night," Missouri says, "It was you and me, walking the beach at Iwo, vivid as can be, up to the graves, searching for names, people I haven't thought of in years. Seems like we spent the whole night looking." His voice cracks and he stops.

I wait. Don't know what to say. Finally, "Haven't thought about that in years. The article you read must have triggered it." I pause, then, "If it hadn't been for you, I'd have never walked to those graves . . . and would have regretted it the rest of my life."

Another lengthy pause, then, Missouri says, "We're two fortunate guys, both of us married to the same wife we started with, families, my career beyond what I could imagine, and I think you'd say the same. Lots of guys didn't land with their feet on the ground when they got back. Some could the first go-around, but couldn't the second, Korea the nail in their coffin. But you and I survived—and prospered. Anyway, you were on my mind this morning, been on it all day." Missouri stops. I wait for something else, but that's all.

"Fortunate," I say, wanting to say more, unable. I've seen him once since I married; about four years ago he came through in a station wagon with Marge and three children headed for the Gulf. But talking today, it's just like we were walking a beach, peering off the back of a ship, or on top of a mountain in Hawaii bragging about wild game—all last week. He hasn't told me a lot today, same me to him. But we understand a lot.

"When you coming to Kansas City?"

"I'd like to someday," I say.

A moment later we hang up. I'm glad he called. Hope he's saying the same to himself. I know he is.

FORTY-FOUR

Sunday dinner: roast, rice and gravy, butter beans, rolls—just like my childhood. Betty doesn't often go all out for Sunday dinner, like Mom in years past. Even Mom's thrown this towel in. She and Dad have the energy to get to church on Sunday, but that's about it. From what I hear, nobody makes a big Sunday dinner. But today, we have a guest: Bobby Joe Martin, ninth-grade friend of Tom's. Father died last year of cancer, same time Travis Farrell, the preacher, corralled me into teaching ninth-grade boys. Wanted me to teach eighth-grade Sunday school, but boys bounce off the wall at that point faster than I can catch, so he let me settle for the ninth grade. Tom's there now. Don't know what or how I'm doing other than I'm trying. Today their hormones were exploding in unison, Tom's the worst of any of them. Didn't have an hour like that all week—even when I lost one of our biggest clients, Hoppy Pearson. An hour afterward, end of the sermon, my pulse still over a hundred.

"Going to pass the roast, honey?" Betty says, her face saying, "Let's eat."

I pass the roast (took me all of forty seconds to carve), rice, gravy, butter beans, rolls, Betty saying, "What did you all cover in Sunday school this morning?"

Tom speaks, his fork of roast beef midair, "The world's first recorded redneck."

What the . . . my thought stops as Betty says, "Please go on."

""Yes, first one," says Tom. "Esau. First thing off, his father, Isaac, marries Rebekah, sister of his uncle, Laban. Guess that made her his aunt. He married his aunt!"

"Tom, I don't remember any of that being in the lesson," I say.

"I know. Read it in the Bible. Genesis. Anyway, when Esau was born he was 'red all over,' not just on his neck, but that part of the body would be included."

"Tom, we've taught you not to judge people by color," I say, a true statement, although I'm trying to head the conversation in another direction. I've had enough fun for one day.

"I know . . . behavior,'" Tom says. "Next thing I read, he's marrying two women in one year. How would you feel if I did that?"

"Upset," I say, starting to say more, until I look at Betty, who's laughing. She's laughing! Thinks this is funny, and I'm uptight as ever. Been like that a lot lately. Constantly serious . . . responsibilities.

"His folks were upset too, but not because he married two women. It was 'cause they were Hittites. Read that in the Bible too," Tom says, grinning straight at me.

I look across from Tom at Bobby Joe, our guest, subdued smile, observing, listening, just as he does at Sunday school. Don't know what he's thinking, ever. Just know he's there most Sundays. Tough age for a boy to lose his father. No telling what goes through his mind.

"Anyway, Esau . . ." Tom resumes his conversation without comment, ". . . worked in the fields, and liked to hunt while Jacob hung around the tent and liked to cook. Mama's boy. Yep, the story of the redneck and mama's boy."

I chew on roast beef, as Betty smiles and says, "Well, is that all there was to it?"

"No," Tom says, more serious this time. "Esau trades his birthright to Jacob for a bowl of soup, just 'cause he's hungry at the moment. What a dummy. Also a redneck."

"Go on," Betty says, listening to every word.

"Later, Jacob and his mom trick Isaac, his father, into giving him the blessing, not Esau. They are deceptive; they lie to him," says Tom.

"Do you think that was right?" Betty says.

"Heck no," says Tom.

"Why do you think that happened?" Betty comes back.

"Not sure."

Not sure? I spent the better part of an hour distilling pure truth, and my own son comes away "not sure." Actually, I'm not sure why they acted that way either, except for greed. Nevertheless, none of them were listening to a word. They need someone else teaching. I'd do better with adults. I'd reason with them. How does one reason with a ninth-grader?

"They did the wrong thing," says Bobby Joe, first words I recall him saying since we sat. "I mean, they basically lied—and stole."

"That's correct," I say.

"In the end, things worked out. God's good came from evil; the twelve tribes of Israel came from the sons of Jacob. God's hand was in it," Bobby says.

Someone was listening, I think. Some one. At least one. I ponder, what to say? Tom's being cute; Betty thinks that's funny. No, look, her face has turned serious.

"That was excellent, Bobby," I say, nodding, wondering if he was listening today, was he also listening last week? The week before? My heart and mind connect, if only for a moment. Need to be a little more patient next week. I chew on the roast beef and that thought.

"Anyway, Esau's descendents were all Edomites. 'Edom' means red. Get it? Jacob's descendents were Jews, and Esau was the 'father of the rednecks.'" Tom gets the last word in.

FORTY-FIVE

"Well, you got to play just before the half. Coach thought you could get the team down the field passing," I say, trying to console Tom.

His face is long.

"You also led that drive when you went in, late third quarter," I say.

Tom shrugs.

It's a tough senior year. Guess a lot of athletes go through this, most. But Tom's my son—that's different. His hands kept growing, as well as his height to match his long feet. Was scheduled to be the starting quarterback this year. Pass the ball. Then came integration, a new coach, and the wishbone—the offense where they run the ball . . . then run it some more. Need a fast running quarterback . . . not Tom.

Change comes—sometimes slowly, sometimes overnight. Integration in Oak Leaf had been gradual: no riots, no marches, pick which school you want to attend, choice is free, most folks get along, then a court order. One school, not two. Immediately, in Tom's senior year. Springtime, he's the quarterback. Fall, he's on the bench. New coach says, "Run the football."

"I'm proud of the way you've played, your effort," I say. "As hard as it is, you need to keep your chin up. So far you have. Don't let that change."

Tom looks up, nods. He's grown so fast. Yesterday, he was born, and today, he's taller than me—a blur. Don't want to see him hurt, want his path to be smooth. Trouble is, it's not that way for anybody; some folk's bumps come later, but they will be there. It's been a big adjustment combining two schools into one, especially for a senior. Oh, but in the end, it was probably the right thing for society. On the other hand, a seventeen-year-old doesn't look at it that way; neither do most forty-something-year-olds.

"Look what Mom's left out for you," I say, looking at the spread of choices for making sandwiches she prepared before retiring exhausted. It's going on midnight. We're exhausted, too.

"Not hungry," says Tom.

Don't blame you; you didn't play much, and your team lost. Why not spoil him a little, I think, as I start to fix Tom a sandwich. "Turkey, roast beef, cheese, or all three?" I say.

"Roast beef and cheese," Tom says, after hesitating a moment.

I apply mayonnaise, mustard, roast beef, cheese, and for good measure lettuce and pickles, and pour a glass of milk. "Here," I say, sliding him the sandwich. "What you don't eat, Pistol Pete gets." I smile.

Tom smiles, takes a bite of sandwich, a gulp of milk. He's hungry—just didn't know it. I watch as he takes another bite; dark fuzz surrounds his chin. Shaved this morning. I look at his arm muscles; he's lifted weights since junior high. Back at his face, still young, no wrinkles.

"What you staring at?" Tom says.

"Your face," I say, totally honest.

He shrugs, blushes a little, keeps eating.

"Want another?" I say.

Still chewing, he nods. I repeat the procedure.

Minutes later, Tom stands, starts to carry his dish to the sink.

"Leave it there," I say. I'll put it all up." Then, "Mom and I are proud of the way you've kept your head up. So far, this year hasn't turned out the way you thought it would. Things that seem so important right now, someday may or may not be. For now, keep your head up and your feet moving forward."

Tom nods, heads toward bed. Don't know whether he heard what I said. Don't know if I said the right words, just know I tried. I place the tops on the mayonnaise and mustard, then look down at Tom's plate, a quarter of a sandwich left, a good treat for Pistol Pete, but not enough. I remove another piece of bread, a slice of turkey, put them on the plate, and open the back door, awakening Pistol Pete. He rises slowly (as he almost always does these days). I drop the food. Although the rest of his body is slow motion, his jaws aren't.

"Happy dog."

FORTY-SIX

I sit, reclined in the recliner, my study of the Sunday paper exhaustive, my expertise in world affairs, sports, and the funny papers immense. Tom's first weekend home from college, Ole Miss. Tried to convince him to go to my alma mater, Mississippi State, their arch rival, but it wasn't to be. Gave up trying to persuade. His future. His dreams, not mine. Great weekend—till he starts to pull out, Betty all teary-eyed just like the day he left for college. Been up twice to football games and saw him all of an hour both times.

"Why doesn't he want to be with us?" Betty had asked. "I can't understand."

I can. Boy wants his space. Also wanted a fresh start after a tough senior year in high school. Looks like he's getting it; also looks like he's got his focus. Hope he keeps it.

I glance over the paper at "Sleeping Betty," knocked out on the couch. Cooked all weekend, the grand finale, Sunday dinner, that main event followed by the cleanup. She rests.

Ring . . . ring . . . I lay the paper down, reach for the phone.

"Gunter Wall?"

"Yes."

"Mr. Wall, Rob Sturgis, Mississippi Highway Patrol."

"Yes," I say, blood pumping through my body, concentrated in my chest.

"Father of Thomas Wall?"

"Yes," again.

"Your son's had an accident. Ran head-on into a bridge. Must have gone to sleep. He's dead."

I say nothing. Numb. Pumping of blood gone. Lifeless. Thoughtless. Vacant. Void.

"Mr. Wall . . . Mr. Wall . . . Mr. Wall?

"Yes."

"Sir, I didn't know how to tell you, other than to tell you," a voice of concern, empathy.

I don't know what to say, what to do.

"Taking your son to . . . Car's totaled, hauling it . . . Number to contact us is . . . Give it some time, call this number . . . Had to run a blood alcohol test, a formality, a requirement, but he must have dozed off. Car a quarter mile back saw it happen."

Can't comprehend, half-listening. I get a pen, a pad. I write down a number and Rob Sturgis hangs up the phone. I stare at Betty. She stares at me, knows something is wrong. Knows the worst, before I say a word, eyes already moist.

"Tom's dead," I say. "Ran into a bridge, halfway to Ole Miss."

Betty's sitting upright, blank, silent. I start to rise. Body's shackled. Get up, Gunter. Get up, Gunter! I say loudly in my mind. I rise, weight on my shoulders, arms, legs unbearable. I almost fall back. Across the room I go, one foot in front of another, hardest walk of my life. You've been here before, Gunter. You've been here before, the words in my mind. Then, no you haven't; this is different.

Memories flash in ten short feet: a baby, learned to crawl, seven-year-old birthday, the dinner table, walking off a football field, and today, getting in a car, watching it disappear down the street. I reach the couch, one arm around Betty, now two, seated right next to her I squeeze and feel no more life than the dummies I practiced on in basic training.

I struggle to talk, yet I say nothing. Silence fills the room. I squeeze harder. No response.

"What do we do?"

What is she saying?

"How do we get Tom back here? I want my boy."

Right now she's thinking a step ahead of me; I can't think that far. Used up my mind and body just crossing the room and squeezing her. Finally, I gather enough energy to say, "I don't know. I wrote down a number to call." I sit a moment longer, then say, "Let me go outside before I call. I need open space."

Betty nods, leans back on the couch as I rise, head out the back door, Pistol Pete rising slowly, perplexed look as I pass. I stop, look across the lawn, in the trees, then up in the sky inhaling, exhaling, trying to free the pressure within my body. I turn, pound the house with my hands time and again. I look down at a bewildered Pistol Pete.

God, a boy's supposed to live longer than a dog!

FORTY-SEVEN

Front row of the church, Betty next to me, her mother next to her, Mom, my other side, Dad next to her; all of us years Tom's senior. Incongruent. The church is overflowing. I'm the bank president, and everybody knows Betty, involved in town and church, Tom's friends galore. He was well liked . . . and respected.

Closed casket is in front of us, Travis Farrell, a man five years my junior in the pulpit begins to speak. "Let's pray," he says, as heads bow.

My mind drifts, a thousand places at once, his words unheard by me. My thoughts then settle on a moment in this same church, same preacher saying, "I baptize you, Thomas Everett Wall, in the name of the Father and of the Son and of the Holy Ghost," with twelve-year-old Tom in the preacher's arms emerging from the water within the baptistery, Betty's hand in mine, her grip tightening as Tom comes forth from the water. My thought is interrupted by human movement around me. I open my eyes.

"Whenever a person of youth passes on, I am asked why? It's the same question I ask. I used to try to explain this to family and friends in theological terms, like 'God allowed, or caused it to happen. In time we will see why'—and perhaps we will. I have also learned that, while still in our earthly state, perhaps we won't.

"A young boy, five years old, that's my first recollection of Tom when I first came to Oak Leaf. His parents, Gunter and Betty, had him here every Sunday at that time, and continued to do so until the time he went off to college a month ago. I, as many of you, watched Tom grow from a small boy, through grade school, junior high, and high school—normal stages of life to this point. Tom grew spiritually, as he grew educationally, and physically. Six years ago he was baptized in this sanctuary. I remember the moment well, although I needed some help from Betty and Gunter as to exactly when."

Travis pauses, gives a brief smile to Betty and me. My mind drifts as soon as his eyes cut away. Mere mention of the words "six," "grade school," "high school," "baptize," evoke memories. Tom's waist high, darting out a door to play, dinner still on his plate, Betty and I finally giving in, letting him go. We stand at our back door as Tom tosses a stick, Pistol Pete retrieving. We're at the dinner table, the three of us, Tom no longer eye level, his height a notch above mine. Memories, pleasant memories flow, for the moment blocking out the pain of his death.

"If we aren't given the answer to 'why?' what are we given? First, memories. I encourage Gunter and Betty, as well as the rest of us, to recall those moments that you value. Savor them. Relive them in your mind. Share them." Travis pauses.

Relive them in my mind. Woke up this morning, two or three o'clock, my mind racing, memory after pleasant memory, then, "Tom's not here," the jolt of reality. Haven't shared those memories with Betty yet, nor she with me. Twenty-one years we've known each other. Knows me like no other, and I her. Yet, this last couple of days—a barrier. Betty's distant. Can't get through. I reach out and hold her, clothed bodies together, and yet not. Can't explain—Betty . . . or myself.

"A few minutes ago, when recalling Tom's life, I referred to 'normal stages,' his progression of life until Sunday afternoon. Please don't take this harshly, for harshness is not my intent. Truth is, Tom has gone through another normal stage. For those of us here today, myself included, that's hard to say, even hard to think. And yet why do we gather weekly? We gather collectively to worship the Lord, great, all-knowing. So much we don't know . . . so much. But we are given a promise, that of everlasting life, not in our bodies as we know them today but renewed ones in the presence of the Lord. We, as believers, have that to look forward to. It's a promise. Betty," he pauses, "and Gunter. You will see Tom again."

The last words plant in my mind—a seed in fertile soil, unseen. Faith is . . .

A prayer, out the church in the car, on to the cemetery, all a blur, my mind drifting the whole time. Graveside, tent shading the late September sun, my eyes looking up, through massive oaks, cotton fields beyond, white as white can be, then back to the casket. To my side, corner of my eye, Betty sits erect, motionless, staring.

Travis Farrell, stands before the coffin, Bible in hand, "I read from Paul's first letter to the Corinthians. 'For this corruptible must put on incorruption, and this mortal must put on immortality. So when this corruptible shall have put on incorruption, and this mortal shall put on immortality, then shall be brought to pass the saying that is written, Death is swallowed up in victory. O death where is thy sting? O grave, where is thy victory? The sting of death is sin; and the strength of sin is the law. But thanks be to God, which giveth us the victory through our Lord Jesus Christ. Therefore, my beloved brethren, be ye stedfast, unmovable, always abounding in the work of the Lord, forasmuch as ye know that your labour is not in vain in the Lord.'"

He closes the Bible, prays, the crowd leaves from the sides and behind us, and although I never look behind, I know it's a crowd. I sense it. Then cars pass, one, then another, many, through the path between the oaks, to the road back to town, then gone, leaving behind Betty, me, my folks, her mother, Travis Ferrell, gravediggers, our drivers. Travis shakes my hand, hugs Betty, then leaves, as do my folks and Betty's mother, leaving Betty and me, our driver, the gravediggers. We sit, stare, say nothing. Time passes.

"It's time," I say, standing.

Betty hesitates. I reach out, my hand back of her arm to coax her as she slowly rises. At the back of the tent a young man stands, silent.

I recognize him, but for the moment am at a loss. That's . . .

"Mr. Wall," he says, extending his hand timidly as we near. "Bobby Joe Martin . . . sir."

Bobby Joe? I think, still disoriented, all of life so confused at this moment. Then, Bobby Joe, Tom's friend, just graduated with him. Known him for years. Today, grown-up looking. "Yes, Bobby Joe," I say, delving deep within to smile, as I shake his hand.

"I'm so sorry, sir," he says.

I nod, Betty does likewise.

"Sir, I don't know what it's like to lose a son, but I did lose my father when I was thirteen." Bobby Joe pauses, then, "It hurt. Hurt like a knife in my heart. Anyway, I wanted to tell you I thought the world of Tom. He was there at a time in my life when I needed a friend—and so were you."

Me? What did I do? I ask myself, perplexed.

"The lessons you taught me on Sundays helped me settle back in, sort through things. I just wanted to say thank you for Tom, and to you."

"I appreciate you saying that," I say, fighting not to cry.

"If you ever need anything, sir, let me know. Same to you, Mrs. Wall."

FORTY-EIGHT

I lie in bed, pillow propping me, Betty to my side as I read in silence, same routine as last night, and the night before. It's not that Betty and I don't talk. We do. "When will you be home?" "What's for dinner?" "I'm tired." All so different than before Tom died. All so different than most of our marriage. I reach for the light and start to turn it out, when Betty rolls, facing me, not touching me.

"I've been doing some thinking," Betty says.

Great, I think, those words are a preface for something at best negative, oftentimes disastrous, occasionally kooky. I say nothing, play the part of the bank president.

"There's going to be an opening in first grade; teacher's going to have a baby in February, and she's going to stay home," Betty says.

I start to interrupt, but don't.

"I think I'll apply."

"Do what!" I say. "You can't do that."

"Can't do what?"

"Well, what I meant to say is, 'there's no need,' " I say, thinking I've chosen better words this time.

"No need," Betty says, eyes glaring, teeth gritted. "How do you know? Tom's been dead almost three months, and you keep saying, 'things are gonna work themselves out. Just give it time. Time will heal things.' Well, I've already figured out that time by itself doesn't heal anything. You go to work everyday, all day, and before nine o'clock I'm done for the day."

"Well, you've got lots of time to see your friends. Lots of time for service work," I interrupt, without thinking.

The glare intensifies as Betty says, "You're not listening."

I start to interrupt again, but don't.

"I mean, you do something with your life everyday, and I did too, until recently. I spent eighteen years serving you and Tom. I changed diapers, cooked, fretted, and didn't mind for one minute, because that's what I was supposed to do. Well, Tom's gone. Hope to see him again someday, but it won't be while I'm alive. I've done my grieving for almost three months, and I came to the realization this week that I'm still alive; I'm not the one who died." Betty stops, arms crossed, her look straight at me, piercing.

"But, Betty, honey. You don't have to go to work. We've got more than enough money. We can find some service work."

"You're not listening to me! You're not listening to me! You're not—" Betty pounds my chest with both fists, once, twice, a third time.

She's never struck me before, nor I her. I'm in shock, blood pumping through me wildly, like my body is to explode, but I don't move. I don't speak.

Betty reclines, doesn't speak. We lie in silence, light still on. Finally, Betty, voice calm, says, "I can't have another baby, and we're too old to adopt, but my life's not over. I went to school to teach children, and if I had never married, I'd be doing it to this day. There's a possibility for me out there right now. The school is at a pivotal point—folks uncertain, second year of full integration. I was a good teacher. No, I was a great teacher, and I can be again. Besides, I think it would be a good example for the town for the bank president's wife to teach."

Betty pauses. "No, that's not the real reason. Lately the words of Tom's friend, Bobby Joe, have rung in my mind like a bell that won't quit ringing. 'Lessons you taught me.' Can't quit thinking about those words."

FORTY-NINE

Sunset, an orange ball through the haze, half-exposed, glistening, sinks slowly, as we sit mountaintop—twenty-one years married today. No year of marriage like this past one. Our only son died ten months ago. Tested to our limits, both of us.

Hard to explain, a wound deeper, far more piercing than those of the war. Strange, I came back from the war and went through the motions of life, one foot in front of another, sometimes feeling pain, other times dead. But, I always kept putting one foot in front of the other, most of the time slowly. This time had no choice . . . not really. I'm in charge of the bank, so I'd better show up—and that I did. Putting one foot in front of the other is easier this time. It's the times I stop . . . sometimes in the office when the door's shut. Other times at the house in the living room when Betty's not present. Times in bed two or three in the morning, Betty asleep, other times in bed with Betty awake.

These moments of despair have become less frequent. Prayed to God like never before—that is, with the exception of a time two or three months after Tom died. I went through the valley of hollowness, and came out of it when Betty pounded me on the chest. The removal of the wall between us (the one built when Tom died) didn't start that night. In the short run, it got taller, sturdier, broader, almost impenetrable, each of us adding bricks to its height and depth.

Betty began teaching first grade in February. Soon after that we quit adding bricks and started removing them. We? Yes, we. Can't explain it, how we got distant and angry to start with, because we had never been that way. Also, can't explain how we started getting more civil, less distant. Somehow, we just stayed together. Yeah, that was it for a while. "Stayed together." No, "under one roof" explains it better. Wasn't much "together" in it emotionally, physically.

Strange, the physical, all my tenseness in the pit of my chest. I'm sure Betty had that, too, but hers was more a flinch in her abdomen, lower pelvic area. Out of nowhere, riding in the car, watching a show on television, reading a magazine, she'd reach both hands like she had just been stabbed. At first I didn't ask. Then I did, and she'd shake her head. Finally, a couple of months ago she talked. Birth of a child, death of a child, all tied to the area of the womb. "It all goes back there," she said.

Soon after that, I came home from work late one day, tired, emotionally spent. School year was over, so Betty had time on her hands again. She led me to the dining room for the first time since Easter Sunday—candlelit, dusk upon us. We sat, oddly enough, at opposite ends of the table, Betty's eyes fixed on me to the point of discomfort as dusk turned to darkness.

She said, "Leave the dishes, I'll get them tomorrow," as she rounded the table, extending her arms, tugging me upward, then down the hall into the bed, the room totally dark. First the buttons to my shirt, then my shoes, my pants, underwear. Then her blouse, skirt, bra, panties, our skin against skin for the first time since Tom died.

Bewildered, perplexed, aroused, never all those at once. Betty and me, close as ever months earlier (or so I thought), then distant as enemies, gradually seeking and finding peace. Then this.

Moments later, we lay beneath the sheets, bodies unclothed, my hand in hers as she began to cry.

"Why are you crying?" I said.

"I don't know."

Didn't know, or wouldn't say? I didn't ask. That was two months ago.

So, here we sit today, the sun dropping downward, more rays than orb. Same place we stayed twenty-one years ago on our honeymoon, same cabin. Today has been a sustained, emotional high. I've had one or two before in the course of my life; like the day I viewed California's shore from the front of the ship returning from war. The feeling in my chest, arms, thighs, when I stepped on the dock, then onto the shore. I can't explain it, a mixture of pleasure and hope, causing me, if only for a day, to forget my pain. Today has been similar—only different in that it's been shared with another. No wall.

"Are we going to spend the night out here?" Betty says, gently tugging on my arm.

"Not unless we plan on getting arrested. They might do that if they caught us out here naked," I say.

Betty smiles, we stand, walk, enter the cabin, cross the sitting room to the bedroom, a light in the closet keeping us from stumbling. Then onto the bed.

Betty unbuttons her blouse, me my shirt, the pace brisk for both of us. She giggles, I laugh. Yes, I laugh. Done that more in one day than the past eleven months combined. All clothes off, I pause upright, my knees on the bed. Betty atop the covers lying down. With the light from the closet, I view her head to toe, then back up again, settling on her face. It's fresh, smiling, youthful. Yes, youthful, more so at this moment than I can remember. I stare at her face.

"What?" says Betty, perplexed.

"Just looking," I say.

She smiles.

I pause a moment, then lean down and kiss, my body collapsing on Betty, my skin against hers as she wraps her arms around me. I'm smiling too, even on the inside.

FIFTY

"Thinking about buying the Parson's place," Robert Rugetti says. "Three hundred acres."

"How much are they asking?" I say.

"Eighteen hundred an acre, but I won't go over sixteen."

I start to shake my head, but don't. Have to force myself. Land prices are going up and up. Cotton and soybean prices aren't. Those opposite forces can't go on for long, I think, as they've been doing it for a while.

"Stop and think what you were paying five years ago," I say.

"Nine hundred," Robert says. "But, they're not making any more land."

"Not making any more land. Not making any more land," I repeat in my mind. Everybody coming in for a land loan says that. Maybe I should say, "But you're not making any more money." All it would take is a drop in crop prices or a spike in crop loan interest rates, and nine hundred an acre makes sense again.

"How much land do you have now?" I say, knowing the exact answer already.

"Four thousand acres, give or take," Robert says.

"And how much of it are you still paying for?"

"Gunter, you know the exact amount, and to the penny, what I owe," Robert says. "What's this game you're playing?"

"Robert, the seventies are coming to a close."

"Yeah, in three months. So, what's your point?"

"What I mean is, you've had a nice run. Or should I say we've all had a nice run. I appreciate loaning you money. I appreciate loaning a lot of people money. But, here's my concern. Has the price of cotton doubled in the past five years?"

"Who are you kiddin'?"

"Soybeans?" I say.

"Nope," Robert says.

"Then why the price of land?"

" 'Cause they're not making any more of it."

"What do you plan on using the land for, Robert, a shopping mall?"

"Eight miles outside of Oak Leaf? Hell no. I'm gonna grow cotton on it."

"And sell it for the same price you'll sell it for on your paid for land," I say.

"Are you telling me not to buy the land?" Robert comes back, indignant.

"No, not at all. I'm merely suggesting you don't buy it now at sixteen hundred dollars an acre. I think you should wait and pay twelve hundred, maybe even a thousand."

"Are you crazy?"

"We both know the answer to that. After all, I was among the first and last to try to go across Lake Knox in a car. Only thing is, before you go calling someone else crazy, you might want to do a little self-examination," I say.

"Speaking of that, the craziest of all is Hoppy Pearson. I hear he's on thin ice again. People aren't buying planes from World War II for crop dusters like they used to. Folks want something newer, faster, more dependable. And there's a limit to eccentrics, even in New York and California. Can you believe that?"

I nod, smile, listen. A tinge of Italian accent comes through when Robert gets animated. He's animated.

"Give the land purchase a little time," I say.

"How long?"

"Three years, four maybe," I say.

"Three or four years! There you go crazy again," Robert says, his animation at the next level, hands moving wildly.

"Yeah, I think I'll be picking up some Mark IVs in the next year or two. It's a hunch. A strong one."

"Repossessing cars?"

"Yeah, the expensive ones."

"So, you don't think I should buy more land . . . at this time?" Robert says, solemn, serious look. "You've never told me this before."

"I've never thought it before."

Robert shakes his head. "Came in here today knowing what I wanted to do. Now I don't know."

"Think about it. The Parson's place is not the only piece of land that will ever come up for sale. And wouldn't it be nice to get five hundred acres for the price of three hundred. This time, just be patient," I say.

Robert stands. "I'll call you back, let you know," He shakes his head as I stand and walk him to the door.

I return to my chair, stare at the mahogany desk, then glance up, my eyes on the bank lobby, the goings-on, the bank clock reading a quarter of four.

"That most unusual man from Missouri is on the line," Lynette, my assistant, says on the intercom.

"Put him through," I say.

"Did I interrupt you counting money?" Missouri says.

"Gave up," I say. "Much too large a number to keep up with, and that's just the part that's mine," words I would never say locally. "What do I owe the honor of this call to?"

"Boredom, I guess. Law practice comes and goes. At the moment it's gone, but it'll pick up again. At least it has every time so far. No, just thought I'd check in. It's been a while and I just wanted to see how you're doing."

"Hanging in there," I say. "Bank board thought about us expanding, buying another small bank or two, the very thing I tried to get them to pursue about three years ago. Now, I don't want to," I say. "Timing's bad. How about you?"

"Practice of law is feast or famine. Fortunately, I've had more feasts this past year. Good thing, two of the five are in college, and two more right behind them. Only got one out of college so far. I'll be working till I'm eighty."

Missouri's voice softens. "Friend to friend, can I ask you something?"

"Yes," I say, detecting the sincerity in his voice.

"I don't know whether I should talk about my children. On the one hand, I figure you want to know, but on the other . . ." Missouri pauses.

"Missouri, I want hear about your children for as long as you want to talk. It couldn't please me more," I say, knowing exactly what he is trying to say. It's been eight years since Tom died. The pain I still feel comes during moments of quiet, not in the midst of noise or people. Maybe I'm in the car driving, or it's late at night when I'm reading or when I'm looking across an open field after the cotton's been picked—and yes, the middle of the night, in the dark when I awake, memories of Tom, as well as occasional memories of war.

That tough marine couldn't have been more sensitive in his own way when Tom died. I called him about a month after the funeral, the first time I had the strength to make the call. We talked for the longest time. He calls me unscheduled whenever something unique (at least to him) happens and that's every couple of years. I'll call him in between.

Missouri starts up again, "Did I tell you about the time ten, twelve years ago when I pulled up to a stoplight, Marge and me on the front seat of the station wagon, three on the next seat, and the two youngest in a pop-up seat facing backward. They had the back window rolled down and were peeing out of it. Thought about reenlisting in the Marines that day, leaving Marge behind with them. She's the one who took advantage of me those times, if you know what I mean. Five in ten years. Five in ten years! I'll be working till I'm eighty."

Missouri pauses. Wow! I think he's as revved up as Robert was. Am I the one doing this to them?

"How's Betty?" Missouri's voice softens, more serious again.

"She's fine," I say, meaning it. "She's wrapped up in teaching first grade—so much so she could do it till *she's* eighty. You can't imagine a woman more in love with what she does. Hey, and we're fine. She's got me into taking a trip every year, the two of us. Went to California last year."

"Not to Camp Pendleton?" Missouri interrupts.

"No, but we did make it to Beverly Hills. That hotel is still there, but different. All fixed up. Started to call you and ask if you would pay for a room, but I got to thinking about you paying for five children."

"How many daiquiris did you have this time?"

"None," I say and start to make a cute remark about what I did do, but I refrain. "So what else is going on?"

"You won't believe," Missouri says. "I was buying a cup of coffee at some fast-food place yesterday and started to pay for it. Little girl says, 'No need, got a policy we don't charge for coffee with senior adults.' If a young man had said that to me, I'd be over the counter on top of him, like he was Navy. But with the young girl, I just said 'thank you.' But, I'll guarantee you this, it'll be twenty years before I set foot in there again. Are we really that old?"

"No, Missouri, fifty-five's not old anymore, particularly for a fellow who's working till he's eighty."

A moment of silence comes, Missouri finally saying, "Heck, we're both lucky guys. Fortunate all the way around." He gets quiet again, finally saying, "Come see me sometime."

"I need to do that," I say.

A moment later we hang up. I stare at the mahogany thinking fifty-five, that's not too old—and not too young—then, Betty and I should go to see them someday. We really should.

FIFTY-ONE

"Still can't believe it," Robert says, shaking his head. "It's been two months, I guess."

I nod, agree.

"He was so successful. Made more money than you and I could count, then he lost most of it. Still can't believe it happened," Robert says, head shaking from across the mahogany desk.

I can, I think. Saw it coming twenty years ago. Hoppy constantly pushed the boundaries of life. Merely a matter of when and how, not if. When interest rates hit twenty percent, even the rich quit buying toys. Hoppy could hardly give them away—or so I heard. Took to delivering them himself, so he could save a dollar. Plane he was delivering to the multimillionaire up East crashed in the mountains of North Carolina. Left behind wife number three, and a twelve-year-old boy—not to mention two grown children from wives one and two.

Strange. Time plays tricks on you. The day he died I had two flashbacks: the duel and the car in the lake. It was like they'd all happened the same week, but they hadn't. Still, in my mind it seemed that way. So much went through my mind in the days following. Grew up with Hoppy, knew him all my life. But when I went to visitation at the funeral home, his wife hardly knew me. Son didn't. Lives drift apart. And if I live to a hundred, I'll not forget him pulling me out of a frozen lake. Fact is, I should have never been on the lake in that car to begin with. Didn't have the courage, or the common sense, to say no. I can see that today clear as clear can be. Other fact is, if Hoppy hadn't had his wits about him and the courage to act, I'd have drowned that day. Looking back, I know that for a fact also.

So there I was, almost a total stranger, saying to his wife and son, "When I was a teenager, he saved me from drowning." And them standing before me, a crowd in front and behind me, the two of them looking perplexed, not a clue as to what I was saying. And yet, it was important to say it. It was true. The moment was also awkward, and I felt awkward inside. The man's dead. In some way, because of him, I'm alive. Can't explain it.

And I feel for his wife and that child in particular. Don't know the details, but word's out his company is folding. They've got that burden, as well as the emotional. Said a prayer for them. No, several.

"You there, Gunter?" Robert says.

"Yes," I say, not knowing what I've missed.

"Well, there's one thing I'm glad of," Robert says.

"What's that?"

"You didn't let me buy that land two years ago."

"What do you mean, 'Didn't let you buy the land?' You decided that yourself."

"You know what I mean," Robert says. "Three hundred acres at sixteen hundred an acre, on top of the land I already owe on, and in addition to crop loans. This twenty percent interest rate is for the birds. Wisest business move I ever made, not to buy. I'm gonna make it. Gonna make it fine. Lot of folks aren't."

That's right. Never had a time like this since I joined the bank. Got folks that aren't going to make it. Lots of them. With these interest rates, in a year's time a family can't pay for a doorknob on their home mortgage. We just finally had to quit lending on most loans. Regarding defaults and bankruptcies, ultimately the bank is going to be okay. I thought things were going to be tough, but not like this.

"Tell you the truth, Robert, my motives were purely selfish," I say.

"How's that?"

"If you lost your land, I wouldn't have a place to go and spend time in the woods."

"Never have been able to figure you out on that one," Robert comes back. "Only thing those woods are ever used for is cutting firewood, and you going out there. The land's worthless."

"Oh, but it's not," I say. "Rabbit hunted on it with my dad, my brother, and with Tom. Got more memories there than I can count."

"But, you don't rabbit hunt anymore," Robert says.

"No."

"Well, whatever. You're welcome to go there for the rest of your life."

"Thank you," I say, glancing at my watch.

"Guess I'd better be going," Robert says. " 'Bout time for you to shut this place down."

"Yes it is."

Robert stands. We chat a moment longer. He leaves. I work awhile reviewing loans. I too leave, drive home, hug Betty, turn on the news.

Hardly ever watch the news. Never home early enough, but today I am.

"Staggering interest rates continue. No end in sight, the final words from the business front. Today the body of Vivian Lemur was found in her Los Angeles home, her death an apparent suicide, an overdose of pills. She had been dead for almost two days."

Footage of Vivian from the 'fifties flashes across the screen, pale smooth skin, perfect smile, shapely body, graceful gait. She waves, crowds all around her, then a scene from a movie, and another.

"Lemur was one of the top box-office attractions of the 'fifties. However, her career began to slide in the early 'sixties, her last movie made in 1965. The three-time-divorced actress had lived in near seclusion for the past decade. Vivian Lemur, dead at age fifty-seven. She is survived by a brother."

Look, anchorman is all smiles, turns on the smile quick as a light switch. "The story of two panda bears when we come back."

Oooh, the volume! That man standing in a furniture showroom. Punch the remote.

Silence.

What difference does her dying make to me? Happens to everybody. It's because when I left California on that boat heading across the Pacific, she was an unfinished dream. On a boat, on a mountain in Hawaii, no girls around, only thing I had was a memory, that of the last girl I visited with, to that point the prettiest girl I'd ever met. So, the memory of Vivian goes from a seed in the ground to roots, to a trunk, to limbs, to leaves, to flowers of all colors: blue, yellow, red, purple, small, large, ever-changing. This became what I thought about when I got a moment alone, staring at Hawaiian sky, closing my eyes at night, all of it a dream, a pleasant dream, a dream of hope, something, someone to look ahead to for when I returned after the war. Never saw her again—I mean, in person. Me, just a kid from small town Mississippi. Probably would have never given me the time of day if our paths had crossed. But she gave me a dream, a pleasant reoccurring one in the midst of my loneliness and fear. She gave me a reason to look ahead.

My life's turned out fine. Plenty enough pain—lost my son, the greatest pain I ever had. But I've got important things to do every day . . . and I've got Betty, together over thirty years.

Vivian Lemur didn't fare so well. Sad. Tragic. Makes me wish I could have done something. Maybe if I hadn't passed out . . . who knows? What if I had seen her when I came back from overseas, explained to her the dream. She'd have looked at me like, "you're peculiar, a psycho, weird"—or would have laughed. And yet she gave me that dream— pleasant, hopeful. So yeah, this moment I feel like I've been kicked in the stomach.

"Gunter . . . Gunter . . . Gunter!"

"What?"

"You look like you're in outer space. Are you okay?" Betty says.

"Yeah."

"Well, you don't look it." Betty seats herself next to me, pulling the remote from my hand, replacing it with her grasp, her hip and thigh pressed against mine.

"Just a lot on my mind," I say.

"Tell me."

No, I think. That would serve no purpose, no way to explain. Would bring up more questions than answers—life has taught me that. "I think some food would relieve my woes," I say. "What's for dinner?"

"Baked chicken, still in the oven," Betty says, knowing I've changed the subject, that I've not told her what's on my mind. She releases her hand, moves her hip and thigh a few inches away. Life's taught her some things too.

FIFTY-TWO

Betty, me, candles flickering, fire roaring, blanket around both of us, close, snuggled on the couch. Ice storm, no electricity, a romantic moment on most occasions—tonight, just trying to keep warm. What a day. Bank's got to keep going. Three generators—one for the branch, two for the main building—just to run the essentials. May have to try to get somebody to drive two hours for a gas haul tomorrow to keep the generators running. No, two hours of normal driving, but on these roads? Schools are out until who knows when, so Betty's at the house. Power lines down for a hundred miles. Nothing like this one in my lifetime. It'll be weeks. Life's constantly got its challenges.

Betty moves closer, head on my chest. "Know what I was thinking?" she says.

Strange, this time I don't. Oftentimes I do, after almost forty years together. "What's that?" I say.

"It takes an ice storm to bring out the candles and a fire."

"Yeah," I say with a light smile and a chuckle.

"We ought to do this more often." Betty's smile glows in the candlelight. "We have quiet times like this when we go away together. We ought to do this more often when we're at home."

"Guess it's the tension of day-to-day life," I say. "Plenty enough of that to go around. Stuff on my mind."

"No excuse," Betty says.

She's right, I think. Again, I'd probably be an old stick-in-the-mud if it weren't for her. Heck, I was a young stick-in-the-mud when we met.

"Lying here tonight my mind's wandering," Betty says. "You know, no television, no newspaper, just quiet, the only sounds our breathing and the crackle of the fire. A moment ago I was in the backyard, sitting in a lawn chair under that big oak, Pistol Pete chasing Tom as he ran around its trunk."

I picture this as Betty speaks, vivid as if I'm in the lawn chair.

"Couldn't think those thoughts years ago—not without pain," Betty says. "Not that there isn't a trace of that when my thought starts to fade. But up to that point it's pleasant. In some ways, seeing Tom in my mind now is closer to actually being with him than it was a decade ago. While I don't think about dying at this time, I see it on the distant horizon. Couldn't say that of myself in times past."

"Don't say that word," I say, interrupting.

"What's that?"

"Dying."

"You weren't listening. I also said 'on the distant horizon.' "

"Yeah," I say, tenseness leaving my body as quickly as it entered.

"Know what else I was thinking?" Betty says.

"No."

"I was thinking of the day we met."

"Yeah," I say, my body smiling, if there is such a thing.

"You looked so young."

"Love at first sight," I say, hoping the answer this time will be "yes," my answer for her.

"No, it took five or six looks. My love for you warmed slowly, like a crock pot," Betty says. "But I did trust you. 'Trust at first sight.' Still do."

My thoughts go back to the day we met, Betty's thought the stimulus. I see her in the bank lobby, my heart leaping, fluttering, the girl I must pursue. And then minutes later we meet, a surprise encounter when I'm not pursuing, Betty right next to me, youthful, clean, beautiful. A meeting of coincidence? No, couldn't have been.

The fire pops, sparks flying against the screen bring me back to the present. Betty smiles, the same smile she gave me at the drugstore counter that day almost forty years ago. No, this time it's deeper.

FIFTY-THREE

I sit at my desk. No wait, it's not "my desk," it's the bank's. So easy to confuse things. Turn seventy next month. Retire next month, not totally my call. I work with Thriftsmart . . . Thriftsmart, not Bank of Oak Leaf. Those two names don't sound like they belong on the same planet. Been like that for over a year.

How many times has this run through my mind? Can't count. For years I tried to convince the board we needed to grow, do it by acquiring banks in other small towns, become a household name in this part of the state. Only time they took me seriously was just before interest rates went to over twenty percent. If we'd have tried it at that time, the whole ship would have sunk. Tried to get them to do it later and every time I brought it up, "What would happen if right after we made the purchase, interest rates went to twenty percent? Can't think of such a thing. Answer is 'no.' "

I remember Oak Leaf when I first moved here, five years old, a few streetlights downtown. Place was growing with oil mill people moving here during the Depression. Oil mill closed last year. Consolidation. Seems like that's what is happening to everything, including banks. Yes, that's what happened; we got "consolidated."

"Better act now. Don't know if the opportunities at this price will come up again." "Everybody loves it." "Train'll leave the station, and we won't be on board."

What train? They closed the passenger depot twenty years ago, and the freight train quit running last year. No oil mill, no need for freight trains. And downtown? Yeah, "down" town—not even half full. First, the stores started moving to the edge of town when the four-lane was built. Then folks started getting on the four lanes to do their shopping elsewhere. "Bigger places, that's where the deals are." Just imagine thirty-something years ago when I had to sell that idea of letting Aaron Johnson, a black man, buy a building for a grocery store in that same downtown. He's still there. Town would suffer a loss if he closed. White folks drop in to buy stuff there now. "It's so convenient. Don't have to get on the four-lane and go elsewhere!"

Anyway, you either grow or shrink. Town quit growing, and the bank quit growing, so the board went shopping and found a buyer. "Thriftsmart." Here I sit, looking at a bank lobby so classic it could go in the Smithsonian, and outside the sign says "Thriftsmart."

Speaking of the Smithsonian, I could go there too. "Dinosaur Exhibit." Yeah, that's where they'd put me, right between a stegosaurus and tyrannosaurus rex. "Survived a flood and one of the two great world wars, but he couldn't survive banking. "He failed to adapt," the prophetic words of Mr. Terry, Oak Leaf's superintendent, spoken on my high school graduation night.

So, the new "financial services company" says they want me to stay on until I'm seventy to ease the transition. Whose transition—mine or theirs? Have yet to figure that out.

When I came on as bank president, James Street orchestrated the deal. He trained me to the hilt, then passed me the baton. This last six months I've had thirty-five-year-olds coming in from out of town to instruct me. Oh well, I was only thirty-seven when I took over the reins. But I know ten times what these guys know. I could teach them . . . Never mind, they talk, they don't listen.

Hey, we used to give out a gold watch when someone retired. Imagine that today, a gold watch—digital.

Well, the other night on the couch it's Betty and me, the TV off, and we start talking. (Smart woman. Knew to cut the TV off. Knew we needed to talk, me going first.) I start giving her my dinosaur speech. She listens, let's me talk till I've run out of things to say. Then she starts asking questions, making comments. You lent the money for this business, that business, this farmer, that farmer. Husbands died and had never taught their wives the difference between a credit card and a savings account, and you took the time with them. If you hadn't stood up to the board when interest rates went through the roof, bank might have folded.

Strange. I never gave Betty the details of any of those. Never. Kept people's finances confidential. But, she could pick up from my general comments. Very accurate. Very understanding.

An hour and a half later she says, "Well if you are a dinosaur, I've liked dinosaurs since I was a child. Maybe now I get to love one."

FIFTY-FOUR

A quarter of the sun protrudes over the haze of a North Carolina mountain, Betty's hand in mine, this the view from our condo balcony. No more cabins—all bulldozed. Cabins didn't make it, but Betty and I did, fifty years today.

"I liked the cabin better," Betty says.

"Yeah, but this place is climate controlled, big glass all across. Sit inside and view it all, or just open the sliding glass door and walk three feet—perfect for me, two years shy of eighty."

"Liked the cabin better," Betty says.

We sit, quiet time together, more of this the past eight years than the first forty-two combined. We've traveled together, not once a year but three or four times. Nothing expensive, just going places together, some we've been before, others not—still creating memories.

Describe us? Retirees of almost everything but life itself. Betty stayed with teaching till I was retired from the bank. "Was retired." Yeah, that's a good way to say it. New bank just moved on without me after I helped with the transition. I thought I had a few more good years in me. Still do. Quit teaching ninth-graders at church a year or so after that. Just couldn't connect with a boy almost sixty years my junior. I didn't have a clue. Still, I felt a sense of purpose doing what I did. Retired myself on that one. Folks at church are just too nice to tell you to move on. Two days a month Betty and I do volunteer work at a hospital. We visit with . . .

"Gunter. Gunter Wall! What planet have you drifted off to this time?"

"What's that?" I say.

"I can tell when you're not here. I've been carrying on a conversation with myself the past minute."

"What about?"

"Never mind," Betty says, shaking her head, slightly perturbed.

The sun's just peeking over the top of the mountain—more rays than sun. Sat out here the past two nights till it was gone, replaced by countless other suns, tiny dots in the dark, the moon a half one, bright as bright can be from a mountaintop. Don't do this at home. Too many trees. No, we just don't do it, except on cool, clear nights in the fall.

". . . so, we need to dig up those bushes," Betty says.

"Uh-huh," I say, just catching the tail end, wondering what bushes she's talking about. I do these "uh-huhs" more than I used to. Mind wanders. Fortunately, it hasn't wandered off.

"Are you hungry?" Betty says.

"A little bit."

"I'll go fix us each a sandwich."

A sandwich? I think. What if I had suggested that on our anniversary, say, forty years ago? "What are we doing for our anniversary?" Betty would say. "I don't know. Thought maybe you could make us some sandwiches," I'd say. Once. Yeah, that's the exact number of times I could have said that. Then, might not have been here tonight—that is, with Betty.

I stand, extend my hand to assist, open the sliding glass door, guide her through, my hand on her arm.

"But the kitchen is that way," Betty says, pointing, my guiding her the opposite direction.

"I'll be hungrier later," I say. "I might even make the sandwiches."

"What? What are you trying to do?" Betty says from the doorway of the bedroom.

I try again, all my might, this time getting her six inches off the carpet.

"Gunter, you're gonna kill yourself. And what would I tell my friends? A seventy-eight-year-old tried to carry me into the bedroom."

"Yeah, tried and failed," I say, half-kidding, half not.

Betty shakes her head as I catch my breath, recompose.

"All right, come on," Betty says, this time her guiding me. "Same old, same old, fifty years in a row. I'd think you'd get tired of the routine . . . tired of me."

"Never."

Betty pulls back the bedspread and sheet, seats herself on the side of the bed, leaving me standing as she removes her tennis shoes, then starts with her blouse, a button at a time. Next, off come the bra, pants, and panties.

"Gonna take your socks off?" I say. "Kind of like you in that two-piece."

"No, my feet get cold," Betty says, leaning back on the sheet, head on the pillow in her "two-piece."

"What?" she says, staring straight at me. "What are you looking at?"

"You."

FIFTY-FIVE

"Can't believe it's November," Betty says.

"Wouldn't have known if I hadn't looked at the newspaper," I say. "Also said it was Wednesday. No need to keep up with what day it is unless one of us has a doctor's appointment, or it's Sunday. 'Didn't see you at church Sunday, was one of y'all sick?' 'No, just forgot what day it was.' Hasn't happened yet, but it will."

Betty doesn't laugh, says, "Gunter, most times I can believe you can't remember what day it is, but we had two dozen trick-or-treaters last night."

The fire in the *chiminea* has turned to coals, red hot. Here we sit, Betty and me on our patio since mid afternoon. Built the fire two hours ago; jackets came on when the sun went down. I take my eyes off the coals, look up, countless stars, three-quarter moon with a fall tint, no clouds.

"Know what this reminds me of?" I say.

"What?"

"Top of a mountain in Hawaii. My platoon gathered around a pit, Missouri's another, coals foot and a half deep, with a ram on ours and a pig on his. Made the grills out of barbed wire."

"You did what?" Betty says. "A pig and a ram on barbed wire? I can describe that in one phrase: 'Missouri, a most unique man.' "

"Yes. Anyway, those were the brightest stars I've ever seen. That night stands out in my mind. Actually, that day and night. One of the best times in my life."

"Gunter Wall, we've been married over fifty-five years and you've never told me about that."

"I haven't?"

"No."

"My platoon, Missouri's had the weekend off. Let us go to the top of a mountain above Camp Tarawa. Nothing up there but some concrete block buildings, food, hot beer . . . lots of hot beer."

"Concrete block buildings? Hot beer? One of the best times of your life?" Betty says.

"Yeah. Highest mountaintop I've ever been to. Shot a ram; the only one I've ever shot. Brooklyn helped me drag it down the mountain, to the jeep."

"Brooklyn? Did everyone you served with have the name of where they were from?"

"No," I say, "Just a handful: me, Missouri, Brooklyn, Big Tex (a tall guy in Missouri's platoon), and Frenchie—a kid from south Louisiana."

My voice breaks by the time I say "Louisiana." Tears form in my eyes, an uncontrollable reflex, my emotions torn between the memories of the ram hunt and the fire, and the deaths of Brooklyn and Frenchie, all this over sixty years ago.

I clear my throat, brace, take a deep breath. A smile comes to my face. Yes, tears to smile. "Well, Brooklyn had never driven a jeep before, or anything. Thought we'd never make it back to the platoon, the two of us bucking like we were bronco riders. Got back and everybody was mocking us—and Missouri and Sarge, too. Missouri shot the pig. Truth is, I think most of them had got into the hot beer. Well, we dug these pits, drug in some volcanic charred trees, put down some barbed wire, and had a cookout. I remember sitting around those pits, coals red hot, guys talking, me looking at their faces, young, oh so young. Then I would gaze up at the stars. Stayed up all night . . . didn't want it to end."

"I've met Missouri. Where are Brooklyn? Frenchie?"

"Dead. Died on Iwo Jima."

My eyes again moisten. Strange, I'm smiling and tears are flowing. Can't explain.

"Anyway, tonight, the clear sky, the stars, the coals . . . brought back memories," I say. Then, "Know what was missing that night?"

"No."

"You. If you had been by my side, I'd have been the most envied man on that mountaintop."

"If any woman had been by any man's side that night, he'd have been the most envied man on that mountaintop."

I start to agree, but don't. Wisdom. "I'd have been more envied than anyone," I say.

"Why have you never mentioned this to me before?"

"I don't know. Really don't. It was such a fine day, such a fine night. Guess it's a bit painful. I mean, so many sitting around that fire were wounded; so many died. I've discussed about everything in life with you, but not the war. Never wanted to. Wanted to push much of it away. But I will say this."

"What?" Betty says.

"To this day, I've never respected any men more than those I served with—dead and alive."

Silence follows. I gaze at the coals, then at the stars.

"Never roasted a ram or a pig," Betty says, breaking the silence. "But, I do recall a big fire, my Uncle Jed's farm, early fall when I was twelve or thirteen. I helped gather firewood. Didn't stay up all night, though."

"Never told me that before," I say. "Anything else you've been holding back on?"

"Won't say," Betty says, her smile radiant, the coals providing the light.

Betty's smile diverts my attention from the stars and the fire. "I prayed for us to have a long life together, the night of your surgery, the day Tom was born. Prayed on the way to the hospital. Prayed the whole time you were in surgery."

"You have told me that more times than I can count. Still makes me warm inside, every time you do. God's granted us a long life together."

I smile.

"Are you hungry?" Betty says.

"Sure."

"I'll go warm us up some potato soup in the microwave. You just stay here and enjoy the fire," Betty says, rising slowly, her trip to the door lengthy.

"I'll help," I say, starting to rise.

"No, enjoy your fire. Doesn't take much to microwave."

I keep my seat, enjoy the fire. Another few weeks, and it will be too cold to sit out. Time passes as I watch the coals dim slightly. I look upward, start to count stars. Can't. Too many, far too many, the heavens so expansive, so incomprehensible. Can't fathom, I think. Then, like a bolt of lightning from the cloudless sky—Betty! Should have called me in. Might just be her being nice, letting me have a bit of solitude. But still, I ought to check.

I rise, pushing mightily on the wrought iron chair arms, straining my thighs. I shuffle across the patio, through the door, to the kitchen. I stop—most abrupt stop in all my eighty-three years. Betty's facedown on the kitchen floor, motionless.

I stare—head to toe, then back again, my heart pounding, blood rushing wildly. I walk toward Betty, fast as I can, fall to my knees, try to turn her. Try again. Again! Got her turned over. I put my hand against her neck, against her heart. Nothing. I place my ear against her nostrils. Breathing? Breathing! None.

"Betty! Betty! What now? What now? . . . I'll call 911. Where's the phone? Where's the phone!"

I crawl two feet, place my hands on the counter, lift myself, adrenaline throughout my body. Phone's on the counter. I reach, dial, listen to the phone ring the other end, a person picks up. "Come quickly," I say, interrupting the lady on the phone before she can complete a word.

"Sir, what's the matter?"

"It's my wife, my wife! She's on the floor. No pulse. Send an ambulance. Send an ambulance!"

"Sir, you're at—"

"407 East Meadowlane, Gunter Wall."

"We'll send an ambulance."

I push the button, leave the phone on the counter, drop to my knees next to Betty, placing my hand in hers. I hold it tight.

No response.

"They're gonna be here any minute," I say. "Any minute now . . . what's taking them so long? What's taking them so long!"

I get quiet. Don't move. I wait.

Knock on the front door.

I place my hands on the counter, rise, walk toward the front of the house fast as I can, open the door. "She's on the floor in the kitchen," I say before they speak, two men.

They dash toward the kitchen, the direction I point, leaving me to follow. I turn, head that way, quickly as I can.

"She's dead, Smitty," I hear one of them say before I reach the doorway. "Has been for a while."

I stop in my tracks, my mind racing a thousand directions at once. Of all the emotions of my life, varied as they've been, never this exact one. Young Tom, my folks, Everett, my dying troops, mountaintop in Hawaii, day I first saw Betty, day Tom was born, time with Betty—fifty-five years.

"Sir . . . Mr. Wall?" the young man says from in front of me, having entered the room, my not noticing.

"Your wife, she's . . ."

"Dead," I say. "I knew. I was just hoping."

"I'm sorry, sir, it's— "

"Do me a favor," I say. "Would you two young men step outside for a moment?"

"But, sir—"

"I'll be fine. Just want a moment alone with my bride. Won't take but a moment. I'll come get you."

"He'll be all right, Jim," the young man says to his partner. "We'll give you a moment," the other young man says, directing his partner toward the door with his head.

A moment later, I'm on my knees, both hands on Betty's wedding hand, my clasp a gentle one.

"Sorry I waited outside by the fire so long. Used to be the bank that kept you waiting, now it's a fire. You've been so patient with me. You were just taking care of me, weren't you? Been doing that most of my adult life. I was one lonely soul when I met you. Did I tell you it was love at first sight? Yeah, countless times. That was one thing I did right. For the things I didn't do right, please forgive me." I become silent.

"I'm smiling at you. Wish you could see my face," I say, stroking her hair, looking at her face, a face once smooth as cream, now cracked and creased by years of life. Same person. No, a better person, better than the day we met.

"Wish you could tell me about joining Tom. Oh, I'd like to see him, too. Well, someday I'll see both of you." I become quiet again.

"Today has been one of the best of my life. Why, just a while ago I was looking at you—so radiant, the coals of the fire giving me just enough light to see your smile. Remember what I'd say when you'd ask me countless times what I was looking at? Remember?

" 'You.' "

FIFTY-SIX

"Come on in," I say from the doorway. "Can I help you with that cake, Marie?"

"No, I've got it. Just need to get it to the kitchen," she says, entering, Robert Rugetti, her husband, basket in hand, right behind her.

"Hello, Robert."

"I'd shake your hand, but it takes me two hands to hold a basket now. Marie's fixed you a month's supply of lasagna, and a quart of her homemade salad dressing," Robert says, towing behind Marie, who is halfway to the kitchen.

"Made us some coffee," I say, bringing up the rear.

"Really, Gunter, it's getting late and—"

"We'd love some," Marie interrupts.

Moments later, Marie has the cake on the counter, lasagna and homemade dressing in the refrigerator, and all three of us are sipping coffee.

"Sure you don't want to have some cake with me now?" I say.

Marie and Robert both shake their heads, saying, "No," in unison.

"Almost couldn't fit that lasagna in the refrigerator. You can freeze it if you like. We waited a couple of weeks before coming by 'cause we thought you might need it more now. Matter-of-fact, we're gonna bring you something every month. Robert and I were talking about that just the other day."

"Oh, you don't need to do that," I say.

"What else are we gonna do?" Robert says. "Get tired of watching TV. Only get six hundred channels on the satellite dish. If I don't watch out, that remote might graft to my hand."

"Yeah," I say.

"No, Marie and I were talking, and Italian food is just what you need. Besides, it'll give me an excuse to come see you."

"Sounds fine to me," I say. "And no, Marie, I'm not going to freeze the lasagna. Some of that other food may just go to waste, but I'm gonna have lasagna tonight."

"Cotton crop was poor this year. Had that drought all summer. Last year it was the hurricane. Dumped as much rain on us as I can ever remember at picking time." Robert pauses, sips coffee, then, "Don't know why I get so worked up about farming. Don't own the land anymore; cash is in the bank, and my three sons are running things. Worked all that out a decade ago."

"It's your sons, and your grandchildren," Marie pipes in. "You want them to do well."

"That's not all," Robert says. "I was in those fields from age five to my seventies; it's in my blood." Robert waves his hands as he speaks. Reminds me of his grandfather, and his father. I smile.

"He cuts on the weather channel every morning at five," Marie says, head shaking. "It's his favorite channel. I think he's addicted."

Robert gives me a grin, waves his hands once more.

"Are your sons gonna let me come out to that tract of land in the woods?" I say.

"Are you crazy?" Robert says, hands now waving like windshield wipers on full speed.

"Yes. But you've known that for decades."

"How many years since you were last out there?" Robert says.

"Twenty."

"You know, one of my grandkids, Eddie—Robert Junior's youngest— just started rabbit hunting out there. I had no idea there were any rabbits still in the Delta, but that patch of woods has them. Imagine that. Anyway, he's got a beagle, just like you used to."

Beagle? The mention of the word creates emotions, multiple types, shooting through my body like lasers, head to toe.

"Anyway, when do you think you'll be coming out?" Robert says.

"Saturday," I say.

"I'll tell Robert Junior and Eddie."

"Either of you need any more coffee?" I say.

Both shake their heads as Marie says, "We'd better be going."

"Wait a second, Marie," Robert says, this time motioning with one hand. "Did I ever thank you for convincing me not to buy that piece of land about twenty-five years ago?"

"Actually, it was twenty-seven, and that's about the number of times you've thanked me," I say, smiling.

"Well, today I'll make it twenty-eight. Times were hard the years following and we almost went under. If I'd added one more ounce of debt, we would have lost it all. My grandfather came here from Italy with all his possessions in one bag and that's about what my family would have been left with if I had made that purchase. So, thank you. Now we can go, Marie," Robert says, standing as he speaks.

Thirty minutes later I'm dishing lasagna on a plate, placing it in the microwave, pouring Marie's homemade dressing on lettuce, then sit down to eat a feast.

What's that? Phone rings right when I sit down, area code 816 on the caller ID. I search my mind, start not to answer, then realize who it is.

"Mississippi, that you?" comes from the other end.

"Yeah."

"Not waking you up, am I? It's six o'clock; thought it might be past your bedtime."

"No, but don't call past ten," I say.

"Don't worry. Haven't stayed up that late in over five years."

"Well, what have you been up to today, Missouri?"

"Let's see. Hmm . . . I went to the office and opened my mail. You know, it's a good thing having two sons follow you in a law practice. Gives me a place to go hang out for a couple of hours. Have all my bills sent there."

I shake my head.

"Tell you what I didn't do today," Missouri says, baiting the hook.

"What's that?"

"Didn't go to the doctor, and didn't take Marge—a good day."

I smile, say, "How is Marge?"

"Better. She's over that crud she had two weeks ago when we talked. Hey, other than taking six different pills a day, she's fine. I got her beat. I take eight. Can you imagine?"

"Yes," I say, counting mine in my mind.

Things get quiet for a moment, then, "How are you holding up?"

"Fine," I say, pausing, then, "Truth is, it's kind of quiet around here. Lonely."

Missouri's silent on the other end. Must be listening, really listening.

"Fifty-five years waking up next to the same person every day, then two weeks ago that all changes." I pause. "You know, your situation is different than mine. Five children. Yesterday I was in my attorney's office updating my will, just in case. I'm leaving a little to Betty's two nieces, the rest to the church and charities. Even had to make arrangement for who is going to make arrangements. Imagine that! Anyway, I'll adjust. Folks around here have been good, checking on me and what not. Hey, even got folks calling me from Missouri."

A moment of silence, then, "Well, just wanted to say hi," Missouri says. "If you ever want to talk, call anytime—even after ten."

"You know," I say, "It's kind of crazy. Couple of days ago I was recalling the two of us peering off the back of that ship the afternoon we left Iwo Jima. More Marines on board than one could count, and we were the only two back there staring toward Japan."

"Yeah, I remember that."

"Well, the strange part is, it seemed like just last week, you standing there, tall, emaciated, unshaven, looking off the back of that boat, sun going down. Had a lot of memories of long ago the past few days . . . a lot of memories." I go quiet.

Missouri stays silent, then finally says, "Well, I'll be checking on you."

"Look," I say, "really do appreciate you calling." I start to hang up, but don't. "Missouri?"

"What's that?"

"It's been almost twenty years since I've seen you, although we've talked on the phone more times than I can count. You came to Oak Leaf the first time while I was still in Japan just to let my folks know I was gonna make it. I knew Mom was fretting over me, but I didn't realize until almost three years later how concerned my dad had been. You came to Mississippi to be in my wedding, and have come through Oak Leaf four times on the way to Florida. I had such good intentions to bring Betty up to Kansas City to see you and Marge. Even had it scheduled two years ago when I got sick. All those times I could have made it and didn't. It's a sin. I didn't do what was right."

"Mississippi, quit that nonsense. You've always been there and I've always been here, and we've both always known it. You know what you mean to me and I know what I mean to you. In life, that's what matters. Now, we better hang up quick before we both go to getting soft. Okay?"

"I appreciate you."

"Same on this end."

We hang up.

I've gone soft. Tears are pouring down both cheeks and I know he has tears, too. I just know it.

FIFTY-SEVEN

W ho could that be?

Doorbell rings a second time.

I'm coming," I holler, thinking I surely don't move like I used to, as I head to the front door, finally reaching, opening it.

"Mr. Wall," the young man—that meaning early fifties—says, tone of voice like he has circled the block a time or two before gathering the courage to get out of the car, come to the door.

I search my mind. Know who he is. It's just been a while. He's older. It's . . . "Bobby Joe Martin, come on in," I say, thinking, my goodness, it's been a decade, he has gray hair.

He nods, gives a smile of relief. "Wasn't sure I'd catch you."

"Don't do a lot of traveling these days," I say, ushering him through the living room to the kitchen. "Coffee or a Coke?" I ask. "Coffee's already made. More than I can drink; still haven't gotten used to making it for one."

"I'll have some coffee," Bobby Joe says, "I can get—"

"No, have a seat," I say, motioning to the table. "What do you want in it?"

"Black."

"Well, you've got to bring me up to date," I say, carrying the cup to the table, placing it in front of Bobby Joe, seating myself.

"Sarah, my oldest, is out of school, teaching English at Franklin High. Bobby Joe Junior will be graduating from Ole Miss next spring—we hope," he says, smiling with his last comment. "Julie is still teaching grade school, and I'm still practicing accounting. Been doing that thirty years now. Can't believe."

"How's the practice?"

"Excellent. I really started doing well when my gray hair became the majority. Guess folks think I know what I'm talking about now."

"That was my biggest problem when I became bank president—not enough gray hair. Ultimately, they retired me, 'cause all I had left was gray, and not much of that. Perception carries a lot of weight—too much. But that's life."

"Sorry I missed the funeral," Bobby Joe says. "Mrs. Wall was so kind, helpful to everybody. I was away in Memphis seeing a client."

"Ton of folks there. Betty came here in 1950. Heck, she taught over five hundred first-graders. 'Miss Wall, this,' 'Miss Wall, that!' 'My favorite teacher.' 'Best teacher I ever had.' Amazing, isn't it? She only taught school for two years until Tom died, and I tried to discourage her from going back then. I was definitely wrong—terribly so."

"I guess you're allowed one or two wrong calls if you live to . . ."

"Eighty-three. No telling how many wrong calls I've made, but marrying Betty wasn't one of them. Great life we had," I say, smiling.

Smiling? Yeah, I'm smiling. All those people, one after another, saying what she meant to them. Makes me smile, all the way to the core of my soul. Better enjoy the moment. It'll be over before I know it, and I'll go lonely, face turned from sunshine to rain.

"Quite a pile of pictures you've got," Bobby Joe says, commenting about the mounds in front of us, some still in boxes, others scattered on the table.

"Yes," I say. "Haven't looked at some of them in so long. I had to dig deep in my mind to remember the settings. Had them stored on a shelf in our bedroom closet in these shoeboxes. Look, there's a picture of Tom's seventh birthday. Betty took these before I came home with a dog. Didn't take any more after the dog and I arrived. She went into shock, then into orbit."

"That's me," Bobby Joe says, pointing in the background, just behind a saucer-eyed Tom, poised to extinguish seven candles.

"Hmm. Never would have guessed. You look a bit different now," I say, smiling. "Maybe it's the gray hair."

"Maybe." Bobby Joe returns the smile, then, "What's in that small box?"

"Oh that, the cigar box." I reach, open, pull out its full contents, one handful. "These are pictures of Mom, Dad, my brother, Everett. Don't have a lot. A picture was something precious back then," I say, looking at the black and white, now tinted yellow. "That's Dad and Mom in front of their first house—first house meaning the first one they owned, and the only one."

"You favored your father," Bobby Joe says.

"Guess so," I say, holding the photo a little closer, studying Dad, then Mom, wondering how the both of them felt at the time. An answered prayer—their home, not rented.

I look up from the photograph of Mom and Dad. "Oh, they were fine people, both of them. Although I've known some great men during my life, none had a more lasting impact on me than my father. He was bedrock, a moral man if there ever was. Wasn't big on talk. He just went about doing the right thing. And he loved my mother."

"Really?" Bobby Joe says, a warm smile on his face.

"Mom died of cancer about three years after young Tom died. Came on fast and she was gone in no time. Hit me hard, but nothing like it did Dad. His heart starting wearing out on him as soon as Mom passed away and he was dead within six months. That was a tough year for me, as you can imagine."

Bobby Joe is listening intently and I feel like talking.

"Now, that's my brother, Everett," I say, pride in my voice.

"What branch of the service?" Bobby Joe says, pointing at the photo.

"Army," I say, looking deeper at the photo, as if it is a great painting. What was on his mind, I wonder. Whole world was on fire when this was taken, and he was heading to fight the fire. Did he think he was coming back? Did he know? I start to tear up.

"What happened to him?" Bobby Joe says, obviously noticing my mood shift.

"Died in Europe, February, 1945," I say, sorrow mixed with pride. "We were gonna go places together. Ended up on near opposite ends of the world. I made it back, and he didn't—like a lot of people."

"My dad was in the Army," Bobby Joe says. "The Germans didn't kill him—cancer did."

I remain quiet, guard my words, then say, "Fact is, because he came back from the war, he had you, and you've had all the opportunities of your life. Now me, I hope to see Everett again. Sometimes hope and faith may be all we've got, but that can be a bundle. Now, losing your dad when you did had to be tough on you—and on your mother. Had to be."

He nods, eyes look like he's thinking, says, "You sound like you're still my Sunday school teacher."

"Only chance I've been given in over a decade," I say, half kidding, half not.

"Where'd you get that box?" Bobby Joe says.

"Which box?"

"Cigar box. Haven't seen one of those in years."

"You wouldn't believe," I say.

"Try me."

"That box contained every cent my folks had when the flood came in 1927. Every cent. We were rescued from a rooftop with the clothes on our backs, a couple of blankets, an ax, and that cigar box. Everett and I weren't even wearing shoes. Feet so cold, you can't imagine. Dad stuffed that box in a bag so he wouldn't let go of it or get it stolen. By the time we got to the hills, it was almost empty. That, my friend, is the most important cigar box you'll ever see. Since my folks passed on, I've kept these treasures in it: pictures of Dad, Mom, Everett. Know what's ironic?"

"What's that?"

"Dad had enough money in it to let us survive–and another family, too. He paid to get some folks on board a boat, when most would not have. Probably less money in that box than I've got in my wallet right now, but it was enough. Enough for us to survive and provide a little charity–charity that probably meant sink or swim for that family. See that single dollar bill you're looking at right now? Dad left it there as a reminder that we were provided for with surplus. All those years sitting behind that big desk at the bank, responsible for tens of millions, I thought about my father and that cigar box more times than I can count. A good model, my father."

I get quiet again. We both are. I'm reflective.

"So, what brought you over from Franklin to see me on a Friday afternoon?" I say, thinking we haven't crossed paths in over a decade, one of Tom's good friends growing up, but that was so many years ago.

"Mr. Wall," he says, pausing.

"Call me Gunter," I interrupt.

"No, you'll always be Mr. Wall, even when I'm eighty–out of respect. He pauses, looks at the table a moment, then looks back at me, continuing, "You helped me more than I can tell, when I was fourteen. You, Tom, Mrs. Wall–but mainly you. You helped me keep my feet on the ground, encouraged my faith and hope."

Me? I think. Had Bobby Joe over to the house a few times for a meal. His Sunday school teacher, struggling to get a word in edgewise, when sometimes I felt like I needed to tie half of those boys down with rope?

Never was sure whether any of them listened. Hmm . . . second time he's told me this. Basically said the same thing thirty-five years ago at Tom's graveside. That memory flashed back just a moment ago.

Bobby Joe looks at me sincerely and says, "Anyway, I just wanted to say thank you."

FIFTY-EIGHT

"Whoo," faint, distinctly beagle. South end of the woods, me on the north. That bark, a statement or a question? "Whoooee . . . whooee." There he goes again. Must be Robert Rugetti's grandson's beagle. First sound of life I've heard today, other than my own breathing and a few birds. I almost beat the sun here this morning, a good two hours ahead of that dog. Couldn't sleep—like Christmas Eve as a boy when Mom and Dad would scrape together enough money for a gift or two for Everett and me. I'd lie in bed, eyes open, heart pumping, full of anticipation. But never like last night.

Never had a day like today, remembering my life seventy-nine years back to the morning of the flood, the memories as vivid as the yellow and red leaves on that sweet gum tree before me. It was the events of significance in minute detail: expressions on faces, tones of voices, joy, pain. It's as if my whole life happened this morning. I relived it—an answered prayer.

I have been with people who helped me when I needed help, but no one more so than Dad. He pulled me from turbulent waters as a child, and emotionally lifted me as an adult when I was struggling to put one foot in front of the other. He always led by example, doing what was right, whether it was helping a family stranded on a rooftop or encouraging a worker down at the oil mill. He was so much more than my biological father. He gave me more than a last name. I was an heir to his example as a great man, just as Everett was. And soon there will be no more Walls, just as with James Street, whose only son died. I am a part of his legacy, too, although my last name is not Street. He believed in me when I had all but lost belief in myself. He taught me wisdom and to "always do the right thing" as I watched him treat people fairly and honestly. It was a motto to live by.

I have known many to die: Everett, Jimmy Street, Sarge, Brooklyn—so young when they gave their lives—their paths so brief. I have breathed the *free air* they left behind for over sixty years.

I was nursed and nurtured as a child by Mom, an emotionally fragile woman, so pained later by the loss of Everett. She was so caring—no doubt ever of her love for me, even to this day, over thirty years since I lost her physical presence.

Along the way I have shared a common thread of life with others, my shared thread with Missouri lengthy and ongoing. I do so regret never driving to see him; it was always him to me. But I never regret a minute I have spent with him—particularly the time on the phone this week.

I have had a constant companion along my life's crowded roadways, as well as on its lonely paths, oftentimes agreeing, other times the internal friction almost boundless. With the shared vision of "till death us do part," the path was never too narrow for two. Betty was my companion till in death she departed.

As for young Tom, at his funeral the preacher said, "Whenever a person of youth passes on, I am asked why? I have answered 'In time we will see why,' and perhaps we will. I have also learned that while still in our earthly state perhaps we won't." To this day I don't know why. I do know I loved him and that he loved me, and for now that will suffice. It must.

Did I lift, did I lead, did I do what was right for others?

Oh, what is this? I'm cold—felt it come on suddenly—especially my feet. Here, I'll move my feet a little, wrap my jacket a little tighter, and adjust my seat on the canvas of this chair—uncomfortable after a while, not quite a recliner, is it? It's odd, but today I spent more time on the years before I was thirty than I did the rest of my life. It's as if I had to hurry things. Wonder why.

Would you look over there? That cottontail just snuck out of the briars. Could hardly hear the patter of his feet. Has no clue I'm here. Or does he? A sly rabbit, maybe? Knows I don't have a gun. And even if I did it wouldn't matter. Everything is so vivid: the color of the leaves, even the brown, the blue of the sky between the oaks so cloudless, pure.

"Whooee . . . yip, yip, yip . . . yip, yip, yip. Yip." A staccato, a little closer, but a ways off. He's chasing a giant rabbit, a cane cutter. Or his mind might be playing a trick; no rabbit.

Years ago, I would have declared to Everett that it was my skill that brought the rabbit out, no other reason than to get him riled up. Last thing in the world I'd do now. Back then we would sit on stumps, or fallen trees placed on the ground by nature or old age. No canvas chairs! Ham and biscuits, and apples, Dad, Everett, me—a memory worth a hundred times all the bank deposits in the world. Yeah, at one time me a sapling, later a tree, now a sapling. I've shrunk. Hey, but I know a lot more now than I did then. Sort of like when Everett graduated from high school, and Dad had only been through the fifth grade. Dad knew so much more. And Everett—never fully got the chance, did he? Died young like Tom. And me, I've had the gift of a long life.

Oh! There it is again. Oh! Pain in my chest. Now in my arms, more severe now. Started soon after I got here this morning. No, that's not the truth, is it? Started a couple of weeks ago, a day or two after Betty died. Indigestion. Thought that's what it was—or did I? Don't lie to yourself, Gunter. That's not really what you thought it was the second time or the third. Trying to be a tough marine? Maybe. You know, I'm not sure I know that answer. One thing I do know. I was supposed to come out here today and I did.

"Yip, yip, yip . . . yip, yip, yip . . ." Can't be fifty feet away. Either that beagle's got a nose for the rabbits or he's plum crazy. Sounds young. Can't turn a rabbit back. Maybe not strong or fast enough to sight it; he's operating on faith. Haven't heard a shot yet, but he sure sounds happy!

I'm smiling. I'm smiling. Pain in my chest and arms like the moment I was struck on the shoulder with the shovel that night on Iwo Jima— only, this time it's not subsiding and I'm smiling!

What a day. It's all so vivid right now, every minute, every second, every leaf, every twig, that pure sky. It's so real . . . yet, not more than what I've relived the past couple of hours.

Oh, that pain is getting worse. Never had pain like this . . . *God, you've spared me. My pain's been emotional, hasn't it? We've had to deal with that quite a few times, haven't we? Can't get around those parts if you live eighty-three years; just comes with life. Forgiveness . . . over the course of my life, I've asked for plenty of it. Is there anything else? Anything?*

Today has been a good day. One of the best days of my life.

Oh, it's worse. It's worse! Like an ice pick, chest and arms. I've been spared a lot. And been given prosperity.

Remember? Remember that night in my bedroom when Dad had encouraged me that day. That nightmare? So many I had. You helped me tone them down, helped me to overcome them. You helped me regain the person I was intended to be.

And Betty . . . that day in the drugstore, almost jumped out of my skin when I turned and saw her. She spoke to me the first time. Then later, I thought she was gonna die, the day Tom was born. I asked for a long life, for the two of us. And you granted us fifty-five years. When will I see her again? How will I recognize her? And Tom? And Mom and Dad? And Everett? Others—others I remembered today. Oh, I've read and been told the playing field's different, relationships and such. But I really want to see them. And, am I going to be in your presence? I've believed all these years. I have hope.

"What's that? What's that!"

"Yip, yip, yip . . . yip, yip, yip . . . yip." Right in front of me. Just took off after that cottontail. The dog's not crazy. He's chasing a real rabbit—at least this time. Young thing, that beagle—not much more than a puppy. Eager, that's what he is. Look at him go! Running a circle. He *can* turn that rabbit, lead him right back to where they started.

Oh! The ice picks! The ice picks! Chest . . . arms. I'm falling forward. On the ground. Got a little control left. A little control. Gonna turn myself over, not facedown. Look at that sky, so pure, cloudless, right between those oak trees.

"Yip, yip, yip." Still barking. So close.

It stopped. The barking stopped. What's that? Warm, moist, my cheek, my forehead.

"Hey. Hey, little fellow. You know something's wrong, don't you?"

Oh, the pain. The pain! Chest! Arms!

"You're licking my face. You know . . . you know, don't you? You can just sense it. Your tongue is so warm. So warm. Only place on me that is. Takes my mind off the pain . . . my last pain."

What's that in the sky? A cloud? A cloud! No, there are no clouds, yet I hear a roar, a rumble.

It's a river, brightest of bright, flowing straight toward me and this time I am not afraid.

I will be lifted from the waters.